Five Names

ALSO BY ADAM LYNDON

DETECTIVE RUTHERFORD
BARNES MYSTERIES
Book 1: Devil's Chimney
Book 2: Beachy Head
Book 3: Burnt Out Secrets
Book 4: The Chalk Man
Book 5: Five Names

FIVE ~~NAMES~~

ADAM LYNDON

Detective Rutherford Barnes Mysteries Book 5

Joffe Books, London
www.joffebooks.com

First published in Great Britain in 2024

© Adam Lyndon 2024

This book is a work of fiction. Names, characters, businesses, organizations, places and events are either the product of the author's imagination or are used fictitiously. Any resemblance to actual persons, living or dead, events or locales is entirely coincidental. The spelling used is British English except where fidelity to the author's rendering of accent or dialect supersedes this. The right of Adam Lyndon to be identified as author of this work has been asserted in accordance with the Copyright, Designs and Patents Act 1988.

No part of this book may be used or reproduced in any manner for the purpose of training artificial intelligence technologies or systems. In accordance with Article 4(3) of the Digital Single Market Directive 2019/790, Joffe Books expressly reserves this work from the text and data mining exception.

Cover art by Nebojsa Zoric

ISBN: 978-1-83526-885-8

AUTHOR'S NOTE

Modern policing is awash with acronyms and abbreviations, particularly those — such as "PACE" — that can be pronounced phonetically. In the interests of authenticity and procedural accuracy, this story employs both in dialogue. The reader will find a glossary of these terms at the end of the book.

PROLOGUE

The cocktail dress gleamed black as an oil slick in the soft light of the hotel room. She slid it on and swept a pair of teardrop earrings from the top of the mahogany dresser into her palm. She moved over to the sash window and gazed out onto the wide, neat pavement, at the street lights made to look like Victorian gas lamps.

The Mayfair street was empty. It was still early, but she was curious to know if he would come. The mark was successful, intelligent and confident; despite all that, she knew it would be easy to overcome his defences once his ego came into the equation. So predictable; you could practically set your watch by it. Maybe he would go along with it even if he *did* deduce he was being rolled; maybe a kiss from a beautiful woman in a cocktail dress was worth being defrauded for.

There was a gentle knock at the bedroom door. She tutted. She wasn't expecting anyone. Nobody knew she was here.

"Would you like your bed turned down, madam?" A muffled, timid voice, with a hint of an accent. Eastern European. Maybe even Romanian, like hers; she couldn't tell for sure through the closed door.

A fierce judder of rage rose up inside her. The service industry in this country was overpopulated by her people.

Why were they not represented in the boardrooms, the committees, the top universities?

The anger impelled her to open the door. She could at least teach this young, wide-eyed imbecile how to be less timid, more assertive. Maybe she would train her, recruit her.

She opened the door — and she herself became wide-eyed.

The housekeeper stood motionless, hands splayed out to the side as if trying to maintain her balance. There was a hand around her throat and a pistol to her temple, both belonging to a well-dressed man with brown curls and spectacles standing behind her.

Then the housekeeper's face changed. Her body relaxed. Their eyes met. With the barest hint of a smile, she stepped off to the side, giving no indication at all that she had just been used as a human shield.

The well-dressed man made eye contact and pointed the gun directly at her. Without breaking his gaze, he reached inside his pocket and passed a thick envelope to the housekeeper. Briefly, she fingered the banknotes inside and then disappeared away down the corridor. The plush carpet deadened the sound of her footsteps.

Anchored by the weapon, she stared into the black tunnel of the barrel. She had survived Ceaușescu's depredations, had grown up with a steely resolve to defy the will of men, had suffered the arduous journey to escape, only to find herself unable to quell the cold swell of fear and panic that rose up inside her, so incongruous in the soft lighting and expensive decor of the surroundings she'd paid so much for.

Her .22 was in her clutch bag. At least six feet away, on the dresser. Stupid. She hadn't brought it with her to the door. A split-second's carelessness that would cost her more than she could afford.

Frozen in the doorway, she searched the man's face, reading it for some kind of tell that might dictate the best tactic for escape. But although there was something behind the eyes, something that said he could show kindness and empathy if the conditions were right, it wasn't bright enough for the here and now. He had buried it in favour of his current purpose.

There was only one tactic. She knew, even before she moved, that she would not be quick enough.

But she tried anyway.

"She isn't . . ." she began, pointing down the corridor to where the housekeeper had gone.

Then she spun round, dived for the clutch.

She heard the suppressed *zippp* noise, felt the impact on the back of her head. Her eyes stopped working an instant before her hearing did — she heard her own head collide with the corner of the dresser — but the spark of life had left her before her body hit the soft carpet.

* * *

Duquesne "Duke" Kenley took a moment. The assault had been brief, and — besides the thud of her head striking the mahogany dresser — practically silent. A fountain of red had sunburst across the room, spattering the floral curtains, pile carpet and polished furniture.

He listened. No commotion. No sounds out of the ordinary. He took a deep breath and shut his eyes, concentrating on the wave of nausea that was flickering in his gut. It didn't come naturally, but it was getting easier to kill. Besides, she'd wanted him dead, so it was a clear case of him or her. Stratton Pearce was already dead. Now it was a full house — he was free and clear. What good was a bounty if there was no one around to pay it?

He pulled a handkerchief from his pocket, folded it over his palm and used it to gently pull the bedroom door shut on Roxy Petrescu's corpse.

PART ONE:
NEW YEAR'S DAY, 2015

CHAPTER ONE

The New Year's air was like a cool blanket on his face, the tiniest hint of warmth radiating from a crisp January sun. The South Downs rose up on the horizon; there was birdsong in the trees, and the distant shush of traffic. If not for the near-unshakeable conviction that he would be lynched the moment he set foot outside, Duquesne Kenley considered that it was almost worth the four-plus years in prison for the feeling of being free.

Almost.

Three years on remand. No hint of a trial. The right to *habeas corpus* patchy at best. Then Kenley, with the help of his silver-haired, surf aficionado, South Australian lawyer Robert Peverell, had attempted to take control of his own destiny with a tactical guilty plea and Oscar-winning demonstrations of remorse and conversion to Christianity. Between them, they'd succeeded in reducing an almost certain double-digit sentence down to something more palatable.

As a result, coupled with time served, he'd only had to serve another eighteen months for some — in Kenley's view rather sketchy, given that he'd been attempting to prevent loss of life — charges of causing death by dangerous driving times three, no insurance, aggravated vehicle-taking and criminal damage. It was curious how much quicker the time went for a convicted inmate — that is, one with a confirmed sentence end date — compared with a remand prisoner, who often didn't have a clue when they were going to get out until about a week before it happened.

He kept his pace steady and his eyes front, an elastic band of tension telling him to keep his wits about him, that the attack could come from anywhere.

He walked down the steep drive from the gatehouse to the roadside, in the same now musty-smelling clothes he'd been arrested in, camo-green duffle bag slung over his shoulder. He resisted the urge to look back at the imposing fortress of HMP Lewes with its fuck-off flint walls and razor wire crowns.

The urge evaporated completely when he got to the road.

There she was, waiting by a yellow Porsche Carrera. Arms folded, half a smile on her face, leaning on the front wing of the roadster with a confidence he had not seen before.

This. This was what four and a bit years inside was worth. More, even. He'd do a thousand years for this woman.

Nervous energy and excitement doing laps around his insides, he made his way over, having to force himself to keep his guard up, to remember that it was easier to mount an attack when your quarry's attention was fully focused elsewhere.

But none came, and for a fleeting moment he allowed himself to be engulfed by her arms, her hair, her perfume. God, it was blissful. Like waking up after a thousand-year sleep under the ice.

"I've missed you," she breathed, her arms warm around his neck.

"I don't believe you," he whispered back.

She removed one of her arms and he felt the tips of her fingers run gently over the front of his jeans. He'd been inside for almost five years — she knew what she was doing. It was all part of the manipulation, and he found he didn't actually care all that much. She could be a quadruple agent and he still wasn't sure he'd be able to summon the defences to deal with it.

He enjoyed the tableau for what it was. A moment. Even as they parted and she tossed him the car keys, he knew there were only a handful of roads out of town.

He was a career criminal — well-groomed, educated, strictly business, but a criminal nonetheless. She knew that, but she didn't know he was a murderer, even if she suspected it. She was a divorced cop with a small child and a bright future. That meant one of two possibilities. One, that she was edging towards chucking it all in to be with him. Or, two, that she was, consciously or otherwise, expecting Kenley to clean up his act, put his past behind him and move forward on the right side of the law.

So, which eventuality was the more likely?

Even as he belted up and floored the delicious V10 engine and the floorpan hugged the road like a magnet, even as he roared towards the green hulk of the distant Downs, he knew which it would be. Despite the prison time, despite the risk of having to reset your whole life to zero the minute you get caught, despite vendettas being far easier to enforce when you're in that life than when you're out of it, he knew he wouldn't be able to resist the thrill of taunting capture and then the euphoria of getting away with it. Knew he couldn't live the life of a working man.

Duquesne Kenley knew that forbidden fruit tasted the sweetest.

* * *

Detective Inspector Rutherford Barnes stood at the bus stop outside HMP Lewes, hands in his pockets, flanked only by two teenagers and an elderly woman. He didn't think the buses would be running today; then again, he hadn't thought prisoner releases happened on a bank holiday either.

It was mild for January, a low and lazy winter sun caking the face of the South Downs, pockmarked shadows dotting the flint walls that rose up along the perimeter of the building.

The place was like an anchor, Barnes thought grimly. Or a black hole. Everything came back to it. He'd visited prisoners here as a young DC; he was here again halfway through his service. And long after he was gone, the prisoners would still rotate in and out of the redoubtable stone walls like Dickensian spirits.

He would have been reasonably comfortable with this notion had he not seen the man he was interested in stroll cheerfully out of the gatehouse like he was returning from a Caribbean cruise. Duquesne Kenley, also known as Ben Blackwater, Michael Quayle, Chris Peake and a shopping list of other aliases, was trotting down the steep driveway to the road with a spring in his step and the breeze teasing those thick Iberian curls. How the hell had the bastard kept his tan, Barnes wondered.

He was wearing a maroon shirt under a grey suit; even the gym holdall slung casually over his shoulder looked new. Add a slo-mo camera and a winning bleach-white smile and all he was missing was the catalogue.

The bus squealed into the stop and Barnes stepped back to allow the people around him to board. There was a slight hiatus while granny rooted around for change, and so Barnes moved carefully in front of the bus to keep his eyes on Kenley.

As he reached the kerb there was the growl of a revving engine. Barnes started, scanning around wildly for any sense of a threat.

The yellow Porsche convertible pulled over and stopped, half on, half off the kerb. A woman stepped out of the driver's seat — tall, blonde hair cut in a stylish bob, caramel sweater, jeans and nosebleed heels. She left it running, leaned against the bonnet and folded her arms, posing like the centre feature in a glossy tabloid.

DC Natalie Morgan waited, and Barnes saw Kenley appear while Kenley strode down towards her. He dropped the holdall on the ground in order to give her his full attention;

she flung her arms around his neck, pressed herself against his body and he reciprocated like a man who had not had any kind of physical contact for almost five years.

Which, Barnes supposed, he hadn't. At least, not the kind that could reasonably compete with DC Morgan.

She responded to his eager kiss and, just at the point where someone walking past would possibly have suggested politely that the pair of them might like to avail themselves of the privacy of a room in a country hotel, Natalie removed one of her arms from his neck and held her hand at the small of her back. She formed an "O" with her thumb and forefinger, never once turning her face from Kenley's.

Barnes touched his lapel mic.

"We're set. Stand by."

Morgan finally broke away from the embrace, bent down to collect Kenley's holdall from the ground — Barnes noting that he seemed perfectly happy to let her do so — and they walked the few steps to the Carrera.

The bus pulled away, leaving Barnes alone and exposed at the stop, now looking more like someone who was conducting amateur surveillance than someone waiting for a bus. He shifted awkwardly, and as discreetly as he could, scanned three-sixty. No armed hordes charging down the tall man in the suit, no zipline buzz of snipers ensconced in the hillside loosing off rounds, no roadside IEDs from passing courier vans.

Kenley didn't notice. He made it to the Porsche unscathed; Morgan went around the front towards the driver's side, then paused, turned, and offered him the keys. Kenley cupped his hands like he was second slip at Hove's county ground, and she tossed them over to him.

"What the hell is she doing?" Barnes muttered.

They swapped places and Kenley gleefully revved the engine. Morgan kicked off her shoes and stretched her legs out on the dash; Kenley dropped the car into gear and pulled away towards the A27 like the Furies themselves were on his heels.

"He's away. Don't lose eyeball," Barnes said. "And, for whatever reason, subject is driving."

CHAPTER TWO

PC Pete Lamb staggered out of the Cameo nightclub, the cold air hitting his system at about the same time as the cocaine. There was a shout behind him; some twenty-year-old in a purple shirt getting into a chest-beating match with the door supervisor. *Only one winner there,* Lamb thought.

He looked up, far above the noise and commotion on the street, at the building that housed the nightclub itself. All the years he'd been coming here, he'd never actually looked at the place before. A squat, dirty beige block that was somewhere between a garage and a three-storey Grecian villa.

He turned back and concentrated on crossing the road, moving carefully around two seagulls squaring up to one another in some kind of homage to the human tableau at the nightclub's entrance.

He chalked up his maudlin state to the shots and the blow. Standard physiological reaction where he was concerned. Despite his intoxication, he cobbled together the faculties to pat himself down — wallet, warrant card, keys, phone, all present — and get himself to the opposite pavement unscathed.

He weaved east down the street, thinking about a KFC, then deciding that at two in the morning, a static, concentrated space like that was a pressure cooker for trouble.

Another shout, this time at the taxi rank. It was a man and a woman arguing with a taxi driver. The gist of it seemed to be that the pair of them were too pissed for the taxi driver's liking, and in response he was getting exaggerated attempts at sobriety and don't-you-know-who-I-am *fnar-fnar-fnar* for his troubles.

Lamb tilted his head as he approached, and frowned. The woman had about four inches at least on the man, and if Lamb hadn't known better, in her denim skirt and pink heels, he'd have said she was a tom.

Trouble was, he did know better. She was Chief Superintendent Theresa Baily from Operations. He'd only ever seen her with her hair up in a tight bun, and hadn't realised quite how long her brown mane was.

Lamb passed them; Baily didn't notice him, but the man did. His eyes narrowed — Lamb wondered if the man was trying to place him, but then realised he was trying to work out whether he himself had been made or not.

Lamb couldn't help himself.

"Evening, sir," he said.

Assistant Chief Constable Gabriel "Gabby" Glover didn't acknowledge him, just stared him out. His eyes were red and glazed with intoxication — even though Lamb was pretty wired himself, ACC Glover looked off the charts.

"Missus got the kids, has she?" Lamb said. He was grinning.

Baily had been swaying a little too, but at that, she shut her eyes momentarily. When she opened them, she was staring at nothing.

Glover stepped past her, his attention fully on Lamb, and stopped when their noses were practically touching. It was funny, Lamb thought, despite his rank, out of uniform he just looked like a football hooligan.

"Just slide on past, fella," Glover said. "Keep on walking. Don't bait me."

"Why, sir, I wouldn't dream of it. I need to cut loose on my downtime; stressful job like yours, Lord knows you must need to as well."

Glover inched forward. "You really want to do this?" he said. "I know who you are. You're on your ninth life. Borrowed time. You want to end your career this way?" He rubbed his own nose with the back of his finger, and then pointed at Lamb's face.

"Sir, that sounds like a threat."

"Come on, Gabriel, can we just go?" Baily tugged at Glover's hand. "We can walk."

"You are his friend?" the taxi driver said to Lamb. "He is too drunk. I cannot take him. Please help him. I am polite. He tells me, 'You should go and learn to drive in your country.'"

Lamb looked at Glover in mock horror. "Oops," he said. His grin got wider, and then some degree of cold clarity filtered through his vodka-and-coke-infused bravado. The taxi driver had just technically alleged an offence on the part of an extraordinarily senior member of the police service, which meant Lamb had a handful of options.

"No, he didn't," Baily said, turning her attention to the taxi driver. "He said nothing of the sort."

Lamb's eyes flicked from one side to the other. The taxi driver didn't know he was a cop. He could just walk away. He could tell the taxi driver to report it.

Or he could make an off-duty arrest.

"You are police?" the taxi driver asked.

Lamb started. How did he know that? Was it that obvious?

Glover eyeballed him, a faintly goading smirk on his face. "Come on, Constable. Tell him." He inched closer and leered. "So, what are you going to do?"

Lamb held his gaze, thought about it, and then raised both his hands and started sliding past the tableau towards KFC.

"That's it, Officer. Keep moving," Gabby hissed.

"Ma'am," Lamb said, tipping an imaginary hat to Chief Superintendent Baily.

He moved on down the street, his bravado temporarily blunted as he wondered whether the likelihood of his name being called for a random drugs test when he was next on duty had increased exponentially in the last four minutes.

At the door of the takeaway, he turned. The confrontation with the taxi driver had not been diminished by his moving on; if anything, it was growing more heated. It had become a matter of principle, a question of honour. What was clear was that neither senior officer had given Lamb a second thought.

And that was what finally burrowed through to his coke-addled brain.

He stalked back up the street.

"Oh, Christ, he's back." Glover rolled his eyes and mimed snorting a line off a tabletop.

"Come on, sir, let's not make a scene. I'll drive you home."

"You? You're three sheets to the wind. More than I am, in fact," Glover sneered.

"Just go home, Officer. This is none of your business," Baily said, pointing a purple talon at Lamb's chest.

"Officer? You *are* police!" the taxi driver said, not missing a beat. "This man has racially abused me. I want to make a statement."

"Look, mate, I'm not in a position to take your statement. I'm off duty, for starters, but—" here he eyeballed Gabby narrowly — "I can make a call."

He stepped back and pulled out his phone. He dialled 999.

"Yeah, it's PC Pete Lamb, here, off duty," he said, his tongue thick. "I need to report an incident to a supervisor. It's, uh, a little delicate."

He looked up momentarily. Glover was shaking his head. He mimed a toilet flushing and, pointing his finger downwards, drew circles in the air, pointing at Lamb with his other hand as he did so.

Lamb described where he was and what had happened, and then ended the call.

"Cops are on their way," he said to the taxi driver. "Let's all just sit tight, eh?"

"I cannot wait. I lose money. I need fare," the driver said, pointing at a bored-looking couple standing about six feet behind Glover and Baily.

The driver beckoned the couple over and made an exaggerated show of opening the car doors for them.

"What do you mean, you can't wait?" Lamb said. "You want to make a report, don't you?"

"Tomorrow," the driver said. "I am busy."

"I'm not being funny, mate, but tomorrow could turn into next week if you don't strike while the iron's hot. Know what I mean?"

The driver shrugged. Lamb grabbed at the collar of his *Scarface* T-shirt and pulled him away from the car.

"Listen, you're not going anywhere," he hissed. "You started this performance in the first place, you little drama queen. You're about to blow open a world of shit, so you can just about bloody hang on and see it through. *Comprende?*"

The driver chewed the inside of his cheek, staring at him belligerently, but eventually nodded. Lamb stared away down the street, trying not to make any more eye contact with Gabby than was strictly necessary, and, after only a couple of minutes, was relieved to see a marked Freelander, blue lights flaring, cruise around the corner and turn onto Langney Road from the pedestrianised area by the Curzon cinema.

Well, maybe "relieved" was a bit strong. Through either some entrenched sense of duty or a kind of inertia borne of the fact that he'd gone to the trouble of calling the real cops, it was now all about the waiting, and he'd all but forgotten the idea of walking away.

The Freelander pulled alongside the odd little tableau. It made no logical sense that Lamb should be more worried about an on-duty supervisor than an off-duty ACC, but he nevertheless took several deep sniffs and rubbed the end of his nose and inspected the back of a finger.

Inspector Georgia Brass stepped out of the Freelander and pulled on her dice-band bowler, adjusting it as she did so. Lamb swallowed. The Pretoria-born former cycling champion, with her fatless jaw and silver hair, was a long way from being wet behind the ears. One might almost suggest that a call to two pissed, very senior off-duty police officers squaring up to one another was just the kind of thing she relished.

She had a supervisor with her whom Lamb recognised as Acting Sergeant Jill Rough. Rough looked nervous enough for both of them. The two of them approached, Brass's eyes glistening as she sized up the scene. She whispered something in Rough's ear and they split, Brass heading to Glover and Baily as she barked instructions, while Rough made a beeline for Lamb.

In retrospect, it was pretty neat. Rough seemed to buy Lamb's holier-than-thou, *sans*-cocaine tale of how he noticed the fracas and attempted to defuse it, but called in the professionals when he realised who was involved. Let's not forget, he said to Rough while indicating the taxi driver, that there's a victim of crime at the centre of all this.

Rough eyed him, then went to compare notes with Brass, who met her at the bonnet of the Freelander. After about thirty seconds of this, Brass went back to Glover and Baily and ushered them gently to the car. Rough tossed her the keys and then turned her attention to the taxi driver, who started solemnly to give his account, as if the potential seriousness of the situation had finally started to dawn on him.

As Brass opened the rear door of the Freelander, Lamb thought that Glover's previously pompous expression had turned into something quite different. In fact, if he hadn't known better, he'd have said the ACC looked almost green around the gills, especially when he attempted to get in the front passenger seat but was instead steered to the rear by a gentle-if-unyielding Inspector Brass.

Ah well, Lamb thought, as he turned on his heel and headed off down Langney Road in search of a kebab, *at least the boss got his ride home.*

* * *

When Lamb booked on for early turn three days later, he was neither surprised nor indignant to find Inspector Brass waiting for him by the locker room entrance. It was twenty to seven in the morning, and Lamb figured the impeccably turned-out Brass had already been at work for an hour at least.

"Constable Lamb," Brass said, in that low BBC World Service broadcaster voice of hers, twenty-five years as a UK resident failing to completely obliterate the edges of her Afrikaans lilt. "Will you come with me, please?"

Lamb obediently followed her into the main patrol building, remembering the old adage that the biggest mistake most newly promoted supervisors make is trying to be chums with their former peers. *No danger of that here*, he thought.

The patrol base, a former management site for the huge and long-defunct gas holders in the adjacent Finmere Road estate, was a single-storey office long enough to bowl a full-length off-cutter in and still have enough room for a tenpin alley beyond it. Brass's office necessitated a walk across this open-plan office, and despite being very familiar with this particular drill, Lamb nevertheless found himself lowering his head as he trailed behind Brass.

He hunched his shoulders and tucked his chin to his chest even further when he saw the command team's new secretary sitting at the end of a row of workstations. She evidently hadn't found her own space to work in yet, and so had opted to hot-desk with the masses in the patrol office.

Hot being the operative word — Lamb had gone doe-eyed for her the moment she'd set foot in the building. Every feature was straight out of a glossy magazine — she was in her mid-twenties with a mane of tousled champagne-blonde hair, and she tottered about on eye-watering heels as if balancing on a unicycle. A couple of times Lamb had attempted a casual look to see if there was anything on her ring finger — she couldn't possibly not be taken — but so far his efforts had proved inconclusive.

Lamb passed her desk, catching a waft of some exquisite Parisian scent. She was engrossed, brow furrowed, in whatever she was working on, and didn't look up as he passed. Given the circumstances, Lamb considered this a blessing.

Besides, he realised as the office door slammed shut behind him, other than recalling that it was a little unusual, he'd actually forgotten her name anyway.

The whole lab-rat-on-a-perp-walk thing was made worse by the fact that the offices themselves were floor-to-ceiling glass, with only a token white frosting forming an infographic — made up of words like "trust" and "integrity" — around the middle to protect the occupants' corporate dignity.

There were two men already in the office — an enormous seventy-something individual with a bald brown head and a tweed three-piece suit, who was sitting in Brass's chair, and a second man standing by the filing cabinet who had some kind of medical kit with him. Brass remained by the doorway.

"Good morning, Mr Lamb," said the seated man, with a broad grin and an accent that was straight out of Repton circa 1942. "Detective Chief Inspector Marlon Choudhury, Professional Standards. This is a random drugs test."

Lamb swallowed. "I see. Anyone else you're randomising, or just me?"

The man called Choudhury beamed at him. "We won't be a minute."

He wasn't wrong. With the swift, accomplished movements of a seasoned practitioner, one who knows his material extremely well, the man standing by the filing cabinet took a step forward and yanked out a clump of Lamb's brown locks with a pair of tweezers.

"Ow! Jesus," Lamb said, rubbing the back of his head. "Have a care."

The man dropped the brown shafts into a clear exhibit bag, sealed it, and then presented a form to Lamb for signing.

Lamb stared at the piece of paper and looked to Choudhury for a prompt; Choudhury responded by leaning across the desk in a surprisingly rapid movement to thrust a heavy, gold-plated fountain pen into Lamb's sweaty palm.

Lamb thought for a moment, and then signed the form. The man slipped everything into a large cardboard envelope and scurried off with his curly brown prize.

"Can I go now?" Lamb said. "They'll come back clean, you know."

Choudhury leaned back and steepled his fingers. The chair creaked ominously.

"You made an off-duty report the other night. During some late-night revelry in Eastbourne town centre. Some, ah, *questionable* behaviour was alleged against a certain senior officer and the officer he was with."

"And you're here to, what? Pay me off? Shut me up? Sweep it all under the carpet?"

Choudhury frowned deeply, and his eyes disappeared momentarily under a thick white monobrow. "Certainly not. But it is fair to say that the nature of the allegation is broadly, if proven, incompatible with his rank — it would be for anybody, but in his particular case the potential damage to public confidence is significant. Seniority is fragile in that way. Ironic, wouldn't you say?"

"And?"

"And you are a key witness. You called 999. You asked for a supervisor, presumably recognising the gravity of what amounted to an otherwise trivial bout of alcohol-fuelled mudslinging in a taxi rank outside a nightclub."

"So speak to the taxi driver."

Choudhury's eyes narrowed. "An action that is already in train," he said. "And one that does not, even if fruitful, absolve us of our obligation to investigate the matter as fully as possible. You should know that."

Lamb raised both his hands in an exaggerated shrug. "I wasn't a witness. I saw the fracas, walked over, saw the boss and the cabbie mouthing off at each other, and decided it was above my pay grade when the cabbie made an allegation."

"And what was this allegation?"

"That Gabby — excuse me, ACC Glover — told him to go back to his own country."

"And you didn't hear that?"

"I did not."

"But the allegation was made in Mr Glover's presence and hearing, yes?"

"He was stood right next to me."

"Then it is admissible hearsay, no?"

Lamb felt a bead of sweat break on his brow. "I suppose it is," he said flatly. "But look, I was pretty well lubricated myself. My recollection may not hold up in court."

"You let us worry about that."

"What did he say? The driver?"

"As far as we can make out, his motives are pure. As a witness, he presents as credible, consistent and competent. Not to mention the fact that he was the only sober person within a fifty-foot radius. He has worked out that Mr Glover is in fact a police officer; beyond that, he doesn't really have any idea of his standing."

"And the boss? Is he . . . what did . . . is he in the shit?"

Choudhury leaned across the table. "Mr Lamb, we'll need your statement."

"He'll make my life hell. I'll lose my job. This is just the first pass," Lamb said, indicating the long-departed hair thief with his thumb.

Choudhury rubbed his nose as if he were trying to pull it off. "Mr Lamb, we've not met before, but I am aware that you are something of a frequent flyer within my department. If this ends up being the way you finally vacate the office of constable, at least you'll be taking some of the dead wood with you."

Dead wood? Lamb grimaced. He was no fan of Gabby Glover, but was that any way to speak of a senior officer who was technically innocent until proven guilty?

Choudhury stood, buttoning his tweed jacket over his tweed waistcoat and thence across his enormous stomach.

"One more thing," he said. "There will likely be a decent amount of media interest in this story when it finally breaks, possibly with a hefty cash incentive to get it there. But however tempting it might be to set yourself up with a post-employment insurance policy—" he slid a single sheet of paper across the desk to Lamb — "don't be that guy."

"What's this?"

"Non-disclosure agreement. Boilerplate, but with a couple of additional clauses referencing the Official Secrets Act and *yada, yada, yada*," Choudhury said, somehow, Lamb mused, making *yada* sound like *RADA*.

Lamb suddenly just wanted to get out of there. He scanned the form and then scribbled his name at the bottom.

"And Mr Lamb?" Choudhury said, holding out an open palm.

"Yes?" Lamb said, confused.

"My pen."

CHAPTER THREE

"Report," Kane said.

"Nil so far," Barnes said. "They went to some Airbnb country cottage, shut the front door, and haven't been out since. His phone hasn't moved. Billing suggests it's barely been used. We're not listening, of course . . ."

"You won't get it. There's no way you'll get authorisation to put a bug in the house. It's above my pay grade, anyway," Kane said.

"As a honeytrap, she's possibly too effective," Barnes said. "I seem to remember that happened last time. He shacked up with her and suddenly lost interest in his gang's enterprises — which was half the reason he became of interest in the first place."

"You're telling me this now?"

"Just thinking out loud."

"You're going to lose them. The surveillance teams, I mean. We can't just click our fingers and they appear. There's grumpy superintendents queuing around the block waving bids at the centre — any number of burglars, robbers and horrible OCGs that would possibly constitute a more compelling case for what amounts to a fairly precious resource."

"What about the threat to his life?" Barnes said.

"What threat? He's survived this long, hasn't he? There's no intelligence on that."

"Keber want him dead. They have done for years."

"Even if that were true — and I'm not saying it isn't — a honeytrap UC is not the way to handle it."

"But boss, the man is a killer. He's committed at least two murders, maybe even three. One of those was a police officer. I've seen more police colleagues killed than anyone else of my rank and service, and he's been in the wings for all of those. If we can take him out—"

"Take him out?" Kane interrupted.

"You know what I mean. Lock him up. Put him away. If we can do it before he gets his feet under the table, then we might be able to stop our town going the same way as so many other seaside towns have gone."

"Are you done with the editorial?"

Barnes was silent, his insides humming like a racing car on the starting grid.

Kane held Barnes's gaze. His icy grey stare was almost hypnotic. "Listen to me, now. You and I both want Duquesne Kenley put away."

"Do we?"

"Of course we do. But we don't *know* all those things. We suspect they might be true. You've never had tunnel vision as a detective. Don't start now."

Barnes took a deep breath and exhaled. Kane was right, of course. Superintendent Samson Kane, the black sheep of the police family, the man who had gone from spiky-haired garage band reject to senior police officer in less than five years. Barnes found it increasingly easy to forget this trajectory, probably because Kane was now part of the furniture. These days, every time he opened his mouth — that is, if you shut your eyes to the pink tattoo-removal scars — you would think you were talking to a seasoned veteran. Even the instances of thumb tacks being scattered underneath his tyres had dried up.

Well, a bit.

"I can keep the surveillance teams on it for twenty-four more hours. That's it. After that, they'll be redeployed."

"Understood," Barnes said with a sigh.

"Get her debriefed, make sure she's not gone completely rogue, and then wind it up."

"Sir."

* * *

Kenley put the holdall down carefully on the kitchen floor of their country retreat. It was some kind of expensive-looking charcoal-coloured ceramic tile, and he didn't particularly want to activate the breakage premium.

He stared across the island worktop at Natalie, feeling no self-consciousness whatsoever, no awkwardness, no nothing. He felt naked, and completely vulnerable.

"You're looking pretty intense," she said, taking two wine glasses from the cupboard.

"I've not had a drink in almost five years," he said. "Not had a woman in almost five years. Not touched anyone. Barely tasted fresh air. Not had a decent meal. It's kind of tough to know where to start."

"As in, what you should eat first?" She didn't look up, instead concentrating with mock-seriousness on inserting the corkscrew into the bottle.

"You know what I've come to realise?" he said, trying not to dwell on her comment in case he ended up vaulting the island block and ripping her clothes off. "It doesn't matter to me that you've been put up to this."

"I—"

"Ssh, Natalie. It doesn't matter to me. Fruit tastes better when you steal it. And if you get away with it . . . well, it's worth getting caught once if you get away with it the other nine times."

Natalie had stopped unscrewing while he talked. Now she looked at him. "You're saying we'd be better together if I was married? To someone else, I mean."

"Probably, actually."

She folded her arms.

"I've got no defences, Nat. No reason to be anything other than completely honest. Most women want that from their men, don't they? Openness, honesty, intimate disclosure of their feelings and all that. I'm doing that now. And the fact is, we're hotter because I know being with you is getting one over on Rutherford Barnes."

She sighed.

"I feel naked, Nat."

"Have a drink and shut up."

She slid a full glass across the countertop to him. He took it, his hands trembling; every second, every movement hummed with electricity.

"How did you find this place?" he said.

She shrugged. "Google."

"Not on the list of DI Barnes's approved safe houses?"

She sipped the wine, and eyeballed him.

"Look, you had a shot across the bows five years ago," he said. "Ditch me or lose your job. A doe-eyed young probationer with no ties might have seen the romance in that and told the Force to stuff it. But you have a kid. And you're too smart to be so reckless. Which means you're here with the blessing of your superiors. A honeytrap."

"Kenley, look—"

He held up a hand, and set the glass down. "I've got to take it easy. My tolerance is way down. All I'm saying is I'm good with that. The question is, are you going to let them know that I know? Where does that leave you? That makes you, what, a triple agent?"

She didn't answer. Her eyes began to glisten. He moved around the island, close to her.

"You could be a good man," she whispered. "I know you could."

He gently tilted her chin up, so she was looking at him.

"You did it before. Your . . . gang was going to kill all those people, and you stopped it. You left me that message. Isn't that something you could do again?"

He leaned down and kissed her. "I'm not sure."

CHAPTER FOUR

Lamb was only a few minutes late for briefing. He kitted up and paraded with the rest of his section, then grabbed the keys to a marked Focus and headed out on his own.

It would, he knew, generate some chat in the office. Lamb generally liked to hold court and remind everyone of his presence for at least half an hour before getting kicked out by a supervisor to actually go and respond to some calls, but the near miss with the PSD guy had caused his heart to drum in his chest so hard he thought he was having a coronary.

He'd laid off the coke for a couple of days — even if, God knew, he was craving it now — but had been up late with the whisky again. He knew it was always a risk to drink before earlies, but somehow neither Brass nor Choudhury seemed to have noticed the stink that he knew must be coming off him in waves. He was more worried about that than about the hair sample.

He called up for a job off the queue, figuring something mundane would keep him occupied as well as scoring him a couple of long-overdue brownie points with management.

There was something about the Choudhury guy that had unnerved him. Somewhere between an Indian Sherlock

Holmes and some theatrical defence advocate, he always seemed to be two steps ahead, knowing exactly what you were going to say, sometimes before you did. Not to mention the fact that the guy was the oldest police officer Lamb had ever seen. What was he, seventy-five? Eighty?

He'd been right, of course. Lamb had been on borrowed time since the year dot. On balance, he had done well to carve out twelve years' service without getting the boot. Now here he was, doing the right thing, and he was at risk of it happening again.

The job he was on his way to had been on the stack for about five days, and the controller hadn't concealed her relief when Lamb called up for it. Some woman reporting some other woman giving her a load of gob on Facebook. There were many jobs like it, and no one had got to it because it had been trumped by more pressing matters on a fairly regular basis. Much like those all-you-can-eat restaurant buffets, Lamb mused, where the new food got regularly ladled on top of the stuff that hadn't been eaten, until there was this congealed inedible sediment at the bottom that, given half a chance, would probably jump up and run off.

Unfortunately, the Facebook woman was going to have to wait a little longer. The controller, now sounding disappointed, diverted Lamb to a call in Ratton Manor. The front door of a house had been reported as being wide open, with both householders' cars absent from the driveway.

Something of nothing, perhaps, but it was a nice area, and the neighbour that called it in was concerned about intruders. Most likely the owners had forgotten to close the door on their way to their doubtless high-flying careers.

Lamb turned into Ratton Drive, a secluded private road on a steep climb ascending the eastern face of the South Downs, and cruised up at a slow speed. He whistled as he scanned for the one he was looking for. It was all high flint walls and sandblasted iron gates and creeping wall vines and stucco Grecian columns. More money up here than he could ever hope to make, even if he opted to become a professional cocaine dealer.

Not the sort of place that tended to warrant many requests for the local constabulary. Lamb certainly didn't think he'd ever been up here.

Maybe, then, it was more likely to be something than nothing. Lamb sat up a little straighter, and tuned in his inner police radar up one notch from condition yellow — chilled but aware — to condition orange: this may still be nothing, but better to switch on.

"Sierra-Oscar from Echo-Romeo-three-zero-one," he said into his lapel mic.

"Three-oh-one, go ahead."

"Reference my assigned, any intel on location?"

"Nothing of note," came the reply. "Stand by one."

Lamb found the house and frowned. Gates closed, front door wide open. Meaning the occupants had left the door open but gone to the trouble of closing the gates? Possible if the gates were automatic; highly unlikely if they'd had to exit their vehicle and go back to secure the gates before heading off into the wild blue yonder of the morning commute.

Intruders-on suddenly bumped itself up the list of possible theories. With a highly inelegant scramble that took him the best part of a minute and made him thankful for the secluded location, Lamb ascended the ten-foot metal gates and dropped down onto the gravel driveway like a bronchial walrus.

He rolled onto his feet as if steadying himself on deck a yawing ship, and racked his baton. Exposed on the open spread of driveway, he moved quickly to the front door and pressed himself to the white stucco of the front wall.

He strained to listen. Nothing. Just the birds in the trees and the faint reverse alarm of a bin lorry from a few streets over.

He poked his head around the doorframe and took in the hallway. Varnished wooden floor, intricate rug, mahogany hall table with a sprawling green perennial in an ethnically chic pot, deep red walls and framed, individually lit artwork forming a runway down to the white space of the kitchen at the end of the hallway.

Lamb whistled. He was the last person on the planet to have any appreciation of fine art, but — the eminent suitability of the glass-fronted frames for snorting cocaine off notwithstanding — this stuff was clearly worth thousands. Even the idiot methadone-addicted creeper burglars that Lamb interacted with on a daily basis — both on duty and off — couldn't have failed to realise that the stuff in the hallway alone was worth a stint inside if you could just offload it.

"Hello?" he called. "Anyone home? It's the police."

Nothing. But he sensed . . . something. He wasn't sure if it was just too silent, or if a human can sense another human, even if . . .

He pushed forward into the hallway, just as his phone began to bleat the tinny strains of the Pogues' "Sally MacLennane" in his pocket. It rang out, then stopped, then came the double buzz of a text message notifying him of a new voicemail, then it rang again. And again.

He quickly cleared the kitchen, hallway, lounge, dining room and what he presumed was a study or maybe a drawing room — even though it didn't look like much drawing went on in there. It could have been the bar of a boutique hotel.

No signs of a disturbance, no broken glass, no trail of blood. He moved back to the hallway, raised his baton so the tip was resting on his upper arm, and ascended the stairs, his back flat to the wall.

The stairs were wide and circled back onto a mezzanine of sorts. All the doors leading off the upper landing were open.

Except one.

There was a note taped to the door of the closed room, in an untidy felt-tip scrawl:

ELLA DON'T COME IN CALL 999

Lightning fired through Lamb's system.

"Oscar from three-zero-one . . . get me an ambulance," Lamb shouted, racing up the remaining stairs.

He planted a boot against the door. It popped open.

He took in the scene in a flash. A whitewashed bedroom, sparsely decorated, fake posies in a white ceramic pot on the dresser — a spare room? In his peripheral vision, a yawning square of black against the white — an open loft hatch.

Two feet swinging gently in front of him, like a flag in the breeze. A rope looped around a joist, crushing the throat of the body in front of him like a python squeezing an egg.

Lamb wrapped his arms around the legs, wedged his boot on the bedframe and tried to shove them upwards, but it was too far off the floor and he couldn't get sufficient purchase. He was aware of his phone still going in his pocket, the controller trying to get him back on the air, the fact that the body already felt stone cold, even through the fabric of the black pleated trousers.

He let the body hang for just a second longer, long enough to drag the bedframe over by four or so feet; he climbed onto the white wooden frame end and wedged himself underneath the body, using his shoulders and back to force it upwards and redistribute any available slack to the neck. Although this was a precarious balancing act, it at least gave him the use of his hands as well as offering a degree of longevity in the position — trying to hold a body up using your arms from underneath was not an exercise that could be performed for any useful length of time.

Lamb barked into his radio for some backup and for the ambulance to get a wriggle on, and then started flailing his arms above him to try to find a pulse point around the feet and ankles.

Nothing. At least, nothing he'd call conclusive anyway.

Sirens in the distance. He shut his eyes and tried to decide if they belonged to a police car or an ambulance, and decided he couldn't call it. They stayed distant for longer than Lamb was comfortable with, and then all of a sudden they were reverberating around the leafy canopy of Ratton Drive.

The two-tones stopped suddenly, and Lamb began to yell.

"Hop the gate! Upstairs, north bedroom."

Shuffling and scrabbling. Boots on gravel, to the front door. Footsteps running up the stairs. Lamb heard radio chatter, and when it didn't mirror his own, he realised with relief that it was the paramedics that had won the silver medal for their response time.

A man and a woman in grass-green coveralls appeared in the doorway. The female paramedic rummaged in her go-bag while the other one shouted questions at Lamb while he pulled an antique-looking upholstered wooden chair over from the dressing table. The paramedic climbed onto it, produced a vicious-looking snub-blade Gerber from a pouch on his belt, and used it to hack at the taut rope.

Lamb yelled as the rope gave way; two-hundred-plus pounds of dead body suddenly shifted forwards onto his back in its entirety, causing Lamb to double over further and then lose his precarious balance on the end of the bed, bashing his chin on the wooden frame on the way down.

The paramedics, assisted by Lamb, rolled the body over onto its back. Lamb, in a slight daze, jabbed two fingers into the fleshy, bulging neck for a pulse, then the three of them performed a carousel of intense-but-short CPR, though even to Lamb it was evident that it was a futile enterprise. The yellowing skin was as cold as stone, the eyes had fogged over with a dark blue tinge and the feet were dark red with lividity.

"Zero output," said the male paramedic. "Rigor and hypostasis. Corneal clouding. He's been swinging here at least an hour, maybe two. Confirming RoLE. Speak now if you object, or forever hold your peace."

"Works for me," Lamb said. "Thanks for trying anyway."

The paramedics stood, snapped their gloves off in a kind of ritual, and then began filling in forms.

It was only then, with the shirt torn open and defib pads plastered all over the place, that Lamb finally got a good look at the corpse's face — at the same time realising that, despite a thick rope where a tie should have been, it was wearing the black epaulettes, white shirt and black trousers of a police uniform. Even with the blackening eyes and lolling tongue, the fuck-you arrogance somehow remained, and Lamb recognised the dead face of Assistant Chief Constable Gabby Glover.

He stood from his squatting position, and steadied himself on the wall. Now it made sense that his phone had been going bonkers as he pitched up on scene.

As if confirming the point, Inspector Georgia Brass appeared in the doorway, the combination of the bowler pulled low over her eyes and the ultra-fit countenance somehow making her appear like Dr Death herself.

"Constable Lamb," she said, removing the hat. "You shouldn't be here."

"If you're standing me down, I'll be happy to go, ma'am," Lamb answered.

"It's a conflict for you. You're a witness in a misconduct case involving the deceased. Now I've got to lock it down as a crime scene to prove you didn't push him out of the loft hatch yourself."

"You are joking."

"I tried to call you."

"It's a bloody suicide — cut and dried."

The paramedics exchanged glances.

"Any family here?" Brass said.

"No," Lamb said. "Pretty sure there isn't."

"His wife works at the hospital. That's just round the corner. No kids that I'm aware of." Brass was talking to herself as much as anyone else.

"Someone ought to let Chief Superintendent Baily know," Lamb offered.

"Don't you worry about that," Brass said. "I just want your full statement — including how, out of all the patrol resources available on the District this morning, you happened to be the one that rocked up here."

"I think there's probably less patrol resources available than you think there are, guv," Lamb muttered.

"Thank you, Constable. You may stand down and go and start on your statement."

Lamb made for the door.

"And Constable Lamb?"

Lamb turned.

"Don't breathe a word of this to anyone. *Especially* Chief Superintendent Baily."

CHAPTER FIVE

Haven stretched her back and sighed, a muzzy feeling in her head. She'd spent the entire day in the conference room, servicing a never-ending train of different meetings, all in the same room. She'd barely had a chance to grab a cup of tea and nip to the bathroom, let alone grab any lunch. And all she had to show for it were pages and pages of notes that required tidying into some kind of coherent structure.

When she'd first started as a secretary, her trainer had warned her that not only could her minutes eventually end up being the centrepiece of murder trials, public inquiries and jury inquests, but that the outcome of such events could *hinge* on the integrity and accuracy of her output. This had instilled in her a kind of diligence that had kept her on the edge of a nervous breakdown for most of her secretarial career.

She logged off the computer for the day, bound the day's papers with a giant bulldog clip, packed them away and headed out, the fresh air from the Levels like a cool, rejuvenating tonic.

She should go to the gym, really. She'd been on her backside all day. Head straight there and beast herself on the cross-trainer for forty-five minutes. Book a class or two. Get into good New Year habits and stick to them. If she headed home first, she knew full well that would be her indoors for the night. If she didn't go tonight, avoiding it tomorrow would be easier, and then she'd forget all about it, and then she would slide into middle age like an enormous potato covered in butter rolling down a hill.

Then she remembered that she'd left her gym bag by the front door, and wrote the day off as a big fat dead loss. She may as well order Domino's and Haagen-Dazs and flake out in style.

She walked to the pink Fiat, figuring the fifty or so steps to get there counted as something, and fumbled around her in coat pocket for her keys.

She couldn't find them. She placed the bundle of meeting papers on the roof of the car, put her handbag strap between her teeth and continued rooting around in her pockets.

The pockets conclusively eliminated, she moved onto the handbag.

There they were, the little buggers.

The day having successfully broken even, Haven started up the Fiat, the radio resuming — having been rudely silenced at eight that morning when she arrived at work — its deafening broadcast of Katy Perry's latest release, and she roared out of the car park and away home.

* * *

By the end of the week Kenley had pulled together enough cash to get him started. It had been an indelicate operation, involving retrieving rainy-day hedge funds (in the literal sense) stashed before he'd elected to throw himself at the mercy of the judicial system, offloading some jewellery, and a small amount of thievery and fraud — none of which, he remarked to his reflection in the mirror, had been taken from anyone who wasn't going to be recompensed by a respectable financial institution within a week.

It made for sad viewing. A dirty bundle of cash stuffed into a Sainsbury's bag. He placed it on the kitchen table of the overpriced Airbnb country retreat and made a rough estimate. Twenty-five thousand or so, maybe a little more. If they stayed here much longer he could easily rinse a chunk of that on takeaways and fine wine.

He fingered the keypad of the new pay-as-you-go phone, then typed a message. *I'M IN THE MARKET. LOOKING FOR A COUPLE OF PASTRIES.*

He didn't send it immediately. Instead, he walked outside, the fecund aroma of the surrounding greenery mixing with the smell of the recently stained decking. It was still daylight, just about, but the circle of trees created a layer of darkness that killed off the last shreds of slight warmth from the January sun.

He looked at his watch. Nat would be back soon with food. She was in full-on nesting mode, or honeymoon, or something. She knew — they both did — that this was some artificial gateway to the future; they were stuck in a rose-tinted holding pattern, and whichever path they took out of here was going to determine a whole hell of a lot.

He looked down at the phone. He knew it would gnaw at him, that after they made love in front of the fire again tonight, she would see the slight distance in his eyes. But the alternative was deleting the message and going off to sell cars or something. It boiled down to feel like shit now, or feel like shit later.

He hit SEND, and headed back inside.

* * *

"He knows," Natalie said, removing the tiny tracking device from the heel of her shoe and passing it to Barnes. "He knows, and he doesn't care."

"He told you that?" Barnes said, stamping his feet. The three of them were wearing hi-vis jackets and hard hats and were standing by a workbench, the only furniture in a freezing, empty warehouse on an industrial estate between Eastbourne and Pevensey. The inside was the size of an aircraft hangar, and their collective icy breaths drifted off into the darkness.

"Fronted me up five minutes after we stepped inside the house. Said he knew I wouldn't risk my career and my child by coming back to him unless it was an official authorised deployment. Said that he didn't blame me, and that he would rather take that than not have me at all."

"And did he . . ."

"He also said he was going to get a job in Tesco or something, but if he was of a mind to sink back down into heavy scores, he wouldn't be telling me about any of it — for my own protection," she added.

Barnes looked at Kane, and then slowly replaced the device in a small black case on the workbench.

"She's blown," Kane said. "We're done."

"Hang on a minute," Barnes said. "This could play."

"What are you suggesting? A triple agent? He's not going to tell her anything."

"He doesn't need to, necessarily. He . . ."

Barnes looked at Natalie. She seemed remarkably stoic.

"DC Morgan — Natalie, sorry — would you mind giving me and the superintendent a moment?"

"It's fine. I need to go and get Max, anyway."

She took off the hi-vis and hat. Kane took them from her.

The loading bay door was a square of light framed by the dark warehouse. Barnes waited until she'd walked out of the gloom and into the cold winter sunshine. She disappeared around the corner, arms wrapped around herself, and Barnes turned back to his boss.

"This is going to stop. Now," Kane said when Barnes opened his mouth.

"It's not a dead end. She can still provide info on peripheral activity — his movements, cars, who's in his life, even his moods."

"She's compromised. Not only that, we're putting someone undercover who we knew already had an emotional connection with the subject before we even started the deployment."

"It's not an undercover operation. It's a vetting interview — well, several vetting interviews — triggered by disclosure of a change in personal circumstances. Happens every day."

Kane looked down at the workbench. Barnes traced his gaze to the small case containing the recording device.

"Look," Kane said, "public inquiry backwards . . . it doesn't play well. You've got three times the policing experience I have — surely you can see that?"

"Yes, but—"

"And even if he was planning on spilling his guts to her, he's keeping his nose clean."

"That we know of."

"Barnes, there's no intelligence. Nothing percolating. We can't what-if until we're blue in the face. We have to go where the intel takes us." Kane placed his hand on Barnes's shoulder. "I know you know all this. You're going to have to let it go. Take Tamsin out to dinner. Bare your soul. Speak to a professional. Put Duquesne Kenley in a box and lock him away."

"She's holding back."

"She's got a kid, Barnes. She wouldn't put Kenley before him, but let's not put her in a position where she has to make that choice, eh?"

Barnes looked at his feet. "Okay. You're right, sir."

"Now look me in the eye and say that."

Barnes's eyes suddenly felt heavy, like there were iron poles locking them to the floor, but he did as he was told, even against the prickle of defensiveness that he knew most police officers felt when they were instructed to do something. It was the paradox of the service — a disciplined hierarchy that relied on lawful order, but that didn't mean anybody liked it. Barnes didn't like taking it from anyone, but Kane was an exception.

He looked at his boss — and then there was another prickle. He looked back at the loading bay door. He couldn't quite zero in on it, but . . . something about the way she walked. Too fast. Head down, focused on her feet. Like she was hurrying to get out of the rain — on a cloudless, bright day.

Like something wasn't right.

His phone began to trill in his pocket, and the prickle disappeared like a dream, breaking his concentration. He stepped away from Kane, then, as the conversation unfolded, stepped back and put the phone on loudspeaker.

"Boss," Barnes said. "You're probably going to want to hear this."

CHAPTER SIX

Barnes looked down at the body on the slab. The mortuary was cold and silent, the only sound the gentle ticking of a clock somewhere.

He was aware of his own chest rising and falling in slow, deep movements as he stared at Gabby's blue-white face, trying to work out how he was feeling. He'd had no love for the man, but that was a drop in the ocean of loathing that the deceased had reserved for Barnes. It had been a dislike materially linked to Gabby's senior position, a position of significant power.

And now that had gone. In an instant, Barnes had the upper hand, the last man standing in a duel that had lasted practically all of Barnes's sixteen-year career. The work facade had crumbled, Barnes's sudden acquisition of intimate knowledge giving him inverse seniority. There was nothing more subordinate than being dead, he thought.

Why had he done it? Barnes tried to kick the feeling that it was a final two-fingered salute to Barnes himself — even he wasn't that egocentric. There was a box of items on his desk that might hold some answers — phone, laptop, diary — but that would take time. There was nothing to suggest anything other than a suicide, which meant — despite his rank, and in contrast to the might of the major crime machine when it was wheeled out to play — that it was Barnes and Barnes alone delving into Gabby's past. A get-to-it-when-you-can enquiry, a one-man show to build a file for the coroner to tell the world what everyone already knew.

Barnes couldn't believe Gabby would have been happy with that kind of ignominy. He'd have much preferred to die a hero, with the pomp that went with falling in the line of duty.

As would we all, if we were honest with ourselves for thirty seconds, Barnes thought.

Maybe, he thought, as he left the mortuary and climbed out of the basement into the hospital proper, that in itself was an indication of the old man's state of mind. To his irritation, he found he was feeling a stab of guilt, of remorse. Maybe he should have asked the old bastard how he was doing now and again.

"Mr Barnes."

Speaking of old bastards, here was one that held the key to the secret of longevity. Barnes would have to ask him about *that*, and preferably sooner rather than later. He must have been pushing eighty, and showed no signs of slowing down at all, let alone retiring.

"How you doing, Marlon? It's good to see you."

They shook hands. It was like gripping the paw of a grizzly bear. Choudhury's skin was smooth and brown, and there was an aroma of sandalwood about him. For about the millionth time since meeting the man, Barnes had thought him an odd fit for policing, for the sartorial nose alone. Then again, next to Samson Kane, Choudhury looked almost boring. Maybe the world was moving on at last, Barnes thought.

"This is a straight suicide, Marlon. There's going to be a pretty big ripple effect within policing, but it's suicide. Dare I enquire as to the interest of Professional Standards?"

"You're starting to sound a little like . . . what's the phrase? A chip off the old block." Choudhury beamed at him.

"Unlike you to lose track of your idioms," Barnes said.

"I must be slipping in my dotage."

Barnes smiled. "I very much doubt it. And you haven't answered my question."

Choudhury sighed. "Maybe nothing. But the suicide of a senior officer warrants some scrutiny, wouldn't you say?"

Barnes shrugged.

"I take it he didn't leave a note?" Choudhury said.

Barnes shook his head.

"A shame. Does that seem strange to you?"

"It is what it is," Barnes said. "It does happen."

"A simple 'I'm up to my scrotum in gambling debts' might have allowed me to prioritise my caseload a little easier. However — and now he is dead, the need for discretion is loosened ever so slightly, I'm sorry to say — he was under investigation for a drunken fracas while off duty, with racist overtones. Not only that, but in so doing, his attempts to remain inconspicuous while out on the town with a woman who wasn't his wife rather went out the window.

"And there is the curious circumstance of PC Pete Lamb, who is of interest to me. Do you know him?"

Barnes eyed him. "You know I do, if only tangentially. He was on the fringes of a death in the line of duty case a few years back. A complete clusterfuck, with a past generation of bent coppers slipping their tentacles around the present, even if it did eventually lead me to Duquesne Kenley. You must remember it."

"I do indeed. Mr Lamb was and continues to be a regular presence in my in-tray, as the saying goes. Mr Lamb happened to be off duty during the aforementioned fracas and manoeuvred himself into being a key witness."

"Clever."

". . . and then happened to be first on scene to the report of Mr Glover's suicide."

"Not beyond the realms of possibility."

"No, indeed. But still odd, and worthy of some further scrutiny. Clever?"

"Pardon?"

"You said 'clever'. As in: Mr Lamb being the key witness in the case against Mr Glover was clever. As in: he did it deliberately? Know you something of this?"

"Well, no, not exactly. You're the one who used the word 'manoeuvring'."

"Indeed."

Barnes puffed his cheeks out and exhaled.

"My advice with this one is to go back to basics," Barnes said. "Go where the intelligence and the evidence leads you. If Lamb and Gabby had history, then you'll find it. If they didn't — well, it's a small town."

"Perhaps we could compare notes from time to time."

"Don't we always?" Barnes said.

"I'm grateful."

"What about Chief Superintendent Baily?"

"She is on my to-do list, if for no other reason than that she is a key witness — whether she likes it or not — to the taxi rank episode, even though some might say that is something of a moot point now."

"How did she take the news of his death?"

Choudhury's eyes widened. It was the first time Barnes had ever seen the man caught on the hop.

"I've not told her."

"You haven't? I assumed . . ."

"Well, as investigating manager for the coronial process, next-of-kin would naturally be on your list of actions."

"Except she wasn't his next-of-kin. She was the other woman."

Now it was Choudhury's turn to expel air. "There will be a formal announcement circulated in due course, I'm sure."

"That won't be for a couple of days yet. You're thinking she should find out in the same way as the rest of the rank-and-file? Seems a bit harsh."

"I imagine his widow would say that's precisely all she's entitled to."

"Does she know? The wife, I mean. Does she know he was having an affair?"

"Another question I'll put back to you, Mr Barnes."

Barnes stared at the ceiling for a moment, his hands on his hips. "Did you come here just to compare notes, Marlon? Or to tell me in no uncertain terms just how much is not in your remit?"

"Well, as I say, any allegations of misconduct involving Mr Glover are now largely inactive. The circumstances surrounding his death may give rise to some more, ah, endemic concerns about the state of something rotten within the upper echelons of the big house that necessitates further investigation — or they may not. And if they do not, then, well, my interest starts to wane. Apart from PC Lamb. *He* interests me."

"The gift that keeps on giving. Well, if I find something that will be of interest to you — and trust me, I'll be looking — I'll call you," Barnes said.

They shook hands again, Barnes's mouth pursed in the same *here-we-go-again* expression he wore every time he crossed paths with Marlon Choudhury.

He walked back through the hospital, toying with the idea of grabbing a cup of tea, but then he caught a waft of disinfectant and bodily fluids of some description at the same time as a scream echoed up the corridor from A&E, and instead he quickened his pace.

He mulled over how best to approach the whole Theresa Baily thing. Keeping her in the dark on the basis of an illegitimate and unrecognised relationship seemed a bit brutal — feelings were feelings, after all — but perform any action that had even a whiff of special treatment and he risked the unfettered wrath of Mrs Glover.

Frankly, the whole thing felt a bit above his pay grade. But, as it was, he needn't have worried too much about it.

She was waiting by his car.

He'd never met her, but knew she was a chief superintendent from Operations, and he had seen her on television once or twice.

Her hair had been in a tight bun on that occasion, however; now it was falling about her shoulders in dark brown tresses. She was wearing a navy-blue tracksuit and trainers, and had kind eyes the same colour as her hair. Barnes felt a stab of pity.

"DI Barnes?" she said, seemingly unsure of what to do with her hands.

"Ma'am," Barnes said, with a slight nod.

She extended a hand, looking momentarily grateful that she had found something to occupy them.

"Theresa, please," she said. "You're DI Barnes, yes? You're investigating Gabriel . . . ACC Glover's death?"

Barnes didn't answer, mainly because he didn't think he'd ever heard the man's first name before.

"I'm sorry, I know this isn't the way of doing things, but . . . nobody will tell me anything."

I was just having that conversation with PSD, Barnes thought.

"I'm not . . . his next-of-kin. I have no claim or right to know anything, officially, but I spent more time in his bed than anyone over the past year, and he shared secrets that he'd never shared with anyone, not even his wife."

Now there was an image Barnes could have done without.

"I know I'm not legally allowed to know anything," she continued. "But morally, ethically, surely I'm not just A. N. Other?"

Barnes finally spoke. "What is it you want to know exactly, Theresa? It's terribly sad, but it's a straight suicide. I'm pulling together the file for the coroner, I'll attend the inquest, it'll be a verdict of suicide and that'll be that."

She eyed him. "Kind of clinical, aren't you?"

"If his widow knew I was speaking to you one on one before I've had a chance to speak to her, she'd throw up a major stink, with my name in the middle of it. You know how it goes."

"Did he leave a note?"

Barnes shook his head. She frowned like she didn't believe him.

"What about his phone? Laptop?"

"All in good time. But this isn't a homicide enquiry. It's not a corporate manslaughter. Not neglect. There were no warning signs."

Her eyes began to glisten.

"No warning signs — am I right, Theresa?"

She gave a little staccato shake of the head.

"Look, there needs to be a decision about how we communicate with you officially, if at all. That's a decision far above my head. But I'll throw you what I can, okay?"

"Like a dog for scraps."

"Your words, not mine. I know you're hurting. But I'm afraid there are quite a few people saying you've no business hurting."

She exhaled steadily, like she was trying not to go to pieces, then turned and walked away in the direction of the hospital helipad.

"Ma'am?" Barnes called.

She turned.

"How did you know he was dead? If you've had no official notification, and wouldn't have had cause to go poking around our systems, how did you actually find out?"

From a distance of about twenty feet, she looked thin, her face drawn and worried. You would never have pegged her as police, never mind a senior officer, but then, he thought, we come in all shapes and sizes.

"He sent me a message," she said, eventually. "The night before. Told me he'd had enough. He was in pain."

Barnes chewed this over. "The night before?"

"I tried to call him, find out where he was, get some help. I almost called his wife. But I didn't. And now he's dead."

"I'm going to need to see that message," he said. "At your convenience, of course."

* * *

Barnes took a deep breath and crunched his way across the gravel drive, marvelling at the chirping wrens and gently rustling cherry blossoms overhanging the private road, masking the traffic to a distant hush. As he walked, a sudden spiral of thoughts slowed his pace: was he too junior a rank for this? Should he have brought someone with him? Should he record the meeting? This was the widow of a chief officer, after all.

None of which stopped him completely — he was old enough and ugly enough these days to know that's how he himself rolled. Besides, he was an SIO talking to the widow of a suicide victim, nothing more. He'd spoken to hundreds in his time. He'd locked down the spare bedroom, searched the scene, ordered the seizure of the loft hatch cover and ligature and dutifully accompanied the body to the mortuary. The next-of-kin was the last tick in the box.

The front door opened and a waft of cigarette smoke, incense and something else greeted him as he stepped in out of the cold at the invitation of a woman in her early forties, who clearly took pride in her appearance. She had, Barnes noted, a good four inches on the deceased.

"Mrs Glover?" Barnes said.

"Ms Short. I've been using my maiden name for a while now. But please call me Ella."

She was red-eyed, but otherwise impassive. Barnes wondered if she'd numbed the pain with a small cocktail or two — over the counter or otherwise — or if she didn't deign to be too demonstrative with her grief in front of the help.

He kicked himself inwardly. People grieved in all manner of ways, rich and poor. He could hear Tamsin in his head: *You inverted snob.* Maybe it just boiled down to the fact that he still couldn't quite believe anyone could stand Gabby enough to be around him, much less marry him. Still, the instant reversion to the maiden name was a new one. In that sense, she seemed to be all business.

He followed her from the hallway into the front room, forcing himself, for her benefit, not to glance up the stairs, even though she had her back to him.

He sat down on an upholstered chair and took in the room. The aroma of incense was stronger here. It was like the lounge of a country hotel, all long floral drapes and thick red walls and polished mahogany furniture. Not a hair out of place and certainly no real sense of having been lived in. Barnes sensed that this was room where business was conducted — financial management, academic study, death planning. Barnes imagined the accountant sitting here, or Glover hearing cases being put forward for intrusive surveillance in the dead of night with the door shut.

He flipped his notebook open, more for show than anything else.

"I'm sorry for your loss. I'm just here to give you how I'm seeing everything, and then you can tell me if you think it about stacks up, or if you're holding any cards that mean I should look at things differently."

She opened her mouth. Barnes held up a finger. She closed it again.

"That is to say, this looks like a suicide. That means the resources that get put to it are, well, just me. That doesn't change based on why he did it. It would only change if it was something made to look like suicide that wasn't."

"And what do you think?"

"I think it was suicide. You disagree?"

She gave a slight shake of the head. Holding it together, Barnes thought.

"Which means we're only really looking at the why. Experience suggests if he didn't have a documented history of depression or mental ill health, then it was something — something he'd kept to himself — that was on the cusp of becoming public knowledge. Often it's gambling, getting fired, another woman."

"Experience suggests that?"

"Well, my experience."

"I've had the chief constable visit me at home since he died. A personal call from the ACPO president. A note from the chief exec of the commissioner's office. Twenty-four hours solid of the tabloids queuing up at the garden wall. How much experience do you have, exactly?"

"Sixteen years' service. Fourteen as a detective. Five as a detective inspector." Barnes forced himself to keep steady, not to be sideswiped by the grandstanding. "Was he . . . did he have any history of being mentally unwell?"

She shook her head. "He was a typical bottler. Saw expression as a sign of weakness. If he was moody — and he could have some foul moods — he could go days without speaking. Whenever things didn't go his way, he took it personally. Saw it as an affront to his masculinity, his intelligence. Made him feel ordinary." She suddenly clamped her mouth shut, like she'd said too much.

"So it's possible that he was depressed and nobody knew?"

"If you'd suggested he was depressed to his face he'd have thrown you out."

"We didn't find a note," Barnes said. "Does that surprise you?"

She thought about that. "No. No, it doesn't surprise me."

"You think he was punishing you by not giving you any answers?"

"Well, I didn't think that. Now I do."

"I didn't mean—"

"To be honest, when Gabriel got up in the morning, his first thoughts were of Gabriel. It was never any different. So this is pretty well on-brand."

Barnes thought about that. "What about the other triggers? Gambling, et cetera. Did he mention the fact that he was under investigation at work?"

Barnes was careful not to mention any more of the detail of that particular episode, and especially not the close proximity of Theresa Baily. But Ella didn't seem surprised. She just gave an enormous sigh, like she'd been holding her breath.

"Look, Mr Barnes, I hold a senior position at the hospital. I also run my own business. I own the freehold on the premises and am chairman of the board. I have an annexe out in the garden that I use as an office, which nobody else has access to. We have separate bank accounts. Gabriel travelled a lot — national work, operations. If he and I had dinner together at home once a week we were doing well. We'd take it turns to talk about our respective weeks, and that was that."

"I'm getting a picture."

"You are, are you?"

"Just a picture. Not necessarily *the* picture. You have any kids?"

She eyed him. "No." In his head, she added, *Thank God*.

"So what you're saying is that it's entirely possible he could, say, rack up a ton of gambling debts and you'd be none the wiser?"

"Precisely."

Barnes thought about it, let it go. It was a bit too convenient; if he'd been thinking about homicide, he'd have pressed a little harder, but he wasn't.

"Let me put it another way: do you know or suspect anything that ought to lead me to revise my suicide hypothesis? Or, indeed, do you object to that hypothesis?"

"Object?"

"Well, look, the chief constable may have been to pay his condolences, but what he's saying to me is he doesn't want ACC Glover's widow voicing public concerns about how wrong the police have got it. This will hit the papers."

"It already has, but so far it's nice and vague," Ella Short said. "Provided it stays that way, I will raise no objections. Certainly not in public."

"There'll be an inquest."

"Naturally."

Barnes put away his notebook.

"Thank you, Mrs . . . Ella. And, once again, I am very sorry for your loss."

He got up and made for the front door. In the hallway, he stopped and turned, a deep frown on his face. "Why do you think he did it where he did?"

"What do you mean?"

This time, Barnes did look towards the top of the stairs. "The room. It's a spare room, yes?"

"I don't see . . ."

"He could have done it anywhere. The woods, the garage, the cliffs. Why do you think he chose here? That room, specifically?"

"I suppose . . ."

"Did you sleep in separate bedrooms?"

"I beg your pardon?" Ella edged around him and placed a hand on the front door catch.

"You've portrayed an idea of two very separate lives. I just wondered if you had separate bedrooms."

"Is that relevant to anything?"

She opened the door and Barnes obediently stepped backwards over the threshold. The wrens had grown particularly brazen in their current rendition.

"It may be nothing. I just wondered what your thoughts were. Logistics, or certainly expedience, can often determine both the most appropriate site and method. There can also be a world of difference between being found by a dog walker and being found by your spouse. Sometimes it's done to punish, sometimes it's done—"

"Speaking of done, I think we are done here. If you persist, I shall be contacting your boss."

"The spare room, Ms Short. What are your thoughts?"

"Because it's the only room in the house with a fucking loft hatch," Ella said, and slammed the door.

CHAPTER SEVEN

An emergency call was just that. Receive, assess and dispatch. Ninety-nine times out of a hundred, background research was undertaken to give the responding units a better idea of what they were rolling into, but it had to happen in tandem — they couldn't sit around waiting to get the ins and outs of a duck's arse before they deigned to show up.

This is undoubtedly what had happened when Lamb had been sent to Gabby Glover's house. A good-faith call made by a neighbour, sufficiently credible to warrant an emergency response, meaning the nearest available — and willing; this was a stranger notion than many gave credit for — unit was directed to attend, stat. So, Lamb had started rolling; it wouldn't have taken long for the people behind the scenes to establish that this was the home address of a senior officer. The multiple missed calls on Lamb's phone had been from both Brass and the control room inspector.

Lamb carefully removed his hairpiece, grateful that it hadn't let him down when the marauding plucker with his tweezers had pounced. He placed it gently on the white polystyrene head in his bathroom, resisting, for the eight-thousandth time, the urge to find a black felt-tip pen and draw a moustache on it. He snorted a line of blow off the glass front of his last — his only, in fact — framed commendation certificate, collapsed backwards on his sofa and felt a little better.

As a career patrol officer, even one who had so often flown close to the sun, he had seen most things. It was irritating to him, then, that he could not seem to dislodge Gabby's death mask from his mind. To start with — extra-marital activities aside — he was surprised to learn the man was married. Lamb had only encountered him personally a handful of times, but he knew enough about him from other sources to understand that he was an arrogant tyrant. Who the hell could stand him enough to have married him? And of all the things that could have likely blown back on him, it was a drunken argument at a taxi rank that caused him to throw a rope over a loft joist? Lamb couldn't work it out. You didn't get to the heady heights Glover had reached by giving a shit about things like that.

That was quite apart from Lamb's discomfort at his own proximity to both Gabby's drunken misdemeanour and his subsequent demise. Too close for comfort. Was he somehow responsible? For all his bluster, had Glover, in the morning's sobriety, realised that he was suddenly up against it, thanks to the presence of Lamb on the scene?

SENIOR POLICE COMMANDER FOUND DEAD AFTER ACCUSATION OF DRUNKEN RACIST OUTBURST AT CABBIE; JUNIOR WHISTLEBLOWER RAMS HOME FINAL NAIL INTO CAREER COFFIN

Well, when you put it like that . . .

The coke began to kick in properly, and Lamb's mind began to race. Cocaine was possibly not the drug of choice for someone on the cusp of PTSD.

He scraped the inside of the wrap with his fingernail and rubbed it onto his gums. Scraping the barrel, literally, figuratively and everything else in between.

He looked at his watch. Gone midnight. Still early.

He picked up his phone and keyed a quick text.

Need re-up. 100 tops.

He hit SEND with a deep sigh. The reply came three minutes later.

20 min boi. Usual place.

Lamb rubbed his face and then headed out, pausing for a moment to look at his front door. Borrowed, like everything else in his career, in his life. Owned by a former colleague. Former friend. Bastard died a hero in the line of duty; Lamb had gone to the funeral and then claimed first dibs on the guy's flat at a discount, like he was circling for carrion.

That had been nine years ago. 2006. The place had been trendy back then — a series of apartment blocks in blue and yellow overlooking the Sovereign Harbour lock, connected by steel girders and a wide boardwalk designed to resemble an ocean liner in some obscure nouveau-art way.

The fresh air felt good. A robust south-westerly swooping along the boardwalk cleared his raw sinuses, and he headed down to the lock, the gates clattering in the wind.

He felt better for the walk, and he headed over to Langney Point, clomping across the shingle at the Martello Tower until he got to the promenade, and then headed west until he reached the series of small buildings at Harbour Reach. Blue iron gates barred the way to the public toilets, while the ice cream kiosk was shuttered closed, metal tables and chairs stacked in a very final-looking way.

He stopped at the car park. There were a couple of estates, some trucks — dog walkers and night shore fishers mainly. He leaned on the pay-and-display machine and waited for the moped.

He checked his watch. Twelve minutes to walk here. Meaning eight minutes to wait.

Sure enough, after another seven minutes there was the whine of a scooter engine, and a bike appeared at the junction with the Ramsay Way estate, a brightly coloured thermal food box mounted on the rear.

The scooter climbed the short ascent of Harbour Reach into the car park; the rider dismounted, and walked, engine still running, to the nearest dustbin. He discarded what looked like a bundle of McDonald's packaging into the bin, then rode off without so much as a nod in Lamb's direction.

Lamb walked over, fighting the urge to look around him, and fished the wrappers out of the bin. He carried them over to the ice cream kiosk and perched on a bench that was sheltered by a tile lip overhanging the kiosk.

The edges of the wrapper flapped in the wind as he gripped it in his palm and counted the bags. There they were, nestled inside like a cluster of frogspawn. Lamb suddenly felt warm, and he got up to go, stuffing the papers into his jacket.

He thought about calling in sick tomorrow and having a little party tonight. Maybe even calling in some company. He thought he might even have a bottle of something sparkling in the fridge. There was that cute little journalist that would do anything for some blue pillow talk. Or he could just go old school and call up one of the massage parlours off Seaside.

He passed the end of the building line, and a wide expanse of black shingle dotted with scrub opened up in front of him, with an accompanying swirl of wind.

The wind filled his ears; if it hadn't, he might have had enough warning to duck, flinch, shield himself somehow. But he didn't, and something hard and metal flew out of the darkness around the corner of the building and collided squarely with his skull.

Fireworks on the horizon, great flashes of purple and lime green exploding out at sea. Stars plummeting into the Channel from the farthest reaches of space. Waves roaring up on the beach like angry lions. And a ringing in his head like a million fire alarms.

He didn't wake up suddenly. For a long time he wasn't sure if he was awake or asleep, if he was seeing or dreaming. It took a while for him to understand that the sound of the breakers on the shingle and the feeling of the promenade's cold grit against his cheek were most definitely real.

He had no idea how long he'd been out, and was disappointed to find that he was still on his front on the ground and not in some warm hospital bed being tended to by a nurse in a too-small uniform. It was still dark, still cold and still bloody windy. He had fallen awkwardly, his hands trapped under his front, and when he shivered, ripples of pain like a swing saw cut through his brain, turning it into salami slices.

He tried to get up, but his legs were weak and the ground was see-sawing like a bad hit on the Starship *Enterprise*. There was a dark patch the size of the dinner plate where his face had been. He touched it, then touched his face and decided the wet circle of blood definitely belonged within him, not without. There was a white lump in the centre of the circle that he quickly identified as one of his incisors.

No anglers, no dog walkers rushing to his aid; nothing had changed while he'd been falling down a rabbit hole, but on the farthest tip of the horizon, over by Hastings, the faintest edge of pink was beginning to kiss the black canvas draped over the sky.

He checked his watch, but couldn't focus on the dial. He staggered to the edge of the promenade, but stopped short of the beach, figuring he was unsteady enough on his feet. He was strangely compelled by the sound of the waves and the stars he could still see. White globules of ice bobbing along on the breakers, having tumbled headlong to Earth from space.

No.

Not stars, but . . .

Something.

There were at least seven of them. White objects, larger than footballs but smaller than dustbins.

He rubbed his eyes, then doubled over in pain. His eyes felt as though they had no lids and he'd just pressed spoons coated in chilli sauce onto his eyeballs.

He staggered down the shingle to the water's edge. The tide was going out, and the breakers were hissing a little less vehemently now.

He stood on the mud flats, one arm clutching his side, completely unable to gauge how far he needed to stand back to avoid his feet getting soaked.

He squinted. The white things were getting closer. They were definitely real, and they were not stars.

They were coming in, so all he needed to do was wait. Just wait and . . . not die.

The pink edge of the sky widened gradually, like an opening flower, the first reaches of dawn beginning to spread across the world. If he was going to die, this would seem a pretty moody vista to go out with, but something was telling him he was not going to die just yet, that he was still just a washed-up cokehead cop with a mashed-up face, a ruptured kidney and a missing tooth.

Something bumped against his foot. He looked down. It was a sack, thick white polythene bound with bungees and secured tight with carabiners.

He bent down; the thing was heavy, but he was very reluctant to use his other arm for anything other than holding his extraordinarily painful side.

He grabbed hold of one of the bungees and dragged the sack up the beach into the lee of a huge wooden groyne spearing into the water like a limpet-encrusted finger.

He slumped against the wood and sat down heavily on the shingle, dragging the sack towards him. It weighed a ton. He prised the seal open like a kid delving into his Christmas stocking. The contents were double-bagged, and below the polythene skins was a rucksack covered with air-filled plastic that he presumed acted as a buoyancy aid. Lamb's face was completely numb, and he was only partly aware of blood from his wound spotting the white plastic.

He reached inside and felt around. His hand closed around a hard item, also wrapped in plastic.

He pulled it out. It was a brick, easily weighing a kilo, the wrapping stamped with some kind of abstract logo incorporating a snake's head, an arrow and a stop sign.

He rooted around in the sack. At least thirteen more in there, maybe more. Instinctively he looked around him, and then wished he hadn't. It felt like there were knives in his brain.

Once the stars stopped dancing before his eyes, he looked out to sea again. There were, he was fairly sure, at least seven more sacks bobbing in the water. Fifteen bricks per sack meant at least 120 bricks in total. If his estimate of a kilo a brick was right, that was a 120 kilos of . . . something.

He suddenly thought to check his pockets. His keys were still there, along with his wallet and phone, meaning that whoever brained him with the metal bar had wanted to fuck him up just for the sake of it. Nice.

He found his front door key and plunged it into one of the bricks. It took a bit of manipulation, but the end of the key eventually pierced several skins of thick polythene. There was a lighter, translucent plastic underneath it — beyond that, some kind of fine white powder that clumped together when the moisture in the air hit it.

Lamb dabbed the tip of his little finger against his tongue, dipped it into the powder, and pressed the resultant sample into his gums.

He sat and thought about it for about half a minute, and then decided he had 120 kilos of some very pure shit indeed.

He stood up, steadying himself on the groyne. The pink was stretching across the sky faster than he would have expected for the time of year, which meant he had to act fast. The corner of the sky was reddening with every minute as the sun threatened to make an appearance.

He looked back up the beach. Dog walkers, anglers and cyclists were a very clear and imminent risk — once they worked out there were pressies appearing on the shore, even lifelong abstainers would descend into a cocaine-grabbing frenzy.

He figured he could wade in and grab at least three of the sacks and only get his knees wet; the remainder were still quite a way out. He would take that, he figured; that was still eighty kilos in the hand.

And then what? He was fifteen minutes' walk from his flat. He wasn't going to be able to carry eighty kilos on his own all that way on foot. It would be easier to put Inspector Brass on his back and run there with her.

The dawn began to spread with increasing speed. What was he going to do? Pack as many bricks into his pockets, cut his losses and disappear? Or stash them for later?

He looked around. That would be very tricky indeed — the toilets and kiosk would be barred shut for some time yet, which meant his only option would be to bury the sacks under a mound of shingle — and you could bet your bottom dollar some overeager bloody Fido would sniff them out well before lunchtime.

Daybreak was going to beat him to it. Shit. The spread of pink was growing paler, a wash of light in which everything gradually became clearer.

Including the blood on his face and hands. He held up his phone and took a quick snap of himself. Jesus. That was a lot of blood. Probably explained the extreme cold he was suddenly feeling, the light-headed, swimmy sensation and the sudden, unbelievable loudness of the waves.

He admitted defeat and called 999. Ambulance for him, police for the drugs.

Some calls just happen to generate a fast response, and, on reflection, off-duty officer just happens to be out for an early morning constitutional as a hundred kilos of coke washes up on the beach did sound a bit odd. Almost immediately, he heard the sirens from the Hammonds Drive patrol base less than two miles away. Possibly he should have kept his occupation out of it.

He figured nothing ventured, nothing gained, and he grabbed five of the bricks and buried them under a pile of shingle in the lee of the groyne. He stepped back to inspect his handiwork, then, as the parachute of blue lights began to coat the promenade, he figured it would have to do.

CHAPTER EIGHT

Lamb trudged into work to be debriefed, still grumbling to himself about having had to pay for a taxi from A&E. They had patched him up and sent him on his way, having made some token noises about keeping him in for observation as a result of the head injury. Lamb had taken the hint and vamoosed, not wanting to dwell too long on the fact that the shortlist of candidates to come pick him up was pretty, well, short; not only that, the names that did feature were either unwilling or unable.

He was a victim of a crime, wasn't he? And his own blue brethren didn't want to come get him.

Jill Rough was the duty supervisor that had attended the beach — as a PC, Lamb remembered her as being pretty good fun. Now she had some stripes she seemed to be cut from the same cloth as Inspector Brass — unsmiling, robotic and clearly not believing a word Lamb said about the assault and the drugs.

It was still early when Lamb arrived at the patrol base — a pale winter sun had yet to fully defeat the night.

This time of day, the car park was still pretty empty. He saw something on the ground in one of the empty bays, and went to pick it up.

It was a bundle of papers, bound with a clip. They were mostly handwritten notes, with some typed minutes of meetings on paper headed with the police crest — marked, he noted, OFFICIAL SENSITIVE.

Oh dear, oh dear, he thought, scrutinising the handwriting for some sense of the author's identity. The i's were dotted with hearts, and double exclamation marks had been used liberally — mainly, he noticed, on prompts and notes to self.

There. In the bottom corner of the third page. Identity confirmed.

ACTION FOR HAVEN!! REMEMBER TO GET FUNDING DATA FROM PREVIOUS SET OF MINUTES!!

Haven. The unbelievably hot secretary. *That* was her name. Beautiful, he thought. The day was looking up.

He walked around the back of the building, and groaned to himself when he saw Inspector Brass's extraordinarily expensive bike chained to the cycle rack.

Lamb popped into the gents — then wished he hadn't. He emerged into the corridor just as Inspector Brass walked past.

Brass turned and deliberately caught Lamb's eye as he was zipping himself up; Lamb avoided her gaze and headed for the briefing room, wondering if life could get any more awkward.

"Wash your hands, Constable," said Brass.

Lamb stopped, thought about it, then obediently returned to the bathroom.

"My office," Brass called, just as the door swung shut.

Lamb did as he was bidden — noting en route that, to his disappointment, the secretary called Haven was not in yet — and was unsurprised to see DCI Marlon Choudhury in the same seat as he had been less than a week ago.

"Constable," Choudhury smiled, putting down the papers he was reading. "Please do take a seat. You've rather been through the mill, I see."

Lamb did as he was told.

"You're probably wondering whether I just camp out under the desk," Choudhury said.

No danger of that, Lamb thought. The man was too well turned out. Today's outfit was a grey waistcoat over a dark blue shirt with a lemon-yellow bow tie and cufflinks that would have had magpies fighting among themselves. A dark overcoat hung on the back of the chair. He was just missing the Panama hat and the silver-topped cane, Lamb thought miserably, but had to admit that the old codger did look the absolute business.

Lamb touched the dressing on his face. He turned as Inspector Brass walked in, and winced as something jarred inside his spinal assembly.

"Here we all are again," Choudhury beamed, spreading his hands to his audience of two.

"Too soon for my drugs result, I'm guessing," Lamb mumbled.

"Indeed," Choudhury said, the smile never faltering. He laced his fingers across his enormous belly. "We are here to unpick the tantalising narrative of your exploits over the last couple of days."

"Am I in trouble?" Lamb said.

"That," Choudhury said, fiddling around in a battered leather briefcase, "remains to be seen."

He found a bone-white clay churchwarden's pipe in the bottom of the case and clamped it between his teeth.

"Just to recap," he said, tamping tobacco into the end, "you were a key witness in an allegation of racially aggravated public disorder, while drunk, levelled at a senior officer. Very senior," he added, with a wink.

"That self-same officer committed suicide — at least, that is the preferred theory at present — a mere three days later. As luck would have it, you were first on scene."

Lamb looked at the floor.

"Then, approximately six hours ago, you were out for a pre-dawn stroll when you were attacked by someone with an iron bar or similarly heavy blunt instrument. On coming to, you intercepted seven or so parcels of what is suspected to be a Class A controlled substance, which just happened to bob up on shore as you were coming round. You investigated these parcels, and then reported the whole matter."

Choudhury leaned across the desk and clasped his hands. The pipe remained unlit in his mouth.

"That about right?"

"I haven't done anything wrong," Lamb mumbled. "It's all as I reported."

"Mr Lamb, without putting too fine a point on it," Choudhury said, in an even tone, ". . . says you."

* * *

Lamb left the office forty minutes later, feeling decidedly dejected. They'd not served him with papers nor thrown anything official his way — part of the reason being he'd given them his side of events and hadn't told them to go poke it by saying 'no comment' every ten seconds — but had merely asked him again to go over the two police reports he himself had made. Which was fair enough.

Except, of course, that wasn't what they were asking. Every comment and nuance was loaded with meaning. Choudhury and that bloody wink of his. They weren't believing a word, even though it was — well, the vast majority of it — all true. They'd taken great pleasure in ladling scorn into every reaction.

And then his day improved.

Haven the secretary was at her desk, forehead etched with that perpetual frown as she concentrated on whatever was on her screen. Some might have said that frowning round the clock was likely to age her prematurely, but Lamb thought it was gorgeous.

And now he had an in.

"Good morning," he said as he approached her desk, only remembering when it was too late to turn back that he looked as though he'd been in a car accident.

She looked up, and he realised that the frown was more pronounced than usual. A sick look of dread and despair was scored into her otherwise flawless skin — one he knew he himself had worn on many a previous occasion, usually when he encountered Choudhury or one of his PSD ilk, but not nearly in quite so endearing a fashion — and he knew he had lucked out.

"I'm sorry to bother you," he said. "My name's Pete."

She offered a thin smile. It was clearly strained; despite her palpable state of worry she remained polite, even if he did detect the effort at restraint keeping her from rolling her eyes.

"Do these belong to you?"

He held out the bundle of papers. Her eyes widened, and she made a scrambling grab for them in a waft of perfume.

"Oh my God. Where did you find them?"

"Out in the car park. On the ground."

She placed an impeccably manicured hand with pink fingernails across her eyes — left hand, no ring, Lamb noted gleefully — and took deep, relieved breaths.

"I'm such an idiot. I must have left them on the roof of the car."

She took the bundle and sat back down, flicking through the pages one by one.

Lamb smiled. "I didn't steal any."

She spluttered laughter — huge, hitching gasps that caused Lamb just a moment's unease. What was the cure for hyperventilating?

"You have no idea how relieved I am. Thank you so much. I literally thought I was going to lose my job. I was just trying to work out how to tell my boss."

"You're welcome."

"No, really. You must let me make it up to you."

Lamb kept his expression as neutral as possible, while his imagination momentarily ran away with him.

"No need. All in a day's work."

"That's very sweet, but you've just rescued me from the dole queue."

"Honestly, it's fine. We all make mistakes. I'm just glad you're not in any trouble."

She smiled — a proper one this time, and he felt his insides melt.

"How are you settling in? I guessed you were new, sitting out here with the rank-and-file. So who do you, you know —" Lamb nodded at Haven's keyboard — "look after, I guess."

"Assistant Chief Constable Glover," she said, her voice a hushed mixture of pride and mild awe.

Lamb tilted his head, a sudden knot in his stomach. Hadn't she been told? She must surely know the late ACC was currently being held on ice in the hospital basement. She couldn't still be arranging meetings and organising the work life of a dead man, surely? Lamb was experienced enough to know there were some controversies surrounding his death and that there would be a delay in the wider workforce being officially notified by mass circulation, but they surely wouldn't leave the secretary hanging, would they?

"Are you okay?" Haven asked. "You look a little pale."

"Am I? I do feel a little dizzy. I lost a fair bit of blood, you see, and . . ."

"Oh, you poor thing," Haven said, jumping up. "Here. Take my seat."

Tempting as it was, Lamb didn't trust himself not to spill the beans, and so he reluctantly carved out a quick exit strategy.

"That's very kind of you," he said. *"Merci."*

"Je vous en prie," she replied, with a flawless accent. *"Si je peux vous aider à nouveau à l'avenir, n'hésitez pas à me le faire savoir."*

Lamb blinked, thought he might pass out, then managed to nod and smile.

She spoke French. He was doomed.

"You've, uh, been in the wars?" she said, pointing at the dressings.

He swelled his chest just slightly, momentarily forgetting the imperative to leave.

"That's also in a day's work, I'm afraid. It's been a busy week. Drug dealers, suicides, assaults. Blue light run to blue light run. New Year, you know."

It was only partially untrue. She went slightly gooey-eyed. *Leave 'em wanting more,* he thought.

"Well, take it easy. Hope your day picks up from here."

He made to go.

"Hey."

He turned.

"I'm really sorry, but . . . I forgot what you said your name was. You know, with all the distractions."

She looked embarrassed. It took the edge off an otherwise red-letter encounter, but only slightly.

"It's Pete."

"Thanks, Pete."

He trotted off, just as Inspector Brass emerged from the office looking ever so slightly put out. Choudhury had remained inside the office, and so Lamb could only surmise that she'd been turfed out of her own domain.

Lamb didn't exactly skip past the inspector, but he did give her a little wink. He couldn't help himself.

He spent the morning eyeing Haven from a distance. He kept an eye on his emails too, in case official notification of Gabby's death was circulated and he could rush to provide a shoulder for Haven to cry on.

He got to about lunchtime and then, when neither Choudhury nor Brass showed the slightest interest in speaking to him any further, he told Rough his vision was blurry and he thought he might have a concussion. Rough looked more irritated than worried, and told Lamb that he should book in sick and get rechecked at A&E.

Lamb didn't need telling twice. He didn't go back to hospital, however, but headed straight back down to Harbour Reach to keep observations on his makeshift hide from a distance. The parcels themselves — the bulk of them anyway — had been loaded onto the back of a police van and had trundled off to God-knows-where in a convoy of ARVs containing tense-looking armed officers. It had been quite an impressive sight, all told.

Lamb watched and waited, walked up and down the beach, never letting the hide out of his sight. The wait was interminable, not least because the drilling in his head was getting louder — maybe he should get checked out again at the hospital after all — but when the sun finally began to give up at around half three, Lamb scrambled inelegantly down the shingle to where he had secreted the bricks.

As his feet were quickly submerged in seawater up to the ankles he realised, with no small amount of relief, that he'd completely omitted to consider the tide times in his haste to bury the treasure that had literally landed in his lap. More luck than judgment, he thought, as he scrabbled around in the stones to find the bricks. Although, he thought, if he hadn't had the presence of mind to come down and spend all afternoon reconnoitring the spot, they could conceivably have all been washed away. Again.

But, no, there they were. Five sealed bricks of party food. A little for himself and whichever hot guests might choose to share it with him, peddle the rest for a sensible figure and he might, just might, with a little bit of sound investment advice, have enough to exit policing for good. He wouldn't be greedy, wouldn't look to become a career dealer or anything — just a one-hit wonder to get him over the hump and away from shift work, moaners and bleeding-hearts.

It wouldn't hurt to spend a little on Haven either, he thought. Take her somewhere nice, once he'd worked out the most effective method for asking her out. She'd be bruised when she found out about Gabby, so he would need to be around for her to lean on. He needn't push things; just being there when she needed a friend would suffice.

But then how to tell her that he was being investigated for potentially being an indirect trigger for Gabby's suicide? He'd have to think about that. He'd like to be up front with her from the off, but, well . . . maybe he'd see exactly how cut up she was about his death first.

He shoved the bricks into a rucksack and scrambled up the beach, his feet squelching in his shoes. He reached the promenade, scanned three-sixty for any signs of trouble, but felt reasonably comfortable that anyone wanting to rush him didn't exactly have the element of surprise — it was either open land or water for at least a hundred yards in every direction.

Got the drop on you last night, though, didn't they? said a smug voice in his head. *Yes, but it was dark, not to mention a sucker punch*, some other voice retorted. Nevertheless, he quickened his pace and elected to keep well away from the ice cream kiosk.

He rushed home, a five-kilo payload proving surprisingly heavy after fifteen minutes of brisk walking. Well, as brisk as he could manage, anyway. His head was killing him, and his wounds seemed to swing from being on fire to being so numb he thought all the blood had drained out of him.

He tipped the bricks onto the sofa, admired them for exactly five seconds, and then stuffed them into the DVD drawer in a flash of sudden paranoia that told him Marlon Choudhury had been surveilling him all afternoon.

For a moment, Lamb's instinct was to put the bricks in the communal bin store, or throw them back out to sea. For all his professional shortcomings, extracurricular pursuits and insalubrious company, he wasn't connected enough to be able to offload the gear safely or at a price worth paying. The obvious choice would be his go-to dealer, but he was street-level; besides, as far as Lamb knew, *he* was the one that smashed him over the head with an iron bar. Lamb needed someone more senior.

He paced the flat in a state of nervous tension, unable to concentrate on anything else, the bricks like hot coals burning a hole through his sofa.

As darkness fell, he began to feel slightly less discomfited — but then another thought occurred to him, somewhere between paranoia and self-preservation, and he ran to the kitchen for his Gerber.

He found a seldom-used PVC tablecloth, spread it out on the lounge floor and wiped it down carefully. Then he slit open each brick and poured the contents out onto the tablecloth, surfing through them with the edge of the knife.

For about half a minute, he was content that there was nothing to look at besides a mound of beautiful pure white sugar.

And then he saw it.

He gently dug the tip of the Gerber into the pile of white, then carefully withdrew it and held the point up to his nose.

It was tiny, a small blue square, thinner than a credit card and half the size of a SIM card.

"Oh, shit," Lamb said aloud.

A tracker. A bloody tracker. Of course it was. How the hell could there not be trackers scattered throughout a bulk shipment of marine-transported Class A? And he had just led both an unhappy supplier and an even unhappier recipient straight to his door.

Not paranoia.

A healthy dollop of self-preservation and investigative nous, neither of which had kicked in quickly enough to get his nuts out of the vice.

Stupid, stupid, *stupid*.

He went to the kitchen and fried the tiny blue chip on the hob, then, as carefully as he could, scooped the bulk of the gear into a collection of plastic tubs preserved from past takeaways and secreted them in his cupboard. He wiped down the tablecloth with disinfectant, bundled it into a bin liner, double-bagged it and pulled on his shoes to take the whole lot down to the bin store.

He opened the apartment door and peered out into the corridor. He'd been worried about a task force of Choudhury's goons turning up, but given this latest development, it would have been preferable to the exasperated drug lords that now knew where he lived.

Nothing in the corridor. A TV playing faintly somewhere behind the paper-thin, new-build walls. He took cautious steps down the corridor, his injuries throbbing like an irritatingly persistent distress signal.

He took the stairs down to the basement level and out into the car park, still cursing his own stupidity, and stared at his allocated bin. Not wanting to repeat his lapse in intelligence, he lifted the lid to the one next to it, and placed his bundle of contraband in there instead.

The underground car park was a tunnel below the boardwalk servicing the tower blocks, and was dotted with sickly yellow arc lamps. The sound of cars pulling in and out radiated throughout the parking tunnel with some kind of weird reverberating acoustics that kept Lamb spinning nervously on his heel and scanning for threats.

Lamb's feet clunked on the metal gantry steps up to the boardwalk, suddenly very aware of the chill air and the wind whistling through the steel stanchions of the enormous — and suddenly, to Lamb, hideous — design. If he had chanced upon Marlon Choudhury leading a team of PSD officers in through his front door, search warrant in hand, he would have breathed a sigh of relief. Career-limiting it may have been, but it was far preferable to the alternative.

As if in response to Lamb's thoughts, his burner phone gently buzzed in his pocket.

He pulled it out and read the message.

U GOT MY BRIX

Not a question, not an accusation. A simple statement of fact.

Lamb's heart bounced up to his gullet and back down again. He dropped the burner, and spun on the spot on the synthetic grey carpet in the apartment block's hallway.

He patted his pockets. He had nothing on him. No phone, no car keys, no wallet. Front door key, that was it. He could make a run for it, but he needed some supplies first.

He looked at the time. Early evening. The tracker would have shown the parcels landing. Lamb's bricks had sat there for, what, eight hours? ten? before he'd come back for them.

Time enough for both the sender and the recipient to realise that they'd gone astray. But if that were the case, and they had a fix on the location, why not retrieve them there and then? Why had they not come for them? Had they hedged their bets on the police laying a trap for them and kept well away? Had Lamb's own vocation bought him a few extra hours while they weighed that up? Or were they watching and waiting — waiting to see if some greedy, selfish, dishonest passerby helped themselves and claimed finders keepers?

Once a tracker was involved, none of the explanations was particularly comforting, but he was going to have to chance it.

He avoided the lift and took the four flights of stairs to his floor, his footsteps echoing in the yellow-and-blue walled stairwell. His wounds were throbbing by the time he reached his front door, and he decided he was in no particular hurry to find out whether they were just the *hors d'oeuvres*.

He shoved his wallet, phone and keys into his pockets, and crammed some other essentials into a rucksack. He stood for a moment in the middle of the apartment, suddenly aware that this flat could end up housing not one dead cop, but two, and it was a legacy he did not particularly want to bequeath anyone.

He made for the front door, and then stopped. He eyed the kitchen cupboard. He didn't have long to make a decision, and so, after a rapid assessment of the pros and cons, he shoved the plastic containers of pure cocaine into his rucksack, along with the few worldly possessions he could not live without.

Then he ran to his car and sped out of the underground car park, the engine echoing in the confined space, and he drove out of Eastbourne, feeling that it was entirely possible he wouldn't return.

CHAPTER NINE

Barnes shut his eyes and replayed the previous day's events in his head. Ella goes to work, giving Gabby the green light to proceed uninterrupted. She wasn't going to the shops, or nipping to the post box, so he expected her to be gone all day, meaning a cry for help was unlikely. He meant to see it through. Neighbour reports the open front door, thinking there might be an intruder on the premises. Patrols respond and find Gabby's body, not warm, but they attempted CPR anyway. No note.

The open front door might have otherwise been out of place, but in her initial account to patrols Ella had already confirmed that Gabby left the house first. They hadn't found his car yet, but it was still likely that he'd parked up out of sight somewhere, waiting for his soon-to-be-widow to go to work, then walked back to the house once he knew she had left for work herself. His state of mind suggested that he didn't notice or wouldn't have bothered with niceties like closing the front door; either that or, deep down, he was secretly, maybe even subliminally, hoping to be discovered and rescued. That being the case, it would stand to reason that he was punishing her for something. But that somehow didn't chime. For all his intolerable professional demeanour, he did seem to love his wife, infidelity notwithstanding.

No note.

Barnes opened his eyes. No note — that they knew of. That didn't mean there hadn't been one. He couldn't immediately imagine that removing a suicide note from a crime scene would be of much interest to anyone — it wasn't like it was a bundle of cash — but it couldn't be discounted.

He flicked through the file until he found the incident dispatch details and scene log. A single-crewed patrol was the first responder, followed by a bunch of paramedics. He checked the timings — forty-seven minutes had elapsed between the neighbour's 999 call and Barnes pitching up on scene. Plenty of time for things to disappear from the scene.

He had no proof, of course. And not every suicide left a note. Many did — people so ill they couldn't think straight, family men battling an inexorable decline in mental health who wanted to leave an explanation to their family. Often these cases had been battling depression for years. People who made bad choices and kept secrets and told lies in ever-decreasing circles that threatened to catch up with them — well, they quite often made overnight decisions, taking the path of least resistance. These cases might not have taken the time to give their loved ones any closure.

Barnes brought the name up on STORM — PC Pete Lamb had been the sole police responder. He tilted his head. He was familiar with *that* name. This was where it would have been really handy to bounce it off Marlon Choudhury. But if he went to PSD on an official footing they would want to know all sorts of ancillary information that Barnes was disinclined to provide.

He looked at Lamb's duties on the timesheet — he was showing as on sick leave, but his inspector, Georgia Brass, was on duty.

She answered on the second ring.

"Brass."

"Georgia. It's Rutherford Barnes."

"Hello, Barnes. How can I help?"

Not a single nicety, which suited Barnes. He wasn't sure if that was from a lifetime of giving off *save-the-pleasantries* vibes himself, or because Georgia Brass wasn't given to providing them anyway, or both. A perfect match.

"Pete Lamb. He's one of yours, yes?"

"What's he done now?" she said, which already told Barnes more than he was expecting. "Another substandard file to CID?"

"No. Well, not that I'm aware of. He was first on scene at ACC Glover's suicide. I just wanted to discuss it with him, but I see he's off sick."

"Yes, that's right. He's been in once or twice, though. You might catch him if you give him a call."

"He's not ill, then?"

"No. He was assaulted off duty. On the seafront. Pretty nasty, by all accounts, but I still question what he was doing there."

Assaulted. Of course. He'd not read the file in any detail, but the assault investigation had landed in the lap of one of his DCs.

"What happened? I don't think we've formally interviewed him yet."

"Supposedly — and, I hasten to add, this is his version of events — he was out for a run at two in the morning and got spontaneously and randomly mugged. Personally, I think it's bullshit."

"That point of view could be described as undermining the prosecution case."

"If it gets into a courtroom, I'll eat my hat. And yours," Brass added. "Besides, this mugging happened at more or less the same time and place as those packages of cocaine washing up on the beach. You're not telling me you think that's a coincidence?"

"Is PC Lamb . . . ?"

"I'm staggered he's kept his job this long, the amount of times he's flown close to the sun. The man is a disgrace, and a bad advert for the service. He . . ."

She stopped, and took a breath.

"I apologise. You get my point, though. What is it you're interested in? You mentioned ACC Glover's suicide?"

"PC Lamb was first on scene. I've got no proof, but I've a suspicion — and it is only a suspicion, mind — that he may have removed something from the scene prior to locking it down."

"'Something'?"

"A suicide note, to be exact. I don't even know that there was one."

Georgia Brass went quiet. Barnes assumed she was mulling it over, but then he saw from the incident log that she'd arrived on scene not long after Lamb. Twelve minutes, in fact. Not long at all.

But long enough.

"It isn't beyond the realms of possibility," she said. "They had that thing."

"Thing?"

"The PSD thing. The set-to at the taxi rank. If there was a suicide note, then isn't it plausible that Lamb might have been namechecked in it? He might have pocketed it on that basis."

"It's a possibility. There's no evidence of that, though," Barnes said. "But there's certainly no other cut-and-dried motive for the suicide."

"Not the affair?" she asked.

"Not according to his widow. The usual theories — financial ruin, blackmail, punishment, severe mental ill health — are all just that: theories. A suicide note would shed some light on that. Maybe open up some new lines of enquiry."

"If there was one."

"If there was one."

"You almost sound like you're looking for work," Brass said.

"I don't like people interfering with my scenes. Where can I find PC Lamb?"

"At home, I guess. Like I said, he could well pop into the office. Give him a call. He's only recovering from being beaten up. He's not contagious. At least, I don't think he is."

"What's his domestic situation?" Barnes asked.

"Single, far as anyone knows. Lives on his own. That's half the problem. Still thinks he's eighteen and in uni digs."

"He went to university?"

"I doubt it. It's a figure of speech. He needs a good woman to get him to grow up a bit."

"Anyone on his radar?"

"Too many, I'm sorry to say. Latest one in his crosshairs is the late boss's new secretary. Haven, I think her name is. He thinks no one has twigged, but he practically pants like a dog whenever she's around. I guess she's out of a job now."

"Useful to know. Got his home address?"

"It's a flat in the harbour. Hang on . . ."

Brass gave Barnes the address. He thanked her and headed out, feeling the hint of excitement that he still got when a line of enquiry led somewhere on the back of a hunch.

It was an area familiar to Barnes. He thought back to night patrols on a pushbike and foot chases through the concrete jungle that was Sovereign Harbour's residential arm, a maze of brick walls, cycle paths and twittens, and bridges over the lock gates.

Almost too familiar. As he drove to the very end of Pacific Drive and into the car park in the undercroft under the boardwalk, he realised he recognised the address. He parked in one of several visitor bays and, having identified which of the six towers he wanted, walked up through a basement stairwell into the building proper.

He used a trades buzzer to get into the main foyer from the entrance vestibule, and then, unable to quite explain why, took the stairs up to the fourth floor.

He pressed himself to the wall as he moved along the corridor. The front door to the apartment was caved in, maybe from a sledgehammer, and although it was technically locked shut, it had buckled so much that Barnes was able to lift the whole door, frame and all, clear into the building. He forced the gap a little wider and manoeuvred himself through it.

He'd been here before. The flat had belonged to Lamb's one-time patrol crew partner, Jefferson Riaz, one of far too many officers that had fallen in the line of duty on Barnes's watch. It wasn't a record he particularly liked to dwell on — he'd never done the research, but he was sure that, statistically, he was an outlier and then some. Barnes wasn't sure if Riaz had owned the place or rented it, but, either way, his erstwhile partner appeared to have taken possession of it after his death.

And the shirt off his back, Barnes thought.

In any case, the flat had been trashed. Burgled. Seat cushions carelessly tossed aside, chests of drawers upended and emptied, DVDs pulled from a shelving unit and flung onto the floor like a domino rally. The place stank of old socks and rubbish. From the stink alone, Barnes reckoned a few days at least since anyone had been here.

Someone looking for something specific? Or some*one* specific? Barnes was pretty sure Lamb hadn't reported this formally as a standard burglary. Did he even know? Barnes looked around the flat again, trying to assess whether Lamb had packed up in a hurry and left, but without Lamb, or someone that knew him present to tell him, it was difficult to make that assessment with any accuracy.

He called the number Brass had given him for Lamb. To Barnes's complete lack of surprise, it went straight to voicemail, and so he called the control room to arrange for the premises to be boarded up. He went out onto the balcony — the salt air, as ever, a welcome release from the stuffy indoors where people carried on all sorts of lives within their four-walled concrete boxes. He peered over the glass frontage, just in case Lamb had taken a header off the balcony and was lying in a blood-spattered starfish on the boardwalk below.

The control room told him at least half an hour before board-up arrived; Barnes thought about getting a PCSO to relieve him, but figured that wasn't really cricket, and so he knocked on some of the other doors in the corridor to try and narrow down the timeframes.

His knocking went unheeded at two of the flats; he slipped a calling card under the doors. Of the remaining two, one was a guy in his thirties who was keen to get rid of Barnes post-haste, which Barnes ascribed to the stink of cannabis drifting out of the property, while the last one was occupied by that most reliable of public-spirited neighbours, a widowed lady in her late seventies. She did not speak particularly fondly of PC Lamb — and clearly didn't know he was a police officer — and from what Barnes was able to glean, the various comings and goings at all hours, not to mention the noise, were not in keeping with an upmarket retirement harbourside community that had paid through the nose for a certain standard of living. Barnes didn't say anything, but the retirement community seemed to be in the minority in comparison with the single-male, recreational-drug-using residents who apparently just wanted a base from which to party.

The list of complaints were difficult to pin down to a particular chronology, but from what she said, Barnes's assessment of the flat having been vacant for about three days was more or less bang on. Prior to the rude attempt to kick the front door in, Mrs Busybody hadn't personally clapped eyes on Lamb for about a week.

Barnes thanked her and made a mental note for that PCSO to pop round and soothe her troubled brow. As he walked back down to the car, he put the likely series of events in order in his head. PC Lamb comes into the fortuitous possession of a commercial quantity of controlled drugs, immediately uses it as a hedonistic way to live beyond his means, but has the presence of mind to absent himself from the workplace first.

Either that, or he was missing.

CHAPTER TEN

Five thirty in the morning seemed to be a busy time for the emergency services, Kenley mused, as an ambulance with the blue light show going sped past him in the opposite direction on the other side of the central reservation.

It stood to reason, he thought. That was the time things were discovered. You wake up and find the person lying next to you, the one you've shared a bed with for thirty years, isn't breathing. You go outside to de-ice the car, only to find it isn't there. You come downstairs to put the kettle on and realise there's a hole in the window and squares in the dust where all your electrical appliances used to be.

As he passed Gatwick, he moved over to lane one and set the cruise control to sixty-five. He'd thrown the gun in the Serpentine immediately before leaving Mayfair, but it didn't hurt to be cautious. Traffic was light, and he should still be back in Eastbourne for his nine o'clock appointment without ragging the rental car.

He drummed his fingers on the wheel, telling himself it had been necessary, trying not to imagine Nat's face were she to find out. After all, it was kill or be killed, wasn't it? Hunt or be hunted? He'd have done it sooner, but had to be quite sure first that Rutherford Barnes had pulled his surveillance effort off his tail.

He didn't have a lot to play with when it came to getting back in the game. The gun, some stolen museum-piece revolver lump of shit, had hardly been easy to obtain.

He wasn't starting from scratch, exactly — he had the carrier bag of grubby cash — but all his networks, his contacts, his scores and hot leads were now embedded within the Keber group. Keber's senior management had wanted him dead even *before* he'd wiped out four of their foot soldiers back in 2010.

But they'd made no move. No threats. No attempts. No clumsily executed contract on the wing by a methadone-dolly clutching a plastic fork.

He'd heard nothing. Even when he'd been lying in his hospital bed, when he was at his most vulnerable and Keber was at its most disagreeable, there had been no approach.

He didn't like it, but he'd come to get used to it. Three years of silence and he'd almost — though not completely — forgotten about it. It wouldn't do to become complacent, however. That was the time the collectors were most likely to close in on the welshers.

Which was why Roxy Petrescu had to go.

Kenley parked near the Saffrons without any difficulty and walked towards the probation office.

He had a bit of starting capital. Now he just needed a bit of commodity to raise his profit margins. Get him back in business. The alternative was a cleaning job organised by his probation officer, and he'd rather throw himself off the end of Eastbourne Pier.

Kenley didn't like his probation officer. He was a wily old sixty-something veteran who saw you coming a mile off. Kenley would not be able to give him any bluster, and his conditions were strict: curfew, non-association, gainful employment, suitable accommodation and no substance use.

Most of these Kenley was relaxed about, but the gainful employment was likely to prove problematic — any gaps in the CV and the officer would automatically assume he was dealing, although Kenley had made it quite clear he was not going to be working in Next.

The accommodation point also required some thought — his three-bed company semi had no doubt been sequestered under POCA — and even if it hadn't, Keber might still be watching it in the hope he would make an appearance so they could splatter his brains all over the walls. The architect of revenge, Stratton Pearce, was thankfully no longer of this earth, but that didn't mean Kenley's elimination wouldn't still be useful for transactional purposes. He still had a mouth on him, after all.

He might have to get his head down in one of the insalubrious seafront dosshouses for the sake of appearances while finding something that was actually suitable, rather than what Her Majesty's National Offender Management Service deemed suitable. Nothing too flashy — two-bed apartment in the harbour with a decent balcony and a bit of space would suit him fine. He could have gone to stay with Nat, but they weren't quite there yet, and the Airbnb thing wasn't long-term — it would rinse them both inside three months.

It had been a week since New Year, but three-quarters of the probation office looked to still be on leave for the Christmas holiday. Kenley wasn't too sorry about this. He passed a vial of clean urine to the PO and left the office, having been careful to dial down his usual front by a couple of notches. Once the PO finally stopped believing he was being fed a bread bin full of bullshit, he would likely either think Kenley was a cocksure fool, or come over all patriarchal and start harping on about missed potential and all that bollocks. Kenley's mood was grim, and if the PO started doing the father-you-never-had routine, Kenley couldn't promise he wouldn't put the idiot in the hospital.

He walked down towards the town hall, past the Saffrons bowling club, geriatric cheers echoing over the high flint wall. He carried on down Grove Road, intending to stop in at the police station to sign on, but found it shuttered and boarded up with a commercial TO LET sign sticking out of the brickwork. He shook his head. Maybe he'd missed more inside than he'd realised.

This thought was amplified when he reached the railway station. The road outside it was like a Formula One pit lane, with red-and-white barriers demarcating a very complicated network of temporary lane closures. He'd also intended to step inside the Gildredge as a line into some information, but it had apparently been demolished along with the rest of the shops on the east side of Terminus Road, and replaced by colourful hoarding advertising an artist's impression of the science fiction, garden city wonderfulness that would soon be the new shopping centre.

Why bother? Kenley thought. Just somewhere else for the fourteen-year-old drug dealers to congregate and kill each other with zombie knives.

Kenley suddenly felt that four-plus years were a lot longer than he'd given them credit for. He had — perhaps naively, having never previously served prison time — assumed he could more or less pick up where he left off and reinsert himself in the pecking order, especially now he was free of Keber's iron talons. Walking into a likely pub and ingratiating himself with the bottom feeders seemed as good a place to start as any — but the pub was now a pile of rubble.

Figuring the bottom feeders must have gone somewhere, he cut into Hyde Gardens and checked the public toilets and recycling area tucked behind the motorcycle bays, but, to his surprise, the usual gaggle of cider-soaked urchins was conspicuously absent. He listened out for the usual shouts and yells coming from the main pedestrian shopping thoroughfare, but there was nothing.

He kept on along Terminus Road towards the sea, intending to head for the promenade and start scouring the beachfront shelters, but when he got to Debenhams he turned into Langney Road and found himself outside the Curzon cinema. There was nothing much on he wanted to watch, but the faded, salt-bleached blue hoarding and the missing red letters announcing THE VERY BEST IN FILM ENTERTAINMENT on the white pick-and-mix display board made him stop in his tracks. He hadn't actually been here since he and his father were turned away from a James Bond film — the first ever to carry a 15 rating — on the basis that Kenley was too young at the time.

He climbed the steps into the dark foyer and spoke to the teller sitting in the gaudy orange box office, who gave him a green ticket for the latest *Hobbit* movie. The smell of worn nylon carpets and popcorn was suddenly intoxicating, and Kenley had to concentrate to keep himself focused on his purpose.

He climbed the impossibly wide stairs to the mezzanine level, trailing his fingers on the sticky, varnished wooden banister, imagining the art deco building to have been some ostentatious hotel back when bathing suits were knee-length and Edwardian Londoners flocked to the sunshine coast for constitutional well-being.

He stepped inside screen one, the main circle, and paused in the back of the auditorium. The carpet was worn to practically nothing and a central section of the seating area had been roped off with yellow-and-black workplace safety tape, with a series of buckets collecting drips from the ceiling.

He stood in the darkness. There were a couple of silver heads on one side of the auditorium, munching popcorn and chatting during the nonsensical trailers, but the place was otherwise unoccupied.

Then he saw a dark form huddled in the front row, right over to the far side by the fire exit, and decided that it was an auspicious place to begin his hunt.

The man was barely discernible. He was skinny, all in dark clothing and had sunk into the seats with his hood up. He was sort of sprawled half on, half off the seat, and his bare white foot was all that was visible in the darkness.

The syringe was wedged between his toes — Kenley appeared as he depressed the plunger, and he yanked the needle out just as the junk hit his bloodstream. This wasn't good for a coherent response, but it did mean that Kenley could yank him up by his neck and drag him out of the auditorium without too much in the way of resistance besides stifled protests and muttered curses.

As they hit the light out on the mezzanine, the man groaned; Kenley spun him around and grabbed him by the front of his hoodie. Kenley swung the man round by the collar, causing him to crash against a four-foot glass display box containing a yellowing release poster for Clint Eastwood's *Unforgiven*. He stank of old socks and urine.

"Fer Christ's . . ." he squealed, his eyes screwed shut. In his dreamlike, junked-out state it was clear he hadn't yet orientated himself to the nature of the assault. Kenley smashed him against the glass again. It made an almighty *thunk* on the otherwise silent mezzanine, besides the muffled hum of the movie soundtrack on the other side of the auditorium doors. "You're gonna break the friggin' glass."

"Poster needs updating anyway," Kenley said. "When did that come out? 1992?"

The man unscrewed his face. Kenley recognised him and realised he'd lucked out — Liam Lawrence had been a permanent fixture on the glossy blue benches up and down Terminus Road for as long as Kenley could remember, and his failure to elevate himself in any way, shape or form up the social ladder was, accordingly, matched only by his usefulness as an ear-to-the-pavement trailsniffer.

"Kenley!" Liam squealed as his cloudy eyes regained a small degree of focus and widened with fear. "What the fuck is this? You back from your holiday, then? We could have just met in Costa. What you want?"

"Well, you're right, Liam," Kenley said, making a show of straightening out Liam's tracksuit top. "I'm back, and I need in."

There were footsteps in the stairwell. Kenley turned. Mr Prabh, the cinema's proprietor, house manager, usher and box-office teller was halfway up the stairs, an alarmed look on his face. He'd presumably come to see what all the noise was.

"This lad was spoiling the viewing experience of your other punters," Kenley called to Mr Prabh, keeping his eyes on Liam. "Chewing too loud. I'm just removing him."

Mr Prabh hesitated. "I'll call the police," he said, without conviction.

"Please do," Kenley said. "They'll be interested to know that you're permitting the use of the place as a shooting gallery."

He turned to look at Mr Prabh, who stood for a moment longer, and then slunk off back downstairs.

"I need in," Kenley said again. "What can you help me with?"

"I don't know anything," Liam said, looking at the floor. "I can't help you."

Kenley rammed his fist into Liam's solar plexus, jinking left in anticipation of the plume of yellow vomit that was indeed forced from Liam's stomach and narrowly missed Kenley's ear.

Liam slid down the pink vinyl wallpaper and curled himself into a ball. Kenley allowed him a minute or two to recover, then squatted down beside him and slid a tightly rolled fifty-pound note into each of Liam's nostrils. He moved his mouth close to his ear.

"Hundred quid there, Liam," he hissed. "I can buy wholesale, I can move bulk, I can run point on logistics. The one thing I don't have — yet — is muscle. I need you to put your ear to the ground and tell me what's moving and who's moving it. I need to jump back on the gravy train, reinsert myself in the supply chain, know what I mean? If you don't — well, let's just say that Clint Eastwood won't be the last thing to rain down on your head."

Liam groaned.

"Don't leave town," Kenley hissed. "I'll find you in less than twenty-four hours."

CHAPTER ELEVEN

Kenley parked the rental Insignia bearing fake magnetic Hackney Carriage plates outside the Sally Army and watched the entrance to the Bourne pub from the driver's seat. In ninety minutes he saw three deals take place, two brawls and a screaming match between a bald man in a tracksuit and a woman with huge hair who was screeching like a harpy. The cool, dark interior of the car was like a warm bubble, and for just a moment he thought about getting on down to the job centre. But then he remembered that no fruit tasted so sweet as that to which you are not entitled.

He wondered if that's why he and Natalie were doomed, if that was why he'd come over all bloody noble and do-the-right-thing with her. If she'd been married, it might have been a different story. He could have remained the mysterious, enchanting other and whisked her off to the excitement of hotel rooms and *faux*-conferences. Like the sodding Milk Tray Man.

Eventually, he saw Liam Lawrence slink out, with a furtiveness and urgency about his walk that suggested he had not yet opted to get high and that his mind was as clear as it was likely to get, but that also bore the hallmarks — in Kenley's view, anyway — of someone thinking about travelling light and getting the hell out of Dodge. He'd told Liam twenty-four hours, but he'd given him twelve, and that was now looking like a sensible play.

He put the car in gear and rolled slowly forwards along Langney Road, both sides of the road lined with cars parked outside the once-opulent Victorian townhouses. Liam was walking fast, head down, fists jammed into his pockets; Kenley accelerated forwards and round the corner, and parked the car at an angle across the pavement under an amber street light.

He leaned against the car as Liam rounded the corner.

Liam's eyes widened. "Kenley? This is . . . you told me—"

"In a hurry there, Liam? You're not avoiding me, surely?"

Liam shrugged. Kenley opened the car door.

"Get in."

* * *

"Is this a real taxi?" Liam asked as they headed along the seafront.

"Thinking about an honest profession?"

"I can't drive. I always wanted to learn, but . . . you know. Good cover, though. Bet no one looks at you twice in this. See, that's why you got to where you got to. Brains. The fucking *GQ* barnet don't hurt none neither, I expect. Bet juries fucking love you."

"You're babbling, Liam, which makes me nervous. Makes me worry you're about to feed me ten types of bullshit."

Kenley pulled the car over by South Cliff, just where the road began to incline sharply up in the direction of Beachy Head. The parking bays were all empty, the Channel and the Seven Sisters invisible in the blackness.

But they were there.

"So." Kenley turned in his seat to face Liam.

Liam took a breath. His eyes narrowed. "Let me just say this. You're freelance now, yes? Those big strong Keber arms not wrapped around you no more?"

Kenley took off his spectacles and rested them on the steering wheel. He was silent.

"You said it yourself: you have no muscle. So why would anyone — including me — think you're a serious bet? What does anyone have to gain from throwing you some work? Sorry to say, Kenley, but once you fall off the property ladder, it becomes—"

With the speed of a cobra striking, Kenley jabbed Liam in the nose so hard it caused the back of his head to bounce off the passenger window glass. He felt the nose crumble under his knuckles, and Liam shrieked. His hands flew to his damaged face. Blood began to pulse out between his fingers. With his victim distracted and both his hands occupied, Kenley grabbed Liam by the hair with his left hand and bounced his face onto the dashboard — once, twice, three times — then pulled Liam towards him so his ear was only inches from Kenley's mouth.

"You said it yourself, Liam. It's the brains that get you places. But it's not just that. It's will."

"Who the bloody hell is Will?" Liam said, sobbing through a mess of blood and snot.

"Not Will, you moron. Will. The will to have a vision and see it through, dealing with all and any obstacles along the way. You've just tried to assert yourself a little higher up the food chain than Nature is comfortable with, and you've been put back in your rightful place. Now, stop the posturing and tell me something useful before you become a permanently missing person."

Liam sucked air in through his mangled face, making a horrible slurping sound, and got his crying under control.

"A couple of days ago, a wholesale shipment lost a package. Washed up on the beach at Sovereign Harbour. Five or six rucksacks, fifteen kilos in each. Old Bill got most of it — but there's five kilos missing, apparently."

"Who's the consignee?"

"This ain't the Godfather. What do you mean, consignee?"

Kenley pinched the bridge of his nose and took a deep breath. "The recipient. Who was expecting the gear?"

"Dunno. Don't think it was meant to land here. Somewhere out west. It fell off on its way there. Either way, far as I can gather, someone over there wants someone over here to recover it. Bit of a local favour. County to county."

"And there's a price?"

"Double contract. Finder's fee for recovering the gear and returning it to its rightful owner — or at least, the local broker — plus a contract on whoever's holding it."

Liam went quiet. Kenley leaned towards him. "And?"

"And what?" His tone was sullen.

"Don't hold out on me now, Liam."

Liam exhaled, nickering like a horse. "I think a cop's got it."

That was interesting.

"Oh, yes? Why might you think that?"

His words were slow, like his only trump card was being forcibly extracted from him. Which, Kenley supposed, it more or less was.

"I'd been down on the beach a couple of hours before the shit washed ashore. Slinging to this cop I know. He keeps short-changing me, and won't pay, so I hit him with a crowbar."

"You what?"

"I hit him with a crowbar."

"I'm impressed, Liam."

"What am I meant to do? You don't assert yourself, people take the piss out of you your whole life. Anyway, I left him lying there, and he must have found the stuff later on. Bet you a pound to a penny."

He shook his head and kicked out at the car's bulkhead.

"If I hadn't hit him, he wouldn't have won the lottery."

"Lottery jackpot is no good if you've stolen it off someone else. So how do you know that the stuff landed when and where it did? You got someone on the inside? In the police?"

Liam turned to Kenley. He looked almost flattered that Kenley might have thought that about him. "Not me. But, you know, a shipment that size — trackers and shit. Besides, it's an open contract. May as well have put it in the *Friday-Ad*. Every street slinger I know answered the call. This is what we were told."

"But you're hoping for a head start because you happened to be down there anyway. Right place, right time."

"Something like that."

"Who else knows? About this cop?"

"Nobody."

"Where might I find him?"

Liam shrugged. "In a jam sandwich booting around town somewhere, I guess. I don't know where he lives."

"Got his number?"

Liam passed his mobile over. Kenley keyed the number into his own mobile — then, just for fun, sent a message: *U GOT MY BRIX*.

"You gonna do it?"

"Huh?"

"You know. Off him."

Kenley looked at Liam as if he were stupid. His thumb hovered over the keypad while he considered something. "Does this cop trust you?"

"Pretty much, I guess. Why?"

Kenley reached into the rear footwell and brought out the carrier bag full of bloody banknotes. He dropped it in Liam's lap. "There's thirty grand there. You're going to broker a sale."

"Thirty grand? For five keys of wholesale Colombian white? I can hear him laughing from here."

Kenley shrugged. "He sells it to me at a discount, or else he ends up as fish bait, with no product and no money either. This way, everyone is happy."

"There'll still be a contract on him." Liam sounded disappointed.

"Don't you worry about that. Set it up for tonight."

"Tonight?"

"Tonight, Liam. This offer is on the table for one night only. You pay him up front — gesture of goodwill — then all he has to do is hand over the product to you. You deliver it to me, and we're good."

Kenley peeled off a bunch of fifties from the carrier bag and passed them to the wretched street dealer.

"That's your commission," Kenley said. "There's more where that came from. You do anything really stupid like lose, spend or steal this money, and I'll drop you into a wheelie bin full of boiling water. And you know I can find you anywhere."

Liam was silent. He was looking at the sea.

"Liam."

"What?"

"Look at me."

Liam did as he was told. He swallowed.

"Tell me you understand."

"I understand."

"Good. Now get out."

"Come on, Kenley. A lift back to town, at least, eh?"

"Walk will do you good."

Liam reluctantly did as he was told. He made to shut the door, then stuck his bloody face back in the car. "One more thing. It's not hit the news yet, but it will. Cop suicide. Happened around the same time."

"The cop you hit?"

"No way. That bloke is cannon fodder. The suicide was a top-brass officer. Very high up."

"Why'd he do it?"

Liam shrugged. "Fuck knows. But that's good info, Kenley. About the suicide. It's not in the press yet."

"And?"

Kenley put the car in gear. Liam leaned further into the car.

"Look, Kenley. Take me along with you."

"What?"

"Take me with you. I'll work for you, be your runner or something."

"No thanks."

"Come on. We'll split it evenly . . ."

Kenley scoffed.

". . . all right, sixty-forty. You said you need muscle. I can run for you."

"Kick the habit, put on fifty pounds, then we'll talk. Unless you can get me a gun?"

Liam was silent.

"Didn't think so."

Kenley released the handbrake and accelerated away up King Edward's Parade. Liam yelped and took evasive action just before the passenger door swung shut on his head.

Provided the product was good, this was a win. It put him back in the market for more, plus he would buy out the contract on the cop's head, and then Kenley would own him.

This is good, Kenley thought as the car growled along the wide-open avenue.

I'm back.

CHAPTER TWELVE

Lamb sat on the edge of the bed in the motorway Travelodge, shoes and jacket still on, stomach and airways tight with nervous energy.

He glanced down at the carrier bag full of bundles of grubby cash — and then at the containers of cocaine next to it.

He was already regretting keeping some back. He'd been offered a lifeline by Liam Lawrence, acting as some kind of broker for God-knows-who — someone willing to pay in advance, anyway — and he'd dug himself further in by only putting up some of the coke, bulked out by some amateur cutting attempts on Lamb's part.

But the offer price had been ridiculous. A piss take. Take it or leave it, Liam had said, so Lamb hadn't really seen that he had any choice. It had been an impulse thing, and he was already regretting it.

He took a shower, grimly thinking: *Lamb on the lam*. Despite all the practicalities of survival racing through his brain, he just couldn't dislodge the thought of Haven. She was literally taking over his mind, and it occurred to him that their only interactions to date had been fabricated coincidences over her workstation. He was twenty miles from his place of work and absent, so that was no longer an option.

He thought about it. He was only off sick, though, not suspended nor on gardening leave. He still had access to his work phone, and he'd had the presence of mind to note down her mobile number off the system before going off sick.

He spent a good half an hour drafting and re-drafting a text message that didn't seem too weird or creepy, given that she herself hadn't actually given him her number. In the end he gave up, unable to settle on a suitable collection of words. He mulled over calling her, but decided that was no better. Eventually, he decided to engineer another chance encounter while trying not to be seen actively stalking her.

In the end, he drove to the station. He did a recce of the car park, being careful not to get too close. As far as anyone was concerned, he was still off sick with significant head and face injuries, and should have been in bed. He drove slowly past the station, peering through the ten-foot fencing, but couldn't see anything. He headed down Hammonds Drive, reversed into the loading bay of a pallet factory, turned around, and repeated the exercise two or three times before deciding — aided by crawling cement trucks and car transporters — that it was too painful.

He pulled up on the kerb — illegally parked, but he wasn't letting a carrier bag of dirty drug money out of his sight — and got out, pulling up his hood as he did so. He scanned the car park, encouraged by the thought that she stood out in so many ways that spotting her car would be no great shakes.

If, indeed, she was even working today. He wasn't sure, and could have kicked himself for not doing better research before getting tonked on the head.

Then he saw it. A flash of pink in the far corner, in among the greys and browns and dark blues, and he got a flutter in his stomach; maybe he was already a little bit in love with her. He tried to manoeuvre himself a little better so he could read the number plate; he couldn't, but consoled himself with the fact that there couldn't be that many hot-pink Fiat 500s around the station.

Now what? He couldn't go in. He looked like a street mugger that had lost a fight with an artic, and he had no business being here anyway. He could engineer a sickness absence meeting with his supervisor — bit weird for it to happen in the office rather than at home, but, he figured, it wasn't like he had swine flu or anything — but his team were not on duty until much later tonight, by which time Haven would be home and in the shower or something.

He tried not to think about that too much.

He cut his losses, tried to chalk it up as a win, and then got in his car and drove back to his Travelodge.

* * *

Kenley drove the rental car along the long dirt track away from the farmhouse and onto the lane back into Eastbourne. A more fitting reflection of the divergence between the bubble he and Natalie had been occupying and the real world could not have been found — in ten minutes he was away from country lanes lined with leafy oaks and heading through an industrial estate near Pevensey with fly-tipped rubbish and a group of kids fighting in a bus stop.

He'd left Natalie sleeping off the wine and the sex, having kissed her gently and told her he'd be back in an hour or two. The honeymoon bubble was bursting for her too — she was beginning to miss Max and the distance he knew she was starting to see in his eyes was gradually being reflected in hers.

It was gone midnight, and the roads were quiet. He was on Eastbourne seafront in less than ten minutes, the sea black beyond the royal-blue promenade railings. He cut back inland and headed into town, to the disused Caffyns showroom opposite the town hall.

The Edwardian building, with its tiger-striped pillars and stone features that Kenley surmised had probably once been described as *baroque* or something, had once been an impressive hub of local commerce. Now the plate glass display windows were covered in chipboard hoarding lashed with graffiti, while the forecourt, such as it was — essentially a wide expanse of pavement immediately outside the building — was surrounded by Heras fencing. The concrete was broken up where persistent weeds had punched their way through. The row of workshops abutting the Saffrons grounds were empty, the garage doors left wide open.

Kenley parked some distance away and walked across to the site; the moon was like a torch in the clear New Year sky and he felt a little exposed. With some difficulty, he climbed over the brick-and-flint wall at the side of the building and headed for the former workshops. He was wearing a hi-vis and a hard hat — even at this time of night, he knew from experience that it could be the difference between someone driving past bothering to pick up the phone or not.

He waited there in the shadows, getting gradually colder. When Liam was ten minutes late, Kenley sent a message:
WHERE U

When there was no response after five minutes, he called him. It cut straight to an automated operator telling Kenley the phone was off and he should try later. Kenley tried again several times, with the same result.

Had the little shit actually ripped him off? It would take some serious *cojones*, but it was nevertheless a remote possibility that Liam was testing his property ladder theory, or that Kenley had underestimated him, or both.

Thankfully, Liam's presence wasn't strictly necessary. They'd communicated earlier in the day to make the arrangements, and Liam had confirmed he'd bought the product and was in a position to hand it to Kenley. But it was a dead drop. Kenley only wanted him here to keep him on a short leash. He just had to hope the little bastard hadn't, in fact, fled with his money.

He moved to one of the chipboard hoardings and wedged his arm behind it. It was loose from repeated use and he slid inside easily.

He took a moment to allow his eyes to adjust, not wanting to use his torch. The moon was bright, and the hoardings were not a perfect fit to the windows, so shafts of bright white light were creating a ghostly pale glow inside the room — almost enough to see, but not quite.

The showroom stank. Urine and mouse droppings. The once shiny floor was covered in a carpet of debris and muck, and the open-well staircase up to the first floor was covered with decorators' equipment, the balustrade draped in dust sheets.

He edged forwards to the drop site, which was under a hatch in the floor used to run cabling through. He squatted down, swept away the dirt and old cardboard that had been placed there to conceal the hatch, and pried the cover loose.

He reached down into the gloom and felt around, trying to banish irrational fantasies of losing his balance and tipping forward into a twenty-foot-deep snake pit.

His hands closed around the canvas bag. He hauled it out and replaced the cover. He unzipped it and felt three solid items. He had yet to check them properly, but on first inspection he was satisfied enough.

He stood up, and stopped.

Sniffed.

What was that? Not urine, not mouse droppings, not damp or mildew.

Something else.

He recognised it.

Iron.

Blood.

He hadn't caught it when he came in, but, he now realised, it had got stronger since he'd moved further into the showroom.

Knowing he should just take the spoils and go, he inched further forward into the room. The moonlight was bursting to come through the windows, but the hoarding held it at bay.

There was . . . was there something — someone — here?

Kenley kept perfectly still, straining in the dark to hear. There was no sound at all, even in the always-busy town centre a hundred yards away, the one-way system of Little Chelsea devoid of traffic. The silence was like a tornado in his ears.

He blinked, trying to work out if his eyes were growing accustomed to the darkness, or if the moon was shining brighter, or both, or neither.

He took a step back, about to spin on his heel to leave — and then he saw it.

Definitely something there. The moonlight was making something glisten in the darkness. Twenty feet away. He thought maybe it was broken glass, or . . . no.

Something wet. A leaking pipe?

A voice inside his head was screaming at him to get out of there. He'd got what he came for, there was no flashing blue cavalcade descending on the abandoned showroom, so why hadn't he gone? If he stashed the gear and didn't hang about, he could curl up next to Natalie before she woke up and their little honeymoon break came to an end.

But while his brain was giving him directions, his body was refusing to listen. He took a step forwards, and then another.

Some distant part of his mind was telling him he had killed before, he had looked stone-cold killers in the eye and not backed down, had done his time without major scars. And yet the physiological reaction was no different than it would have been for Billy Bob Three-Bed Semi — thumping heartbeat, stomach doing cartwheels, oxygen blasting through suddenly clear sinuses.

He crept forwards, suddenly wishing he'd been able to procure another sidearm after he'd thrown the antique revolver away, but, since ostracising himself in prison, he'd lost access to a lot of resources that he'd previously taken for granted. That's why he was here in the hush of night, collecting bricks like a brain-dead street dealer, consorting with bottom feeders like Liam Lawrence.

There was a smaller glistening thing just above the bigger glistening thing — and then in an instant, like a magic eye picture suddenly clicking into place, he realised the smaller thing was an eye, and the bigger thing was a patch of blood spreading across the fabric adorning the body that was propped up against the wall.

He inhaled sharply, and decided the time was right to chance bringing out the torch. He swung the Maglite round and flicked it on, and saw the sorry state of a man slumped against the wall, his tracksuit sodden with thick red blood, his face mangled with injuries. One of the eyes was sunken back into his face under a swollen pink mess that resembled lean turkey mince, which was why it wasn't glistening.

This might explain why Liam Lawrence wasn't answering his phone. Kenley's instincts tumbled over themselves — call for help, check for a pulse, put the poor bastard out of his misery — but he quickly rationalised that the more he involved himself, the more likely he was to be incriminated somehow — erroneously or otherwise.

His foot squelched down in something wet; he looked down and shone the torch beam along a slalom trail of blood from the chipboard hoardings to where the body sat. Kenley was no detective, but it seemed pretty obvious that the unfortunate soul had either crawled or been dragged here.

Kenley brought the torch down for another look.

"Holy shit," he said aloud.

He blinked. Liam had died cradling armfuls of his own viscera, which were *really* glistening, and making a wet slapping sound like somebody stirring a pan full of just-drained boiled pasta.

Kenley covered his mouth with the back of his hand, and inched forwards, unable to explain to himself why he was not back in his car. He certainly had no intention of rendering first aid, or calling the cops, or even calling an ambulance. This poor sod was way beyond that.

Then Liam made a sharp sucking sound, and Kenley flinched like someone had woken him up with a firework.

"Jesus fucking Christ!" he yelled, dropping the torch. It clattered onto the once-polished floor and rolled away, the beam picking up dirt and debris as it went. "Are you . . . ? Holy shit. Liam? Are you alive?"

Liam continued to inhale through his mouth. It sounded like there was bubble wrap in his teeth.

Kenley backed away; it took a moment of scrabbling around in the dark, but he managed to summon the presence of mind to retrieve the torch as he went — leaving any items behind at this particular crime scene would be insurmountably stupid.

He took tentative steps backwards, his feet crunching on the carpet of crap, drugs held tightly in hand, his torchlight beam fixed on the heap of entrails against the opposite wall. The choking, sucking sounds emanating intermittently from somewhere around its mouth grew fainter as he moved away.

He shook his head and, out of some childlike irrational fear, only turned his back on the thing when he reached the exit.

He stood on the street, the night air a welcome relief after — he now realised — the cloying stink inside the showroom. He listened. No sirens, no running footsteps, no indications that he had been stitched up by . . . well, who? The shortlist ran to a good few pages, even with Stratton Pearce's demise. This little tableau was a bit different, however — it had been put together by someone twisted and calculating enough to eviscerate another person and leave them just about breathing, but also to rig the scene so as to put Kenley in shit up to his armpits if he made the wrong call.

But he was still here, in the cool night air, still breathing, still carrying his package, so, if it *was* intended for him, maybe it was just a little warning. A little parlour trick.

He walked a few steps, and then his usual nerve evaporated — he pulled the hard hat off his head and sprinted around the corner to his car. He fumbled with the lock and got in, gulping giant breaths in the silence. Whoever had wanted to spook him had done a good job, he thought irritably.

He scanned the street. No lights, no curtains twitching, no curious dog walkers. He gave thanks to whoever and started the engine. He'd pulled one-eighty and had — inexplicably — driven back past the boarded-up, once-opulent building when he saw the telephone box by the town hall's main doors.

Just as he was about to floor the car down South Street and away, he thought of Natalie's face and pulled over.

He pulled on some latex gloves and covered his mouth with a surgical mask from his glove box. He lifted the receiver, dialled 999, and asked for the ambulance. The operator asked him if the patient was breathing.

"Only just," he said. "Meads Road, next to the town hall. The old Caffyns garage. In the boarded-up showroom."

"What is your name, please, sir?"

"Don't spare the whip. He's not got long. He's been well and truly gutted."

"Sir . . ."

Kenley replaced the receiver, jumped in the car and drove as steadily as he could, taking back roads out of Eastbourne, back to Natalie's warm bed, thinking he would quite happily never set eyes on the damn place again.

When he got back to the Airbnb, he took a moment to compose himself. He sat in the car on the gravel driveway, the dead engine ticking, the cold soaking through the car the moment the heaters were switched off.

He got himself together. He wanted to share his fear and panic at what he'd found, wanted to curl up beside Natalie and have her tell him all would be well, but he couldn't. It wouldn't do, on any number of fronts. He wondered what a psychotherapist would tell him about his ability to compartmentalise.

And besides, when he finally entered the lodge and crept into the bedroom, he saw the bed was made and the wardrobe empty.

She was gone.

CHAPTER THIRTEEN

Barnes was so engrossed in Duquesne Kenley's nominal record that he didn't hear Marlon Choudhury enter his office. He'd been scrolling through the latest intelligence reports in the hope of being able to scrape together enough to mount another surveillance case, but, in the absence of any new updates that he himself was not the originator of, had finished up staring at the man's profile picture. He could see why he'd succeeded, why he'd evaded capture time after time. The thick wavy brown hair edged with rust, the Castilian features. He didn't have the spectacles in his custody photograph, but Barnes had never seen him without them, and they made him look like a leading man volunteering at the local library.

The eyes, though. The eyes were cold.

Choudhury usually only popped up in pockets; like a wraith emerging from the fog, he would appear long enough to impart some form of abstract wisdom or other, then would fade away again, sometimes for months at a time.

"Marlon. It's two in the morning. Don't you have a home to go to?" Barnes said.

"I could ask the same question of you. Except, now I know the answer. I'm pleased your life has found some light. I'm glad for you."

Barnes nodded. "I appreciate that. I mean it, though. You have over half a century's worth of policing service. What's waiting for you at home?"

He immediately wished he hadn't asked. Marlon Choudhury, ever stoic and unflappable through sheer longevity, suddenly assumed a sorrowful countenance that Barnes had not seen before. Barnes imagined an oak-panelled study, a slab of mahogany desk bearing green bankers' lamps, floor-to-ceiling classical works with *Don Giovanni* playing quietly from unseen speakers, a pair of green leather Chesterfields next to a fireplace.

He imagined one of the Chesterfields suddenly standing empty, and the murmur of conversation drying up over time.

"You're coming around a lot, Marlon," Barnes added hurriedly, before the older man had too much time to think about the question. "And I know it isn't just me you're interested in. Your constant presence usually means some shit is about to go down."

Choudhury didn't speak, but hefted a cardboard box onto the desk.

"What's that?" Barnes said.

"ACC Glover's widow called the Chief. Asked about the DI with the bad attitude and the chip on his shoulder."

"I wouldn't have won any money betting on that," Barnes said.

"She also said something about you having sad eyes, which is why she won't be making a formal complaint."

Barnes leaned back in his chair. "That, however, is a surprise."

"The Chief was all fire and brimstone, and then he called me. I visited Mrs Glover — or Ms Short as she apparently would like to be now known — and then this was brought to the station later in the day," Choudhury said, pointing at the box. "For you, by all accounts."

"What's in it? Do you know?"

Choudhury just gestured to it. Barnes stood, and lifted the lid off the box as if he were opening the lid on the fossilised remains of the Holy Grail itself. The cardboard was stiff, dusty and smelled of damp.

He peered inside, the ambient noise of the night shift outside his goldfish bowl reducing to a muffled hum in his head.

In this box was the life and times of the late Assistant Chief Constable Gabriel "Gabby" Glover, handed over — perfectly willingly, it seemed — by his grieving widow.

Barnes pulled out a framed photograph. Gabby as a probationer, a thatch of strawberry-blond curls covering his head. He was beaming at the camera in a stiff pose, the parade ground of the long-defunct Ashford Police Training Centre in the background, alongside an older woman that Barnes assumed to be his mother. He was seated, dressed in a brand-new dress uniform, custodian in his lap, the woman standing with her hand on his shoulder. Gabby's uniform shirt was blue, rather than white, and Barnes put the photograph at around the mid-1980s.

"Jesus. Look at his hair," Barnes said. "And I don't think I ever saw him smile. Certainly not like that. What else have we got in here?"

He began to rummage once more.

"Look at this. Keepsakes, photographs, old letters, journals. This must be all his personal belongings. She handed this over?"

Choudhury shrugged. "Front counter were not particularly assiduous in their record keeping, it seems."

Barnes continued rummaging, and then stopped. Underneath a mound of photographs and a burnished silver jewellery box faded to brown, there was a sheaf of papers held together with a clip. The brutal red stamp of CONFIDENTIAL caught Barnes's eye.

There were more similar bundles underneath.

"Marlon," Barnes said, "there's work stuff in here. Case papers, by the looks of it. Crime files. Intelligence reports. Stuff he shouldn't have had in his loft."

"If I had a penny for every crime report that turned up somewhere it shouldn't . . ." Choudhury said. "Still, it's a moot point now, I suppose. It isn't like we can prosecute him. The main thing is they have returned to the bosom of the family, where they belong. Our family, that is."

By the time Barnes reached the bottom of the box, he had no less than twelve confidential and highly sensitive reports on individual officers — each thematically different, but each individually commissioned by Gabby Glover. Only the dead man knew why.

And names. Names he recognised.

Jefferson Riaz.

Samson Kane.

His own.

He was dimly aware of Choudhury still standing silently by, maybe observing Barnes's reaction. Resisting the urge to evict the older man, lock the door and read them there and then, Barnes placed the stack of reports in his desk drawer, locked it and thought about swallowing the key. They would have to wait until later.

As it turned out, that was a timely decision.

The door to his glass office rattled, clanked and burst open. A young uniformed sergeant stood there, twenty-five at the absolute most, radio held halfway to her mouth. She looked pale and, frankly, stressed out.

"Don't you knock?" Barnes said.

"Sorry, guv, I—"

"I don't think I know you, Sergeant . . . ?"

"Jill, guv. Jill Rough. Acting up. Only got my exam a couple of months ago."

"Well, it's good to meet you, I guess. Do you always look this nervous?"

"I, no, well . . . Guv, you're going to want to see this."

* * *

Since Acting Sergeant Rough was interrupting a shift that was already twelve hours old, Barnes figured she could act as his driver too. She hit the blues and they spun through the Birch industrial estate, all car auctions and kitchen showrooms, and back out onto Lottbridge Drove.

The roads were empty at that time of the morning; it took them less than a ten-minute blast along the seafront, and then they were in the town centre. The whole road outside the town hall had been closed off, and a constable on the cordon lifted the scene tape for Rough to drive her car under.

Barnes saw the phalanx of patrol cars outside the old boarded-up Caffyns garage, supplemented by a fire truck and some enormous lighting rigs that were being lowered off the back of a liveried lorry.

They stopped, and Barnes got out to survey the scene.

He turned to Rough. "Who's the duty inspector?"

"It's Ma'am Brass tonight. She's over at Hastings dealing with a missing person. Said she'd be right over."

"Nice big scene cordon. Did you organise the lights too?"

"I did, sir."

"Who's at the scene?"

"Nobody. We haven't been in yet."

"You didn't check for vitals?"

"Ambo did. They called us after confirming death. Fire prised off the hoarding to get them in."

Barnes was momentarily distracted by the sound of retching. Over Rough's shoulder was a firefighter with sweat-plastered hair, doubled over, vomiting into a storm drain.

"Okay, Jill. You've done a thorough job of *not* mucking up the crime scene prior to my arrival. Well done. Be sure to mention this when you go for your promotion interview."

Barnes ducked under the tape and approached the showroom, watching the two guys from Ops Planning as they unfolded the enormous yellow metal legs and hooked up generators.

It was a slick operation, and they had a full blast of light like a solar flare into the disused showroom in less than fifteen minutes. Unlike natural daylight, however, it only pointed in one direction, and certainly didn't eradicate all the shadows.

He pulled on a scene suit and stepped forwards to the building's edge, peering in through a hollowed-out section of the wall that had obviously housed a plate glass window some years ago. Its new clothing, a square of rotting chipboard, lay on the ground a few feet away.

The interior of the showroom was as you might expect after years of disuse — it stank of mildew and droppings and urine, while the once shiny floor was almost hidden beneath nameless crap.

The body was slumped up against the far wall, sitting in a puddle of dark red that Barnes could smell from twenty feet away. It was the endpoint of a thick red stripe that led from the rear of the showroom, possibly from an office or a fire exit. There's your first point, Barnes thought. He'd either been dragged to his final resting place or had crawled there.

The head was lolling forwards, the hands hanging limply to the side, fingers turned up in a silent appeal, like he'd been cradling something in his lap and then his hands had fallen away the second the final spark of life had left him.

Barnes took a careful step forwards, around the edge of the wall to avoid disturbing the scene too much. He didn't go too close — even as a seasoned detective he knew not to upset the senior SOCO too much before they'd even arrived — but close enough to see that the deceased had, in fact, been cradling something in his lap pre-mortem.

His own insides.

CHAPTER FOURTEEN

Aware of his inability to function for longer than twenty hours without sleep, Barnes locked the whole thing down and grabbed four or five hours at home, somehow managing to do so without waking the girls. Despite a brief but frank exchange of views with Georgia Brass about resources at the station, he was still able to get back to the scene before the day started to properly wake up.

Once Clive Brynn, the crime scene manager, was happy — or as happy as the grumpy old bastard tended to get — Barnes ordered the arc lights to be manoeuvred closer to the enormous square hole in the side of the listed building. It was a slow, rather painful process to watch, but after a while they were in position and fired up, flooding the former showroom with a powerful white halogen beam.

Nowhere to hide now, Barnes thought, stepping inside the scene and using the foot plates that the CSM had placed around the edge of the showroom to make his way over to the body, still slumped against the wall in a sitting position. With the addition of the lighting, and the stark contrast between the strangely neat circular pool of blood and the white walls, it now looked like the centrepiece of some bizarre modern art tableau.

Cameras clicked and flashed. Clive Brynn stood impassive, scanning the scene. He was a tall, solidly built Lancastrian with bright, hard eyes and a Burt Reynolds moustache that had been a permanent fixture on his lip for the entirety of his twenty-seven years' service.

Barnes moved closer to the body.

He'd seen some sights, but nothing like this. The body was male, and, at first glance, maybe late thirties. The head was folded forwards, showing Barnes a widow's peak and thinning crown that, for some reason, reminded him of a crop circle.

The body seemed to be furiously regarding his own lap — which, given that it contained armfuls of its own viscera, was probably what he had been doing shortly before death. There were smear and streak marks in the blood pool near his feet and legs, suggesting to Barnes he'd been kicking and thrashing before death, probably in a state of extreme agitation.

He looked at the trail of blood from the body that led back to the rear of the showroom, where offices and a kitchen area had once stood. Crawled or dragged, he wasn't sure — the former was more likely, but Brynn was writing in a notebook and seemed to be in a state of furious concentration, and Barnes didn't want to interrupt his thinking. He would ask permission to go and follow the blood trail shortly.

He moved closer and squatted down, staying on the foot plates, forcing himself to look away from the lapful of entrails and focus on the other details — age, weight, height, tattoos, other injuries, body temperature, anything out of place. The sight at his feet was impossible to ignore, but had to be blocked out in order to assess the thing as a whole — well, almost a whole, anyway — otherwise you just became a gawker, and he wasn't getting paid for that.

It took concentration, however, and he needed to get closer.

"Can I look?" Barnes said.

"In a minute," Brynn said, not looking up from his scribbling. "Pathologist coming out to this?"

"I sincerely hope so," Barnes said. "I need to check the rest of the scene."

"Stay on the plates."

Barnes turned, trying not to look directly at the beams. The arc lights were at an angle outside the building, positioned to zero in on the body. This meant that the other end of the showroom was still dark. He took out his Maglite and notebook and began to scan the showroom.

He made a note: check current ownership, market status, length of time it had been disused, contractor, security and maintenance access. There were a few bits of rubbish, but not much, nothing to indicate that it was regularly being used as a squat or anything, suggesting that the Heras fencing and hoarding had been largely effective to date.

He did a walkthrough of the building and found nothing fresh to indicate a break-in. Some of the upper ox-eye windows were smashed, but the breaks didn't look new, and were just as likely to have come from kids practicing their tee-off swing out on the playing fields. Besides, judging by the ornate stone fixtures and scrolled pillars around the place, the building was probably listed — the original glass wouldn't have withstood much.

Barnes climbed the stairs, keeping his hands to himself. The Saffrons Rooms themselves — formerly offices and a high-end private function room, now the company boardroom — were all locked.

He kept the walkthrough cursory, and returned to Brynn after a few minutes.

"Well?" Brynn said, not looking up from his notebook.

"Nothing here. Nobody else."

"You're thinking maybe he broke in through a window, gutted himself on a broken shard of glass, then dragged himself over here to expire?"

"I wasn't thinking that." Barnes gestured around the empty showroom. "There's nothing here to steal."

"Getting in out of the rain, maybe."

Barnes didn't dignify that with an answer, but looked from Brynn to the heap of bloody mess and back again.

"Anything on an ID?"

"Nothing obvious. Face is a mess. Haven't looked in his pockets yet."

"Okay. We'll need to cross-check the misper reports."

Brynn glanced up, as if to say: *We?*

"And think about intelligence on the locus. It will become clearer once we know who he is."

"Was," Brynn said.

"There's no blood outside," Barnes said, mainly for his own benefit, his eyes shut. "So it's unlikely he was injured in the street and was just taking refuge in here to escape his pursuer."

"If you say so."

Barnes opened his eyes. "We'll need to rip it up. Full itemised forensic search of both floors. PolSA-led search of the perimeter. I'm thinking maybe this was a prearranged meeting that went wrong somehow."

"Oh yes?"

"At least two sets of footprints in the dust," Barnes said, pointing over at the centre of the floor. "Hey, what's that?"

"What's what?"

"Here, pass me a footplate."

Brynn obliged, and Barnes moved over to where he'd been pointing at the footprints. The dust and debris was not evenly spread and so it was difficult to pin them down with the naked eye, but there was a more or less linear trail approaching the body from the other end of the showroom. In the centre of the floor, the pattern became rather more chaotic in the dust, and seemed to be concentrated around the lip of an underfloor hatch.

Barnes squatted down and pointed his Maglite at the hatch. The cover was not sitting flush, and was resting on the outside of the hatch itself by about half an inch.

Like it had been replaced in a hurry.

"This has been moved," Barnes said. "Look. There's marks on the top surface. Suggest you start here."

He stood up and went outside before Brynn could answer, intending to stretch his back in the January sun and get some fresh air into his lungs.

"Oh, Jesus."

Despite the disembowelled body, the interior of the building had been locked down and preserved so quickly that it was in a controlled state of calm.

Unlike the outside.

The uniformed contingent had closed Grove Road outside the town hall, two PCSOs in blindingly yellow, fresh-out-the-packet hi-vis jackets funnelling all traffic into Little Chelsea and turning it back on itself at the one-way system. A small group of people armed with confetti and champagne flutes, who had apparently turned up early to begin preparations for a wedding in the town hall, were being shepherded grumpily back down Grove Road in a cloud of perfume and lilac dresses. On the north side, the road was closed at the bowling club, with traffic directed back towards Gildredge Park, and to the south at Grassington Road. It was a huge cordon, inducing chaos for the normal run of everyday life.

And it was, to Barnes's eyes, a thing of beauty.

Inspector Georgia Brass had arrived from Hastings, and she was waiting for him on the pavement with her arms folded and, under the bowler pulled low over her eyes, an unsmiling expression. With the crowds gathering on the barriers behind her, Barnes half expected to be ushered away from the fans into a waiting limo. He could hear rotors thudding overhead, but Barnes didn't want to look up in case it was Sky News and not a police helicopter.

"This scene wide enough for you?" Brass asked.

"It's perfect, thanks," Barnes said, thinking that coming from anyone else, it would have sounded sarcastic; in Georgia's case, however, he knew it wasn't.

"You're going to have to speak to TV," she said, pointing back over her shoulder with her thumb.

"All in good time," Barnes said, suddenly thinking it might be nice to go back inside and spend some more time with his inside-out corpse.

He surveyed the activity. You've just slaughtered another human in about as gruesome a fashion as could be imagined.

Where do you go now? Which direction? What are you thinking?

He looked over at the barriers at the junction with Grange Road.

Barnes scanned the faces. *Are you here?* he thought.

Hiding among the crowd, moving amid the audience, anonymously soaking up the gasping wonder of the activity that you, and you alone, had caused with a single swift movement of the blade.

He says jump, we'll say how high, Barnes thought. Because we have to.

He zeroed in on a face at the cordon, and took a couple of steps towards the barrier.

He squinted, brow furrowed.

A familiar face.

Tina Guestling.

She saw him and smiled.

"Hey," Barnes said to the PCSO manning the barrier. "Let her through."

It took a moment, because she was walking with a cane, but Barnes took her hand and guided her under the tape and around the barrier. Her movements were slow but graceful.

"Detective Inspector Barnes," she said, leaning forwards to peck him on the cheek.

"Tina Guestling." He shook his head. "It's good to see you."

"It's Flagstaff now," she said, holding up her ring finger.

"Congratulations," he said.

"Well, a woman should know when to move on," she said, and winked. "Coming up on our first anniversary."

"Good for you. Seriously. You look good."

She did too. She'd always been a head-turner — tall, built like a swimmer with dark hair and olive skin. Today she was wearing some kind of chocolate-brown trouser suit and looked all business.

"Well, I try," she said. "Quit the fags before the wedding. Haven't quite managed to phase out wine, but it's a marathon, not a sprint."

He looked down at the shiny black cane. It demanded his full attention for a moment.

"This is for life," she said, no trace of regret in her voice. "But I'm used to it. The South Downs Way just takes a little longer, that's all. And I always hated bloody squats anyway. I'm all about upper-body strength these days."

For a moment, Barnes couldn't speak. It was because of him she had the cane.

"It's been too long," he said. "I haven't seen you since the awards ceremony."

And he felt bad for that.

"I'm sorry," he said. "For not being better at staying in touch. You know I'll never forget what you did for me."

Her eyes glistened.

"That means more to me than a stupid bravery award," she said. "Much as I'd like to keep you in my bathroom."

For a moment, the sounds of the street were tuned out. She had saved Barnes's life, his wife's life and that of his two girls, as well as indirectly making sure the man that had badly wanted him dead was off his back for good. She had put herself in harm's way to do all that, and was lucky to be alive. How do you repay that?

"So what have we got here?" she said, as if sensing his awkwardness. She gestured at the street scene.

He looked around, and then pulled her gently further inside the cordon. "A terrible mess, is what. One deceased, adult male. Stabbed and, it appears, eviscerated."

Her eyes widened. "Christ."

"No victim ID, no suspect, no motive."

"Sounds like you need Intelligence, then," she smiled.

"That's why you're here?"

"Don't sound so disappointed. I'm heading up my own team these days. If I'd just wanted to catch up with you over a beer I would have picked a more intimate setting."

"I just meant, you don't often see Intelligence down at crime scenes."

"You can't do anything with the enquiry unless you've seen it yourself."

Something he'd been saying to his young detectives all his life.

"Well, it's fantastic to have you back on the team," Barnes said. "But do me one favour."

"Anything."

"When the time comes to get tactical on the bad guy, promise me you'll stay in the office."

"Anything grab you about it?" she asked, when she'd finished laughing. "Besides the obvious, I mean."

"Well, other than feeling a little like the Beatles landing at JFK, it's a pretty ordinary scene," he said, gesturing around the street.

And it was — beyond the barriers, at least. Traffic, pedestrians, street furniture, commemorative benches, public phone box.

Barnes frowned as something occurred to him. A fairly basic building block in a murder investigation, one might say.

He called Georgia Brass over.

"Who called us again?" he asked her when she approached.

"Ambulance."

"Yes, yes, but who called them? It's a locked, empty, boarded-up building. Who would have had cause to call them?"

"Are you asking me to get hold of that 999 call?" Brass said.

"Yes, please," said Barnes. "I think that would be a very good idea."

CHAPTER FIFTEEN

Lamb checked the package once more. There was no way any moisture was getting inside — it was in an airtight plastic container and had been quadruple-bagged before being placed inside a sports holdall and then sealed again inside a heavy-duty polythene garden sack — but it didn't hurt to be sure.

He carefully lowered it into the murk, waiting for the faint tell-tale sound of the surface of the water rippling as it was disturbed, then he hooked the cord around the rusted hook embedded in the wall of the shaft, gave it one final check, and then replaced the heavy iron manhole cover. He dressed the surface of the cover with some foliage as a garnish — probably unnecessary, but it made him feel better. He was trying not to think too hard about the fact that he had just sealed almost a hundred thousand pounds — thirty grand cash, the rest a liberal estimate of the cocaine he'd held back from Liam Lawrence — in watery catacombs on the cliff edge.

He was no chemist, but what he did know enabled him to cut the bricks by just enough to claw back almost a couple of kilos of the stuff, sufficient to survive and have a good time for the next three months or so. He was making the assumption that the supplier — some potbellied accountant in

Bogota or somewhere — would be reasonably happy with this arrangement, but the real loser in this chain was the intended recipient, whoever that was, who had likely paid up front for the consignment. Lamb had pegged this individual as some local drain-brained flophouse bail jumper with neither the wit nor the guile to do anything about being had, so he didn't waste too much time thinking about it. Besides, that was for whoever had slung him the grubby thirty thousand to worry about. The potbellied accountant was more of a concern.

He stood up and stretched. Beachy Head was bathed in January's afternoon half-light from the sky's dark grey underbelly, foot-long blades of brown and green grass sprouting from the humps and ridges like the crazy hair of a hunchbacked troll. It was popular as a visitor spot, but when the temperature dropped and the last shreds of daylight disappeared over the Channel, the only people you'd see up here were the police and the chaplains — and the deeply troubled individuals they were likely there looking for.

Lamb had chosen the Beachy Head playing fields for this very reason — provided he didn't come here at two in the afternoon on a sunny Saturday, the likelihood of his being spotted was low. Not only that, but there was only one road in or out, and the sprawling landscape meant it would be very difficult for anyone to follow him without him spotting them.

Lamb stepped out of the cluster of waist-high shrubs and onto the edge of the sports field. He surveyed it for a moment. It was a well-kept square of green, cut into the clifftop at, in his view, great personal risk. It was the only perfectly flat part of the entire twelve miles or so of coastline that made up the Seven Sisters. You couldn't ask for a more beautiful vista during a Sunday club game in July, but it would only take one over-exuberant catching attempt on the eastern boundary rope, and . . .

Lamb shuddered, and climbed up the verge. He scrambled back up the slope to the main road, knowing it was all too easy to become disorientated. You could traverse the gentle undulations quite happily from east to west, thinking the drop was some way off — then a wrong step or two to the south and you'd be over the edge and plummeting. At its most narrow, there were just fifteen or so steps from the road to the cliff edge, albeit that was closer to Belle Tout and much further south of Lamb's current position. Accidental falls were not common, but they did happen.

With this in mind, Lamb made a point of scrambling up the verges to cross the road. He headed for the pub, thinking a pint would both soothe his nerves and throw off any potential tail. He scanned the landscape as he crossed, watching for incongruous pedestrians, crawling vehicles or artificial ice cream vans.

After putting away two pints in quick succession, he walked out to his car. He'd parked as far away from the pub as possible; never mind the drug dealers on his tail, parking too far away and walking in would likely attract attention from the chaplains that patrolled the clifftop looking for souls to save.

He felt curiously liberated — not to mention lubricated — at the prospect of driving while over the limit. He figured that with the amount of prospective indiscretions hanging over his head, tacking a drink-drive charge onto the end wouldn't really add much to the indictment. He partially regretted that sentiment as he snaked back down Upper Dukes Drive, whose one-eighty hairpin bends required his entire concentration and then some.

As he cruised down King Edward's Parade, the enormous white palace of the Grand Hotel rose up on his left. Bathed in an amber wash from the ground lights, the building looked extraordinarily inviting, and for a moment he thought about relocating from his shitty Travelodge and making the most of what felt increasingly like a limited amount of time left to him on this planet. Take Haven to a black-tie dinner and dance. Get a sea-view suite. If they came for him, he could even go out in a blaze of glory from the first-floor mezzanine overlooking the Great Hall in some kind of homage to *Scarface*.

He woke early the following day, thinking about Haven, and hit on an idea. His team were on earlies today, and so he sent a text message to his supervisor on the pretext of coming into the office to hand him his doctor's note, and, if the man was free, maybe a kind of return-to-work-plan-type meeting?

Why don't I just come and see you? You should stay home if you're sick.

Lamb went cold. The last thing he needed was his sergeant knowing he'd moved out of his flat in the dead of night and hadn't told anyone where he was living. Another police regulation breached.

That's ok. Be good for me to see the team. I'm going stir crazy. I'm not infectious, anyway, just very sore.

The reply took a while to come through, but it was at least in the affirmative: *Fair enough.*

Lamb drove to the patrol base and parked; as the enormous steel gate slid shut behind him, he felt rather relieved to be sealed off in a secure-ish compound.

The meeting was perfunctory. His skipper clearly didn't like Lamb and didn't seem to be believing much of what was coming out of his mouth. That was okay. That suited Lamb. He was only going through the motions in any case.

All thoughts of his wobbly subterfuge went out of his head when he saw Haven. As ever, she was staring at the screen in fierce concentration, like she was playing the computer at chess, losing badly and trying to work out her next move.

As he walked over, he saw she'd only put on minimal make-up and her eyes were pink-rimmed. For some reason he thought of a rabbit that had been plucked out of laboratory obscurity in order to have the latest perfume tested on it. While his first instinct was one of marginal disappointment — she didn't look quite as glamorous as on previous occasions — he nevertheless reminded himself that she was probably grieving, and that was a definite in. Lamb would be a rock so solid she would think he was Scafell bloody Pike.

Lamb put on his best, most sincere, most empathetic expression and headed over to Haven, noting she did actually have a sort of turquoise shade on her eyelids and a diamond nose stud that twinkled under the strip lights. Both features — along with a tiny dagger tattoo on her wrist — indicated *fun* to Lamb, but he couldn't quite articulate why.

"Hey," he said, softly, with his best look of doe-eyed sympathy. "Haven."

She looked up, clearly not able to immediately place him.

"Pete Lamb. We met the other day."

"Oh . . . oh, yes. Of course."

Maintaining pleasantries seemed to be something of an effort, and he suddenly felt genuinely bad for putting her under the strain. She was obviously hurting.

"How are you healing up?" she managed, touching her face.

"Just fine, thank you. How are you doing?"

She looked confused, like she wasn't sure who knew what, or — more to the point — who was allowed to know what, or . . .

"It's okay," he said. "I know. I . . ." Here he swallowed, tilted his head up and shut his eyes momentarily in, he thought, a tremendously convincing piece of theatre. "I was the one that found . . . that found him."

Her hand went to her mouth, and she gasped so loudly a couple of heads turned.

"Oh my God. You? You found him? You poor thing. That must have been . . . oh, you poor thing. Are you okay?"

Her reaction was better than he could have hoped for. He knew he was being a ham, but he wasn't going to disembark this particular wave in a hurry.

"I'm okay, I think," he said, dropping his voice to a whisper. "A few nightmares. You don't know when it's going to hit you. I didn't really know him, though, so once the technical bits and pieces are done — secure the scene, preserve the ligature . . ."

Another gasp.

". . . my work is pretty much done. At least until the inquest. But you . . . you knew him well."

"I was in the car when I heard. I had to pull over into a layby. I sat there for forty minutes, just crying."

"That must have been horrendous," he said, thinking, *I wish I'd been in that layby with you.*

"I just kept going over and over it in my mind. I'd spent half a day with him only the previous week, going over meetings, action updates, diary admin. I've been killing myself trying to think if there were any signs I'd missed, or whether there was anything I could have done, you know? Oh God, what a turn of phrase. I can't believe I just said that."

Lamb had grimaced at the term *killing myself.* She'd obviously noticed.

"Look, you're busy, and besides, our conversation is probably being fiercely soaked up by at least two DCs with nothing better to do. But it is important to talk. Sound off. Let it all out. And you can ask questions. Who knows, I might be able to give you a couple of answers. Maybe not all of them, but sometimes it's enough to ease the pain a little."

Her eyes had started to brim with tears as he spoke. He was right there with a fresh Kleenex, producing it with the deft flourish of a magician.

"That . . . that would be nice. When were you thinking?"

"This afternoon?"

She looked a bit taken aback.

"Or whenever you feel ready. But the science says the sooner you open up, the less long-term damage you risk doing. To yourself, I mean. What time do you finish?"

CHAPTER SIXTEEN

Barnes watched the Home Office pathologist move around the table, thinking, *I've probably, on balance, spent more time in mortuaries than I have filling up my car.* He was standing slightly back from the action with Brynn and the mortuary technician, the powerful light leaving nowhere for anything to hide on the polished steel and gleaming white bathroom tile surfaces that made up the decor.

At the pathologist's insistence, the pile of entrails that were still just about connected to the remainder of the body were to be preserved, packaged and delivered along with the cadaver, and so they had been unceremoniously scooped and ladled into the body bag along with the owner, and now took pride of place on the steel table between the corpse's green-white legs as an improbable accessory.

Unlike most pathologists Barnes had encountered, who were theatrical and charismatic, this one was an introvert. He scurried around the table lifting folds and poking crevices, all the while muttering into a dictaphone that he clutched in a gloved hand like it was a Fabergé egg. Barnes was only picking up every other phrase, and soon began to get bored. He was already irritated by the fact that it had taken three days to organise the post-mortem.

"Disembowelment was what killed him?" Barnes asked, eventually.

The pathologist lifted his head, looking almost surprised, as if he had forgotten Barnes was present. He turned back to his work before replying.

"Exsanguination killed him," he said, fiddling around with the cranial flap. "The evisceration certainly accelerated that."

"Any other injuries? Anything to help with ID?"

"No obvious defensive wounds. Cuts and bruises around the face and scalp area, and an assortment of miscellaneous minor wounds of varying ages on the hands, arms and legs. At this early stage," he continued, eyeballing Barnes, "all I can tell you about those is that they indicate someone with poor hand-eye coordination, and/or someone who was generally careless or clumsy, and/or someone whose self-care capabilities were substandard. There are capillary bleeds on the lower body, which are consistent with scraping or dragging across a rough surface, which in turn is consistent with your theory that the deceased pulled himself along the floor from where he sustained the injuries to where he eventually expired."

"What about fractures, sprains, things like that? If the killer went straight in with a knife to the guts, I'd have expected some defensive wounds, or some sign of resistance. If he overpowered him first, I'd expect to see that somewhere."

"I haven't quite got to the orthopaedic survey yet," the pathologist said, the merest hint of sarcasm in his voice.

"In any case," Barnes said, apparently not hearing him, "bleeding out would take at least a minute, no? He wouldn't have just lain there in peaceful expectation."

"It's entirely likely he panicked, or went into shock, or both," the pathologist said. "Did you say you have not managed to identify him?"

"Not yet," Barnes said. "SOCO's got prints, but that will take a little while."

"He has a small tribal tattoo at the base of the neck, and a Union Jack on his upper left arm."

Barnes leaned forwards, mobile phone aloft, but Brynn stopped him.

"Allow me," he said, holding up a half-decent camera.

Barnes gestured *be my guest* and stepped aside. "Time of death?"

"Well, my initial assessment is: not that long ago. What time did you say you were called?"

"A little before two a.m. Ambo called us; their informant called from a payphone at the Saffrons five or so minutes before that."

"That sounds about right. He may even have been alive when your payphone caller reported it. I take it he is a suspect?"

Barnes tilted his head: *What's that got to do with you?* "Seems likely," he said. "But why draw attention to yourself when the trail is still warm? It might otherwise have been months before we found him."

"Maybe he was proud of his handiwork and wanted to share," the pathologist said, indicating the pile of guts on the table.

"Is there any possibility he did this to himself?" Barnes said.

This time, all eyes turned to him.

"What sort of question is that?" Brynn muttered.

The pathologist looked at the technician and then back to Barnes. "In theory, yes. But imagine the determination and willpower to see it through. I'd be speculating about a seriously disturbed state of mind."

"Which may or may not show up when you get to the cranial exam. What about under duress?"

"Well, if someone held a gun to your head and told you to eviscerate yourself, you'd opt for the gun, wouldn't you?"

"You'd be surprised, I'm sure," Barnes said. "I'm just saying it can't be ruled out at this stage. No defensive wounds, no injuries that would tend to indicate he was subdued first, which means our best theory is that someone took him by surprise and made a foot-long incision before he had time to react. That's a bloody sharp knife."

"I'm glad you mentioned that," the pathologist said. "I was going to save the incision until last, but since it is the elephant in the mortuary..."

He paused. Nobody laughed.

"...then let's take a look."

He moved around the table.

"I mean, you're right," he said, using a steel spatula resembling a palette knife to raise the edge of the wound. It looked like a huge, red, winking eye. "This was a sharp knife. A surgical instrument, perhaps. A clean cut."

Barnes chewed the inside of his lip, deep in thought, going through myriad different scenarios in his mind, stepping back through the movie, rewinding from the present moment to when this dead body was not a dead body but a live being whose insides were not on the outside.

A drug deal gone wrong? A revenge attack? A message to the family or associates of the deceased? Or a self-inflicted injury?

The building was not used as a squat — at least, not with any regularity — and although the deceased did not sustain the wound in the same place that he'd actually expired, as far as Barnes could make out, he had simply been stabbed in one corner of the building and had crawled or been dragged to another part of the building. You wouldn't carry your own guts around like a bouquet of flowers and *then* try and gain access to an almost impenetrable abandoned car showroom. You'd panic and scream for help.

Which suggested it was some kind of meeting that had gone sour. Or...

"Describe the state of mind someone would have to be in to do this to themselves," Barnes said, looking at the white ceiling.

"This again," muttered Brynn.

"Indulge me," Barnes said, glancing at him.

"Extreme psychosis, excited delirium, some kind of toxic brain activity, perhaps."

"Would any of those things show up on your examination? As a physical presentation, I mean."

"Most forms of encephalopathic conditions present in some way, but certain psychiatric disorders may not. It just depends. The compendium of the differential diagnoses of mental disorders is pretty thick."

"What about pain?"

"Pain?"

"I mean unbearable, indescribable pain. Like there was something inside you that you absolutely had to get out."

"It's possible, I suppose. But this is all speculation. Theories — some more valid than others."

"Everything is a theory," Barnes said. "You just gradually eliminate them, one by one, until you're left with the most plausible."

He stepped back from the table again, remaining silent for the remainder of the post-mortem, while the pathologist resumed mumbling into his Fabergé dictaphone.

Barnes's phone trilled in his pocket; when things had started to wind down, he excused himself from the mortuary and stepped out into the box-like vestibule, a tiled airlock between life and death.

Jesus, he thought, how could anyone not come in here and wonder about the point of existence, or whether it hurt to be worm food, or when it would be their turn to assume the position on the slab.

There was no signal in the vestibule, and barely any in the basement corridor, so he ascended the stairs to the outside world and stepped outside the hospital, passing a smoking room filled with medical staff in theatre blues, the walls stained brown with years of exhaled nicotine.

There's ironic, and then there's existential, he thought.

Two missed calls from Kane. He called him back from the car on his way to the station.

"How's it going?" Kane asked. Barnes thought he could hear a heavy metal guitar shredding in the background somewhere.

"Not so good. Disembowelled victim, no ID, no hot leads on suspect and a media circus up at the scene."

"Sell it to me, Barnes."

"Well, ordinarily, Gabby Glover would be chewing me out about now," Barnes said. "But he's not here."

"The DCC wants the post left vacant for a few weeks as a mark of respect," Kane said. "At least, that's the official line."

"And unofficially?"

"Theresa Baily is acting up."

Barnes raised an eyebrow. That was interesting. "The mistress becomes the heir apparent?"

"So it would seem."

"Rather you than me, then," Barnes said. "Chain of command, and all that."

"So what am I going to tell her about this murder? I don't really want to be bringing her more bad news."

"I don't know that you can avoid it — the injury is brutal, like nothing I've ever seen before. It's like something out of the Crusades. The only good news is that I've downsized the cordons now, so it doesn't look quite so much like Aerosmith are performing at the Winter Garden. We've not released the details of the injury, nor even that we're looking at it as a homicide — and that's only because there's a very small possibility that it was self-inflicted, so the red-tops should be held at bay for now."

"Self-inflicted?"

"Ritual suicide. Psychotic episode. Something like that. Highly unlikely to be the case, however. Soon as we've identified the victim we'll know what we're dealing with."

"Okay. Keep me posted. The big house has its hands full dealing with the aftermath of Gabby's demise — I don't really want to add to it."

"About that," Barnes said.

"Gabby?"

"We've retained the investigation. There's some bits and pieces to tie up, but it's a file for the coroner, no more than that. The only thing going to cause some aggravation is why he did it."

"What does his widow say?"

"She's no conspiracy fan. She's pretty convinced he took his own life. When I pressed her for the reasons, she became a bit cryptic. Seemed to think he had his fingers in so many pies it would be difficult to point at any one thing that might have tipped the balance. The affair — at least, the one we know about — is one angle, but I didn't press that with her."

Barnes decided, as he pulled into the patrol base, not to mention the secret box full of confidential reports and apparently illegal surveillance.

"To be honest, that suits me," Barnes continued. "This murder is going to soak up all my time for at least the next fortnight. Boss, you might want to think about reassigning someone to oversee the investigation into Gabby's suicide."

Barnes said it as politely as he could manage.

"Can't do that," Kane said. "Sorry. The whole thing is as sensitive as a day-old bruise, and the circle needs to stay as tight as possible."

Barnes exhaled heavily.

"Did he leave a note?" Kane said.

"No."

"Really?"

"Really. You don't believe me?" Barnes said.

"Don't be pissed off. It doesn't seem odd to you, the fact he didn't leave a note?"

"You're the third person to say that it's odd that he didn't leave a note," Barnes said. "But they don't, always."

"I guess not."

"This body dropped less than a fortnight after Duquesne Kenley was released from prison," Barnes said.

"I thought you said you didn't have any suspects."

"I don't," Barnes said. "Just seems a bit coincidental, that's all."

"Life's full of them."

"And Roxy Petrescu was found dead in a hotel in Mayfair last week. Did you know that? Shot dead two days after we shitcanned the surveillance on Kenley," Barnes said.

Kane didn't answer. Barnes guessed he'd probably needled him, and he wasn't surprised. Roxy Petrescu, by turns Duquesne Kenley's boss, nemesis, tormentor and hitherto *bête noire* of the Keber group, had finally had the tables turned on her.

"How do you know that?" Kane said, eventually. "I didn't see anything about it."

"There was a total media embargo until the security services were happy it was just a run-of-the-mill assassination or robbery-gone-wrong, rather than state actors or anything like that. By the time it was lifted, the tabloids had moved on. I still have a flag on her record, so it came to me through official channels."

"She slipped through our fingers once and dangled him like a puppet. He probably figured it was kill or be killed," Kane said.

"Two days, boss."

"You'd better find enough evidence to convict him, then," Kane said.

Kane ended the call and Barnes began to set things up for the following day's briefing, which was going to be early, earlier than most people were used to. As he pulled open the heavy steel door to the Major Incident Suite, the cables from the pylons overhead thrumming insistently, Barnes realised he had butterflies in his stomach, and he frowned.

His heels clicked and echoed around the glass-and-steel atrium that formed the lobby, as he tried to think. He didn't usually get nervous before major crime briefings, or any kind of public speaking. He hadn't even got nervous before his last attempt at a promotion interview — *which may have been why you failed it*, he thought.

Then he realised: it was the case itself. He'd handled his fair share of homicides over the years, including colleagues slain both on and off duty — a disproportionate number, actually, for a man of his service. But the majority had been unremarkable, as murders went. One-punch fatalities after too much chest-beating and peacocking outside a nightclub at 2 a.m. Domestic beatings where the perpetrator waited patiently at the scene after calling 999 themselves. Teenage gobshites walking around with blades and all too ready to use them in the name of posturing and street status. Cases that lent themselves to soundbite descriptors for the convenience of public and police alike. If you could understand it, you could process it, could avoid living in fear and confusion. Robbery gone wrong. Drunken brawl. Home invaders panicked. Even contract killing had a place in the psyche of the vast majority of viewers of the six o'clock news without the natural order of things being upset too much.

This one felt different. The answers were not obvious. Victimology, locus, motive, nature of the wound — all head-scratchers. Victim ID was only a matter of time, and a lot of answers would come tumbling down the hill after that, but it didn't feel contained at all. The only thing Barnes could zero in on that made any sense was that the whole case seemed to come back to one word.

Rage.

CHAPTER SEVENTEEN

Kenley was raging. Raging, in a frustrated, helpless way, the likes of which he found largely unfamiliar. It was an impotent rage, the kind of unjust emotion a child would feel.

He wiped his hands on his faux-decorator overalls and stuffed a hose and a long brush into the back of the signwritten Transit, having made a good show of scrubbing the lancet windows of Our Lady of Ransom church. It had given him a good view of the crime scene at the Caffyns showroom, and nobody was giving him a second look.

He prided himself on being one step ahead. He'd very seldom hurt anybody in anger. It was always business. He still — or so he believed — retained the capacity for love, happiness, fear. Like the fear he'd felt on finding an inside-out Liam Lawrence in the showroom, gasping and gurgling like field-dressed game.

But this bloody treacherous cop had ripped him off. Held back on the coke and still took the money. And Kenley, still several rungs down the post-prison property ladder, had yet to reestablish the connections within the ranks to be able to identify the usurper. Liam Lawrence had taken that little snippet to his grave.

He got into the front of the van and pulled out his phone. He dialled Natalie's number twice: both times it rang and then cut to voicemail. His fingers hovered over the keypad, and he made himself put it away. He'd only sent her one message — simply saying *Nat* — since he'd found their bed empty, for two reasons: the first being that he didn't want to leave a trail of incontrovertible written evidence that could be read out by some curly tongued silk in court. To him, that was just suicide. Like killers who hand themselves to the cops on a plate by boasting about their antics on Instabook or whatever. The other reason was that he didn't want to earmark himself as one of those pathetic, obsessive, stalker psychos that can't get over the fact that they were punching above their weight in the first place, and thus end up in the same place as the first group.

And so he fought the urges and stuffed the phone into his pocket.

He supposed, in the scheme of things, it was no particular great shakes. It was a snakes and ladders board; he'd just slid back to the bottom, which meant cruising Terminus Road again for one of Liam's conveyor belt clones in search of some street intel to repeat the exercise to reestablish himself.

But he couldn't let it slide. Couldn't let the cop think he'd got one over on him. Liam had been dealing to this cop. He'd mentioned Langney Point as a regular rendezvous. Meaning the cop probably lived nearby. And with Liam gone, the cop would, sooner or later, be looking for someone else to serve up. And, if he was desperate, he'd likely let his guard down. Slip up somewhere along the line.

And so, Kenley supposed as he started the engine, he would just have to make sure that he himself was front and centre when it came to the list of attractive suppliers.

CHAPTER EIGHTEEN

Barnes sat at the head of the conference table and glanced around at the attendees sitting around him in a horseshoe. His disquiet was reflected in their faces. As a DI, Barnes shouldn't have been running this solo — the SIO for a case of this nature ought to be a DCI as a minimum. But Major Crime were crying "closed for business", and Barnes was PIP3 qualified, so whoever was in charge upstairs had seen fit to leave him be, at least for now. A couple of times he'd thought about taking the plunge and going to Major Crime full-time, but that door had been closed all the time it fell under Gabby Glover's portfolio.

"Okay, welcome to Operation Limekiln. We will be having twice-daily briefings, 0600 hrs and 1800 hrs, until further notice. If you can't make it, send somebody in your place — preferably someone who knows as much as you and who can make decisions about your resources. I'll give an overview and then we'll go round the table for departmental updates. Keep it brief, please.

"The victim is male, aged approximately forty. As yet, no ID has been established but this continues to be a work in progress. Cause of death was exsanguination caused by a fourteen-inch abdominal wound, which in turn resulted in the evisceration of the victim."

Haven Banks was taking the minutes. She was sitting next to Barnes, and he heard her stop typing. Whether it was the nature of the injury that had given her pause or the spelling, he wasn't sure, but he scribbled *evisceration* on a Post-it anyway and slid it across the tabletop to her before continuing.

"Victim was found in the former Caffyns showroom in Meads Road, Eastbourne, following an anonymous report to ambulance from the payphone outside the town hall approximately seventy yards away. This call was received at 0149 hrs on 10 January 2015; the pathologist puts the time of death in the preceding one to four hours. At present we have no motive, no victim ID and no handle on a potential suspect. Areas of focus are ANPR, house-to-house, CCTV in the area, forensic evidence from the respective scenes and the 999 call itself. This is widespread and speculative until the victim is identified, beyond which I expect the trawl to become rather more targeted. In addition—"

The door squelched open at the other end of the conference room. All heads turned.

"This is a closed briefing," Barnes said, not looking up from his policy book.

"Forgive me," said a voice Barnes recognised. He looked up to see Marlon Choudhury standing in the doorway, unlit pipe in his teeth, hands like cable dampers raised in surrender. He was dressed in a navy-blue suit, the panels of which were like the sails of a nineteenth-century clipper, with a white shirt and a salmon-pink tie. His gold cufflinks bore five martlets, golden flightless birds that formed the Sussex crest. An aroma of sandalwood and rosehip drifted into the room.

Barnes leaned back in his chair. "DCI Choudhury. You're very welcome. But, in the nicest possible way, this is a homicide enquiry. What's Professional Standards' angle?"

Barnes addressed Choudhury across the room. A couple of the others busied themselves on their laptops, but most heads flicked back and forth like they were at Wimbledon.

Choudhury frowned, like Barnes had asked a stupid question. It was the most serious Barnes had ever seen him.

"You have a leak."

The faintest murmur rippled around the room, and Choudhury sat down on an empty chair.

"Well, we may as well start with the media update, then," Barnes said, turning to Andrea Hope, the senior media manager, who was wearing a powder-blue pencil skirt and matching suit jacket with a white blouse. She and Choudhury had some kind of sartorial face-off going.

"It's been a slow news week, I'm afraid, so there is a lot of interest in this particular enquiry." Hope addressed the room over half-moon spectacles in a voice that made the Windsors sound like Steptoe and Son. It was, Barnes mused, the closest English could get to sounding French. "We've had to put out a proactive release simply due to the amount of activity at the scene, but it is quite bland. However, on the topic of a leak, one of the nationals has got wind of the nature of the injury, and has asked us to confirm the details."

"Goddammit," Barnes said, shutting his eyes and pressing his forehead to his fist. "Where the hell would they have got that from?"

"We're holding them off at present, but we'll have to give them something before too long," Andrea said.

"Could have been one of the officers on scene guard," somebody offered.

"They've all signed NDAs though, am I right?" Andrea said. "That's a pretty bold step. A red-top would pay well for decent information from an unidentified police source, but not enough for them to survive on forever if they lose their job."

"And besides, none of the scene guards should have had access to that information. We'll need to think about a confidential media briefing," Barnes said. "DCI Choudhury, is there anything you would like to add on that?"

"Only my reassurance that PSD are actively looking into it. Let's not forget, however, that the leak may not have come from a police officer. It could even have been disclosed by the killer themselves."

"Why would they do that?" someone piped up.

Barnes shrugged. "Notoriety, disinformation, a tactical means to try to get a sense of how we are playing it and how far ahead we are."

"I don't know," someone else said. "That feels like a lot of calculation for such a violent attack."

"You may be right," Barnes said. "Which brings us back to someone else who had access to the body between the scene and the mortuary. That includes our payphone ambulance caller — who may also be a suspect. Okay, Intelligence next."

He looked over at Tina Flagstaff. She cleared her throat.

"The SIR's been raised and has been tasked. Other than getting the recording and transcript of SECAMB's 999 call — which is proving bloody slow to get hold of — until we have confirmed IDs, the net has been cast far and wide."

"Slow? Like, red tape slow?"

"Exactly that."

"Okay, thanks." Barnes made a note in his book. "Let me know if you haven't got it by the end of the day. I'll personally go to the ambulance control room and tie myself to a desk if needs be. Carry on, Tina."

"Okay, so we are focusing on trying to match the MO and churning the description through the national systems, as well as prioritising missing people reports and ViSOR prison releases. We've got an ANPR dump of all cars tripping town centre cameras one hour either side of the time of death, but—"

"Give me good news, Tina. There's not that many at that time of night."

She shook her head like she'd just found the chocolate stash of a man whose doctor has told him he needs to eat more vegetables.

"I'm afraid the list is too big to do anything with, even at two in the morning. Proximity to the town centre means the traffic flow never really dries up. It's very difficult to get your car out of town undetected, but it's not impossible. We'll work on whittling down the list one by one, but it will take time."

"Thanks, Tina. That's exactly what this enquiry is going to take — elbow grease. We're going to have to start big and gradually work our way in from the margins. The point is: everything is on the table until we can use a bit of science to conclusively eliminate theories. We're not working on hunches and gut instinct here, ladies and gentlemen, tempting though it may be. And speaking of science, I'm going to come to Scenes-of-Crime next."

He turned to Clive Brynn, who still looked as grumpy as he had done at the mortuary. He held Barnes's gaze for a second, and then looked down at his papers, addressing the room over Harry Palmer spectacles in a cigar-shredded baritone.

"Scene One is the disused Caffyns showroom in Meads Road, backing onto the Saffrons, just outside the town centre on Devonshire beat. It's a listed building, been out of action for about three years since the dealership opened up some new sites in Eastbourne and Lewes. It's still notionally their head office, but it's been out of action all that time. From what we can gather, the fencing and boarding has done a reasonably sturdy job of keeping out the riff-raff — it doesn't appear to have been used as a squat, and the state of the interior is as you would expect. That is to say, there's a lot of dust, debris and animal droppings. There's a few desks scattered about, but in the main it was cleared out before it was shut down.

"Searches are ongoing, and I've policied with the SIO that we will need to do a full examination of the entire ground floor, based on the movement of the deceased prior to expiry as well as the unusual nature of the injury. We don't want to miss anything. The bad news is that this is going to take some time, and also that — as with any public or disused locus — any forensic evidence will be difficult to attribute to any one causation. We might be able to tell you who's been there, but there could be any number of explanations for why. We can only hope that the passage of time will mean any usable trace material is relatively recent.

"There are a couple of points of interest, however. Firstly, while the vast majority of the blood found so far is that of the victim's, there were a couple of microscopic droplets near what we think is the point of entry. We don't know yet for sure that this is actually human blood, but if it is, it will obviously give us another line of enquiry.

"Secondly, in the centre of the showroom is some kind of hatch that leads to an underfloor recess that appears to have been used as an access point for cabling. Around the edges of the hatch itself we found traces of a substance that appears to be cocaine. It's a trace amount, but very early findings suggest it's from the same batch as the packages that washed up at Langney Point a few days ago, and it seems the location may have been used as a drop site for the exchange of drugs on more than a handful of occasions."

There was another murmur around the room. Tina started scribbling furiously. Drug deal gone south, Barnes thought. That would work for the six-o'clockers. That played. He'd be happy to release the details of the injury if he could lean on that as a theory. It also lent a shred more weight to the — admittedly still rather loose — suggestion that it was self-inflicted. A mule felt something pop inside them and panicked maybe.

"Interesting," said Barnes. "More interesting given that the batch doesn't seem to be part of the usual supply chain. It seems that someone has laid claim to these packages and may well be looking to shift them on their own."

"Finders keepers," somebody said.

"You could well be right," Barnes said. "But that introduces a number of additional complexities — not least the risk to whoever has decided to make a quick buck off the gear before the hammer comes down."

"You're thinking it could be our victim?" somebody said.

"Anything is possible at this stage," Barnes said.

Brynn continued. "The fact that it has been used as a communal dead drop gives us some problems, insofar as forensically establishing the identities of individuals' mere presence at the scene will not be enough on its own to convict.

"Scene Two is the body. I won't rehash the pathologist's findings here, but, as the SIO says, cause of death was exsanguination as a result of a bloody large gash in his stomach. The discovery of the body was relatively quick, and so with minimal decomp it's been straightforward to obtain prints. We should have NAFIS and NDNAD results in the next few hours. There are a couple of distinctive — ish — tattoos, which are being cross-checked against PNC, PND, HOLMES and a few other national databases. This is unfortunately taking longer than hoped. All of which is a long way of saying that we don't have an ID yet, but a number of samples have been recovered, which are in the process of being itemised. Once this is complete, myself and the SIO will decide which of these should be sent for analysis. It may be all of them, but I'm not the one signing the cheques.

"Scene three is the phone box. See above in terms of the showroom — it's in the open, is for public use, and even if we get some lifts from it, they are likely to be for intelligence and/or elimination purposes only. However — and to my ceaseless amazement — whoever the responding officers were did a good job of locking it down and preserving it pretty quickly. This was in the middle of the night, meaning people were not exactly queuing up to use it, and so you might get lucky.

"Scene four—"

The conference room door burst open again. Acting Sergeant Jill Rough stood there, again wide-eyed, again looking stressed. Her eyes fixed on Barnes, whose efforts to retain patience with the conveyor belt of interruptions were starting to slip.

"What is it?" he snapped.

"DI Barnes . . . sir. I'm sorry for the interruption. Um, again. We've been trying to reach you."

Barnes looked down at his mobile. Six missed calls.

"There . . . there's been another one, sir."

CHAPTER NINETEEN

Pete Lamb had been nagging Haven for a date for days, and she had been trying to think of ways to let him down gently. Not necessarily because she didn't *want* to go out for coffee — he was certainly persistent, but he seemed sweet enough, and had a bit of a devil-may-care thing about him — but the secretariat was a bit of an island, career-wise, and a reputation for thorough, detailed minute-taking during major enquiries couldn't hurt as a step up.

However, her worry ceased when the entire conference room went barrelling out the door to whatever it was that had been announced, leaving her alone with half-typed minutes and a *could-you-turn-the-lights-out-when-you-leave* feeling about her. She packed up in a mild sulk and walked over to the patrol base.

Pete was already outside, leaning on the bonnet of a large black saloon. It was immaculate, and practically brand new. She was about to ask about it, but then saw the rental car company's logo, a tiny green square in the rear window, and something made her keep her questions to herself. She instead turned her attention to Pete himself, and realised as she did so that he wasn't leaning on the bonnet in any kind of affected pose; if anything, it looked as if he were resting on it for support.

"Are you okay?" she asked, skipping the pleasantries.

"Hello to you too," he smiled. "But thank you for asking. How are you?"

"You seem a little . . . wobbly."

"I'll be okay in a minute. It's being bashed on the head, I think. I get the odd dizzy spell. It'll pass in a sec."

"Should you be driving?" she said, her eyes widening. "Shall we take my car?"

They both glanced over at her hot-pink Fiat 500, parked as it was at such a sharp angle that, despite its diminutive size, it rendered the neighbouring parking bay useless.

"Honestly, I'll be fine," Lamb said. "We're not going far."

He winked as a bit more colour seemed to appear in his cheeks, and she got in the passenger seat.

They headed past the Sovereign Centre and onto the seafront, Lamb making chit-chat, and they crawled along Marine Parade, slowing for the procession of blue lights that had descended on Treasure Island.

"That must be what everyone ran out to," she murmured. "I hope nobody's badly hurt."

Lamb glanced at her.

The sea was like a huge green snake alongside them as they drove, and Haven, for reasons she couldn't quite explain, felt a twinge of unease. She certainly didn't feel relaxed.

"Where are we going?" she asked in a small voice as the road widened out onto King Edward's Parade and inclined towards Beachy Head.

"It's a surprise," he winked.

The unease began to grow, and she felt a flash of panic. She grabbed the door handle suddenly — and then the panic subsided just as quickly as it had erupted. Lamb pulled off the road and onto the crescent driveway of the Grand Hotel.

"What . . . what's this?" she said.

"Well, you didn't think we were going to Starbucks, did you?"

Lamb parked between a Lexus SUV and a Mercedes and permitted the doorman in his bottle-green top hat and tails to hold the door for them both. He stepped aside to let Haven through, and they both stood in the enormous entrance foyer. It was bathed in warm light, a welcome respite from the January drizzle.

A smiling host in a grey waistcoat approached, hands clasped, not even batting an eyelid at Lamb's — admittedly improving — injuries.

"Two for tea, please," Lamb said, winking at Haven. "Or, tea for two. Whichever you prefer. Booking for Lamb."

They headed into the cavernous Great Hall, festooned on either side by golden marble pillars and antique furniture adorned with flowers, their soundless footsteps absorbed by the deep patterned carpet. Haven had no words as they passed underneath a huge chandelier recessed in the ornate plasterwork to be seated in wing chairs in the Lounge Hall, next to a roaring fire and the Palm Court string quartet.

"Wow," Haven said, gazing up at the eight-foot classical portraits and towering atrium. "I feel a bit bad, you bringing me here."

"Too much?"

"A bit... overwhelming, I guess," she said, hoping Lamb hadn't done anything silly like book a room.

"It's only tea," Lamb said, as menus were delivered and tea poured through silver strainers. "It's just nice tea, that's all. Plus, we're less likely to be bothered by nosy neighbours. Don't see many cops pitching up here."

"There's probably a reason for that," Haven said. "Did you win the lottery or something?"

The easy smile remained fixed on his face. "It's only tea," he said again.

After a three-tier cake stand occupied by more baked goods than Haven had ever seen in one sitting was delivered, Lamb leaned across the table, china cup in hand, his face suddenly serious.

"I don't want to waste time on small talk," he said. "I just wanted to make sure you're okay."

"Well, likewise," she said. "I didn't realise that you . . . you were the one that found him."

"I'm afraid so."

"What happened?"

He screwed up his face. "You really want to know?"

She shrugged. "Of course. You said it was good to talk about it."

He exhaled. "I was out on patrol, heading to a job. I got diverted to a suspected break-in report — called in by a neighbour, door wide open, nobody home. I went in and found him . . . in the spare bedroom."

"How?"

He winced. "Hanging. Loft hatch."

"Oh my God," she said, covering her hands. "That poor man."

She looked up suddenly.

"Should you be telling me this?" she said. "Isn't it, like, confidential?"

"The way I see it, we've both been traumatised. Talking helps. If you don't let it out in a way that's comfortable — to someone you feel comfortable with — then you risk all sorts of residual damage later in life. We need to support each other. No one else is going to. They might tell you off, but they won't stop you going wibble."

"Who else knows? How he died, I mean."

He shrugged. "Me, the DI, the wife . . . and the mistress."

Haven covered her face again. Lamb gave her a disbelieving look.

"You're not going to tell me you didn't know? You were his secretary, weren't you?"

Haven flushed. "It was none of my business, but . . . well, I did have an inkling. Couple of times a superintendent from Ops called the office trying to get hold of him."

"Probably not unusual."

"No, I know, but there was . . . something about the way she spoke to me. About him."

"None of the usual deference for rank?"

"Something like that. And then . . ."

"Then?"

"Then his wife called. I didn't know where he was, and told her so. She didn't believe me. She was vile. I think maybe she thought, you know . . ."

"That you were the other woman? Not totally surprising, I guess."

Haven watched as he looked her up and down. She felt another twinge of discomfort. "And then she turned up."

"Turned up? Where? At his office?"

Haven nodded. "She got past the front desk somehow, and appeared in the waiting area. He was there on that occasion. They had a massive ding-dong in his corridor, then she stormed out. He followed her outside and it carried on in the street. I could hear it from two floors up. I had to call the control room to tell them to let me know if they got any 999 calls about it."

"Good thinking." Lamb rubbed his chin and looked over at the quartet. "Do you think that's why he . . . you know, ended it?"

"Because his wife found out? I don't know. My experience, once you've been found out — for better or worse — the pressure lifts a bit."

"Your experience?"

"I'm not just some airhead secretary, you know," she said, only half playfully. "I've got a bit of life experience."

He didn't push it, but grinned and raised his palms in surrender.

"Anyway, I really think he loved Theresa. The super," she added. "But, I suppose, anyone in that frame of mind isn't thinking straight. So I suppose it's possible, I guess. Maybe it all just piled up. That and the other thing."

"Other thing?"

A waitress appeared and refreshed the tea without being asked. Lamb shook his head.

"That's what you pay for," he said. "The service. Anyway, sorry, you were saying. The other thing."

"The discipline thing. He was in trouble. Some night out that went wrong."

Lamb's easy smile seemed to slip a bit. He shifted in his fleur-de-lis wingback. "Did he tell you about it?"

"Not in so many words. He was just in a foul mood one morning, and I asked him if he was all right, and he swore and said something about the bastards trying to slander him."

"Did he seem worried?"

"Well, no. He said he was going to beat them. He never really worried about anything like that. His self-belief was, well . . . I guess you don't get to those heights without a good deal of hubris."

"So you don't think that was the reason he did it?"

She shook her head. "I just can't believe it. Something like that. He'd been through worse."

"Seems like he confided in you quite a bit."

It suddenly sounded like Lamb was fishing. She folded her arms. "He did. Not always explicitly. Some of it — most of it, in fact — I ought not to share."

The easy smile returned. Lamb raised his palms. "Of course."

"Anyway, what about you? How is the head?"

Lamb touched his eye. "Bit tender. Getting there, slowly. I'll be back at work in no time."

Her eyes widened a little. "You're . . ."

"Sick leave."

"Should you be here, then? You know, out and about? Shouldn't you be in bed?"

"My doctor says a bit of indulgence with incredible company is conducive to a speedy recovery." He grinned.

"What happened again?" she said.

He shrugged. "Jumped while I was out jogging. On the seafront. I like to run late at night."

"Jumped?"

"I had my headphones on. Never saw it coming."

"What did they take?"

He frowned. "Nothing. Here, have some of these buns," he said, sliding the cake stand over. "I'll eat them all, otherwise."

"Nothing? Somebody attacked you on the seafront for no reason?"

"You don't believe me?"

She leaned back in her chair. "I never said that."

When the waitress sidled up and spontaneously presented the bill, Haven wondered if this discreet puncturing of the tension was just another part of the silver service, but then she realised it was more likely that they were on a clock and the hotel wanted the table back.

Haven offered to split the bill, but Lamb pulled out his wallet and insisted. She couldn't help notice that the notes in there were in a thick bundle — hundreds, maybe more. They were grubby and weathered, and on the corner of one of the notes he placed down on the plate was a dark brown stain.

Haven was no expert, but she thought it looked like blood.

CHAPTER TWENTY

Treasure Island was a rundown, tired-looking but nevertheless unfailingly popular amusement park — in season, that is. In that strange void immediately after New Year, it sat on the seafront hibernating until the spring school holidays, hunkered down between the promenade and the main drag, a couple of hundred yards east of the Redoubt. A crazy golf course was out front; continuing into the main amusement arcade and out the other side brought you to the main event — a blue lagoon with a fibreglass whale as its centrepiece, complete with jets of water fountaining directly upwards at intervals to the delighted shrieks of the tiny patrons. It was surrounded by a pirate shipwreck climbing frame and similarly themed picnic furniture on a spread of lawn. Like many places whose target audience median age was in single figures, Barnes had driven past it so often he had forgotten it was there, but since Tamsin had burst into his life with her *take it or leave it, time's a-wastin'* outlook — not to mention potty mouth — they had brought the girls here once or twice. He personally couldn't see the appeal, but they had loved it.

Now, out of season, the place was weather-beaten and had a general air of abandonment. A carpet of dead leaves blanketed the grass, the ship's wood looked in dire need of some Ronseal, the lagoon was bereft of water and caked in algae, while the whale itself had faded from blue to some kind of washed-out off-white. Barnes couldn't decide which bits of the pirate shipwreck were actually broken and which bits were part of the design.

The body was lying between a boarded-up ice cream kiosk and a wooden lean-to with a corrugated iron roof that appeared to have been used as a winter storage area for all manner of stuff. The feet were sticking out into the park proper — a passing warden had thought it was one of the street drinkers that occupied the seafront beach shelters taking a rest after a bender, and had clambered over the fence to move them on. When he'd reached the body he'd seen the blue-white discolouration of the ankles. The gap was only just big enough for the body itself, and so the warden had gloved up and then pulled it out by the ankles to try to attempt some sort of first aid. This action had resulted in post-mortem flatulence, skin colder than stone, and the revealing of a patch of black blood on the winter grass large enough to cover a picnic table — at which point the warden had called the authorities.

Barnes pulled into the Redoubt car park alongside a snowplough of marked patrol vehicles, and headed past the main entrance, instead walking up the ramp onto the promenade itself. A blast of cold salt air whipped around his head as he turned to walk along the prom to the best vantage point for viewing the park.

He walked up to the fence, holding it with both his hands like a prisoner longing to get to the other side of it. He took it in. There were uniformed response constables stationed at the exits, having retreated there once they'd confirmed life extinct. It had to be pretty obvious for a cop to pronounce death rather than a medical professional, but even from this distance Barnes could tell it was, indeed, pretty obvious. The gears had thus shifted from "initial incident response" to "crime scene management", meaning the body lay alone in the centre of the park itself, skeletal leaves swirling around it, the hair and clothing flapping in the January wind, giving it a curious sense of animation.

Barnes looked up and down the smooth tarmac promenade. Acting Sergeant Rough had done a good job again, closing it at the Fisherman's Club to the east and the Redoubt car park to the west. It wasn't possible to keep people off the shingle completely — they'd have needed another fifty officers for that, depending on the tides — but Ops Planning were en route with some tarp or something to run along the fence line and protect the scene from view.

It wasn't going to keep the phones on the news desk from going crazy, though. They'd just about been able to keep a lid on the disembowelled carcass in the middle of the Caffyns showroom, but, even out of season, this was going to be a different matter. The body wasn't on display, as such, but it was very exposed and difficult to conceal from view, especially when the news copters began circling.

Scenes-of-Crime arrived and began laying stepping plates from the main entrance to the locus. There was a network of concrete paths looping through the grass — Barnes didn't dwell on the fact that the plates more or less followed one of these paths exactly.

As he stepped towards the body, Barnes found himself again leaning towards "drug deal gone wrong". The park was secure enough out of season, but if a little dope was going to exchange hands it was easy enough to get in and keep out of view with minimal effort. Nobody had any interest in the place in January, not even the all-night, all-weather fishers and dog walkers. But it was secure enough to render the theory that the victim was killed elsewhere and dumped here unlikely. The six-foot iron fence was not impenetrable, but it would be pretty tough to get a dead body over it.

Barnes thought all this while the SOCOs tiptoed around the body, placing yellow scene exhibit markers, taking photographs and generally busying themselves with perimeter activity before they got onto the good stuff. Starting on the outside and working their way in.

The body was on its front. The head, swathed in a thatch of dark brown hair, was facing away from Barnes, with the hands by the sides, palms up. The clothes — a thick fisher's sweater and grubby tracksuit pants — were damp and soiled. Barnes's immediate thought was a street drinker, but that was a leaping assumption. Maybe it was a half-baked hope, one that kept him from coming back to the almost inescapable possibility that this was linked to his other body and that he had a whole world of pain on his hands were that the case.

"Your SOCOs seem keen to move in."

Barnes turned. Marlon Choudhury had materialised beside him. He tamped tobacco into his pipe and blew the expelled smoke upwards. Barnes thought about telling him he shouldn't smoke in his crime scene, that, actually, Professional Standards had no business being here either, but found he was strangely grateful for his presence.

"They can't, yet."

"Pathologist coming out to this?"

"I sincerely hope so."

"Oh yes?"

"Yes. I've got a bad feeling about this one."

"Pray tell."

Barnes shook his head. "When have you ever known a major crime briefing to be interrupted because another body has dropped?"

"It happens, I'm sure."

"Location, time frames, victimology — you can't tell me it's a coincidence that this has happened mere days after Caffyns."

"You haven't even looked at the body yet."

Barnes dug his hands into his pockets like he was foraging for change. "And Duke Kenley out of prison two weeks," he muttered.

"Now, now," Choudhury said, in an admonishing tone that Barnes didn't think many could pull off. "That *is* a leap.

Most unlike you, the local ambassador for logical assimilation and deductive reasoning."

"It's kind of you to say so," Barnes said. "But the little shit is like a non-stick frying pan, and only an imbecile would not think to start profiling nominals of interest against recent prison releases. So, no, I don't think it is a leap at all. The ink isn't even dry on the bastard's release papers."

"And he's walked straight into the arms of our own Natalie Morgan," Choudhury said. "You're keeping her debriefed, I presume."

"Of course."

"So she can vouch for his movements?"

"Theoretically."

"Is this his style?"

Barnes shook his head. Even he had to concede that particular point. "No. Far from it."

The grey January daylight was like the side of a butcher's blade, and it was starting to fade when they finally turned the body over. There was a carefully structured formation in place when it finally happened — pathologist, CSM, coroner's officer, a platoon of SOCOs — and the SIO. The tide was starting to come in, gnarled green-grey fingers clawing at the shore as if trying to get a better look at the crime scene.

Barnes took no comfort in the fact that the victim's insides seemed intact, and that the most immediately obvious similarity to Op Limekiln was not in evidence. But it wasn't a hope he could cling to with any conviction — there were gaping slash wounds criss-crossing the front of the torso, the edges of the wounds curling back like scorched parchment. The upper-left side of the face was black and concave where it had been bashed repeatedly with something heavy. The left eye was buried under an avalanche of contusions; the teeth, by contrast, were revealed in a grin where the cheek had torn on the left side. No murder was gentle, but this one smacked of the same violent rage that seemed to have been enacted on the previous victim. This one hadn't been eviscerated, but it didn't appear to have been for the want of trying.

Barnes, trying to exercise patience by telling himself that the pathologist had at least deigned to come to the scene, took a deep breath, inhaling salt and damp, while the man muttered into his bloody dictaphone. Spots of cold rain fell in his ear. His phone wasn't ringing off the hook, but this was undoubtedly the calm before that particular storm. In a way, he missed Gabby. Missed that he would not be around to receive the worst ever of Barnes's calls, and the hellfire he would be raining down on Barnes at this very moment had he not tied a rope around his neck and jumped out of a loft hatch. Missed that he would not be the one to get the call to end all calls from Barnes, that it appeared they were dealing with Eastbourne's first serial killer since John Bodkin Adams.

CHAPTER TWENTY-ONE

A decent chunk — almost ten years, in fact — of Barnes's sixteen-year career had been spent as a widower. For better or worse, everything centred around work during that period. He could get to the office as early as he wanted, leave as late as he liked. He could eat when and whether he felt like it. He could come home and find the house in exactly the same state as he left it.

But since meeting Tamsin and becoming an overnight stepdad to her two girls, there were other demands in his life. Simple things like doing the school run when he could, or all of them sitting around the dinner table. As if to emphasise the point, his phone trilled with a text message:

Shall I save you some dinner? X

He felt the pull. Not of two masters — work and home — or the tension in the gut of having to say, *I'll be late, don't wait up*, and provoking a reaction, but simply that he had other priorities. Other things he wanted to do. It was too simplistic to say he loved his job, it was more a need. It kept him ticking over. It helped him feel like he was making some vaguely worthwhile contribution to human endeavour. If he hadn't had that, he would have shrivelled away to nothing when Eve died. He still felt that need, but . . . well. He also wanted to sit down with Mags and Ellie over sausages and chips and peas and hear about their day. And he wanted that more. That dedication borne of a barren life was actually counter-productive to career progression was an irony not lost on him. The police needed its members to be at least vaguely rounded and reasonably well-adjusted, not shells of their former selves more at home with the ghosts, even if that meant they had to occasionally get out the door at a decent hour.

It was getting on for seven, with some hours of work as yet required before he could think about getting home. He stared at nothing, knowing he should grab some time for a shower and a meal before getting back to it, glad that the patrol centre's twenty-four-seven status meant the hubbub never really died down.

A serial killer. When *that* news broke, it would be a spotlight on his little corner of the map. The National Crime Faculty would weigh in. NCA. The Home Office. Criminologists. Behavioural experts. Forensic scientists. Maybe even overseas help. Quantico or something. A regular rotation of experts, advisers and *don't do it like that* chirping. The formal announcement rested with him and him alone, but he had no doubts. He just wanted to get it down on paper first.

He had no personal benchmark, but he knew that there could be long distances and periods of time between murders where a series was concerned, and there might be many reasons for this. Opportunity, planning, spells in prison, the ebb and flow of irresistible urges together with shame and the fear of being caught competing to be the primary drivers.

This was not that.

This was two apparently connected murders committed with furious rage two miles and mere days apart.

Blunt force trauma.

Yawning slash wounds.

Evisceration.

Until the first victim was identified — Goddammit, that had to be soon, surely — he couldn't completely rule out random victim selection, and that was going to be a whole world of pain.

Two victims, both white adult males knocking on the door of middle age. All facts that were relevant. Beyond the situational factors, age, sex and ethnicity were the only common denominators at present. But that was relevant too.

Barnes smelled the sandalwood and rosehip before Marlon Choudhury appeared at his door.

Again.

He looked unusually solemn, which worried Barnes. When Choudhury was around, the ship felt a little steadier. There seemed to be very little the man hadn't seen — which, given his age, was hardly surprising. He had more policing service than an entire response shift combined and then some. Mind you, as far as Barnes could make out, most of *them* were barely shaving.

"You ever see anything like this before?" Barnes said.

"A series? Indeed, yes, but quite different from this."

"How so?"

"I have worked three major serial homicides in my time. A continental lorry driver who, over three years, murdered his way through seven hitchhikers — back when such a pastime was a thing — between Glencoe and Biarritz; a schizophrenic inpatient on day release in Peckham who killed a taxi driver and two women meeting for an *al fresco* lunch; and Operation Anagram."

"Tobin? He had an Eastbourne connection, didn't he?"

"Indeed. Well, tangentially. The remains of two women were found in shrubland on Beachy Head in the late eighties. It transpired — albeit some years later — that he had been working in the town around that time. Right place, right time, but little more than that to link him. Your case is different."

"I was afraid you might say that."

"Two victims, similar characteristics, killed days apart in the same ward. The linking of hitherto distinct crimes as a series can sometimes take years — in your case, it's happened in days. There is fury here, Mr Barnes, and someone who is very far from being done yet."

Barnes shook his head.

"Terrific," he said, even though he'd already arrived at the same conclusion. "Maybe that means he — or she, I guess — will make a mistake."

"He, Mr Barnes. This is not the work of a woman. And indeed, yes — he does not seem to be particularly discerning when it comes to covering his tracks. That goes in your favour, naturally. It remains to be seen whether the placement of the bodies has some relevance — one hidden away, the other in nakedly public view. It's too much of a stretch to say yet that this was deliberate, but there was precious little attempt to conceal it. In both cases the bodies had been moved — but not far."

"I'm not going public with a series hypothesis until some hack asks the question. And at least not until the first victim is identified."

"I don't disagree, but, in the nicest possible way, I worry that may be slightly above your pay grade. Have you briefed Superintendent Kane?"

Barnes shook his head. "I'm going to call him in a moment."

Choudhury nodded. "Heavy lies the crown. If the clamour swells, and you are lucky with your first victim ID, you may be able to confine the public narrative to squabbling among drug dealers. I hate to espouse cynicism, but the fact that your victims were not young, attractive females should help limit the media interest. A slightly sad indictment — a life is a life, after all."

Barnes's mobile rang. He kept his eyes on Choudhury.

"DI Barnes. Yes, I'm still here. Okay, thanks. Yes, ping them through."

He ended the call and dropped the phone back on the desk.

"Two for the price of one — IDs on both victims. Profiles being emailed over now."

"Progress." Choudhury smiled. "How were they identified?"

"Victim One is a hit on NAFIS — one of our more loyal customers. Victim Two is a missing person report from around New Year. Description, including tattoos, are bang on the money. We need to confirm it with a fingerprint and DNA comparison, as well as a formal ID, but it sounds good."

"I will leave you to your thoughts."

"What about you?" Barnes said. "Any closer to finding your leak?"

Choudhury shook his head. "No, and I'm not optimistic. It's a difficult one to contain. If you're elliptically asking me why Professional Standards are still hanging around an external murder enquiry, then let me assure you, in simple terms, that cases such as this — series homicides, I mean — have a tendency to tempt people into the most unsavoury behaviour. Or, put another way, to plumb new depths of stupidity."

"I wasn't saying that. I'm always grateful for your counsel, Marlon."

Choudhury nodded, and stepped backwards into the office doorway. "Remember what I said, Mr Barnes, and please don't think I'm being alarmist — but I don't think he is quite done yet."

He slipped away, and Barnes watched him go. Despite his size, the man held himself in such a way as to practically glide through the patrol centre.

Once he'd gone, Barnes turned his attention to his inbox and printed out the victim profile that had landed there.

Victim One was Liam Lawrence, thirty-nine. Barnes vaguely knew the name. He was local and had trodden a hokey-cokey of chaotic drug use to a fragile straight-and-narrow and back again since early adolescence. No employment record to speak of, no particular linear footprint to his journey in life, an infrequent but steady pattern of minor offending interspersed with longish spells of keeping his nose clean and a general impression of someone who lived hand-to-mouth and hustled a living in a largely threadbare way. He was one of Eastbourne's forgotten ghosts, and Barnes was depressed to note that he recognised the template all too well.

The second victim was forty-four-year-old Carl Jessop. Contrary to Barnes's first impression, he hadn't been a street drinker or homeless — and Barnes was cross with himself for making the assumption — but part of the local fishing trade. He'd been found wearing a war-torn cable knit gansey and jeans, and with his weather-beaten skin and brittle hair from a life spent more away from land than on it, Barnes had made the wrong guess.

He had no current record, but, thankfully, one of the more diligent intelligence analysts had dug deep into cross-referencing the description with other records. The trouble was, nearly all of the data on the PNC was only as good as the person doing the inputting. So, for instance, when the arresting officer started working through the C55 nominal descriptor form in the custody block, they might write — if you were really lucky and they were an aspiring detective — *4" diameter red and yellow Superman logo tattoo on inner wrist (R), bottom point facing towards elbow.* Or, as was more likely, they would just write, *Superman tattoo*, or, even worse, *S tattoo*. That did not make for a quick search should it be needed later.

Barnes dialled Tina's number, not even thinking what the time might be, or whether she would still be at work. As it was, she picked up almost immediately.

"Tina, we've got a new intel tasking. Confirmed victim IDs," he said breathlessly, unable to keep the excitement from his voice. "Connections or associations past or present between our victims. Did they meet up? Did Victim One obtain cocaine from Victim Two, or vice versa?

"And timelines — victim movements over the preceding twenty-four hours, then we widen it out. Phone work and financials. ANPR movements on the vehicles of the deceased. I'll get OET and a house-to-house manager on the route and put the FLOs on the next-of-kin updates. We'll regroup first thing tomorrow and gear up for a media briefing, but not until the families have been told."

"Okay, got all that," she said. "No problem. Leave it with me."

"Tina, if there's a needle in this particular haystack, I don't trust anyone else to find it," he said.

"Flattery will get you everywhere," she said. He could hear her smiling. "Do you have a pen?"

"What do you mean? You haven't found something already?"

"ANPR hit. As you know, the dump of vehicles tripping town centre cameras an hour either side of the first murder was massive, and slow to whittle down. When the second murder broke, we prioritised cross-referencing the second list with the first for any similarities."

"And you got a hit?"

"We got a hit. A black Volkswagen Passat estate RF13 CZG. Went through the town centre forty-seven minutes before the 999 call from ambulance reporting the first body. That same car was pinged heading up to Beachy Head at 0307 hours on 14 January 2015. That's a good four hours before Victim Two was found, but—"

"But it's broadly consistent with the time of death. Tina, you little beauty," Barnes said, and not for the first time.

"It needs developing, but it's a start."

"Who does it come down to?"

"It's a rental. No adverse trace PNC, RMS or any of our other systems. Doesn't appear cloned or anything like that."

"We'll need to get the hirer details, stat."

"I've got someone doing that now, but we're not likely to get an answer till the morning. Overnight we're going to build a full inventory of its movements since New Year's Eve."

"Brilliant work. Now I can tell the boss his maybe serial killer is a stone-bonker serial killer."

He ended the call, and stared at nothing for a moment.

Remember what I said.

There was no danger of Barnes forgetting what Choudhury had said.

He isn't done yet.

CHAPTER TWENTY-TWO

Haven excused herself and walked down the corridor to the bathroom, her heels clicking on the impossibly shiny floor. Lamb watched her go, then turned to look down the Great Hall. Beyond the marble pilasters, Persian carpet and cavernous entrance foyer was a small square of grey where the late afternoon had succumbed to the downpour that had been threatening all day. Beyond that, Lamb knew, the snarling Channel was waking up and clawing at the land.

This was technically their second date, and Lamb had opted to return to the Grand on the basis that it was a tough act to follow. He felt like he was floating in an impenetrable bubble of gloriousness — even if he did consider himself rather lucky that she'd even agreed to go out with him again. Her almost-white blonde hair, her scent, the open fire, the soft light from the chandeliers that made her skin glow, the strings — they all seemed a million miles away from his predicament. He nearly blew it last time; he wasn't going to make that mistake again, even if coming here a third time would probably clean him out completely.

His phone buzzed on the table. It was resting against a silver teapot, which trilled in turn as the device vibrated. He picked it up and read the text message.

U cant fkin hide 4eva. Weres my pkge?

So much for the bubble. The cocaine he'd kept back had reduced to a few parties' worth secreted in the battery compartment of a six-cell torch and a Pringles tube hidden in his car's spare wheel well, and he thought about nipping to the bathroom himself for a quick bump. It would certainly help the sudden sick feeling in his stomach. There was something about the wording of the message that seemed to indicate the sender, or people acting for them, had been to his flat. But then, of course they had.

He thought about sending a quick reply — *package gone to a good home, I can pay you what it was worth* — but as he did a quick totting-up of what he'd skimmed off the top, he realised that he would need to top up the fund by a few hundred quid first. He made some notes on his phone and then switched to the calculator. He made a mental note of what the hotel bill was likely to come to, and landed on a figure of nine hundred and something that he needed to put back into the sum before he could repay his mysterious — and pissed-off — wholesaler. He frowned. That much? He hadn't spent that in the last week or so, surely. Besides this — admittedly now rather frivolous — school trip, everything he'd spent had been on survival. Maybe he should look to shift the gear he had left so as to get the money together quickly.

Just as well he hadn't tried to book a suite. He suddenly hoped Haven didn't want to order champagne or anything.

He heard the *clack-clack* of Haven's heels echoing in the corridor; he stuffed his phone into his pocket and just about remembered his manners, standing up as she approached.

"Are you okay? You look a little tense all of a sudden," she said, plonking herself down in a cloud of reapplied perfume that suddenly made Lamb wish that he'd booked a suite all over again.

"I'm fine, thanks," he said, giving her another of his easy smiles. "The headaches come and go, you know?"

She looked concerned. "You want to go? Maybe you should be resting. I probably should head off soon, anyway."

Lamb didn't protest. "I guess I can't keep you here all night," he said, signalling to a waiter for the bill.

"Want to go halves?" she said.

"Don't be silly. My treat. You can get the next one."

The waiter brought their coats and delicately placed a black leather wallet on the tablecloth with a small strip of white paper poking out the top. Lamb took out his wallet, then slid the bill out and read it.

"Are you sure?" she said, one arm in the sleeve of her coat.

Maybe a little more than nine hundred, he thought.

"Pete?"

"Huh?"

"You okay?"

"I'm fine. I'll be right back. Quick comfort break. Sorry."

He left her standing there and padded off down the corridor past a display cabinet of designer handbags and a grand staircase to the gents' equally grand bathroom — stacks of individual facecloths in wicker baskets, brass-and-marble fixtures, a mahogany dado and brilliant white tile.

He stared at himself in the huge mirror. He didn't look good. A little like someone who'd camped out for four weeks in a construction site tunnel and had then been electrocuted upon emerging. A bump was definitely needed.

He reached for his wallet and little emergency baggie therein, only to find his pockets were empty.

Shit. He'd left his wallet out on the table. Not only that, he'd disappeared at settling-up time — she was going to think he was a tightwad who'd bitten off more than he could chew and liked to abandon his dates with one arm in their jacket the minute the bill arrived.

He fixed a mad smile on his face and walked back to the table. He picked up the bill — unable, despite himself, to avoid a minor twinge of irritation that she hadn't taken care of it while he'd been in the bathroom — and then the wallet, which was lying there next to the leather folder containing the bill.

"Do I need to check this?" he said, holding up the wallet.

His broad grin was entirely unmirrored by Haven's grave expression, and his face fell as he realised the joke hadn't landed at all.

He put down some of the dirty cash and guided her out, trying hard not to rush her.

He made an effort to make small talk as he drove her back to her car, but his phone kept buzzing in his pocket, and the conversation dried up.

By the time they got back to the station, the business-hours workers had gone home, and Lamb pulled up alongside her Fiat.

"Thanks for a nice time," she said in a monotone as she opened the door, not looking back at him. "See you around, I guess."

His phone buzzed again, just as he opened his mouth. Her eyes dropped to his thigh and back again.

"Maybe you should just turn it off," she said.

"I'm sorry about that. I will, next time."

She ducked her head back into the car. "Look, Pete, there isn't going to be a next time."

"What?"

That caught him square between the eyes. No next time? As far as he'd been concerned, things were moving along nicely. Couple more dates, a move to next base, then either back to her place or that suite at the Grand he'd been fantasising about — provided he sorted out his cashflow problem, of course.

"I don't want to be blunt, but I ought to be straight with you," she said. There seemed to be a slight tremor in her voice.

"Haven, come on . . ." he said, leaning across the car. "I thought . . . did I do something? I can give you some space, time, whatever."

"It just isn't a good idea," she said. "I like you, but . . . you just seem to have a lot of chaos around you. Maybe you should organise your life a little."

"Is this about the PSD thing? They're always on my case for no reason. It'll all come out in the wash. It always does. Come on, I thought we were having fun."

She didn't answer. Clearly she hadn't been having fun.

"Is there someone else?" he asked, then wished he hadn't. That was a stupid question.

She frowned. "We've been on two dates."

"I didn't mean that, I just . . ."

"Take care, Pete."

She slammed the door. He leaned back over the seats to watch her through the rear window as he went to her car, her head down. *Fuck me*, he thought, *she's practically running. She can't wait to get away from me.*

He drove slowly out of the patrol centre car park, his mind in a whirl of shock, shame, frustration and genuine upset, his phone still going in his pocket.

He stop-started impatiently through a crawl of rush-hour traffic that thinned when he reached the Sovereign Centre. He bombed down Prince William Parade, at least twenty miles an hour over the limit, until he reached Langney Point. He parked on double yellows, then walked to the end of the shingle until only the Martello Tower and the slowly blinking light demarcating the entrance to the Sovereign Harbour lock were in his vista, with the Cooden cliff face away in the distance across the crescent of Pevensey Bay.

Why? Why had she just dumped him like that? He couldn't believe it. Things had been going so well. Obsessing about her while he was still technically in with a chance was bad enough, but it was a fuck sight better than obsessing when she'd just told him she was closed for business. The thought that he might now never be alone in a posh hotel bedroom with her was almost too much to bear.

He was going to end up single and alone and it was all because of Marlon Choudhury, PSD and their bloody-minded ten-year campaign to witch-hunt him into touch.

He shuffled down the shingle, took out his phone and, without looking at the display, lobbed it as hard as he could into the sea with a grunt.

He sloped back up the shore, head down, his footsteps sliding and slipping on the loose pebbles, and then stopped as something occurred to him.

He reached into his pocket for his wallet and flicked through it. Cash count — okay. Cocaine baggie — present and correct. Driving licence and credit cards and general detritus — yep.

Oh, shit.

The note, the A4 piece of paper carefully folded into sixteen that he'd so carefully removed from the bedroom door of Gabby Glover's spare room.

It was gone.

CHAPTER TWENTY-THREE

Haven wasn't sure what to do. She looked down at her watch display, which showed her step count for the day, and figured that if she was going to be pacing up and down like this, she may as well get on the treadmill.

It wasn't in her nature to be nosy, or interfere in matters that didn't belong to her, but Pete Lamb's general demeanour just didn't sit right with her. He was by turns attentive and distracted, funny and morose — and just generally, well, *wired*. Most of the time. They barely knew each other too, and if alarm bells were ringing already then it was best to cut your losses, surely?

And that was *before* she'd rifled through his wallet.

It had just been lying there on the table. She'd felt electric with guilt as she went through it. She remembered shoplifting a Twix when she was about eleven, and how she'd practically crumbled into a pillar of salt on the spot.

It hadn't been a speculative poke around, either. It was the grubby cash she'd seen on their previous date, with the bloodstains on. She was sure they were bloodstains.

She could have just asked him about the cash, of course, but even at this early stage in their relationship — if you could call it that — she somehow knew she wouldn't have got a straight answer.

And then she'd found the note. The carefully folded, single piece of A4 paper carefully tucked into a zipped compartment at the rear, with an untidy felt-tip scrawl:

ELLA DON'T COME IN CALL 999

Haven was no investigator, but she had been in and around police stations a long time, and you tended to soak up a lot of it by osmosis. Besides, even the slowest single-celled drain-brain couldn't fail to work out what this instruction meant — even if you *didn't* know that Gabby Glover's widow was called Ella, which Haven did.

And then, on the back, the strangest suicide note Haven had ever seen. Not that she'd seen many, but she could imagine, and this was just a list of names:

Liam Lawrence
Carl Jessop
Terry Markham
Lee Flathill
Levi Sadler
He is coming.

CHAPTER TWENTY-FOUR

Contrary to what he'd told Marlon Choudhury, Barnes didn't call Kane immediately. He knew he should have done, but his feet had barely touched the ground for two days — plus, deep down, he knew he wanted to have something positive to report before he took that step. The identification of the victims and Tina's golden ANPR nugget seemed to be a good way to expedite that.

Between the carousel of briefings, calls and marshalling resources, pockets of time to actually write down anything meaningful in his policy file were few and far between. Documenting what you were doing, and the reasons for it, was the last bastion of good practice, all in the name of safeguarding against future trials — or, God forbid, public inquiry or jury inquest — going south. And yet, in the heat of battle, it was the thing that came least naturally. Trying to bring some order to chaos was never a bad way to structure your thoughts, but, unfortunately, it wasn't possible to hit the pause button often enough for that to happen.

After the latest evening briefing he went to his desk, and took the time to nail down some of the thoughts swirling in his head and commit some of them to his policy book. He managed a couple of pages before Georgia Brass appeared in the office to complain about resourcing, after which Barnes found it difficult to regain his concentration, and so he grabbed his jacket and made his way out through the back of the patrol centre.

Barnes walked past the enormous prefab evidence store, past the portacabins housing the SIU and under a runway of arc lights to the Major Incident Suite. He paused for a moment, his hand on the cold metal door, a low swoop of biting wind blowing in off the dark Levels.

Kane was in his office, typing furiously. Now edging towards forty, he had taken to wearing half-moon readers, which were a strange incongruity to the remnants of the spiky hairdo, lasered-off tattoos and chin piercing. Then again, Barnes thought, *Strange Incongruity* could have been his stage name.

"I was expecting you to call," Kane said, not looking up.

"I thought this might be better face to face."

Kane stopped typing. He took off the readers, and gestured to a chair.

Barnes remained standing.

"Op Limekiln. Samson . . . boss . . . we have a series."

"Series?"

"A serial killer."

Kane's eyebrows went up.

"Two bodies, discovered four days apart within two miles of one another. Both white men, both local, both — as far as we can make out — working class, and both suffered extensive slash and blunt force injuries. One found in a disused car showroom, one in a seafront amusement park. Closed off-season, but the body was found in a very publicly visible outdoors area. The bodies were moved after death, albeit not far — we think. The dump sites don't seem to be relevant as yet, but they don't quite appear random either.

"IDs have just arrived on both victims. Victim One is Liam Lawrence, thirty-nine, who, as you know, was disembowelled.

Victim Two is Carl Jessop, forty-four. He wasn't disembowelled, but the killer still had a good go."

"Shit. Any motive?"

Barnes shook his head. Kane's radio handset chirped on his desk. He turned the volume down.

"Not so far. Nothing concrete, anyway, but numerous possibilities. Drug deal gone wrong is what we're going with for now, but it's loose. We've only just identified them, so there's work to do, but as yet there's no obvious link between them."

"Then it might not be a series."

Barnes shook his head again. "We need to get a lot deeper before we can say that. We've only done a first pass of exploring potential links so far, but we've identified a vehicle of interest that connects the two. And there's . . . something."

Rage.

"Something?"

"About the injuries. Brutal. Frenzied, almost."

Kane sighed. "Is there any possibility of random victim selection? Are the public at risk?"

"My instinct tells me no, but it's too early to say. Drug deal gone wrong is over-simplifying it, especially with those injuries."

"That's not a convincing line for the media. Too much ambiguity. They'll fill the gaps with scaremongering bullshit. What about suspects?"

"Nothing yet. We've got trace amounts of blood at Scene One that doesn't match the victim's, as well as what looks like cocaine from the batch that washed up at Langney Point."

"That's interesting. Accords with the drug dealers killing each other narrative, anyway. We'll go with that for now until we know more. What about this vehicle you mentioned?"

"ANPR hit — same vehicle in a time and location proximity to both bodies. Not so close as to be definitive, but neither can it be a coincidence."

Kane's eyes roamed the room as he thought through all this, then they settled on Barnes. "Okay. What do you need from me?"

"Deal with the press conference. Help me with resourcing — the house-to-house alone is going to soak up manpower for at least a week, and I'm going to need some wheels greased to call on some of the skills at the NCA and Crime Faculty. Criminologists, behavioural scientists, that kind of thing."

"Anything else?"

"Brief Baily. She'll want to chair the Gold Group, I expect, but the DCC might take it off her, especially if the serial killer line makes it to the press. And, so you know, we think there's a leak to the media, which isn't a great surprise, but still an irritation. Nothing to suggest it's even come from us. We're going to need to think about a closed media briefing."

"Okay, noted. Is there any link to Gabby Glover's suicide?"

Barnes frowned. "No. What makes you say that? Do you know something I don't?"

"Not at all. It was just a thought. Something you said before about the timings. What about prevention? Is he going to do this again?"

"Yes, boss," Barnes said. "I'm afraid this is just beginning."

CHAPTER TWENTY-FIVE

Haven kept the note in an envelope in her glove compartment for three days before she finally couldn't take it anymore. She could practically feel it glowing through the trim, like something out of a Poe story.

When she arrived at work, she slipped the envelope into her bag and placed it under her desk. She looked around nervously, half expecting everyone to somehow know that she was holding a potential crime scene exhibit, and half worried about bumping into Pete, before remembering he was still off sick and didn't sound like someone who was planning on coming back to work anytime soon.

Even towards the end of the day, the office was a hive of activity — being the main patrol hub, it always was, but today felt different. Haven knew the investigation into Gabriel's suicide would have been frenetic, but, as it was so politically sensitive, the bulk of it would have been conducted behind closed doors.

And his suicide note was in her handbag.

But this activity was different. She could just tell. Something about the tempo, the atmosphere, the way people were running about and calling things, with segments of radio traffic and phone conversations humming in the background. There was a total absence of laughter as well. No one was joking around.

The man she wanted, DI Barnes, was busy holding an intense conversation with someone in his goldfish bowl of an office. His left arm was outstretched, the hand resting on something on the desk as he spoke. It looked like he was blessing it, whatever it was.

The door opened and a stony-faced, sour-looking inspector walked out. Brass, Haven thought. She couldn't remember the woman's first name, but thought she might have been Pete's boss. One of the patrol sergeants, who didn't look more than twenty-five, walked up to Brass, who didn't break stride, and the sergeant hovered, looking unsure of herself, before Inspector Brass issued an indiscernible yet obvious admonishment.

After a few minutes, DI Barnes appeared, jacket under his arm, wearing an expression that said Inspector Brass's appearance had not been particularly welcome. He stalked across the office with a thousand-yard stare and disappeared out of the patrol centre's rear entrance.

When he'd gone, Haven decided to wait five minutes before making her move, but found she was frozen to the seat. The ridiculous design of the building meant the whole thing was open-plan, with all the glass-walled offices stretching in a line down the centre of the office, creating a physical wall between uniform and CID.

There was absolutely no way she could get in there undetected, unless she made a point of coming back tonight and creeping in at, like, three in the morning. She didn't think that would work either — it was a twenty-four-seven operation, and besides, DI Barnes seemed to be at work an awful lot.

In the end, she decided her role as a secretary gave ger a veritable arsenal of reasonable explanations as to why she might be in DI Barnes's office. Besides, she only needed to be in there for thirty seconds at most. And if Barnes came back, well, she would just tell him the truth.

Not that it seemed likely. Given some of the snippets of conversation she was picking up, he was going to be gone a while.

She took a deep breath, grabbed the envelope and took the thirty or so feet from her desk to the office in a purposeful stride.

She opened the glass door and scanned the office frantically. She'd intended to either slip it inside his briefcase or leave it on his keyboard, but she could see no personal effects of his, and she suddenly worried that leaving such a vital exhibit on a keyboard might be a bit too conspicuous. For all she knew, Pete Lamb had by now realised the note was missing from his wallet and would shortly be raising merry hell to get it back before it fell into the wrong hands — or should that be into the right hands?

She'd already been in the office longer than she'd intended, and was rooted to the spot, not even looking vaguely like someone who was engaged in a legitimate errand.

On the desk was a large cardboard storage box, caked with dust, and emanating the musty smell of something that had been in a loft or a garage for a long time. It was this object that Barnes had been resting his hand on while he spoke to Inspector Brass.

Haven saw that *GABRIEL* was written on the side of the box in faded marker pen, and decided that would do for her. She gently lifted a corner of the lid far enough to slip the note inside the box, then replaced it carefully, wondering if she should have worn gloves.

She sat back down at her desk, her heart drumming in her chest. No one had paid her the slightest interest. She stared at the office door, suddenly unable to remember if it had been open or closed when she'd walked in, suddenly worried that some orderlies would appear and start emptying the office for the purposes of decorating or running cables through the ceiling. She decided there and then that the next time she saw DI Barnes, she would tell him straight out, and bugger the consequences. She'd done the right thing, hadn't she?

She had nothing to worry about.

Surely?

CHAPTER TWENTY-SIX

Barnes walked back to his office. Kane hadn't asked him if he was up to the job — that wasn't his style, and besides, Barnes trusted that Kane trusted him. Chief Superintendent — or rather, Acting Assistant Chief Constable — Baily might have a different opinion, but time would tell.

Barnes hadn't considered whether there might be a link between the murders and Gabby's suicide, largely because the evidence hadn't pointed to it thus far. But now he was considering it, which meant he was looking out for it. It was practically a logical non sequitur, but, in Barnes's view, that just summed Kane up.

Barnes hadn't mentioned the possibility of Kane acting up as chief super behind Baily. Kane would have just thought Barnes was taking the piss, even though Barnes thought he was eminently suited to it. As he walked, he realised that he was wondering because he was worried. A spontaneous reshuffling of superintendents across the Force — which seemed to happen with arbitrary frequency — could mean Kane was out of Barnes's professional life overnight, and Barnes found himself wondering, purely selfishly, about the extent to which his career had been held together by Kane's presence alone, and what it would mean if he moved on.

There was a laugh from the corner of the office. Barnes looked over and saw a couple of his DCs engaged in conversation, to all intents and purposes making some kind of plan to socialise at one of the looming off-weekends. Barnes hoped not to rain on their parade by introducing a third body and the handiwork of a serial killer who seemed to be operating at pace. Social plans and family events, all that normal stuff that most people did without thinking, they tended to go out the window when the shit hit the fan. It was funny when you thought about it: cancel somebody's day off because someone had mucked up the rota and the office was understaffed, or refuse their leave request because three other people had got in first, and the mutinous reactions could stop a line of tanks. Cancel everybody's rest days for a Big Important Job, however — CBRN attack in the town centre, kidnap of a young girl, serial killer moving swiftly through their midst — everybody dropped everything and came in from all over, no questions asked.

He looked at the two DCs again. It happened in clusters — they went for drinks outside work, their wives and husbands became friends, they made cakes for each other, helped each other with school pickups and stuff. It wasn't something Barnes had ever given much thought to. His social life — such as it was — had always been firmly outside the police circle. He felt the pull of his family when he was working a lot, but that was it. He didn't have time for friends.

Unless you counted Kane, and Barnes wasn't even sure he did really. Drawn to an obvious outsider — one to another? — and probably pushed together by circumstance, largely in the form of the Keber group's various power grabs of the last ten or so years. Yes, they'd blown off steam in the pub from time to time, but only to debrief incidents, explore theories, unpick incubating trauma. If the narrative of the last decade had just been morale and solved crime rates and budgets, he might never have even encountered Kane, other than to ask for money or sign off on custody extensions and closure orders. How hard could it be to make the effort to invite the man over for dinner? Kane had already met Tamsin and the girls, albeit in inauspicious circumstances — even if *inauspicious* was putting it mildly.

When Barnes got back to his desk, a reminder popped up on his phone: ON CALL. He grimaced and looked at the ceiling in a moment's disbelief. He'd forgotten he was on call again. How had that happened? He could really do without it — he'd been thinking about going home after a seventeen hour day, or whatever it was, but now he was on the clock until the following morning. He thought about ringing Kane, see if the boss could coopt someone into a swap, but that wasn't his style, and wouldn't make him any friends on a Friday night either. He wasn't stupid enough to jinx it by wishing for a quiet one, but he could really do without collecting any more brutalised bodies.

His mobile rang three minutes after he sat down. Thinking promotion to chief inspector would be worth the aggravation just to benefit from the secretarial support that the rank was afforded, he eventually answered it with a muttered curse.

"DI Barnes?"

"Who's this?"

"It's Theresa Baily."

The former chief superintendent and now acting ACC. Gabby's lover and, apparently, now successor. Barnes braced himself. This call could go any number of ways.

"What can I do for you, ma'am?"

"Sorry about the phone call. I'd rather have told you in person."

"Yes?" Goosebumps on his shoulders.

"It's Marlon Choudhury. I know you two are friends, so . . . I'm afraid he's had a stroke."

"Shit. How is he?" Barnes said, his insides turning to cold water.

"He's alive, but it's too early to say. Happened last night. He's still in hospital, obviously. The bad news is that it was some hours before the ambulance got to him. He lives alone, you know, so . . ."

A pregnant pause on the line. Barnes drew a line under it. It was fair to say that he had a few trust issues, chief officer-wise.

"Thanks for telling me, ma'am. I appreciate it."

"You're welcome. We'll keep you posted, but, obviously, go and visit if you want to. And by the way, it's 'Theresa'."

Yeah, right.

"Thanks. Goodbye."

He ended the call and stood up, his instinct telling him to grab his keys and get straight down to the hospital.

At the doorway, he checked himself and sat back down. Something was keeping him from going. Fear, maybe. Fear of seeing the last man standing fall, of the indestructible struck down, of the end of eras.

He spent several minutes staring at nothing before he eventually zeroed in on the storage box on his desk. It had been sitting there for days since Choudhury brought it in. The thing seemed to be ladled with intrigue, but the ill-timed emergence of a serial killer had meant that Barnes had practically forgotten about its existence. He remembered the reports he'd locked away in his desk drawer — he opened it, relieved to see they were still in there, and put them back in the box.

When a passing DC paused in the doorway of the office to ask him if he was all right, he got up. He checked his emails, checked his phone for signal and battery — vital for a jobbing on-call detective — checked his watch, shut everything down and hefted the box into his car.

CHAPTER TWENTY-SEVEN

"I shut the door in your face when you were last here," Ella Short said. "I apologise for that."

"You were upset," Barnes said, looking around the hallway. He imagined Pete Lamb searching the house while Gabby swung from the rafters. "I need to ask you some questions."

"Of course you do."

She looked better than she had the last time he saw her. There was some colour in her cheeks and her mouth had lost some of the downturn that she had seemed unable to shift at their first meeting. She was wearing a navy maxi dress with a large gold buckle, and her hair bounced when she walked, like she was in an advert for conditioner.

She showed him through to the front room they had sat in during Barnes's last visit. There were two matching lemon-yellow sofas facing each other across an impossibly polished coffee table. Barnes found himself resisting a powerful and sudden urge to rest his feet on it.

They took a sofa each.

"It's very unusual to make something look like a suicide that isn't," Barnes said. "Usually we pull out all the stops because the family can't believe their loved one would do that to themselves, and that there must be some other explanation."

She shrugged. "He killed himself. Someone did not break in here, overpower him and then string him up. Simple logic."

Barnes tilted his head. "Logic can be a quiet voice when emotions are high."

She shrugged again. "I just want to get on with it. The inquest is an unnecessary distraction, in my view, but the coroner has indicated he'd be minded to release the body for the funeral, which I've provisionally booked for the end of the month. Then there's probate, et cetera. You understand, I'm sure."

Barnes did. He'd seen it before. Box it up, move on. It was a way of dealing with it — sometimes — that people lived to regret. He did wonder if she was wanting to move on just a little too quickly, and not just for emotional reasons.

"In which case, the investigation need not be protracted. My focus is on the why."

"Does that matter?" she said. "The inquest will itemise the cause of death as suicide, or not. Whether it was motivated by financial strife, corruption or the guilt over his adultery finally catching up with him is neither here nor there. His mind wasn't right, so he took his own life. That's as much as the inquest will be interested in."

"Did you ever confront him about the adultery? I mean, was it fact? You didn't just suspect?"

She leaned forwards and slid a drawer out of the coffee table. She pulled out a magazine and slapped it down in front of Barnes.

He picked it up. It was a winter edition of *Country Life*, with the front cover given over to a feature about bonfire activity across Sussex. It showed a picture of a village high street at dusk, thronged with people eating candy floss, holding sparklers and milling about, ostensibly waiting for a parade to start.

The shot telescoped away down the high street; in the foreground, near the photographer's lens, was a couple walking toward the camera. They stood out because the woman was taller than the man, but also because they were holding hands and gazing lovingly at one another. The man was bearing a smile so genuine and incongruous that it took Barnes a moment to work out who it was.

Gabby and Theresa Baily.

"Pretty incriminating, wouldn't you say? This was taken in mid-September."

"Where is it?"

"Mayfield. They hold their bonfire early on in the season, so the light is good and it provides a decent lead-in to the bigger events in October and November."

"You showed this to him?"

"A friend of mine saw it and gave it to me. To his credit, he didn't try to wriggle out of it. What he actually said was, 'What miserable fucking luck.' That was not long before Christmas, three weeks before he killed himself."

Barnes said nothing.

"He'd picked a guest house in what he thought was the middle of nowhere, told me he was going to a conference, and then the pair of them obviously chanced a stroll around the village — I don't know, maybe they got bored of having sex — and walked straight into the photojournalist's field of vision. I can see why they wanted to keep it. It's actually quite a sweet photograph."

Barnes figured she'd done her screaming already, but the anger was still there, simmering below the surface.

"Was she his first affair?"

"She's the only one unfortunate enough to have incontrovertible proof splashed on the front of a coffee table rag, but I had my suspicions."

"Do you think that's why he did it?" Barnes asked.

"No, I don't."

"You don't?"

"No. In my experience being found out can be a relief. Cathartic, even. It's the fear of being found out that drives people to find an alternative exit."

"In your experience?"

"Do you just repeat the answers you get in the form of a question? Yes, my experience. In a past life I retained an occupational interest in mental health. People who can't face the music only have a handful of options. One of them is the coward's way out."

"That seems pretty tough."

"I'm not generalising. I'm speaking about my husband. He couldn't stand being wrong. He would argue white was black with a hubris that had you doubting yourself. And when faced with proof to the contrary . . . well, let's just say sticking two fingers up at me as he dangled wouldn't have been far from his final thoughts."

Barnes thought about this. He tried to assess just how fragile she was. She seemed matter-of-fact about it all, but her words were punctuated with brittle anger and an almost parental *what's he done now* resignation about the antics of her late husband. She seemed to have no interest in processing her loss in any meaningful way, despite her claim to a professional interest in mental health. Box it up and move on. Maybe she didn't want to give him the satisfaction.

"So if the affair wasn't the chief motivator for his suicide . . ."

"As I said to you before, I did not have an intimate knowledge of his work life. One might say I maintained a strictly strategic interest." She tittered. "So I'm not informed enough to speculate on any skeletons in his professional closet. All I can say with any certainty is that our joint finances — from a cursory look, anyway — seemed to be in reasonable order."

"But the box . . . that can't have been all he possessed."

"Box?"

Barnes was beginning to grow frustrated, but he kept it hidden. He couldn't work out if she was deliberately leading him a merry dance or simply passing on stuff she thought might be useful without any great consideration for the why.

"The box of his stuff. The one you brought to the station for me."

"Inspector, I don't know what you are talking about. I didn't bring you anything."

"But—"

"Look," she said. "There are hundreds of boxes of his stuff, of course there are. I haven't finished going through them all yet — I may just put the whole lot in the skip — but I can say with absolute certainty that I have not delivered any to you."

Barnes's mind raced, and he began to tune out what she was saying.

"I'm sorry?" he said.

"I asked if you said somebody brought you a box. Of his things. Who else would . . . Officer, are you okay?"

"Fine. Thank you."

He stood. She did the same and faced him, like she wasn't done with him by any stretch.

"What box?" she said. "You're not leaving? I need to know more about this box."

"I'm afraid I need to go," he said, bewildered.

"Was it her? Has she got a load of his stuff?"

Barnes was relieved that he had taken the sofa closest to the door, and he shuffled towards it, still facing her.

"She has no right to his things!" Ella Short cried. "DI Barnes, I must insist—"

"I'll see myself out," he said. "Thank you for seeing me again, and, again, I'm sorry for your loss."

"No, you don't," she said. "You can't drop that little bombshell and then just leave."

"I'm afraid I have to," he said from the hallway.

"This is unacceptable. I shall be speaking to your boss."

Barnes didn't answer, but instead opened the front door. As he did so, she suddenly advanced towards him. Barnes stepped out onto the driveway and hurried across the gravel.

"You haven't heard the last of this!" she shouted at his back. "I want to know what was in that box!"

So do I, Barnes thought as he ran to his car. *So do I.*

CHAPTER TWENTY-EIGHT

The girls were asleep when Barnes rolled in, and Tamsin was drifting there herself.

"Fuck, what time is it?" she asked, her voice thick with sleep.

"Late. Sorry to wake you. Go back to sleep."

"Coming to bed?"

"Shortly," Barnes said, kissing her forehead. "I'm on call. Got some bits to finish."

She stroked his face, her eyes already shut, and he went down to the kitchen, made himself a cup of tea and settled in under a desk lamp to sift through the contents of Gabby Glover's box of secrets.

It was getting on for one in the morning, but being on call, he was in no rush to get to bed. He'd much rather be awake when the phone rang than in the surreal state of being barely awake having been catapulted from sleep by news of a shotgun suicide, or a double murder, or a live kidnap.

This was not the only box of Gabby Glover's belongings, he was reasonably sure of that. And yet somebody — but apparently not his widow — had gone to the trouble of bringing this particular box to the station for him, presumably in the belief that it would help him find answers.

Did they know what was inside it? They must have done — but what playful purpose was served by not just telling Barnes directly? Why toy with him? He would have to go through the whole box again, focus as much on the keepsakes as the paperwork. For all Barnes knew, there was a password to a secret bank account or a love letter to Theresa Baily hidden behind the foam mount of one of the boxes of long service and good conduct medals.

Despite the bundle of commissioned reports on individual officers — all of whom were, himself included, on Glover's shit list for one reason or another — being unorthodox at best, unlawful at worst, there was nothing leaping out as being an obvious trigger for Glover taking his own life. Not only that, but there was nothing in particular in the reports that came as any great surprise.

Or was there?

It offered an insight into how the ACC rolled, but nothing that was a particular surprise, and certainly nothing that would give him any more insight into why the man had killed himself. He'd conducted at least one extramarital affair, but that didn't fit. His widow, Ella Short, already knew, and he agreed with her that any suicidal impulses may well have evaporated a little once the cat was actually out of the bag. There was no evidence of widespread corruption or seriously declining mental health. He did know that he couldn't — couldn't — go back to Ella again. That ship had sailed.

He found himself wishing Marlon was here to bounce theories off. What would the old man say? Look at it from another angle, or think about what you're not seeing, or go and take a walk and come back to it, or something like that. Think outside the box, in fact.

Jewellery boxes with cufflinks and tiepins inside. Undeveloped rolls of 35 mm film. Commendation certificates. Formal photographs rolled into scrolls nestling inside commemorative tubes. A 1986 programme for the Smiths playing at Wolverhampton Civic Hall. A transistor radio, of all things.

And then, underneath the normal stuff, the stuff you might find in the loft of any middle-aged man, was the stuff that shouldn't have been there. Policy books, intelligence products and crime reports.

Barnes caught something else. A finalisation report. Stamped on the top in thick black typewriter font was *SENSITIVE — OPERATION WOODHATCH*.

Barnes wasn't sure what it was, but something about the bundle burned his fingers. An almost electric energy pulsed through him, like the thing was radioactive.

He sat back heavily in his chair in the half-light, feeling for all the world like he was, in fact, in a goldfish bowl.

CLOSURE REPORT — OPERATION WOODHATCH — SENSITIVE
To: Chief Superintendent Gabriel Glover
From: Senior Investigating Officer Sergeant Brett Dickson, Roads Policing

Sir,
Collision date: 12 March 2006
Location: Cross Levels Way, Eastbourne
Time: 1407 hrs
Conditions: Wet, with glare caused by sunshine
Estimated speed of Vehicle One at point of impact: 50 mph
Fatalities: 1 — Eve Barnes, aged 43 yrs

I write with my final report into the above collision. As you will know, the collision arose from a police pursuit of a Ford Transit flatbed van that had been seen in suspicious circumstances at or near a number of residential burglaries in rural, affluent locations spread across Rother and Wealden Districts.

The van had been spotted by an unmarked patrol car who reported its location. Marked units got behind the van; it failed to stop when required to, resulting in a pursuit through Cross Levels.

The van showed little regard for other road users and drove dangerously in trying to evade police; indeed, the control room inspector in his statement asserts that he was about to abort the pursuit at the point of impact.

The van struck an oncoming private car — the deceased was a front-seat passenger in this car — before a glancing secondary collision with a second car. The deceased suffered catastrophic internal injuries; drivers of both cars suffered only minor injuries. The Forensic Collision Investigator reports the van's speed as around 50 mph at the point of impact, with no evidence of braking.

The van continued off-road, ascending a grass bank before cutting across a spread of wasteland opposite Eastbourne District General Hospital onto Kings Drive. It continued into a residential area where it was abandoned. Reports from the scene indicate there were three occupants of the van, including the driver, but to date this has not led us to any identified suspects, despite a number of enquiries.

All pursuing units stopped at the scene of the collision to render first aid, giving the van driver a small but fruitful opportunity to continue evading police. There was a relatively short time before the abandoned van was found, but this was enough for the occupants to make good their escape. As mentioned, three men were seen leaving the van by a number of householders in the area, but despite the use of several different tactics — including cognitive interviews, sketch likenesses and, in one case, the use of hypnosis — no witness was able to positively identify any confirmed suspects. Media appeals and social media interrogation also proved fruitless, and while forensic material within the van generated a significant intelligence opportunity, it was not possible to prove that those identified from the forensic harvest were actually in the vehicle at the material time. A dog track from the site of the abandoned van led the search into the residential estate, where the trail dead-ended. Enquiries in the area did not progress the enquiry further.

The van itself is believed to be a pool vehicle used by either the Keber organised crime group or a local subsidiary. It has no current keeper and had previously been notified to DVLA as being off-road, and had come to notice for a range of offences including petrol station bilkings, shoplifting and, as mentioned, had been seen in suspicious circumstances at or near several distraction and creeper burglaries in remote, affluent areas spread across Rother and Wealden.

Forensic material, prison intelligence and Crimestoppers information led to the naming of one Stratton Pearce as the driver of the van and the only named suspect to date. A profile on Pearce suggests he was a street-level enforcer and aspiring capo of the Keber group. He had a range of local links and was arrested in 2010 during an armed raid of a slave farm in Rickney, but had been at large after a successful operation by Keber members to break him out of a prison transport while in transit between HMPs Lewes and Belmarsh later that same year. He remained at large until he was fatally shot by armed police during an operation on the South Downs in December 2013 to rescue hostages from a purpose-built underground storage facility that was primarily used as a receiving centre for Class A shipments moved over water.

Pearce was interviewed under caution about his suspected involvement in the collision following his arrest at the slave farm. He obtained legal advice and refused to answer questions, and the level of evidence retrieved to date means that there was insufficient to charge him with any offences relating to the collision. Had we been able to prove he was the driver at the material time, we would undoubtedly have been able to charge him with the relevant driving offences, but it would have still been impossible to prove his intent to deliberately harm or kill the deceased. Despite this, he remains my preferred principal suspect for the offence.

However, given his recent demise and the lack of other investigative opportunities, I believe the enquiry has progressed as far as it can, and has come to its natural conclusion. It is a matter of personal and professional regret that no person has stood trial for this matter and that, as a consequence, I have been unable to achieve justice for the deceased.

You will be aware that the deceased was the wife of a serving officer, Detective Inspector Rutherford Barnes, who was driving the car in which the deceased was travelling. Mr Barnes himself is not suspected of any road traffic offences. Contact with him has been rather inconsistent to date, due to the ebb and flow of available updated lines of enquiry over a prolonged period of time. I do know that he agrees with my hypothesis that Stratton Pearce was the preferred suspect. With your approval, I will contact DI Barnes and advise him of the decision.

I am also aware that Mr Barnes has, over time, embarked on several investigations that have, directly or indirectly, involved Pearce and/or his Keber associates. It is not for me to say whether this has been deliberate or unwitting; nor is it for me to address any concerns that DI Barnes, as a result of his work — and, I have to say, tenacity — may have been actively targeted by the Keber group. This would lend weight to the supposition that Pearce deliberately killed the deceased, but it remains impossible to prove. It is outside my remit, but I would nevertheless recommend that measures are taken to assess the risk posed to DI Barnes by the Keber group, with safeguards put in place accordingly. It is of note that Pearce was fatally shot by police while holding DI Barnes's second wife hostage.

I respectfully submit this report for your consideration of formally closing the Op Woodhatch investigation.
 Sincerely yours,
 Brett Dickson PS CD285

Barnes put the report down, staring at the screensaver on his laptop as it lazily changed colour like a lava lamp. The silence was like thunder. The report contained no particular surprises, but to see so much that he had hitherto suspected but had never had formally confirmed caused the adrenaline to flare in his chest. The formal notification of the investigation's closure alluded to by Brett Dickson in the report had never actually taken place, but Barnes didn't blame him for that. It happened all the time — cops not quite following through on their intentions. Usually it was defensible — too much work, not enough staff, distracted from their to-do list by yet another emergency call, but, Barnes mused, if they could have just got that one small thing right as a collective it would have solved a lot of problems, if not crimes. Maybe Dickson — not unreasonably — had expected Gabby to give Barnes the final update. Maybe Gabby had offered to do so, and it was Gabby himself who had never followed through.

He put down the report, not quite ready to dwell on it too long. It was like the closure he'd never really wanted but could now never escape.

He quickly picked up another report, checking his phone for any missed calls as he did so. It had been right there on the kitchen table, but he'd been so engrossed in the report he could quite easily have tuned it out.

Sir,

As requested, please find below my full report into Superintendent Samson Kane.

Barnes noted that *As requested* had been crossed through with a red biro, a double strike pointing to two bold question marks in the margin.

As you know, Mr Kane joined the service as a lateral entry superintendent in 2010. Full self-disclosure of potentially adverse trace — including his prior arrests — was made on his appointment, and, after due consideration of the circumstances, his appointment was approved. Shortly after his joining, intelligence was received suggesting further past behaviour that may have been deemed incompatible with the police service. However, further developments confirmed that this intelligence submission did not provide any additional detail that had not already been disclosed by Supt Kane himself as part of his application, and its provenance may — I stress may — have been motivated by malice. (The source of this information was later traced to one DS Paul Gamble, whom you will recall remains missing, presumed deceased, with homicide at the hands of the Keber OCG one of the favoured possible theories.)

The lateral entry scheme necessitated the appointment of a senior sponsor, and, as you will be aware, this responsibility was discharged by DCI Marlon Choudhury of the Professional Standards Department, who was and continues to be supportive of Supt Kane's appointment.

For convenience, I have itemised the more contentious elements of Supt Kane's past below. This summary has been researched and corroborated where possible, but should not be deemed exhaustive:

7 January, 4 February and 28 February 1992, Eastbourne, East Sussex. Supt Kane is named as an involved party in further reports of domestic abuse between his parents. The debrief of his mother by officers suggested there were further instances around this time, but they went largely unreported. While other reported episodes — including the GBH referred to below — appeared to have occurred sporadically, the frequency of reporting increased in intensity around this period. At present, it has not been possible to examine with any confidence why this might be the case. I have made initial enquiries with partner agencies — including Children's Services — but the passage of time means that significant effort will be required to unearth archived records and will require further authority — and probably resources — from yourself.

Why not just ask him? **Barnes thought.** *If you're going to go to the trouble of surveilling him, that is.*

12 September 1992, Eastbourne, East Sussex. Police responded to a 999 call from Janet Flathill, reporting assault by her husband, Lee Flathill. A documented history of domestic abuse was noted. On arrival officers found both Janet and Lee with significant injuries; Janet reported that she had been saved from more serious injury by her son, fourteen-year-old Samson, who had inflicted the wounds on Lee in the defence of his mother. Both Supt Kane and Lee were arrested for GBH; the case against Supt Kane was later dropped.

14 December 1992, Uckfield, East Sussex. Police patrols attended a drunken brawl in the middle of Uckfield town centre. Several individuals were arrested for assault, affray, public disorder and drunk and disorderly. Most were juveniles; among them was Supt Kane. He was held in a cell to sober up but at that time Supt Kane was still a cleanskin, and the decision was made to release him without further action after eyewitness accounts confirmed that, again, he had prevented a sixty-seven-year-old individual, who was unrelated to the group, from coming to further harm.

6 January 1993, Eastbourne, East Sussex. Supt Kane was one of four occupants in a vehicle that was stopped and searched under s23 Misuse of Drugs Act 1971. No drugs were found but the driver, Liam Lawrence, 22 yrs, was arrested for driving while intoxicated. No further action was taken in respect of Supt Kane.

17 March 1993, Eastbourne, East Sussex. Third party report documenting Supt Kane, fourteen at the time, as the victim of assault. There is little information on this report, with no direct evidence or information from either Supt Kane or his mother. My assumption is that this was likely a professional referral, probably made by either Children's Services or Supt Kane's school.

18 March 1993. Eastbourne, East Sussex. Report of assault on school premises. A verbal disagreement between a fourteen-year-old Supt Kane and fellow pupil Callum Burt, 16 yrs, led to injuries being sustained by both parties — albeit, by all accounts, Supt Kane came off better. From what I can ascertain, verbal provocation attributed to Supt Kane's heritage triggered the confrontation. This was dealt with as a schools-related incident and was reported to police for information only.

As is evident from this summary, while Supt Kane has had a number of interactions with the authorities as an adolescent, none resulted in charges or convictions, nor were alternative disposals such as reprimands, warnings or cautions applied. I infer on this basis that, as mentioned, the risks surrounding his appointment as a senior officer were deemed tolerable. Put another way, Supt Kane had a difficult upbringing and was given to acting in the defence of others — sometimes violently — but, in the eyes of the law, his actions were deemed to have not met the threshold for prosecution, nor would a realistic prospect of conviction been presented if they had, on the basis that the public interest would not have been served in so doing.

Prior to his appointment, Supt Kane undertook a diverse range of occupations, most of which involved a degree of voluntary or entrepreneurial effort. He undertook work in the charity sector; by all accounts he thrived, as this led to a temporary appointment as a middle manager with the overseas arm of an international aid agency. After leaving this role he started a software company based in Hastings, East Sussex, which he sold as a going concern prior to his appointment to the police. In addition to this, he has worked in medical supply chain services, property development, and has undertaken youth safety and community work alongside domestic abuse support services, which in some cases, led to a significant reduction in street crime in high-deprivation neighbourhoods. I understand that he has also delivered inputs to inmates in HMPs Lewes, Camp Hill and Ford as part of offender rehabilitation schemes.

> *There is very little in his work record that indicates more conventional employment, and while his more enterprising ventures have been largely successful, I am aware there were long periods where he was not receiving any form of documented or legitimate income. Based on what we currently know, there is nothing to indicate Supt Kane has benefited from any kind of unlawful enterprise, but, of course, this does not mean it has not happened.*
>
> *As you will know, the commissioning of this report does not extend to any kind of covert or live-time surveillance of Supt Kane's activities.*

Again, Barnes noted *the commissioning of* had been struck through.

> *However, on the surface of it at least, Supt Kane has not behaved in any way since his appointment to the police service that would give rise to concern, and if more intrusive activities were desired, it is not likely that the current intelligence case is sufficient to support the approval of such measures.*
>
> *Clearly, appointing an individual to the police service whose past behaviour may cast a dim light over their suitability carries organisational and reputational risk. In Supt Kane's case, these risks were deemed tolerable and were underwritten by the Executive. In retrospect, these decisions were made in good faith in the interests of improving diversity of thought within the senior leadership, and there remain no substantial reasons why they should now be deemed to have been unsuitable or incorrect.*

Barnes put down the report, then picked it up again. He was so tired he almost missed it, but skim-read the report again and saw it. There, on page 3:

Liam Lawrence.

His gutted murder victim.

Op Limekiln.

The victim and Kane had history, and the history was writ large in the life box of a dead chief officer.

He thought back — Kane had asked him if he thought the murders were connected to Glover's suicide, an assumption hitherto not considered by Barnes. Was he prompting him? Dropping hints? Did he know full *well* they were connected?

Wide awake now, he rifled carelessly through the remainder of the box's contents, like an anxiety-riddled burglar, filtering photos, trinkets and reports. The sound of the items rattling against the bottom of the box sounded like thunder.

He read, replaced, sifted and scrutinised — and then he saw it. A single piece of A4 paper, folded in half, almost completely concealed by one of the folded-over lid panels forming the bottom of the box.

He pulled it out. Apart from a number of tell-tale fold lines, it was new and clean, and didn't have the faint smell of must shared by all the other items in the box.

He unfolded it.

ELLA DON'T COME IN CALL 999

And then, underneath:

Liam Lawrence
Carl Jessop
Terry Markham
Lee Flathill
Levi Sadler
He is coming.

CHAPTER TWENTY-NINE

Barnes was stunned. Galaxies swirled and collided in his brain. A handwritten, practical instruction in block capitals. Not exactly a suicide note, but its meaning was unequivocal. It needed verifying, testing, handwriting comparisons, all that stuff, but Barnes knew it was Gabby Glover's parting shot. How the hell had it ended up in here? Ella Short? PC Pete Lamb?

He opened up the laptop, pen in mouth, and fired off a number of emails while his brain was active, lining up urgent actions for the morning. The one he sent to Tina comprised just two words: *Call me*.

He formed the presence of mind to glove up and slip the note into an exhibit bag, photographing both sides with his phone before he did so. He sealed it and then added the time, date and location to the bag, along with an exhibit number — RB/1.

He peered at the writing through the polythene bag.

A list of five names — two of whom he knew for a fact were lying in the mortuary, stitched-up skin-bags of organs awaiting disinterested, long-lost families to claim them.

Who were the other three names? What the hell were they doing in the life box of a dead chief officer?

Barnes knew one thing for sure: all three of them were in terrible danger.

CHAPTER THIRTY

One routine that Barnes had never quite managed to master was the habit of going to bed so as to get some half-decent rest when he was on call. He woke with his face on the kitchen table as the girls came bounding downstairs to get ready for school, flying around the kitchen in a hurricane of activity in search of cereal, juice and toast and the component parts of their school uniform. Part of these circuits involved kissing and hugging Barnes as they passed, and he tried to not let his only-half-awake vulnerability dwell too long on the existential wonder of the noise in his kitchen.

He switched the laptop back on, mainly to check he hadn't had any emails of the *WHERE ARE YOU? WE ARE TRYING TO CALL* variety — a constant paranoid fear when he was on call, and one shared by many others. Not that the control room would have bothered emailing. They would have just sent a night patrol to his house to wake him the hell up.

There were no such emails, but there was one from his contact at Children's Services. He frowned. He'd sent the query at God knows what time, and had received a reply at just after seven in the morning. You had to love a pre-existing relationship. The email suggested she was a bit wary about discussing it on the phone or even giving too much away in writing, and so, despite a powerful urge to go back to bed once Tam had taken the girls to school, Barnes typed a quick reply saying he could be at her office within the hour before the day got properly going and he became again sucked into the double murder that was occupying most of his in-tray.

He cleaned his teeth, kissed the girls again and changed his shirt, then drove to Children's Services offices, calling Tina on the way.

"You know you only ever call me when you're out of breath," she said when she answered. "I'd like to think that's the effect I have on you, but I think I'd be wrong."

"Listen," Barnes said, "I found Gabby's suicide note."

"Gabby? ACC Glover? He committed *suicide*?"

Shit. Another cat out the confidential bag.

"Yes, but . . . look, keep it to yourself, okay? You're not meant to know that."

"Why are you telling me, then?"

"The note lists five names written on the back of a sign he taped to the door when he did it. Two of the names are our Op Limekiln victims."

"They're *what*?"

"My reaction was pretty much the same. I need you to start building profiles on the other three for a threat-to-life assessment. I think our killer is working his way through this list."

"It's never just car breaks and burglary with you, is it?" she said. "Okay, leave it with me."

A phrase that, in policing circles, either inspired total confidence or unmitigated terror. In Tina's case, it was definitely the former.

"One more thing: you can't mention a word of this to Superintendent Kane, okay?" Barnes said.

"I don't know if I like that," she said.

"You must promise me," he said. "I'll be in the office in an hour. I'll explain it to you then."

"You'd better," she said, and hung up.

Barnes got to St Mark's House in less than fifteen minutes, which included parking time as an added bonus. The news was talking about some kind of Arctic hurricane inbound from the north, but the no man's land that was the period immediately after New Year was a curtain of grey slate — still and perfectly cold but without even a hint of frost to appeal to the eye.

The senior administrator, Shelley Saunders, was in her fifties and smartly dressed, with a spark in her eye that, to Barnes, meant she had a wealth of experience, experience that was either going to make you pretty sanguine about most things or send you running for the hills.

She met him at reception, holding a brown foolscap file that looked like it had been unearthed from the Temple of Doom.

"Barnes," she said, giving his hand a quick shake and then looking at her watch. "You really want this information, don't you?"

"Strike while the iron is hot," Barnes said, as casually as possible.

She showed him into an empty conference room; Barnes made for the far end of the long table and sat facing the door.

Shelley looked at him.

He shrugged. "Old habits."

"Well," she said, taking a seat opposite him, "this shouldn't take too long. You wanted to cross-reference a report, yes?"

"Yes. It's . . . a little complicated. It concerns a colleague. It's from his adolescence." He checked his own notes. "Spring, 1993. He was fourteen. We have a third-party report raising concern for him presenting with some reasonably nasty injuries. Black eye, bruising, facial swelling, that kind of thing. By all accounts he explained them away as a rugby injury."

"You do know—"

"I know, confidentiality. You can share the information with me as a safeguarding concern, though, yes?"

"That would be true if he were still a child and there was an ongoing risk. But he's not. Which means we would need permission from him to tell you anything from his past."

"And that's going to be my next port of call. Put this to him. Ask him outright."

"You should probably have a long think before you do anything like that. Or at least do a little more research."

"That's why I'm here. Look, I don't need the details. I don't need much of anything. I just want to know who raised the report. My assumption was that it was a teacher or something, but—"

"It wasn't a teacher," she said. The file stayed beneath her palm.

"The thing is," Barnes said, "I can't just go steaming in there and ask him. I don't know what it might dredge up."

"All right, a better question," she said. "Why do you need the information at all?"

Barnes thought about it. As an answer, a silent fuck-you from beyond the grave delivered by a senior officer who was probably getting some kind of posthumous kicks from making Barnes run around in circles probably wouldn't go down too well.

"It's a safeguarding concern. Not for the subject, obviously. But a cold case. A live investigation, with at least three individuals at risk. The third-party material could prove definitive."

It wasn't a lie. It was a vague approximation of the truth. She knew it too. She eyeballed him while fishing out the Data Protection waiver for information-sharing between professionals. He resisted the urge to shrug.

"All right," she said. "Sign the form, and I'll dig it out."

"You don't have it?"

"Relax, it shouldn't take long to find. But it is twenty-two years old. It'll take a little digging. You want tea or something?"

Barnes shook his head. "Thanks, though."

She disappeared off. Barnes walked circuits of the conference table, trying not to zero in on the muffled sounds radiating through the walls and ceiling. The hubbub of a meeting taking place next door. Some kind of building works on the floor above. The strained voices of a supervised child contact session in the room on the other side. The tension was practically oozing through all four walls.

He went over to the window and looked out at the staff car park and the rows of lock-ups beyond. He watched the branches of some sprawling buddleia swaying in the breeze, and wished he'd said yes to the cup of tea.

He continued to circle the conference table for almost an hour before she returned — just before the sheer depressing weight of the municipal building and the activity it contained pushed Barnes into the floor.

She held out a thin envelope. "Well, here you go. You'll have to sign for it."

"I don't need to keep it. I'll make a note."

She slid a sheet of paper out of the envelope and handed it to him. He took it.

"It certainly wasn't a teacher. Not sure of the relationship, but looks like they were of a similar age. Ben, his name was. Classmate, maybe?"

Barnes didn't hear her. He sat down heavily on one of the chairs servicing the conference table. He read the name again, and again, and again, knowing that if he hadn't pursued Duquesne Kenley in so bloody-minded a fashion he might not have immediately latched onto the fact that his compendium of aliases included the name he went by in his formative years — Benmayer Blackwater.

Glover had wanted Samson Kane out of the job. He'd pursued it like a dog with a bone, but every time he'd tried to oust him, every shred of intel, every piece of mud to be slung that he could find, Kane had swerved, deflected or returned serve, and shrouded it all with a sheen of honesty that rendered him largely bulletproof.

But now, from beyond the grave, Assistant Chief Constable Gabby Glover was finally about to get his way.

A secret that Kane had kept from Barnes, one of only two allies Kane had within the service.

Samson Kane and Duquesne Kenley.

They knew each other.

PART TWO:
SPRING, 1993

CHAPTER THIRTY-ONE

When the boy called Samson came into class the next time, he was made to sit at the front. He was late. Always late. Often absent. When he was present, he seemed to be there in body rather than spirit. He wasn't badly behaved at all; in fact, he was quiet, almost studious. But the coiled strength in his body was lost on nobody. It felt entirely plausible that a misplaced word — from either a peer or a teacher — would lead to violence being unleashed.

For fourteen, he was sinewy and muscular beyond his years. He had large ears and a broad back, and wore those hideous black parkas that you got in Woollies with the itchy nylon-fur hoods and tartan lining. He wore black plimsolls instead of shoes — also from Woollies, two pounds a pair — and Ben quickly deduced it was a question of affordability.

He wore the plimsolls for everything, even football practice. In the depths of winter, out on the wet mud, pocked with the stud marks from football boots, he would go slipping and sliding all over the place in those two-quid plimsolls, unable to get any kind of traction and of use to neither man nor beast, despite his obvious athleticism. He nearly always ended up in goal, both because it required less movement, but also because his hands were like plates.

It took Ben a while to realise that he felt sorry for the kid. It was an alien feeling. Most wretches that kicked about the school were generally worthy of not much else than contempt, and most of them did such a good job of hugging the walls that they soon went unseen and then were eventually forgotten. Samson was never going to manage that. Even at his quietest, his most distant, shuffling along the corridors between lessons, he somehow just radiated *fight me*.

The first time Ben saw him in action, it took his breath away. He never actually saw what triggered it, but there were two lines of kids moving between classes like ants on a conveyor belt. One line hugging the left wall moving along the corridor west to the science classrooms, the other line on the opposing wall, coming the other way towards the maths block.

It could have been a muttered provocation, or an accidentally-on-purpose shoulder barge, or a deft flick of the schoolbag strap off the shoulder. In any case, Ben rounded the corner to see the instigator — a solid boy in the year above whose reputation for being the hardest was well-established — being pummelled by Samson, whose face was contorted with rage and exertion as he rammed his fists into the side of the boy's head and nose.

Ben was ushered along to his class as a couple of teachers hurried along to break up the melee and pick up the pieces. He couldn't imagine what the aftermath would have been like, what possible discipline could be meted out that would rehabilitate this violent offender. Expulsion, presumably.

But, no. There were a few absences, but the following week Samson was sitting at the back of the maths class again, and if anyone had previously considered casting some ill-judged witticisms about Samson's economic status his way, then his performance had consigned them to history. He may not have been popular, but it would take only the bravest or stupidest challenger to have a go at this kid. Certainly no one who had personally witnessed his prior exploits could have thought it a good idea. At least, not to his face.

That didn't necessarily mean people were going to queue up to be his mate, however. Ben was comfortable enough in his own skin to know that his motivations were partly mercenary — making friends with anyone that hard had to be a sensible investment — but also because he was fascinated by and felt sorry for this awkward boy.

He broke the ice with lunch. Samson never went into the canteen to eat, he always perched on a low wall by the basketball courts. It was technically against the rules, but a rule that the authorities were presumably content to let slide. And so one lunchtime Ben joined him.

Samson had a metal lunchbox that appeared to be a repurposed biscuit tin, and was munching on squidgy white sandwiches smeared with either Marmite or some kind of chocolate spread. Ben never ventured to enquire — swapping lunchbox items was for primary school kids.

Ben sat next to him.

"You've got a hole in your shoe," Ben said, looking down at his own gleaming-white Air Max 90s.

And Samson did — a threadbare window over his big toe.

"Sega or Nintendo?" Ben asked. He'd considered asking, *Nike or Reebok?* but, judging by the hole and the grey slice of sole flapping loose at the end of Samson's Woolworths plimsolls like a gasping fish, figured he would earn no great kudos from this — not so much an icebreaker as a nosebreaker, maybe. But from the cold, suspicious stare Samson gave him, he might just as well have said, *Hollow point or full metal jacket?*

"I've got a 2600," Samson eventually mumbled, dropping his gaze to focus on his minging sandwich.

"Traitor," Ben said. He opened his mouth to proudly tell Samson about the brand new Super Nintendo he'd just acquired. It was a grey US import — the official UK release still some weeks away yet — but again checked himself. He didn't want to be bragging about that. Even then he wondered just how often he would be self-censoring in the coming months.

"What you got for lunch?" Samson said.

Ben shrugged the question away. "I've eaten."

They sat on the wall, largely in silence, for the remainder of the lunch hour. Samson seemed pretty awkward, but Ben, arms stretched out casually behind him, was comfortable with the lack of conversation — mainly because he was enjoying the curious, befuddled and, in some cases, even slightly awestruck stares he was attracting from the basketball courts, five-a-side pitch and cluster of picnic benches. In some cases he even detected a twinge of regret — Ben Blackwater, savvy enough to make friends with the hardest kid in school before anyone else had. Ben smiled to himself — you didn't get ahead in this life by passing up opportunities.

At fourteen, Ben liked to think he was pretty worldly-wise — he'd been to London without his parents, he'd been on a plane more times than his peers had replaced their underpants and he'd even tried alcohol and tobacco under the watchful gaze of his liberal-on-the-weekend father. When he first visited Samson at home, however, being presented with his first ever soft-porn magazine was an awakening that knocked him sideways. A full-frontal, full-colour spread of some raven-haired, supposedly Eastern European beauty that made Ben think, for some reason, of a gynaecological exam. The cocktail of feelings was overpowering — guilt, shock and a general sense of revulsion tinged with something else that he later supposed was a hormonal reaction. All in all, however, it was pretty gross.

Samson lived in a two-up, two-down council house on the corner of a cul-de-sac north of Eastbourne that led onto the rear of an enormous industrial estate lined with precision engineering firms, plastics manufacturers and bodywork repair workshops. The demarcation between the residential area and the trappings of industry was a thick copse with a stinking ditch running along the perimeter that was filled with shopping trolleys, syringes and pallet boxes that had rotted from being recycled over several summers' worth of homemade camps.

Samson's front garden was about six-foot square and was more mud than grass, albeit it didn't feature any of the discarded domestic appliances and mattresses that the other houses in the row did. As a fourteen-year-old, Ben didn't even register the significant economic divide between them that their respective domiciles represented — that sort of observation wouldn't come until much later in life.

The house number had been painted on the wooden front door in white emulsion by a slightly unsteady hand, and the smell when Ben stepped inside was like nothing he'd ever experienced. All the curtains were drawn and the heating was on full blast, giving dubious cultivation to a cocktail already comprising two-day-old deep-frying, cigarette ash, wet laundry that had been left too long before being hung up and some other smells that Ben couldn't quite zero in on.

Samson's heavily pregnant mother, Janet, was the smoker — she was never without one. Her dark hair was tinged with grey and always pulled roughly back into a ponytail, and her olive complexion, resplendent with a mole under her left eye, betrayed heritage that Ben later theorised as either Balkan or Mediterranean. She smiled a lot and seemed to enjoy talking to and cooking for the two boys when they were together, and despite the constant presence of grease-stained hooded sweaters three sizes too big to cover her bump, she stirred Ben far more than any magazine was ever going to.

Not that they spent much time in the house, other than when they were being fed. They refabricated the camp behind the houses, reinforcing a natural canopy created by a cluster of firs, which in turn benefited from a constant blast of warm air from one of the enormous white metal extractor vents bolted onto the windowless brick rear of one of the industrial units ten feet away, beyond the ditch of black sludge.

They didn't smoke — Ben had offered Samson a cigarette, but he hadn't been interested, which caused Ben's own enthusiasm to wane — and so they ate sweets and drank fizzy drinks while they talked and looked idly at gaming, car and porn magazines. Sometimes they just sat in silence, hanging out, listening to the rain persistently fail to penetrate their carefully constructed shelter. Occasionally, when Janet was occupied, Samson's three-year-old brother, Manny, would join them — and the porn had to be stashed, double-time.

For the most part, the camp was protected. Occasionally they would come in to find the logs had been moved around, or that someone had started a fire or left a beer can or two, but generally it required no effort to tidy up. The late spring weather had been warm and moist, and the cluster of foliage surrounding the camp had shot up, with chest-high clumps of stinging nettles, bindweed and horsetail creating a convenient perimeter wall.

On one occasion, a group of five boys aged about sixteen or seventeen chanced upon the camp. Neither Ben nor Samson recognised them as local, but, to Ben, they just screamed rough. He wasn't sure if it was the narrow eyes, the abundance of jewellery or the Fred Perrys, but that didn't matter. They were bored, and boredom spelled trouble. They were boys who didn't give a shit about trouble, or the authorities, or *consequences*. They just cared about kicks, and kicks had four primary sources — fags and booze, cars, girls and fighting. Ben, for all his relaxed confidence, acknowledged the odds — they were outnumbered, isolated and unarmed, and he had felt the flicker of fear in his stomach.

He'd remained seated on his log, frozen in position with a marshmallow at the end of a stick, but Samson had stood up. This was obviously interpreted as a defiant challenge, for the ringleader stepped forwards and squared up to Samson, throwing fucks and goading the smaller boy.

Samson took a step or two back; the bigger boy, seeing this as a demonstration of submissiveness, lunged forwards, swinging a haymaker with his right fist.

Samson, apparently, saw it coming a mile off. He feinted left, stepped off to the side and, almost effortlessly, used the boy's own momentum to shove him into a four-foot-tall cluster of stinging nettles. He lost his balance as he went in, and he fell into it head-first.

The kid emerged, angry red hives already standing out on his hands, face, neck and arms. He held out his arms in a weird display, and his cronies, seemingly unsure of what to do, stood rooted to the spot. A couple snickered while their ringleader cursed and wailed.

Samson and Ben didn't wait around for the aftermath, but bolted from the camp like escaped convicts outrunning trail dogs.

CHAPTER THIRTY-TWO

Ben couldn't remember the first time Levi Sadler appeared, but he seemed to have become a permanent fixture outside the school gates more or less overnight. He was a tall, bandy-legged skinhead with extraordinarily long arms, who lived in a parka and lolloped along with the exodus of school kids like he was following a parade. He latched onto clusters of children at random like an intimidating beggar, and by turns either attempted to extort money and cigarettes or pressured them into stealing same on his behalf. He was only about seventeen, but as far as Ben and his peers were concerned, he was old enough to have left school, and that was all that mattered. The tightly wound fabric of societal norms that governed the school, that were so ingrained in its pupils as to be invisible, did not apply to Levi, and that — in Ben's mind — made him dangerous.

Ben was easy-going, confident and had an earthy sense of humour. He also had money, and this made him nervous around Levi. He took the same route home most days, and found himself increasingly apprehensive about Levi appearing beside him amid the gaggle of uniforms.

The new mountain bike made Ben doubly nervous. His father had bought it for him a few weeks back as a birthday present, and it was unbelievable. It was a gleaming navy blue with bright orange forks and seat tube, with an ultra-light carbon frame, front suspension, alloy wheels, top-end derailleurs and enough chrome to put a Harley to shame. Ben had been dropping hints about it for months and knew that there wouldn't have been much change out of a thousand pounds when his father paid for it. You certainly couldn't find it on the high street, and it wasn't until he'd acquired an indestructible lock that Ben finally worked up the courage to ride it to school.

It was no coincidence, therefore, that one warm afternoon Ben heard Levi's insistent voice beside him, buzzing like a chainsaw.

"Gissa smoke."

Ben obliged, tapping loose a Marlboro Light without speaking or making eye contact, clamping the bike frame tight between his legs.

"Gissa light."

Ben turned. Levi was holding his hand out. Ben flicked the lighter and proffered the flame, knowing that if he handed over his chrome-plated Zippo with the skull and crossbones design he'd never see it again.

Levi took hold of the lighter in Ben's hand to pull the flame closer; Ben tightened his grip.

"Lighter's da bomb. Where'd yer get it?"

"Nicked it."

"Nick me one?"

"Can't. Got it abroad."

That was a contract Ben did not want to enter into. It was a question, not a demand, but Ben figured making himself as useless and uninteresting as possible would be a sensible strategy.

"Sweet bike. Gissa quick go."

"Sorry. Can't."

"Come on. Five minutes."

"Sorry."

"Two minutes."

"Can't. Sorry."

Levi eyed him, like he was thinking about taking it anyway.

"Maybe next week," Ben added hurriedly, and instantly regretted it.

The stream of uniformed schoolkids eventually began to thin out as they reached Gildredge Park and began to traverse it; Ben was dismayed to find that Levi was still keeping in step with him.

Besides the exodus of schoolchildren leaving by the gravel avenues that led out of the park in the four points of a compass, there were very few people in the park. It was a mild March day, and the thick borders of daffodils led up to Manor Gardens while a row of elms swayed in the breeze. Ben did not want to lead the prick home, and so he parked on a bench, made a point of locking up his bike, casually tossed his bag behind it and stretched out.

Levi stopped too — he was jittery, and alternated between sitting, standing and doing circuits of the bench, all the while encouraging Ben to procure him some form of shiny contraband. Ben eventually decided — on realising there was by now practically nobody else in the park — that he'd made a big mistake, and thanked his stars that, besides his bike, trainers, lighter and a leatherbound copy of *Crime and Punishment* in his rucksack — that he presumed would be of no interest to Levi — he had nothing else of value on his person.

The awkward stand-off was eventually broken by the sight of another school blazer over by the swings — Ben recognised the haircut instantly, even a hundred yards away.

Levi apparently noticed Samson too, and lolloped over; Ben presumed he'd lost interest in him and had gone off looking for another host.

It became apparent that the two had some kind of history. Ben watched the interaction with fascination. He couldn't hear anything that was said, but Samson stood stoic and impassive — clearly not intimidated, but not going on the offensive either — while Levi circled him like an excitable primate indulging in some kind of territorial stand-off.

Levi had about a foot on Samson, and when he suddenly stopped moving about and leaned in close, Ben thought he was going to headbutt his friend. But Samson craned his head up and took hold of the back of Levi's neck — for a moment Ben had the bizarre notion that they were going to kiss, but it became apparent that Samson was whispering something in Levi's ear.

Ben watched, amazed, as Levi straightened up, stook a step back, and then — practically on all fours — galloped off and out of the park.

Samson strolled over as if the interaction had never occurred. No smugness, no pride, no boasting — he'd just seen off the biggest parasite this side of the Watford Gap and took it all in his stride. He was practically emotionless — like an ant, Ben thought. Obstacles fell in his path, he stepped back, sized them up, and worked out a way around them.

"How the hell did you get rid of him?" Ben asked. "What did you say to him?"

Samson just shrugged. "Told him you were going to beat him up."

"Very funny. No you didn't. Come on, what did you say?"

"Forgotten."

"Bollocks have you."

"If I told you, I'd have to kill you."

Samson stopped walking, dropped his school bag and stared at Ben intently. It had the desired effect, and just for a moment Ben thought Samson was going to pan his head in.

Then the tension broke and they both fell about laughing.

"We should go to Ashdown Forest," Samson said as they continued out of the park.

"What's in Ashdown Forest?"

"Trees."

"Very funny. And?"

"Just a lot of open space. Animals, creatures, wildlife. Nature. There's no sodding Levis, I know that. We could take Manny. I don't know how we would get there, though."

Ben thought about this. "My dad might take us."

"No thanks," Samson muttered. "Bit of bike, bit of bus and a bit of hitchhiking. Be an adventure. On your shiny new steed you'd get there in no time. We can get supplies and stuff."

Ben shook his head in wonder. "No Levis. Imagine that."

CHAPTER THIRTY-THREE

It was a carbon copy of any other main commercial thoroughfare in the country — pedestrianised precinct; painted boxwood planters; Clintons, Quality Seconds and all the other asinine shops. But Ben knew he wouldn't have to walk far to scratch the surface.

Ben and Samson strolled down from the seafront, too engrossed in serious debate on a range of heavy topics — Sega vs Nintendo, Reebok vs Nike, Lamborghini vs Porsche — to be too focused on either the journey or the destination.

It wasn't late, but the unseasonably brisk south-westerly blowing in off the South Downs had more or less cleared the streets. The pair of them sought temporary respite from the weather in Mr Wu's, where they ordered prawn crackers, chips and curry sauce before venturing out again, clutching their dinner in white paper bags that were already becoming translucent with grease.

They'd been scoping new places to camp since vacating the previous site after "Nettlegate". Treasure Island had some advantages — it was out of season for another several weeks, the fence was easy enough to hop over, and it had a decent amount of sheltered seating areas. They could board the enormous pirate ship and climb down below decks into the hold and get really comfortable, and no one would have any idea they were there. Not only that, but there was that huge plastic whale to clamber about on, which Manny would have been thrilled with.

There were some downsides — the promenade was right next door, which meant a constant stream of dog walkers, and they'd have to be quiet nearly all the time to avoid attracting attention, and anyway, in a few weeks' time they'd have to vacate the place when it opened for summer.

Manny wasn't with them — Janet seemed to be on an even keel the last couple of days — and besides, Samson didn't want to bring him until it was a definite, otherwise the kid would have been gutted.

They'd reached the pedestrianised section of Terminus Road and were debating about whether to go and eat in the Trinity Place multi-storey while their food was still hot. They were just about to cross Seaside Road when a voice distracted them.

"All right, you cunt!"

Ben turned, startled, and saw Levi Sadler striding purposefully along the middle of Seaside Road. He was clearly primed for violence: the veins were standing out on his neck, his face was twisted in a battle snarl and his body was pumped in a in a rigid swagger. He was clearly paying the traffic no mind at all — the drivers must have sensed his determination, for they swerved round him in a chaos of angry horns.

He ignored Ben and made a beeline for Samson, who resolutely stood his ground with a neutral expression. Levi arrived with outstretched orangutan arms and clattered into Samson with a double-handed shove; Samson didn't fall, but he lost his balance, stumbled and dropped his food in the gutter. Levi swung a wild kick which was short by about a foot, and then went again for another shove.

Ben took a tentative step forward to assist his friend, but realised that so far, the bout hadn't progressed much beyond foreplay. Levi had started the round, but seemed reluctant to engage in any actual fighting until, presumably, Samson swung first.

Samson, it seemed, was only too happy to oblige. He regained his balance and stayed low, and then drove upwards from his hips with a ferocious uppercut that caught Levi square under the chin. He didn't fall, exactly, but sort of crumpled into himself and folded into a ball, covering his head with his forearms. Samson grabbed him in a one-armed bear hug, pulling Levi towards him so he could rabbit-punch him in the side of the head with his other hand.

He was strong and fast, and Ben opened his bag of chips and began to eat as it dawned on him that his assistance was quite clearly not required.

"Come on, leave it out," Levi eventually cried through a mouthful of clothing. "Take it easy."

Samson didn't let up. He was giving this his all, making staccato whimpers from exertion as he got the better of Levi, who had evidently written a cheque his fists couldn't cash. Levi was tall and wiry, but Samson's shorter, square body had the prehensile strength of a sabre-toothed cat.

When it became clear that Samson had no intention of releasing his wretched attacker, Levi began to extricate himself from the battering by wriggling out of his dirty lime-green hoodie until he was able to free himself completely, leaving Samson swinging at an empty garment that brought Dr Seuss to mind.

Once Levi was free, he sprinted back along Seaside Road like a hyena that had realised it could not mount an attack without the support of the clan. To Ben, the reassertion of dominance was like watching something out of National Geographic; Samson might have thought the same, for he dropped the lime-green sweatshirt in the middle of the road, then, as Ben watched, amazed, he unzipped himself and urinated onto the garment in a long, languorous stream. Steam rose up into the cool evening air.

"Come on, then," Samson said, zipping himself back up. He retrieved his package of chips from the gutter and inspected it with an expression that suggested that its brief detour was not insurmountable. "Food's still warm."

"You'd better wash your hands," was all Ben could think of to say.

* * *

"You going to tell me what that was all about?"

"It wasn't about anything."

Ben didn't really have an answer for that, and so he and Samson continued quietly munching chips in the half-light.

They were on the top floor of the multi-storey, tucked away in one of the few corner bays that didn't bear the hallmarks of having been claimed by an intravenous drug user. The concrete was cold and damp; the domestic ambience wasn't quite on a par with the camp, but that was a work in progress, and at least they were dry here.

"Need to get some cushions or something," Ben said. "You know, if we're going to make a habit of coming up here. Pot plant or two as well, maybe."

Samson didn't answer. His face was bathed in shadow; nevertheless, Ben could see that he'd easily come off best — Levi had barely inflicted a scratch.

"Where did you learn to fight like that?" Ben asked, as he produced a pack of Lambert and Butler and lit up. He passed the pack to Samson, who, to Ben's surprise, took one.

"These are seriously cheap and nasty," Ben said. "Sorry. Supply problem."

"We could get some of those decent cigars off your old man," Samson said.

"Oh, so you *are* talking to me."

"Uncle Jimmy taught me. To fight, I mean. Get up."

"What?"

"Come on." Samson sprang to his feet. "I'll show you."

"No, thanks."

"You asked the question, didn't you? Come on. Up."

"Just leave it out, will you?"

Samson got to his feet, flicked the cigarette, brought his guard up and began to bounce on the balls of his feet. Realising there was no other way out of it, Ben reluctantly hauled himself up, inserted the cigarette between his lips and adopted an exaggerated stance.

"You're too square. Get side on, reduce your opponent's target area." He fired some quick jabs towards Ben, connecting only with fresh air. "Power comes from the hips, not the fists. Keep your centre of gravity low."

Ben made a half-hearted attempt to jab at Samson.

"Fights are won in the mind, not the body. Forget bravado, forget anger and fight like you intend to win. Don't do it half-cocked. Most people don't want to fight, even the ones who steam in thinking they're Lennox Lewis. They're all talk. Like peacocks. It's pretty easy to knock that out of them."

Ben poked at him with another tentative jab; Samson blocked it and shoved a fist into Ben's diaphragm. He'd obviously pulled it at the last second, but it still hurt like a bastard, and when he doubled up, Samson got him in a headlock and sat down heavily with Ben under his body, pinning him to the damp concrete.

"Whatcha gonna do now, eh? What?"

"Come on, get off me. I'm tapping out, see?" Ben said in a muffled groan.

Samson released him, sat back down against the concrete wall and lit another cigarette from the pack he'd liberated from Ben's jacket. Ben shook himself off and joined him.

"Jesus, I nearly swallowed my cigarette," Ben said, taking another one from the pack. "We should get hold of something stronger. Something to smoke, or some whisky or something."

"No chance," Samson said, his voice flat. "You fill your boots. I'm not going near that stuff."

Ben turned to look at him. "You learned the hard way, huh? Fighting, I mean."

Samson kept his eyes dead ahead, focusing on some point in the distance, way off across the black car park. "All that shit about hips and stance and stuff. It's all out of a book. It really just comes down to how much you want to be the one standing at the end."

Ben didn't say anything. Samson was off somewhere in his own head, then he snapped out of it and turned back to Ben.

"And if it comes down to it, a rabbit punch to the windpipe or sinking your thumbs into their eyes can usually get you out of most situations."

Ben held his gaze. "What did Levi do to you? Or, more to the point, what did you do to him?"

"I don't want to talk about it."

"The guy's a leech. He plays the big I-am with all the kids in school, and if they don't give him what he asks, he gives them a black eye. But you're not telling me you just refused to steal something for him."

"I *said* I don't want to talk about it." He shoved a final fistful of chips into his mouth, then got to his feet and bagged the rubbish. "Let's get out of here."

* * *

They hopped on the next bus without looking at the route; it took them closer to Ben's house than Samson's. It was down an unmade track lined with thick leylandii with PRIVATE ROAD on a painted sign at the entrance. It was not in particularly auspicious surroundings; there was a sprawling council estate on one side and a suburban estate on the other. Ben figured his house had been there first and the rest had sprung up around it. You wouldn't even know it was there.

"You coming in, or what?" Ben said. He'd never given any thought to the polished hardwood floor, the arabesque wall art or the ornamental Ottoman scimitars on the wall, but, now, seeing Samson's face, he discerned them for the first time.

Samson tentatively stepped over the threshold. "What does your dad do again?" he murmured.

"Works at the hospital," Ben said, omitting his father's actual occupation on the basis that *cardiac consultant* would not be likely to put Samson any more at ease. "Come on. There's nobody here."

They went down a level into what Ben described as a den, a lounge area hooked up with sofa, beanbags and a video games console attached to a huge television, with sliding glass doors leading out onto a Spanish-tile patio.

Samson whistled. "So, you going to follow in his footsteps?" he said, as Ben flopped heavily onto the sofa and grabbed a controller.

"You're kidding, right?"

Samson shrugged. "I would. You know, if I could. You wouldn't have all this if he was driving a bus."

"You need grades. Come on, play some *Mario Kart*. It's two-player split-screen. Toad or Koopa have the best control but they're a little slow. You want some food?"

Samson sat down on a beanbag. Ben opened a small black fridge next to the sofa and tossed him a Pepsi.

"Jesus, how many buttons does this thing have? My Atari's got a one-button joystick and that's about it."

"It's ergonomic. Intuitive. You'll pick it up. A to accelerate, B to brake, D-pad to steer."

"D-pad?"

"Directional-pad. Clue's in the title."

Ben looked at Samson and smirked. He was doing that whole tongue-out, waving-the-controller-around-in-the-air thing that all novice gamers did.

"Anyway, you've *got* the grades," Samson continued. "I've seen your papers. World's your oyster, man."

There was an edge to his tone, but not, Ben had noticed, a malevolent one. If anything, he sounded excited for his friend.

"You've got to use that brain. You owe it to yourself. You owe it to me."

"You've got a brain. It's bigger than mine."

Samson shook his head. "Having a brain is only half the battle. Bet people hold the door open for your dad. Invite him to the Rotary Club. All that shit. That's not happening where I come from."

"You can be anything you want, man."

"'As long as you stay out of prison, I'll be happy.' My mum's words."

Ben stopped playing and looked at Samson.

"Boom! Pole position. Snooze you lose," Samson said. "I'm getting into this."

Ben picked up his controller again. "It's not . . . it's not the work. It's the job. My dad — okay, yeah, he's pretty high up, but he still has to be in the office at a certain time, can't leave until a certain time, phone rings all the time and he has to go back in. Weekends on call."

"Decent wedge, though," Samson said, taking a hand off the controller to indicate the house in general.

"Yeah, but . . . well, you know. Even the president has a boss."

"You think you won't have a boss?"

"Not if I can help it."

"So what are you gonna do?"

"I dunno, man. Something. I need to be my own boss."

"One of my cousins is self-employed. All he does is bitch about having no sick pay."

"What about the rest of them? What do they do?"

"My cousins?" Samson said. Ben thought he looked shifty. "This and that."

"Don't like talking about your family, do you? What's 'this and that'?"

"Exactly what it says on the tin."

"Something illegal?"

Samson didn't answer.

"That's what I'm talking about," Ben said.

Samson scoffed. "What? You're gonna be a big bad criminal? You'd get your eyes poked out, boy."

"That's where the brains come in handy, *boy*."

"Why?"

"You talk about being your own boss, and that's it. It's not just that, though."

"What else, then?"

Ben shook his head and pulled a winsome smile, not taking his eyes from the massive television screen. "I stole a huge bar of chocolate from Tesco last week."

"For Levi?"

"No, not for Levi. For me. I was going to buy it, but then I realised the place was heaving and no one was going to notice. I slid it up my top and then ate half of it once I was clear of the place. And the point is: when I realised I'd got away with it, it tasted sweeter than any other chocolate bar I've ever tasted. And I still had the money in my pocket. No job gives you that."

"Your dad know?"

Now it was Ben's turn to scoff. "Don't be ridiculous."

"So, what? You're telling me you love to steal?"

Ben nodded, like he was bearing down on some huge confession. "Yes, man. I really, really do. And if you can make your living that way, why the hell not?"

CHAPTER THIRTY-FOUR

The front door was ajar. Ben knocked tentatively and then stepped inside. The smell of cigarettes, damp and solidified cooking fat was almost familiar, but the additional cloying, fruity stink of a night of exhaled liquor hung in the air like a cloud.

"Hello?" he called from the hallway, aware of the slightly strained edge to his voice.

A gurgling toddler answered him from upstairs, and Ben climbed the narrow staircase to find Samson and Manny curled up underneath a bunk bed, concealed from the world by a blanket clothes-pegged to the frame to create a curtain. The toddler was snuggled up to Samson, who was reading him *The Hungry Caterpillar*.

"I guess you're not coming out, then," Ben said, pulling up the blanket.

"Mum left me with Manny," Samson said, not looking up from the book. "If we're going out, he's going to have to come with us."

Ben picked up the Atari joystick and squeezed onto the end of the bed, sandwiching the boy between himself and Samson.

"How you doing, champ? Shove over a little, will you?"

Manny ignored him. Ben got involved in a round of *Pac-Man*.

"How old is Manny?" Ben said.

"Three. Product of a particularly cosy making-up session, I reckon. Neither of them planned for a baby at their age. You got new trainers?"

Ben wiggled his feet. "The new Air Jordans. Man, look at the graphics on this thing. It's prehistoric. How do you cope?"

"Your old man spring for them?"

Ben put down the joystick and stared at his friend.

"You didn't . . ." Samson said.

"Get you a pair, if you want," Ben said, resuming the game.

"How the hell did you manage it? There's video cameras, security staff, tags . . ."

"Just got to do your homework. If you're careful, it's just a case of creating a small distraction. The rest is easy."

Samson was silent. Ben could hear his brain whirring.

"Means I've got the boots *and* the money. Sweeter than honey. We could go get something to drink."

"No thanks."

"Something to smoke, then."

"Maybe."

Samson finally looked up, and Ben saw the rings of purple and red circling his eye.

"Jesus," Ben muttered. "This is why you're babysitting?"

"Mum's down the cop shop not giving a statement. Lee's in the cells."

"What happened?" Ben's voice was small.

"What, your dad never knock your mum about?"

"No, never," Ben said, missing the sarcasm. "Hang on, what do you mean: *not* giving a statement?"

"She's not going through with it. The minute the cops turn up, the fear starts to ease off. It's like when you were small and lost your folks in the supermarket. The fear builds and builds and builds until you think you're about to vomit

— then you find them and they hadn't even noticed, and the relief makes you feel stupid. By the time she's told to sign on the line, she'll apologise for wasting their time and then ask one of them to run her home. She'll be home by lunchtime; he'll be out in time for last orders."

"Did he . . . you know," Ben said, indicating Manny with his thumb.

"He slept through it last night. He doesn't always. That's why he's stuck to my side like a limpet."

Ben looked down at the toddler. He was indeed glued to Samson. He didn't look traumatised, but Ben suspected that if he tried to prise him off his older brother there would be serious consequences, and the caterpillar's tummyache would be the least of anyone's worries.

"Let's take him, then," Ben said. "Sun's out. We can feed the ducks."

Manny's ears pricked up.

"What a lovely little family we'll make," Samson said.

"Since when do you give a flying hoot about what anyone thinks about you?" Ben said.

Ben eyed his friend. Samson's tone was even, but he was sharing more than he usually did. Ben wondered if that was because Manny was around. Normally Samson clammed up and got a bit surly whenever Ben asked him about his family or his home life generally. At first Ben hadn't pushed it, thinking Samson was just embarrassed by the gulf between their respective socio-economic origins, but when he started talking about cells and police cars and A&E, Ben realised there was a little more to it than that, and that maybe Samson talking a bit more about it might be good for him. Maybe even for them both.

Samson finished the story; Manny wanted it again; Samson obliged. Ben, distracted from the game by Samson's steady reading, gazed around the box room, then wished he hadn't. There were no curtains, just the orange throw pegged up on the track, fighting to keep out the sun. There was an

MDF chest of drawers on broken runners which was more exposed chipboard than melamine coating and was covered in football stickers. There were more clothes on the floor than in the drawers. A huge poster of Ian Rush was thumb-tacked to one wall — Ben wondered what it was covering. Samson's bed was against the opposite wall, a single divan with a Liverpool duvet and pillow cover that had faded to pink; both the colour and the *Crown Paints* sponsor logo indicated that it was older even than Samson himself. There were barely three feet between the two beds. The lower bunk was Manny's; the upper bunk was equipped with a stained mattress but had no bedding, and seemed to be acting purely as a convenient storage area for all manner of junk — Ben almost asked about it, but something stopped him.

The room suddenly felt hot and stuffy.

"Shall I open a window?" Ben said.

"Window doesn't work. But you can try," Samson said, between the pears and the plums.

Ben got up and pushed the throw aside. The garden was a square of boggy mud with the odd cluster of grass, like a bald man clinging onto what little hair remained. Neat twirls of dog shit were dotted around the place, including atop a long-discarded washing machine whose door was hanging off.

The windowsill was completely concealed by boxes and schoolbooks and old toys; when Ben pushed them aside, the sill and frame were black with mould. He swallowed, then gave up on the window-opening idea, suddenly wanting to leave.

"Come on, then," Ben said, when Samson had finished the third go-round of the story. "Let's take him down the park."

Manny appeared to think all his Christmases had come at once. Ben replaced the joystick while Samson picked up all the clothes on the floor and shoved them into a bin liner that was acting as a laundry basket. Samson got Manny's wellies and anorak on in a way that made Ben think this routine was more than occasional.

They walked out of Willingdon Trees and off towards Hampden Park in the sun. Manny took his trike — which, to Ben's surprise, was new and in good condition — and pedalled ahead. While they walked Ben found he suddenly had a lot of questions, but couldn't think of any that wouldn't make Samson bristle — certainly Ben knew that would be how he'd react if the boot was on the other foot.

So he just talked.

"I've got a sister," he said.

"I know," Samson said.

"Have you met her?" Ben asked, surprised.

"No, just seen her about. You know, around school."

"Oh, right. She's a bit wild. Always having . . . tantrums and stuff."

"How old is she?"

"Twelve."

"Bit old to call them tantrums, then. Tantrums are what Manny has."

"Yeah, she's got . . . a few issues," Ben said, not wanting to say that, since birth, she'd been to the doctor more times for her mind than her body. Instead he zeroed in on Samson's opening. "Manny doesn't look like he has tantrums. He seems pretty chilled."

"He has his moments."

"Where does he think your folks are?"

Samson's mouth puckered with anger. "Far as he knows, Lee's at work, Mum's got an appointment. He doesn't really ask anymore. He'll wake up, search the house, then if there's no one in but me he'll just tell me 'Mummy's got a *poinkment*, Daddy's at work.'"

There was a slight tremor to his voice. Ben left it. Manny tricycled back to them and said he was hungry.

"We'll get you some beans or something when we get back, kiddo," Samson said, ruffling the boy's hair.

Ben suddenly felt the money in his pocket burning a hole through the fabric.

"Let's go and get something," he said. "There's a coffee shop on the other side of the lake. They do sausage rolls and stuff."

Samson seemed to freeze.

"I'll pay," Ben added.

Samson dug his hands in his pockets, his face neutral, his body language uncomfortable. He opened his mouth, but Manny thought the idea was beyond tremendous, and so they headed off, stopping to throw bread at the ducks and watching swans glide low over the water. The water was clearer than Ben had ever seen it, and fat fish shot about under the sun-dazzled surface, head-high reeds moving gently in the breeze.

The proprietor of the coffee shop was wary of two fourteen-year-olds with a toddler, even verging on hostile. Ben knew how to handle grown-ups, however, and with a smile, some loosely complimentary small talk and a bucketload of politeness, she was quickly won over. Ben had overheard his Aunt Imelda — a ripe beauty of thirty-six who was likely the scourge of fourteen-year-old boys everywhere — talk about his *charisma*. He'd looked it up and wasn't really any the wiser — and didn't plan on asking her about it, either. He generally tried to avoid Imelda anyway — no blood relative should have that kind of effect on your hormones.

They ate like kings, with sausage rolls, sandwiches, jelly and chocolate cake, and while Ben tried not to stare, it was clear that Manny and Samson hadn't had a decent meal in quite some time. After they'd finished, they took Manny's red ball with the Ian Rush signature over the back of the coffee shop to the rugby club playing fields and let Manny take penalties, the twenty-metre-high smokestack chimney from the District General Hospital next door watching over them like a stained cigarette as it belched fumes into the air. The sun was warm and Samson seemed to loosen up, grinning as he chased Manny around the field with gusto in furtherance of a tackle that never materialised, the toddler squealing with delight.

They played for forty-five minutes or so; just as Manny started to flag and began to make noises about needing a wee,

Ben spotted a group of men in the opposite corner of the field. They were scanning the park and obviously looking for someone or something.

"Trouble," Ben said, grabbing the ball and gesturing for Samson to scoop up his younger brother.

Samson didn't ask questions, but grabbed Manny and the three of them retreated to a gap in the thick hedge separating the playing fields from the college grounds. They climbed through the gap and flattened their bellies to the earth; Samson whispered to Manny that they were playing spies, which brought about unquestioning obedience.

"Levi," Ben said. "And he's not alone."

"Jesus, you've got good eyesight," Samson said.

"I don't like the look of them," Ben said.

There were three men with Levi, ranging in age from twenty to fifty. The oldest was fat, wearing a white vest and chunky neck chain, and was — for reasons not immediately apparent to Ben — carrying a car tyre.

Ben didn't like it. Like prisons, hospitals and the armed forces, schools were institutions with their own set of societal rules and norms that everyone knew and understood. Disputes between groups of kids were common, as were the rules that governed the thresholds at which the authorities — grown-ups — were introduced. Levi may well have been bested by Samson in the middle of the street, but bringing the patriarchs of his extended family into his quest for retribution made Ben very uneasy. This broke all the rules of engagement and made the whole thing feel more real than he was comfortable with.

"You know them?" Ben asked.

"Mm-hm. Liam Lawrence and Terry Markham. Terry is a mate of Lee's. Not sure about the other one."

"Which one is Liam?"

"That one."

"Shit, that's the kid you pushed into the nettles."

"Yeah, probably. I kicked about with Liam for a little while. Lee thought it would be a good idea."

"You did?"

"Not for long. Just long enough to realise he's a complete bellend. I told him so, and that I didn't plan on hanging out with him any longer. He didn't like that — hence his visit to the camp."

"Are all these pricks related or something?"

"Probably."

"I don't think they're feeding the ducks," Ben said. "Think they're looking for you?"

Samson shrugged. "Possible, I guess. I can't be the only one to have pissed him off, though."

"Does he know where you live?"

"I don't think so."

"We need to get out of here."

Samson helped Manny wee in the bushes and then the three of them looped around the edge of the college grounds and cut back into Willingdon Trees via the main road, circling around Hampden Park by following the tree line around Decoy Drive. Ben figured they could cross the railway line to put a bit of daylight between them and the grim-faced group.

They were just about to disappear from the main road into a network of alleys and twittens when Ben noticed a Vauxhall Cavalier double-parked half on the kerb, half on the road at the densely tree-lined entrance to the park. It was grey, with a red bonnet and mismatched tyres. It was caked in mud and the rear number plate was obscured. There was nothing to say it belonged to Levi's posse necessarily, but it was close enough and there was something tingling in Ben's stomach.

"You go," he said to Samson. "I'll be right with you."

"Where the hell are you going?" Samson said.

"Just get Manny indoors," Ben said.

He ran off without another word, knowing Samson would listen to reason. Keeping low, he ran up behind the Cavalier and peered in the back. It was full of junk, but a shiny new power drill and a case of what looked like fine wine caught his eye.

He tried the handle. The boot was unlocked — through carelessness or nobody-would-dare hubris, Ben didn't know, but he grinned to himself anyway as a thought occurred to him. Getting your mates to stage a punch-up in Olympus so you could walk out with the latest Air Jordans unnoticed was one thing, but, in the moment, he realised that nothing covered your tracks better than stealing stuff that was already stolen.

He yawned and stretched, scratching himself and generally trying to look as bored and casual as he could while he rummaged through the boot, as if he'd been dispatched against his will by the family in the park to recover forgotten picnic items. He knew — instinctively as much as anything — that nothing aroused suspicion more than looking suspicious.

He just had to hope that the meatheads didn't come back.

In the end, he placed the drill, the case of wine and a holdall containing nappies and baby formula on the pavement, and reached up to shut the boot. He resisted the urge to look all around him, and instead wedged the case of wine in the holdall, picked up the drill and sloped off, looking bored. He crossed the road and made straight for the nearest twitten to get himself hidden away from passing traffic. There might be a couple of curtain-twitchers in the estate who would pick up the phone, but he'd be long gone before anything came of that.

Thinking Samson might have exercised some caution in case he led some unseen pursuers straight to his door, Ben made for the camp first. Besides, it was closer, and his spoils were quickly becoming heavy.

He lucked out. Samson was pacing the camp while Manny looked for sticks. Samson's eyes widened when he saw the loot and heard Ben's story.

"Are you insane? What the heck are we supposed to do with that lot?"

"I figured Manny could use the nappies and formula, and your mum might like the wine. The drill we can stick in the *Friday-Ad*."

"They'll kill you."

"Maybe. But they won't report it, eh?" He winked as the logic of stealing from thieves appeared to line up in Samson's mind.

"Manny's a little old for formula and nappies."

Ben shrugged. "Your mum will probably want it. You know, when the baby arrives. It's expensive to buy."

"Baaaaaby!" Manny cried with delight.

Samson shook his head. "I don't get it. Your dad would buy you a drill like that if you just asked him—"

"He wouldn't, actually," Ben interrupted, bristling.

"But he could if he wanted to. You don't need any of this stuff — so, you know, why?"

Ben thought about this, and then gave an honest answer.

"The other day, I was in the corner shop. You remember, they were doing a special on penny chews after Vik Ahmed beat their *Street Fighter 2* record in the back of the shop. It was a few days after that. Anyway, this woman behind me in the queue found a twenty-pound note on the floor between us. She picked it up and gave it to the bloke at the till. You know him, he's a bit simple. Village idiot type. Anyway, the first thing he did was offer it to me and say: 'Is this yours?' I was so surprised I just said no, like a reflex. And I tell you this — I kicked myself for a lot longer than I would have felt guilty if I'd said yes."

Samson thought about this. He didn't seem to agree, but when he shrugged, Ben figured he could see his argument.

"I just hope they don't catch up with you," Samson said.

"Me too. But that's half the fun, isn't it? Besides, we know they won't call the cops."

"Maybe. But we should still think about finding a new camp."

CHAPTER THIRTY-FIVE

Ben knew Samson well enough by now to know that he didn't drink, seldom smoked and generally avoided intoxicating substances of any kind. It didn't take a genius to figure out why, but when Ben popped round the next Saturday afternoon, Samson was wired on something. Ben wondered if he'd just had a fight or if he was gearing up for one, but he was grinning in a way that Ben hadn't seen before.

They went out into the square of mud that passed for Samson's garden, then thought better of it and went down to the new camp — Manny tagging along. When Samson pulled his shirt off, Ben thought his first guess had been right on the money and wished they'd stayed indoors.

Ben balled his fists, thinking he was about to get lamped, then Samson spun round and pointed at his own back like he was posing for a magazine shoot.

Ben stood agog. Stretching across his shoulder blades was a bright red star in a black circle, with THE CLASH — POLICE ON MY BACK tattooed over the top in a white military block stencil.

"Holy mother," Ben said, while Manny clapped and cheered excitedly.

"Great, isn't it?"

"Who the heck did that for you?"

"Uncle Jimmy. He's a dab hand."

Ben moved in for a closer look. Samson wasn't wrong — Ben was no expert, but it looked like a pretty professional job.

"How does he square with tattooing a fourteen-year-old?"

Samson shrugged. "Uncle Jimmy doesn't have much to offer — fags, cider and the odd bit of cash. But he can draw like da Vinci. You'd like him, actually — he seems to have a lot of car stereos lying around as well. Just don't involve me in those conversations."

"Think he'd want the nappies and the fine wine?"

It was an unexpectedly serious question. Samson responded with a don't-go-there look.

Ben touched the artwork lightly. The edges of the skin were still slightly raised, still a little pink.

"Did it hurt?"

"Like you wouldn't believe."

"Manny seems to like it."

"Manny's asked if he can do my next one."

"You're gonna get more?"

Samson shrugged. "Expect so."

"Public Enemy, maybe?"

For a second Ben regretted the remark — but Samson, after thinking about it for a second, just grinned at him. Ben didn't think he'd ever seen him look so happy.

"Well, I don't think Levi is going to give you any more hassle now. Your street cred just went off the charts."

Samson stopped posing and put his top back on. He shook his head, looking genuinely disappointed. Ben even felt himself flush, which was, in an adolescent playbook comprising little more than charisma, thick brown curls and a growing proclivity for elaborate thefts, unheard of.

"Who gives a flying fuck about street cred?" Samson said. He sounded almost disgusted.

Ben put his car back on the metaphorical Scalextric track and gave an impish grin. "People who don't have it, usually."

"What does it even mean?"

Ben shrugged. "We should ask Manny."

Manny responded in the affirmative: "Yeeeaahhhhh."

The new camp didn't feel particularly permanent. It was a bastard to get to, for one thing, and it wasn't off the beaten track in quite the same way the previous site had been.

The Italian Gardens were a well-kept secret at the westernmost end of Grand Parade, a manicured horseshoe of lawns, benches and landscaped flower beds. Despite the careful cultivation, the footfall was relatively light, which Ben largely ascribed to the fact that it was cut into the side of the land somewhere between the lower promenade at Holywell and the unbelievably steep network of paths ascending up to where Grand Parade began to snake upwards towards Beachy Head. If you didn't know it was there, you could walk right past it. Ben and Samson had posted their site above the gardens proper, recessed in the side of the steep cliff face on a carpet of bark and largely concealed by clusters of oaks and Austrian pines. It wasn't brilliant — mainly because the lie of the land was far from being flat — but, provided overexuberant rangers didn't rain on their parade, it was far more agreeable than its condom-strewn predecessor. Manny, in particular, seemed enthralled by the proximity of the sea. Mods, bovver boys and Levi would never think of looking for them here.

They sat down — the older two on upturned logs, Manny on the now-empty wooden case that had previously been full of fine French wine — and Ben produced some snacks, while Samson attempted to resurrect a phoenix from the blackened patch of ashes at their feet.

"It'll do, won't it?" Samson said as he poked the embryonic fire. "We can get some better seats, and a stash for the snacks, all that."

"Should probably get a crib, too," Ben remarked.

Samson stood up. "What's that supposed to mean?"

Ben shrugged. "Your mum is going to drop any day. Six months' time — less, maybe — it won't just be Manny you'll have to look after."

"You don't think I've thought of that?"

Ben was silent. Nothing more was said for several minutes. When he eventually succeeded in getting the fire going — helped along by some firelighter cubes swiped from his father's garage workbench — Ben threaded a marshmallow onto a wooden skewer and passed it to Manny, before recounting his plan for the next attempt at stealing from thieves.

CHAPTER THIRTY-SIX

Ben knew from practice that a disarming smile, impeccable manners and an even temper was all that was required to have the vast majority of adults eating out of his hand. He was often better behaved than many adults, especially those who took it upon themselves to enforce the law with walking sticks and shouts, be it cycling on the pavement, littering or terrorising the neighbourhood cats.

However, the disarming smile and on-tap compliments disappeared the moment Samson's father, Lee, answered the front door. Summoning the effort to be charming could sometimes take considerable resources, and Ben felt a cold lick of fear sap all the energy out of him the moment Lee's icy, suspicious eyes bore into him.

"Yeah?" Lee said, swigging from a can of Stella Artois, roll-up nestled between his fingers, belly crammed into his vest.

"Samson home?" Ben mumbled, reverting to the sullen teenager template and despising himself for so doing.

"Nah, mate," he said, his eyes dropping to the brand new sports holdall in Ben's grasp. "He'll be back later. Whatcha got there? Nothing hooky, I hope."

"No, sir," Ben said, offering Lee a look inside the bag. "Just my cricket gear."

Lee's pupils seemed to dilate as he regarded the equipment. It was nearly new, and Ben suddenly realised he had several hundred pounds' worth of equipment in there — stumps, pads, bats, helmet, gloves, the works. It was a look Ben suddenly realised, to his chagrin, that he recognised. His own eyes had taken on a similar aspect when he'd come across power tools, designer clothing and high-end electricals that didn't belong to him.

"Who is it, babe?" came a lazy female voice from inside the house. "You coming back to bed?"

"Just one of Sam's mates," Lee called. "Be right there."

He turned back to Ben, who wasn't totally sure, but didn't think the voice sounded like it belonged to Janet.

"I just thought we could go down the park. Show Manny how to play, maybe. I can come back another time."

Lee, in the process of closing the door, stopped and opened it again.

"Manny? What you mean, Manny?" Lee growled.

Ben swallowed as he tried to urgently work out what it was he'd said wrong.

"Yeah, we . . . we just . . . we took him for a kickabout the other weekend. Thought he might like to see what cricket is all about. But we don't have to," he added hurriedly.

Lee was chewing the inside of his cheek like it was some kind of self-restraint mechanism, and that if he stopped chewing he might completely blow his stack.

"But, like I say, another time, eh?" Ben said, finally summoning one of his yearbook grins. He started to back away down the short path before Lee was able to dwell for too long on his suspicions. For a moment it looked as though Lee intended to follow Ben down the path and continue his interrogation, but the lazy female voice called again, and Lee pushed the door closed. Ben may only have been fourteen, but even he could see Lee was on a promise.

He found Manny and Samson down at the camp, and wondered why he hadn't just gone there first.

"How'd you get here?" Ben asked.

"Four different buses," Samson said. "Took bloody ages."

"You should have waited," Ben said. "Could have got in my taxi."

"Had to get out of that bloody house," Samson said, ruffling Manny's hair.

Ben was sort of grateful that he'd met Samson's father. It had momentarily taken his mind off the fact that he'd found out — pretty much entirely by accident — that Aunt Imelda was not a blood relative at all. This should have been a source of good news, but the fact that she was instead just "a friend of his father's", whatever the hell that meant, completely tempered any sense of relief.

"I went to your house first," Ben said, while Manny gazed at the cricket holdall, a thumb in his mouth.

"Meet Lee, did you?"

"Your dad? Yeah, I did."

"What did you make of him?"

Even the question seemed to take all the fight out of Ben. The man was like a bear when static and calm — if suspicious — on the doorstep. Trying to imagine him in full flight, pissed and swinging fists like hammerheads around — with Samson trying to insert himself between the brute and his mother — brought on a kind of hopeless fear that Ben was completely unfamiliar with. Not a lot fazed him, but wowsers.

Ben looked at Manny. He was a bit pale, and his eyes were red-rimmed.

"He all right? Seems a bit quiet today."

"He's knackered. Didn't sleep much."

"Thought he'd be right in the sports bag."

Samson shook his head. "He won't, not unless you give him permission. He's always set back a few steps after . . . after . . ."

Ben jerked his thumb back in the general direction of the house. Samson nodded. Ben turned back to Manny, and indicated the sports holdall. "Go on, son. Get involved."

Manny shot forwards like a sprinter out of the blocks, and dove head first into the bag.

"I have to say, they didn't seem . . ." Ben thought about Samson's mother's lazy, almost sultry call, and struggled to find the words. ". . . didn't seem . . . like they'd . . . you know."

Samson shrugged. "Forgiveness fuck." His tone was matter-of-fact, but it nevertheless caused Ben to flinch. "He gets released, throws himself at her mercy, she turns it on thinking it might make him think twice next time. I'm always hearing them having sex after he's hit her."

Despite an upbringing surrounded by Castilian tile and rare fine art, Ben nevertheless considered himself pretty street smart, something he ascribed to the fact that he could insert himself positively into most social hierarchies with his smile and is easy-going nature — his access to cash didn't hurt either, and he wasn't naive enough to think otherwise. But, when he was around Samson, he was learning every day about how other people lived. His own parents were comparatively young, and he'd realised — after a saucy comment from Aunt Imelda one visit — that they were consequently probably still doing it from time to time. But Ben had no concept of this; he never heard it or saw evidence of it — no flirting, no casual innuendo, no unexpected early nights. Maybe he just didn't want to think about it — after all, it was pretty gross, as far as he was concerned. But even if he did think about it, he felt pretty sure it would be borne of something reasonably pure and wouldn't necessarily have all the violent psychological implications that apparently surrounded the trysts of Samson's parents.

Ben looked at Manny again. He was just a pair of feet sticking out of the holdall.

"When does he start school?" Ben asked.

"Couple of years yet."

"Does he go to, I don't know, nursery or something?"

Samson shook his head slowly.

"So what does he do all day?"

"Mum has him. If she has to go down the station, or is doing a shift at the yard, then he'll rotate between aunties and cousins and stuff. Sometimes Uncle Jimmy, but not very often. They'll have him until I get home from school."

"You seem to have him a lot."

"Just how he likes it, I guess. Eh, champ?" Samson called.

Manny gurgled in response.

"How do you feel about it? You know, if there's homework, or a girl or something?"

Samson eyeballed Ben as if he'd asked a really stupid question.

"Spears!" Manny cried, pulling out the stumps and brandishing them like some sort of *Lord of the Flies* survivor. He looked like he might strip down to a loincloth.

"Not quite," Ben said, and showed him how the stumps were arranged. "Now this is your castle," he said, balancing the bails on the top. "My job is to knock it down with the ball. Your job is to protect it with this."

He handed Manny the bat, who took it, wide-eyed, like it was Excalibur, before pulling the pads, gloves and helmet from the holdall. Ben paused before fitting them to Manny; both he and the toddler looked to Samson for approval. When he gave a slight nod, Ben dressed Manny in the protective gear.

"You're a knight, defending the castle, and this is your suit of armour. Keep you safe from the ball."

"He could do with wearing that on a Friday night," Samson murmured.

Ben heard the comment, but didn't acknowledge it, thinking Samson was probably talking to himself. Instead, he made a show of being impressed by Manny in full cricket get-up; the toddler was practically rooted to the spot and rendered immobile by the outfit, and after a moment or two, Ben and Samson burst out laughing. Manny, apparently in on the joke, started laughing himself.

"I wish we had a camera," Samson said. "You like your photo taken, little man?"

Manny nodded eagerly, the helmet bouncing loosely up and down on his head.

"You don't have one at home?" Ben asked.

Samson looked at his shoes and gave an almost imperceptible shake of the head.

An idea came to Ben.

"Wait right here," he said, and ran out of the camp.

"Where you going?" Samson called, but Ben was off on his toes.

He ran out the back of the camp, launched himself across the drop down to the prom and lit out onto King Edward's Parade. He ran west up the hill for ten minutes or so until he reached the bottom of the South Downs Way, and, just before the road began to twist in earnest up towards Beachy Head, stopped at a yellow fibreglass GRIT bunker. Ben scanned around him — unusually furtive for him, but he was in a hurry — then prised the lid open and pushed aside the surface layer of fusty stones. Under the stones lay several zip-tied polythene bags containing various expensive pieces of hardware: a handful of Game Boys, costume jewellery — and a couple of Polaroid cameras.

He re-scattered the surface layer of grit over the contraband, replaced the lid and bolted back the way he had come.

When he got back to the camp, he held the machine aloft like it was the Olympic torch.

"Where the hell did you get that?" Samson asked. "Don't tell me you stole it."

"I did not steal it," Ben said, with a grin. "That doesn't mean it isn't stolen, mind."

Samson shook his head like a disappointed father. Ben wondered if it was almost wishful thinking.

"Where's Manny?" Ben said, the smile dropping from his face.

Samson indicated the sports holdall with his chin. Ben went over and opened the bag, momentarily worried about what he would find there. Manny was nestled on a bed of stumps and pads, the helmet still on, snoring lightly with his thumb in his mouth.

CHAPTER THIRTY-SEVEN

Ben couldn't believe how hard it was to find a suit for a fourteen-year-old. If you weren't going to a wedding and didn't want to look like a top-hatted tit, it was nigh on impossible. In the end he went with his school uniform and some shoes he found buried in the bottom of his wardrobe along with a tie that he pilfered from his father. It would have to do.

The foyer smelled of disinfectant and vinyl floors. He was peering at that day's listings when he was accosted by some officious-looking gnome in a black robe who was right out of *The Never Ending Story*.

"Youth court doesn't sit until Wednesday," the gnome barked.

Ben switched on a winning smile. He'd been expecting this.

"I'm just waiting for my dad," he said, and walked away before the gnome could interrogate him further.

Eventually the gnome went off to do more important things, and Ben returned to the noticeboard of listings. He found one that felt like it would do the business, and then left the court, walking around the park until it was time to be called.

He got back to the court building just in time.

"Parties in the case of Jessop to Court Two, please." The voice over the tannoy was — unmistakably — the gnome's.

A skinny man in a shirt and tie who made Ben look like he should be in *GQ* hauled himself off a bench and loped off to one of the courtrooms. He was accompanied by a fat woman wearing pink and a ratty-looking man in a pinstripe suit, who wasn't much more than twenty. Lawyer, mother and defendant, Ben presumed. He maintained a respectable distance — far enough away to not attract their attention, close enough to slide into the courtroom before the door swung shut.

He sat at the back in the public gallery, right in the corner, pressed up against the wood-panelled wall. The hearing was administrative, and perfunctory, and was over in ten minutes. There was a case summary, however, and details of the defendant's address — both facts gave Ben all he needed to know.

When the hearing was over the door to the courtroom was opened by the gnome, who clocked Ben immediately and glared at him.

Ben stood. "I'm hoping to be a court reporter," he said. "You know, work experience."

The gnome opened his mouth; Ben slid past him and dashed off while the going was good.

* * *

It was a time-intensive operation that required patience and a lot of man-hours, and as Ben hovered around Carl Jessop's address on his bike, in the dark, he figured there had to be a better way to steal from thieves. This was eating into homework time, not to mention cricket time and girl time. And Samson time, he found himself thinking.

Eventually, though — and, thankfully, not as late as Ben had expected — Carl Jessop appeared in an entirely unsubtle get-up comprising a black tracksuit, black beanie hat and black ski mask. He was a complete and total caricature of a cat burglar, and, even at fourteen, Ben wondered what on earth the man was thinking. Why not just wear a suit or a hi-vis? No one would give you a second look.

In any event, Carl Jessop was on his toes. Despite being on his bike, Ben had to go some to keep up — the guy really was like Spider-Man. He was quick, stealthy and silent, and until Ben's eyes adjusted to the darkness, he nearly lost his quarry a couple of times. The new bike was a dream; it ran smoothly and quietly, allowing Ben to keep an otherwise unbroken surveillance.

To say Ben's father would have taken a dim view of his current assignment was an understatement. He would have been aghast, not to mention stunned beyond belief. Most parents with high hopes for their offspring hold on for dear life throughout adolescence, and just hope that the scars incurred along the way won't completely kick the adult aspirations into touch — career, house, family, all that shit. If you asked those same parents what distractions they worried about during those turbulent years, there were, by and large, few surprises. Drugs, joyriding, teenage pregnancy, flunking school, the wrong crowd. Actively surveilling convicted burglars so you could rip them off was not likely to have featured on Ben's father's list.

Not that Ben cared much, and this fact alone meant he knew he was, at some point, going to be a disappointment to the old man. That said, fourteen-year-old Ben already knew that the things his father wanted for him — education, reputation, prospects, respect — would all prove an invaluable cover for the things he really wanted to do. On that basis, dropping the bomb on his father might be stayed for a good few years yet, and would be dictated largely by whether — when — he was caught.

Which would be sooner rather than later if he didn't keep his wits about him. An almighty barking suddenly erupted from the other side of a wooden fence, shattering the quiet as Ben pedalled past — Ben couldn't see the beast, but from the sound alone he could all too well imagine what was on the other side. He swerved into the road, lost his balance and fell on his backside between two parked cars. He cautiously raised his head and peered through the rear windscreen of the one in front. Carl Jessop had stopped, and was looking in Ben's direction. Ben froze, but the burglar didn't waste time. He was off on his toes again, obviously not wanting to hang around.

Ben checked the bike, cursing in a whisper when he saw two tiny grey scuffs on the paintwork. He manoeuvred the bike back onto the path and took off again. He rounded the corner onto a long, straight residential street. They'd moved upmarket now, from Willingdon Trees through Hampden Park into Ratton, and Jessop's congested estate was beginning to thin out — houses with long front lawns and wide driveways were set well back from the road, the cars parked kerbside were infrequent, while the pavements were wide and well-kept, marked at intervals by a straight line of orange streetlights. Jessop should have been easy to spot — but he wasn't. Ben had lost him.

Ben cursed and dismounted the bike. He pushed it slowly along the road, scanning the houses left to right like a spectator up at the Devonshire. He passed two houses, then four, then six. There was nothing obviously out of place. No lights on, no doors open, no more barking.

He was just about to cut his losses and head home — it was a school night, after all, and this way he might at least still be able to haul his carcass out of bed and be just about on time — when his eye caught something off to his left.

He'd almost missed it, tucked as it was down the side of a house at the end of a long driveway, in the shadows, beyond the arc of the street lights. Which, he figured, was hardly surprising. It was a ground-floor uPVC fanlight window, obviously servicing a toilet, about a metre and a half across. It caught Ben's eye because it was wide open, but much wider than the things were supposed to be. The opening mechanism with the limiting bracket on the side seemed to be faulty — or had been tampered with.

It was only about ten inches high, but a well-practised skinny person could fit through it. Ben quickly looked around and then backed away from the street, tucking himself down a similarly gloomy alleyway splitting two large detached houses opposite.

He didn't have to wait long. He was impressed. Ben had been wondering how Carl Jessop was going to fit a sack of swag through the same window, when the front door opened and Spider-Man appeared, a rucksack on his back. Of course, Ben thought. Why on earth would you go out the same way you came in? Ben looked at his watch, the dials glowing green in the dark. In and out, six minutes. He must have done a fair bit of research ahead of time.

Jessop moved off down the street. Ben carefully climbed onto his bike and pedalled after him. He didn't know if he was in for a full night of burgling, or if Jessop was going to call it a night and stash the gear — it presumably depended on how successful his score had been. Although, Ben thought, even if he planned to hit some more houses that night, the rucksack was likely to encumber him, and he probably wouldn't want to risk being caught with it either.

Ben's instinct was correct. Jessop moved quickly, heading out of the residential area and onto an industrial estate. There was a service road leading off the main drag that curved around a bunch of warehouses and workshop units, at the end of which was a dead end marked by a bright yellow GRIT bunker. Jessop fiddled with the opening; it popped after ten seconds and he stashed the proceeds.

All in all, it had been an impressive demonstration. Mesmerised, Ben continued to follow, and over the next couple of hours, he had memorised the locations of grit bunkers in Willingdon, Langney and Meads, all stuffed with the proceeds of Carl Jessop's enterprising.

After the fourth or fifth house, Ben was yawning, and decided he'd seen enough. Jessop loped off after secreting the swag in a bunker near the Roselands industrial estate, and Ben let him go. He'd seen what he wanted to see, and he left Jessop alone to continue his work. Ben counted one, two, five, ten minutes, and then, once he was satisfied Jessop was long gone, he approached the yellow bin, pulling on some gloves as he went.

It took him longer to pop the lock than it had Jessop, but he got there. He lifted the lid, trembling with excitement, feeling like Aladdin discovering the Cave of Wonders. He held a pen torch between his teeth and saw nothing but grey particles of stone. He cursed. Had he got it wrong? Had Jessop spotted him and led him a merry dance?

He stuck his hand in the bunker and felt something hard. He swept the stones to one side and saw it was just a surface layer concealing what appeared to be a decent haul of electronics and jewellery. He almost crowed with delight, but resisted the urge to shovel the whole lot into his own rucksack. The minute Carl Jessop realised he'd been ripped off, he would switch it up and become triple-cautious.

Not that the stuff would be here long. Even at fourteen, Ben knew that Jessop wasn't obtaining Christmas presents for his extended family. The likelihood was that he would need to sell the stuff on as soon as he could arrange it.

Ben pedalled home, brimming with a sense of achievement and excitement that nothing else had yet come close to in his short life, not even the time that Samantha Leonard, eighteen months older and envy of the sixth-form PE students, had touched his crotch over his jeans. It wasn't even the fact that his rather long-shot theory had been validated, that someone else — someone that couldn't complain — had done the hard yards, that there were countless other Carl Jessops out there, that he'd unearthed an untapped mine promising potentially untold free riches.

It was the fact that he'd got away with it.

* * *

In his dream, he was surrounded on all sides by police dogs and blue lights that appeared out of nowhere as soon as he opened the lid of the grit bunker. The sound of his bedroom door opening jolted him from sleep like a Pavlovian reflex — his father never knocked, which kept him in a state of near-constant tension.

"No school today?" his father said from the doorway, carefully knotting a tan silk tie as he spoke. Tall, dark-haired, a suit that even Ben's uncultured eye could tell was extremely expensive. Ben couldn't help it, but the first thought on seeing his father was of Aunt Imelda and all the secrets she held. Many said Ben was a chip off the old block, and maybe they were right.

Ben reached over to the bedside table for his watch.

"Shit. I'm late."

"Language," his father said, looking down at the tie as he spoke. "I'm not surprised. What time did you get in?"

Ben eyed him. His father seldom asked questions he didn't already know the answer to.

"Not sure. I just went for a bike ride in the dark. Helps clear my head. I had lights and stuff, before you ask."

His father nodded. This was not news, and, in any case, wasn't completely untrue.

"Okay. Well, tick-tock. Oh, I meant to say, I saw your friend the other day."

"My friend?"

"Samson, is it?"

"You did? Where?" Ben said, suddenly wondering if Samson had been in for some kind of cardiac consultation.

"In the bike shop. I went to get you an after-market crankshaft. He was in there collecting something, with some brute of a bloke I presumed was his stepfather."

"Lee." Ben hadn't given any previous thought to the notion that Lee might not be Samson's biological father, and realised it had never come up. Was that his own preconception, or his father's?

"The man is a bear. I felt quite sorry for the boy."

"Was he . . . was he . . ."

"No, no, there was no disagreement, although it wasn't exactly a jovial atmosphere. The boy just trailed around after him looking like a scolded puppy."

"That's about right. Thanks for the crankshaft."

"It's on the hall table. I'll help you fit it later. Do you need a lift? If you're late, I mean."

Ben eyed him again. School was out of his father's way, and the man was never late. Ben wasn't sure if it was a theatre day or a consultation day, but either way his schedule would be jam-packed.

"No, that's fine. Thanks."

"Okay, if you're sure. Don't dawdle, then."

He made to go. Ben swung his legs over the side of the bed. His father stopped and turned back.

"You should have him over more," he said. "Samson. It's good that he has you as a friend. That's important, I think."

He left. Ben had heard it all now. He fell back on the bed, covered his head with his pillow and wondered how much weirder his week could get.

CHAPTER THIRTY-EIGHT

Ben hit the ground hard, his weight breaking a thin film of ice on the surface of a puddle. The frozen, stud-churned mud was jagged and razor sharp, and Ben was thankful for the fact that his bright pink legs were cold enough to numb the pain.

"Release!" somebody yelled, and Ben was only too happy to oblige, since discarding the oval ball meant the attention would be on somebody else.

Samson liberated Ben from the tackle, and offered a hand to help him up. They were on opposing teams, and Ben's few attempts to reciprocate by bringing down Samson had been utterly fruitless. The kid was like a sprinting tree, that heady combination of strength and speed — in adolescence, the two were often mutually exclusive.

He consoled himself with the thought that he'd only been playing a few weeks — and, at this rate, wouldn't be for much longer. Lee, Samson's father — stepfather? — had been playing rugby since he was a boy; naturally, Samson had been kicking a ball around from the age of six. At fourteen, Ben was a comparatively late arrival to the sport, and he couldn't see himself getting bitten by the bug. He could think of better ways of spending freezing Sunday mornings.

The final whistle mercifully blew a short time later, and the victorious — thanks, Ben was happy to admit, largely to Samson — mud-streaked home team piled into the showers while the visitors licked their literal and figurative wounds. The adults, who played on Saturdays, made for the bar. Ben sat with Samson, apart from the other kids, watching Lee warily. It was barely midday, but he was, along with his peers, steaming through the pints. There was only one draught tap in the makeshift clubhouse bar — basically a plank of wood in a portacabin — and it was being well and truly rinsed.

Despite the victory, Samson was quiet, a sense of general foreboding coming off him in waves. It didn't take much to work out that Lee's mood was the cause.

He started off fine — laughing and joking, bouncing Manny on his knee and plying the winning kids' team with chips, burgers and squash. Then, after pint five or six, there was a palpable change in his mood. Ben couldn't quite put his finger on what triggered it — a spilled drink, a mistimed jibe, cold food — but it was neither here nor there, really. His face hardened and he became very quiet, symbiotic rage incubating inside him just waiting for a host to latch onto.

Samson was watching Lee like a hawk, and seemed relieved when Lee put Manny down and told him to go and play. Samson shot out of his seat and coaxed Manny over with a sausage.

"What are we doing now?" Ben asked. His legs still felt numb.

"Sssh, just wait," Samson said. "When he's not looking we'll slip out the fire door."

Lee was by now engrossed in a loud, impassioned debate about two-stroke engines or something, and his attention was concentrated on the other man. With any luck, Ben thought, Lee would lose his temper and batter the bloke, then get nicked before he could refocus his attention elsewhere.

They took their leave per the exit plan and slipped out the back of the portacabin onto a shingle path that ran behind the posts along the tree line by the hospital's incinerator chimney and back to the main road.

"Should we, you know . . ." Ben said, jerking a thumb back over his shoulder.

"If you're worried about him realising we've gone, don't. He'll be in there for hours, and likely won't remember a thing."

They debated about whether to double back to Hampden Park, but a bus pulled up as they walked past the stop, which Ben said was meant to be, not least because the Sunday service was hit-and-miss at best. Samson wasn't immediately convinced, but Manny — apparently a lifelong lover of public transport — was thrilled at the idea.

They climbed aboard and realised it was going north up the A22, out of Eastbourne to Uckfield and beyond.

Ben paid the fare and they all took root in the back row. Ben felt Samson relax. There was nobody else aboard.

Ben turned to Samson. "Ashdown Forest?"

CHAPTER THIRTY-NINE

Ben looked down at the destroyed camp. Manny was holding Samson's hand. The kid had his thumb in his mouth and looked bewildered. Ben could feel the anger coming off Samson — not for the desecration, but for the upset to the child.

"Who do you think?" Ben said. It was a facile question, but he wanted to break the silence.

"Doesn't matter, does it?" Samson said. "Could have been Levi, could have been Carl Jessop — if he cottoned on it was you robbing his stash — it could even have been Lee, for all I know."

Samson turned and squatted down to face Manny. He grasped both his hands.

"We're going to fix it, okay, little man?" he said. "Somewhere else, where it can't be found. We'll get some proper seats and a roof. It'll be awesome."

Manny nodded. Ben looked down at them both. He opened his mouth to reinforce the point by saying, *Let's build it in my garden. No one will bother us there, not even my family.*

It was true too. His garden was so massive that once you were in the depths of the trees and vegetation at the bottom you couldn't even see the house.

But something stopped him. He looked down at the holdall containing the cricket gear, then picked it up and slung it over his shoulder. "Come on."

"Where?"

"Over the hill and far away."

"What?"

"Come on. I'll show you."

They ascended the sharp incline of Holywell Drive towards Helen Gardens. The ascent was breathtaking, and Samson slung Manny onto his shoulders after it became apparent that little man's legs were going to turn to jelly pretty quickly. April had brought some warmth, and a line of sweat broke out on Ben's brow.

"Manny," Ben said as they climbed. "That Spanish?"

"Hebrew, I think," Samson said. "Emmanuel. Don't know why they landed on that. Flathill might be Saxon. Mum's maiden name is Kane."

Ben opened his mouth, but quickly decided that he needed to conserve his wind, and didn't continue the conversation.

Once they reached the road, they paused for breath outside Bede's School. They carried on up onto Dukes Drive, then stopped at a kiosk at the foot of the South Downs Way where they stocked up on water and bought Manny an ice cream.

Samson shook his head as Ben paid.

"You ever ask me to pay you back, I'm stuffed," Samson said.

"Forget it," Ben said. "One day you'll be rich enough for the three of us."

Samson scoffed. "Where are we going, anyway?"

They stepped onto the South Downs Way itself, a dry, muddy track worn into the grassy hillside by Foyle Way, and began the climb onto the cliffs proper, the blue dome of sky like a fishbowl of refracted sunlight. The wind began to pick up as they walked, and when they eventually crested the hill it suddenly roared; unleashed, it caught them unawares, and

Samson took a step back to keep his balance, with Manny still on his shoulders.

"Oooh," Manny said. "Windy."

He stuck his tongue out and laughed.

The grass danced like green flames in the wind, and the trees dotted around the hillside were bent flat as if a particularly heavy giant was sitting on them. The wind suddenly yanked Manny's hat off his head and he lurched from unbridled horror to hysterical laughter as they mounted a successful ten-second chase across the hilltop to retrieve it.

Grimy and sweaty, they stopped for water and attempted to clean Manny up after the toddler claimed victory over his ice cream. Samson opened his mouth, but before he could complain, Ben nudged him and pointed to the view of the town below, the rooftops and buildings a broken mosaic of orange and white, the sea like gleaming blue baize.

They moved off again. The track continued up towards the top of Beachy Head, but there was a second path that forked to the south and took them on a slightly more level route towards the cliff edge.

The path rose again, and Ben began to feel the dead weight of the holdall, and his legs become leaden. On balance, he decided, he'd have rather carried Manny.

After forty-five minutes or so of walking, and just as Ben was starting to feel a little less cocksure about delivering on his enigmatic unspoken promise, the path crested again.

"Ben," Samson said. "Will you please tell us where—"

"Look," Ben said.

They stopped at the brow of the path, and looked down at the well-kept but nevertheless deserted sports field. A flat, neat square of green, comprising four football pitches and three cricket pitches. It was nestled in the cliff face, in an enclosed amphitheatre of wild shrubbery rising up on three sides, with a discreet line of gorse demarcating where the southern boundary rope stopped and a five-hundred-foot drop began.

"Holy crap," Samson said. "Look at that."

"Tell me they're gonna find us here," Ben said.

Samson grinned, wider and broader than Ben had ever seen.

They set about arranging the stumps, taking overly precise measurements as if it were the Ashes decider at Lord's itself.

They flipped a coin and Samson padded up first, while Manny sat cross-legged in the centre of the pitch, marvelling by turns at the wild green, the rippling sea, the never-ending sky.

CHAPTER FORTY

Carl Jessop seemed to have slowed his operations a little. It couldn't be seasonal — it was months until anybody would need to access the grit bunkers. Maybe the work ebbed and flowed — intensive stockpiling, and then laying off to allow the law to focus its attention on other, new priorities. It made sense to Ben — all of the grit bunkers that Jessop was using were packed full. Certainly Ben had tailed him for three nights straight, and he either hadn't ventured out at all, or had only popped down to the corner shop for smokes and lager.

Ben decided he'd give it one more night and then think about diverting his efforts back into his art project — it had been woefully neglected for a long time and the deadline was rapidly approaching. In any case, Ben thought, Christmas was taken care of. What he would have liked, he thought, was to just donate the whole stash to Samson, lock, stock and barrel. When it came down to it, he — and Manny — needed the stuff more than Ben did.

The shrill edge of the wind was just starting to mellow as April passed by, and the evenings were gradually getting lighter — there was a pink tinge of daylight in the sky as Jessop left his house.

Ben set off at a distance, his well-practised surveillance methods by now as smooth and silent as his bike, but he knew instantly Carl Jessop wasn't going burgling. He was wearing a blue-and-white checked shirt, new stovepipe jeans and hi-top Cons, and Ben must have been downwind, because he could smell the Brut and hair gel from a hundred yards away.

He was strutting, too — almost swaggering — not moving with that nimble Spider-Man cat burglar gait of his previous outings. Ben figured he was going to strike out — Jessop was going to meet a girl or something and the night would be a bust, but he was reluctant to miss any action.

He tailed him anyway, through Hampden Park and Tutts Barn, and was unsurprised when Jessop made for the pub. Well, the Roselands working men's club, anyway. Even at fourteen, Ben could tell this was a strictly functional establishment, where drinking was a serious business, almost a vocation. The paintwork on the signwritten hoarding had been salt-bleached from red to pink, and the banner advertising live Sky Sports was hanging from one corner.

Ben hung back on the other side of Seaside, using the shrubbery of the Archery rec as cover, and watched Jessop slide on into the club. Some bass-heavy Slade and the chatter of voices punched out into the street air when he opened the door, then it reduced to a muffled hum again.

Ben kicked up his pedal and was about to call it a night, when the door opened again almost immediately, and Jessop came back out.

Ben frowned. He'd just arrived.

But it wasn't just Carl Jessop. He was being followed out by Levi Sadler and two other men. Ben didn't know them, but he recognised them as Liam Lawrence and Terry Markham, the same motley bunch whose vehicle Ben had shamelessly — and expertly, he felt — stolen from.

And bringing up the rear was Lee Flathill.

Oh, Jesus.

Samson's dad.

Samson's dad was mates with *this* lot?

The five men stood in a circle and spoke earnestly over their pints. One of them laughed. A couple of them stroked hands — even to Ben's sheltered and untrained eye, it was obvious they were exchanging items while totally failing to look discreet. Maybe they didn't care. Ben figured even a vanload of hard-as-fuck policemen might check their exits when confronted with this lot.

Ben looked left and right. It suddenly felt imperative to at least try to hear what they were talking about. It was obvious they were plotting something, but Ben couldn't get close enough without crossing what was probably the busiest 30 mph road in the world, and in doing so would be right on top of them and totally exposed.

He looked left, and then right, and then left again — and when he looked back, Lee was staring across the street.

Right at Ben.

Ben recoiled, stumbled back and almost fell over his bike. He made some half-hearted attempt to conceal his face with a tree branch, but it looked ridiculous. He managed to cobble together the faculties to light a cigarette and call over to some imaginary associate behind him, trying to look absolutely casual.

While his back was turned he heard the sound of the door opening as the music and cheering was briefly amplified, and after a minute or two he chanced a look back across the street.

All the men had gone — back inside, presumably. Ben spun three-sixty on the spot in case Lee was waiting to mash his teeth in, but there was nobody there.

Maybe Lee hadn't seen him. Maybe he was just looking across the street. Maybe psychological warfare and mind games was exactly how he liked to torment his prey.

Ben cut his losses and pedalled slowly home, feeling decidedly glum. It was like there was a secret society of dickheads clad in Lacoste polo shirts who all knew each other. If Samson didn't know who his dad's mates were, Ben felt he should impart the information — in the interests of self-preservation, if nothing else.

Ben diverted en route and headed to Samson's house. It was late, but not that late. Manny would be in bed, but Samson would likely still be up. Ben might even be able to grab a cup of bacon fat–flavoured tea with Janet.

When he got to Samson's house, however, he was surprised to find the front door open and a nonplussed Manny standing in the doorway in Fireman Sam pyjamas.

"You okay, little man?" Ben said, looking around. "It's late. Where's your big brother? Where's Samson?"

Ben took Manny's hand and stepped inside the tiny hallway, but moved aside almost immediately to make way for a man and a woman hurrying out.

"Hey . . ." Ben began.

They wore suits and carried briefcases, and the man had a snowstorm of skin flakes all over the shoulders of his dark jacket. They exited the house without looking at Ben.

Once they'd left, Samson gripped Manny's hand and ventured further in.

"Samson?"

"In here."

Ben, relieved, walked to the back of the house and found Samson at the kitchen table — an outdoor picnic table shoehorned into the tiny, laundry-strewn room — drawing a space-age-looking guitar in a notebook.

"You okay?" Ben asked. "What's going on?"

"Not much," Samson said, digging his pen deep into the paper so that it scored lines in the sheet.

"I found Manny outside. Who were those people?"

"From the social."

"The what?"

"Mum dropped."

"Oh shit. Where is she?"

"In hospital with the kid."

"Now I'm a big brother too," Manny said, his chest puffed out.

Ben looked around the house, not quite sure what he was hoping to see. The baby and Janet were in hospital, and Ben knew for a fact that Lee was in the social club, so everyone was accounted for.

Then he realised — other than Manny's proud affirmation, the whole place seemed utterly joyless. He didn't quite remember his little sister being born, but he did remember the atmosphere being a fuck sight more cheerful than this.

"Ah well," Ben tried, "at least they left you here. Didn't lock you in the dog pound."

"They think Lee's a good father. The woman was making eyes at him last time."

"Lee's in the pub," Ben said.

"Yeah, that's standard. Especially with news like this. Probably reckons he's wetting the baby's head, but it's no different than any other Thursday night."

"Turns out he's mates with Carl Jessop and Liam Lawrence too."

"Small world," Samson said, drawing a skull and crossbones, and Ben didn't labour the point.

The picnic table was wedged up against the counter block, meaning only one side was accessible. Ben dragged it out a bit and plonked himself opposite Samson, sliding a basket of washing to the other end of the tabletop.

"So, you got a brother or a sister?" Ben asked.

"Brother," Samson said.

"Cool. Your mum is a bit outnumbered, then."

Samson eyed him.

"Does he have a name yet?" Ben asked hurriedly.

"Bananaman," Manny offered.

"Cool," Ben said.

"I want to see him," Manny said.

"Soon, champ. Soon," Samson said. "If you're a good boy and go straight to sleep, we'll visit in the morning, okay?"

Manny yawned in the affirmative, and Samson finally put down his pen. He hefted the toddler up, put him over his shoulder and left the kitchen. Ben, intending to let the family enjoy whatever pleasure could be cleaved from this strange set of circumstances, followed them out to the hallway and watched them climb the stairs.

Manny rested his cheek on Samson's shoulder, and was asleep before they'd reached the top.

* * *

It was late when Ben finally got home and locked the orange-and-blue steed in the garage. He was hot and sweaty, and too wired to shower or sleep. He took the unusual step of throwing himself into his geography homework, which, this term, was focusing on Central America and the Caribbean. He read for a couple of hours with more or less unbroken concentration, taking in the discovery by Columbus, the colonisation of the territories by the British, the weirdness of the Bermuda Triangle being debunked by tropical cyclones, and the rivers of Grenada — the Balthazar, the Black Bay, the Duquesne.

Duquesne, he thought.

Cool name.

CHAPTER FORTY-ONE

The late afternoon sun settled across the Beachy Head sports field, casting a lazy net of amber over everything and stretching the shadows in a distorted haze. April had melted into May, and the summer had almost arrived.

Ben looked down. The shadow of the stumps on the grass reached away into the distance, almost to the clump of hedges at the treeline. He could feel the grime and stickiness on his forehead, while his gloves were damp with sweat. Dark patches had appeared on the leather palms from a day spent tightly gripping the lump of willow.

It was getting harder to see, but he settled into his stance, focused on the other end of the pitch and waited for the ball.

Samson whipped the ball down so fast Ben almost lost it in the fading light, but picked it up again when it bounced. Short-pitched. A bit ropey, frankly — just not cricket, in fact — to chuck down a bouncer when the light wasn't so good, but he rocked onto his back foot, put all the grip into his bottom hand and pulled his arms round in a textbook hook shot. The leather hit the willow with a heavy, satisfying *crack* — not a *click* like you heard on the telly — and he watched it fly off to the makeshift boundary made up of jumpers and bags.

"Not bad, considering you'd never even picked up a ball a month ago," Ben called with a grin. Samson flushed with what Ben thought looked like pride, in a way that made Ben almost embarrassed.

It was almost four weeks since they had found their own private corner of the world, etched into the cliffs. It was a small piece of neatly cultivated precision, a well-tended postage stamp stuck to an otherwise untamed pedestal at the edge of the world, five hundred feet above the snarling sea. It made Ben think of Alice finally finding a carefully constructed path after fighting her way through Wonderland's impenetrable forests. Despite being obviously looked after, they'd never chanced upon anybody else up here, either casual players or proper grown-up sports teams.

Samson, the once and future spare part, had taken to the great game with gusto, and had revealed a sharp eye and a pneumatic throwing arm. The one thing they were missing, Ben thought, was an actual team. They had all the proper kit, thanks to Ben's father; Ben had proudly announced that it wasn't stolen. The trouble was, if Samson belted down a yorker and Ben missed it, well, there was no wicketkeeper, and it was a long way to go to retrieve it. Manny was keen as mustard, but he wasn't here today, and besides, Ben lived in perpetual fear of a misplaced square cut taking the kid's head off.

The other helmet was on the ground, marking the start of Samson's run-up. When he got there, he picked it up and put it on.

"What you doing?" Ben called. "You can't bowl with a lid on."

Samson responded by doing some kind of strange war dance that was a combination of *haka* and "Agadoo". Ben fell about laughing. He didn't think he'd ever seen Samson lark about like this. Maybe some of the weight on the kid's shoulders was finally starting to lift.

He settled into his stance again, dipped his head slightly, and watched the ball in those massive hands.

He frowned. Samson seemed to be hesitating. His attention was elsewhere. Ben straightened up.

"You gonna bowl or what? We're losing the light."

In the previous overs, Samson had gone striding back to his mark, tossing and spinning the ball to himself as he went, maybe imagining the camera on him, before belting down the field with increasing speed like a 747 about to lift off the runway. Now he was standing stock still, arms by his sides, expressionless behind the face guard.

"There you are, you little cunt!"

Ben spun round in horror, a blanket of cold thorns covering him with dread. Lee was lolloping across the field, bracelets rattling on his wrist, tufts of grey hair poking out over his vest. Six foot two of solid anger, greying black hair cut tight to his square head. His jaw was set in an angry sneer, and he was jabbing at the air with an index finger as he marched towards his son.

Ben tried to rattle through the shortlist of possible transgressions that Samson could be guilty of — home late, untidy room, unattended child . . . or, as was more likely, some irrational combination of a foul mood, beer or resentment that his son might actually be having a better time than him.

Samson spread his palms and wound up a protest, but as Lee closed the gap between them, it quickly became apparent that he had no intention of getting into verbals. He was going to bypass that altogether.

Without breaking stride, he backhanded Samson across the face. The helmet took the worst of it, causing a sprouting of cuts across Lee's knuckles, but the impact was enough to knock Samson off balance. Lee followed up with a kick to the ribs, and Samson went down in a heap.

Roughly, and with surprising dexterity for someone who presumably didn't know one end of a cricket bat from the other, his father pulled off the helmet, sputtering blood over the white fabric, and dumped it on the grass. Once liberated of the protective gear, he hooked a thick forearm around Samson's neck and dragged him bodily off the field.

Ben, rooted to the spot, watched in horrified dismay as Samson scrabbled helplessly at his Lee's arm, his feet just about able to gain enough purchase on the ground to stop him suffocating completely.

It looked like Samson couldn't breathe, couldn't speak, could barely see. As they reached the path, Lee twisted slightly to change course; Ben and Samson locked eyes for a second, each mirroring the other's expression of shock and fear.

CHAPTER FORTY-TWO

Ben was engrossed. Completely and totally absorbed. His grades were generally okay, but nothing had grabbed him like this, which had the additional benefit of enabling him to tune out all the crap and upset of the preceding days.

He'd been putting off the art project, having got it fixed in his head that his teacher would expect it to be some dreary abstract Impressionist crap, but then, halfway through the term, he'd hit on the idea of a graphic design project for a made-up bike shop — business cards, flyers, posters, a logo — which was much more his thing. The best bit was that he'd had to hang back after class to ask his art teacher, Miss Bianchi — who was a total fox if ever there was one — if his project theme was acceptable. She'd breathed, "Yes, of course!" with a smile and he'd trotted off happier than a turkey on the day all Christmases were made vegetarian by law. He'd totally immersed himself in it, and not just because he wanted Miss Bianchi to think he was the mutt's nuts.

The project was due the following day, and Ben, after slaving away every evening that week with almost hypnotic precision, realised he was going to run out of letterset and mounting card at just the wrong moment. He tutted, then sprang up from his desk in horror when he suddenly saw that he had about seventeen minutes before all the shops shut.

He barrelled downstairs and pedalled into town like his life depended on it — which, if it meant earning Miss Bianchi's disappointment, it pretty well did. He perched the bike outside the art supplies shop — and realised he'd forgotten his bike lock.

He weighed it up for half a second: on balance, it would probably be all right; the shop was small and he could keep an eye on it through the window; he knew exactly what he needed and wasn't going to be long.

He took the risk, and when he walked out nine minutes later — seven minutes longer than he'd intended, but apparently 5.27 p.m. on a spring Thursday was a hot time for geriatric craft enthusiasts who only pay in 2p pieces to stock up — the bike was gone.

Ben stared at the empty patch of wall for a moment in sick disbelief. He blinked, and felt the bile start to rise up his gullet. In the end, he didn't vomit, but stalked up and down the street, not knowing what to do. Ben knew for a fact that the bike could take him to town and halfway back in seven minutes if the conditions were right, so the thief could be miles away by now.

He nevertheless jogged around town for fifteen pointless minutes, hoping for a glimpse of it, and just knew Levi Sadler had got his talons on it.

In the end he walked to the police station and made a report, thinking that by enveloping himself in official channels he might feel a little better. Unfortunately, the sergeant on the desk spent more time castigating Ben on his lack of helmet, lights and postcode marking, and Ben left the station feeling even worse.

He walked home in a sick funk — it was a long way, but he needed the time to work out how he was going to tell his father. Miss Bianchi had completely evaporated from his mind.

He arrived home forty-five minutes later and was both relieved and dismayed to see that neither parent was home yet. He opened the front gate — and was suddenly aware of someone behind him. Before he had time to react, he found himself grabbed by the shirt and shoved up against the wall.

"Found you, you little fucking bastard!"

Carl Jessop was all bad teeth, sinew and stinking tobacco breath. His eyes gleamed with righteous anger and Ben felt spittle land on his face.

"I bet you think you're pretty fucking clever, you child," Jessop said. "But I found you."

"What do you want?" Ben said, the shock of having had his bike stolen numbing the edge of the fear he would otherwise expect to be feeling. With that in mind, he scanned the environs in case Jessop had his bike. It seemed an entirely plausible sequencing, but Ben couldn't see it anywhere.

"You've been mugging me off. Taking my shit. You do *not* take another man's shit. The fucking brass neck on you."

"You want it back? You can have it."

"Yes, you're right, I can have it. 'Cos if you don't return it—" here he glanced over Ben's head at the house behind — "I'll tell your father what you've been doing."

Panic rose in Ben's chest, but he fought not to show it. That would mean the bottom falling out of his whole world. Shame. Guilt. His father's disappointment. And worse — discovery. *Capture.*

"Not only that," Jessop said, apparently enjoying Ben's discomfort, "I'll tell *Lee* what you've been up to. Tell him you've been leading young Samson astray. What do you think *he* will do?"

Ben blinked. How could this horrible bloke know all this? Had he been following him?

Jessop offered a sneer. "You jumped-up little rich shit. Sorry to tell you, but you're not nearly as clever as you think you are."

He finally released Ben's top. Ben looked down. There was a tear in it.

"You've got a day. Twenty-four hours to return all my shit."

"I will," Ben nodded. "All of it."

"You will."

"Where?"

"I'll find you."

"Not here. Please."

"Maybe I will, maybe I won't."

Jessop took a step back, and Ben felt the merest hint of relief that he was going, allowing himself to think this horrible day might finally be about to draw to a close.

But, before he turned and stalked off, Jessop fired a punch straight into the centre of Ben's face. The eye-watering, nose-popping pain was like nothing he'd experienced before, and he sank onto the pavement, cradling his wounded face.

* * *

After nobody had arrived home after another half an hour, Ben decided to postpone the inevitable by immersing himself in his own world for a while longer, and so he headed out again and made for Samson's house. He even toyed with the idea of getting to Lee before Jessop did, and giving him his side of the story first.

He had pretty well got used to a degree of uncertainty whenever he went to Samson's house. Sometimes somebody answered and all was normal; sometimes there was no answer at all, despite audible voices from within; sometimes he would find the front door open, and he would call from the threshold. When this first happened, he'd been unsure of what to do — keep calling and wait for someone to come home; walk away, pull the door closed and quietly leave; call someone? Now if it happened, he would do a quick check of all the rooms before closing the door, checking with the neighbours and going home to tell his father.

Today, he was unprepared for what he found. The front door was wide open, but the entrance was blocked by a criss-cross of blue-and-white tape that bore the words *POLICE LINE DO NOT CROSS*. It looked new, but one of the ends had come adrift and was flapping gently in the breeze. There was no activity, no sounds from inside, nothing. There was a police patrol car out the front, but nobody was in it.

Ben wanted to walk up to the tape and peer into the doorway, but he found he was rooted to the spot. All he could see from the end of the short path was the blanket pegged up on the patio doors at the back, creating gloom throughout the house, the sun fighting to penetrate the centre of the blanket like an egg yolk.

He'd been here — a few times now, actually — on the mornings after Lee had been hauled off by the police for one of his outbursts — the ones which, nine times out of ten, Janet had been on the receiving end of. He wasn't quite as inured to it as Samson seemed to be, but he'd been getting used to it. This felt different.

He figured that the police officer wouldn't be far from their patrol car, but suddenly found he didn't want to go looking, wasn't sure he wanted the answers. So he remained standing at the end of the path, fixed to the spot, the urge to leave growing and growing.

The street was completely silent. Just the whispering of the trees and the loose end of the crime scene tape fluttering lazily in the breeze.

Ben didn't know what, but he knew something terrible had happened here.

# PART THREE:
JANUARY, 2015

CHAPTER FORTY-THREE

The phones went nuts. Media, dog walkers, beach cleaners. Even the desk phones in the CID office started to ring off the hook, which was unusual. For a moment Barnes thought it was a technical malfunction, or a fire alarm, but when officers started streaming out of the station like it was on fire and he saw that even the usually stoic Georgia Brass was ashen-faced, her phone wedged under her chin, Barnes knew it was serious.

"Hey," he called over to her. "What's going on?"

"Dead body. On the seafront," she said. "We're going to need you."

Barnes shut his eyes, thinking of the three remaining names on what was increasingly looking like a hit list.

"Any ID?"

"Not yet."

Barnes grabbed his briefcase, go-bag and a couple of DCs and jumped in with Georgia. It was, as it ever was during the day, a rather hairy run along Royal Parade, which was snarled up with pedestrians, traffic and coachloads of senior day-trippers trying to cross the road.

The Italian Gardens were nestled in an elevated platform recessed in the cliff face above the westernmost section of the promenade and below the sheer drop from Holywell. It was a neat oval spread of trimmed lawns crowned with Spanish daggers and a canopy of Holm oaks overhanging the concrete shelters.

Barnes took comfort in the fact that it was reasonably well sheltered. There were vantage points from the beach and the promenade, but the mid-elevated position lent itself well to preservation from view.

Then, he realised, that was because he was expecting the body to be on the ground. He scanned the verges, ditches and flower beds carpeted with fragrant bark chips, before one of the first responders — who looked like he'd mentally tendered his letter of resignation — touched Barnes's arm and pointed up.

"Jesus Christ," Barnes whispered.

The body was thirty feet above the ground, suspended from a lamp post, like some bizarre warning to pirates. It had a hessian bag over its head, and its hands were bound behind its back with what looked like cable ties. The whole front of the body was sodden with black blood, so much so that Barnes thought it looked like complete exsanguination. It was hanging by the neck — the rope had been looped over the top of the lamp post to create a makeshift hoist and then lashed to one of the cobalt-blue iron railings separating the promenade from the beach.

King Edward's Parade began to climb somewhere down by the Grand Hotel. The promenade continued on at shore level, while the road ascended along the clifftop, the two gradually diverging like a yawning trap door. This far west, the promenade was a couple of hundred feet below the road level — and it was a bastard of a steep climb back up. The prom itself stopped about five metres below the gardens. Just a hard stop, marked by some public toilets and a seasonal café. Beyond that was an almost impassable spread of rocks and shingle leading all the way around to Beachy Head and beyond, all along the Seven Sisters to the mouth of the Cuckmere. Proceed beyond the prom at your peril, Barnes thought — he could think of more than a handful of instances where intrepid hikers had found themselves cut off and stranded by the relentless tide.

Barnes stared, and then spun around on the spot. The promenade had been closed two hundred yards to the east. The body would be tough to see from the road above, but from the beach, the sky, the cliffs even, anyone with a half-decent camera could obtain some lurid footage.

It took nearly an hour, with the assistance of HM Coastguard and Fire & Rescue, to get the body down, a SOCO photographing most of that hour while EGT recorded video footage. It wasn't nearly as controlled or forensically careful as Barnes would have liked, but he would have to let that slide. He did not want this on the front pages of the evening news.

It lay there on the prom, still bound, still bagged, surrounded by emergency responders whose features seemed to wear a collective *what now?* expression.

"We should take the bag off, shouldn't we?" somebody said.

"Not till the CSM arrives," Barnes said. "Everything needs to be documented and preserved."

"Yeah, but imagine your family knowing you were lying there like that."

"I said no," Barnes said.

The body was in a bad way. It looked like a sleeping bag that had lost a fight with an InterCity, a tangle of blood-drenched limbs and matted clothing. If not for the bound hands and the bag over the head it might have been difficult to discern which end was which.

Clive Brynn, the CSM, arrived next. He was his usual grumpy self, but Barnes wondered if he detected a flicker of unease in his eyes at this — body number three in as many weeks.

"You again," Brynn said. "Are you the only SIO on the duty rota, or what?"

"If I'm not up to your exacting standards, please tell me and I'll happily stand down. Although I'm not quite sure where you'd get a replacement from." Barnes waved a hand towards the sea.

"Well, this is undoubtedly an Op Limekiln body, so it's a neat touch to legitimately spread your material all over the scene if you happen to be the killer," Brynn said. "You've seen *Dexter*, right?"

Nobody laughed. A couple of the coastguard guys looked over.

"Shall we make a start?" Barnes said, and Brynn started unpacking his equipment.

Number three. There was no possibility that it was actually number one, either — the body had been very deliberately put on display, and would not have remained undiscovered for any length of time. Which meant there was a ticking clock and a closing window for the public inquiry to ask Barnes, *You had the list, so why weren't you able to save them?*

With two more to go, he thought.

The genie was out of the bottle now. The press were going to go crazy. And who could blame them? Barnes decided then and there to appoint a senior officer as a shield, someone to face the public while he got on with the investigation.

Barnes didn't feel out of his depth, necessarily. It was more the fact that a reactive major crime investigation — that is, piecing together every shred of evidence and then packaging that evidence into a coherent and legally impenetrable narrative of what actually happened — was a painstaking process that took months, if not years. But the act that led to it might have happened in the blink of an eye — you could put someone's lights out permanently with one well-aimed slash of the blade. And if their killer continued to drop his victims like flies, then Barnes had some serious catching up to do. There was a school of thought — already echoed by Marlon Choudhury — that said: the more frequent and brutal the murders, the more likely the killer would be caught. Less careful, more indiscriminate, a consistently warm trail.

There was a counter-view that said, Barnes thought grimly, that if you just kept killing, the police wouldn't be able to keep up. It was becoming increasingly apparent that the guy probably didn't care much either way.

There were five names on the list. Would he stop there? Were there more, as-yet undocumented? Gabby knew about them — would Gabby have been on that list if he hadn't punched his own ticket? Had he taken the quick way out?

Despite all this, Barnes realised, there was a buzz in his stomach. Not the buzz of a notch on the career bedpost, not the buzz of public exposure.

The buzz of the hunt.

When the CSM, SOCO and pathologist were all lined up — the pathologist took convincing, but a bona fide serial killer persuaded him, plus it was daytime and the weather was good — Barnes organised the controlled removal of the bag and the cable ties.

He moved the cadaver's head back and forth with a pencil, and it flopped like a gasping fish. It was a shapeless mess — the features were still prominent, but the structure and positioning had started to slide into a ghostly, blue-grey wax pile that resembled the surface of the Moon. Even if this person happened to be Barnes's nearest and dearest childhood friend, it was entirely possible he wouldn't have recognised them.

The force of being hauled upwards by the neck had caused the noose to eat into the black five-inch gash across the throat, creating a sort of hinge that had forced the jaw and head up into a sharp angle.

The throat was stained with a waterfall of blood, but there were also eleven fish-eye stab wounds to the abdomen. Barnes imagined a cross-section of the body seen through an MRI scanner, wounds like angry red meteor trails firing rudely down through the torso.

"Look at what the pressure of the rope has done to the wound," Brynn said, almost in awe. "Few more hours, he'd have been decapitated."

Under close supervision and video camera scrutiny, Barnes gently searched the pockets with gloved hands until he felt something secreted in the damp jogging bottoms.

He pulled out a dull metal money grip the colour of fish scales. He carefully slipped the contents out — no cash, but an NHS prescription exemption card, a National Insurance number, a lottery ticket and a couple of pawn shop receipts. It was a sad state of affairs, but it gave Barnes a name he was entirely unsurprised to see.

Terry Markham, fifty-six years old. Older than the other two victims by about fifteen years, and a local name familiar to Barnes. Not one he knew well, but one that had been in and out of the cells, in and out of the system and in and out of the CID in-tray for years. From memory, his USP centred around enforcing drug debts and cultivating a fearsome reputation in order to haul himself up a rung or two on a ladder that otherwise had no particular interest in whether he lived or died. He was not in especially great shape, but he was still a lump, and Barnes found himself slightly awestruck by the strength that would have been required to both best this street soldier and then hoist him thirty feet into the air by the neck.

Another one ticked off the list.

He stood up and looked around.

Where are you?

This killer was on a mission, and wouldn't stop until all five names were dead, and maybe not even then. That meant planning, logistics, practicalities. Barnes couldn't conceive of a scenario where he perpetrated the act of violence Barnes now regarded on the damp floor of the promenade and then slipped back to a Premier Inn for cheap espresso and a continental breakfast. But maybe he had. In any case, he was hunkered down somewhere — regrouping, resetting, recharging. And then he would come back out.

So, how do you get a body down here? Barnes thought. And why pick here particularly? You've launched a pretty frenzied knife attack on your victim — who, judging by the lack of defence wounds, didn't have time to put up much of a fight — let's say in a house or B&B somewhere. Even if it had happened at one of the fading seafront guesthouses that had found new leases of life as bail hostels — then what? Even in the dead of night, it would be practically impossible to drag a dead body out on foot without someone seeing. Which meant a car — or, more likely, a van — with access to the service roads that were locked and only accessible by the emergency services and local authority.

Unless they'd met here? Coaxed here on the pretext of — what? A drug deal? Repayment of a debt? Probably money — it talked the loudest. If it was for criminal purposes then that would be the easiest way to lure the victim here at three in the morning — he wouldn't have wanted to be seen by a dog walker any more than the killer would have.

The sun was fighting to come out from behind a thin veneer of cloud, turning both the sky and the sea an almost blinding white. The tide was beginning to come in, and the irregular rock pool formations looked like clusters of black bodies, the breakers lapping over limbs twisted this way and that. The waves suddenly felt to him like the inbound cases beginning to pile up; he could call for a timeout, or try to catch his breath, or hold up his hand to stop the traffic — it wouldn't matter. Those waves would still keep coming in and wouldn't stop for anyone.

Where are you, you bastard?

CHAPTER FORTY-FOUR

Barnes glanced around the U-shaped conference table. The air was tight with tension. The other attendees met his gaze — ANPR, intelligence, forensics, neighbourhoods, family liaison, media, HOLMES office manager — and somebody from Professional Standards deputising for Marlon Choudhury whom Barnes didn't know and was instantly suspicious of.

On one of the walls was a large display board bearing photographs of their three victims — Carl Jessop, Liam Lawrence and Terry Markham — with *OPERATION LIMEKILN* displayed at the top in bold capitals. Underneath, Barnes had written the list of five names, with their three victims scored through:

~~*Liam Lawrence*~~
~~*Carl Jessop*~~
~~*Terry Markham*~~
Lee Flathill
Levi Sadler

Haven was sitting next to Barnes, fingers hovering about the keyboard. He looked at her before he started speaking.

"Ladies and gentlemen, we have a bona fide serial killer in our midst. Our three victims are connected by time, location, MO and prior associations. Causes of death were, in turn, evisceration, blunt force trauma and . . . well, the third victim was lynched. After his throat had been cut," Barnes added.

"From intelligence received — much of which is highly sensitive, and cannot be discussed here, I'm afraid; I know that's unhelpful — we have formulated the list that you see over my shoulder. We have reason to believe that the two remaining names may well be the offender's next victims, and that they are at significant risk of harm as a consequence. There is an active threat-to-life investigation running in parallel to this one, whose priority is, unsurprisingly, to locate these two individuals and safeguard them.

"We have no suspects, and our time is going to be best spent getting out there and working the investigation, not sitting around a table. I want to keep today high and tight, so let's spin round the room and discuss the common factors rather than the minutiae of each case," Barnes said.

He looked to his left. Brynn was up first.

"Good morning, everyone. Per the SIO's brief, I'll keep this high-level."

He glanced at Barnes — slightly balefully, Barnes thought. Maybe that was because *not* going into minute detail was not generally in a SOCO's nature.

Brynn continued.

"We have seven main scenes so far: the three bodies themselves, the three locations where they were found, plus the phone box that the first 999 call was made from, on the basis that whoever made that call is likely to be a suspect or at least a sigwit.

"The forensic strategies, agreed with the SIO and the PIP4 coordinator, are, at this stage, primarily concerned with suspect identification, with attribution of weapons, degree of force, deliberateness of the acts and placing the suspect at the crime scenes necessarily secondary objectives. In plain English, that means an absolute fuck ton of exhibits and a very long list of names to work through when we eventually get them. In addition—"

"Good summary. Thanks, Clive," Barnes said, interrupting. "Media next, please."

Andrea Hope, in a peach two-piece and lavender corsage and looking like she was about to head off to Royal Ascot, picked up her notes.

"The press have this now," she said, in her silver spoon voice. "Three bodies and a confirmed link. The nationals are beginning to step over the locals — only Boko Haram and the *Charlie Hebdo* shootings are keeping it off the top spot."

That was a perverse blessing if ever he'd heard one, Barnes thought.

"A couple of outlets got hold of a photograph of Victim Three in situ — before he was cut down," Hope said.

A murmur went around the room. Barnes raised his hand.

"That was inevitable," he said. "Carry on, Andrea."

"Thankfully, they came to me first, and — so far — have agreed to hold fire on publication. We're going to need to brief the media, though, and soon. I recommend a press conference either this afternoon or first thing tomorrow."

"Noted. Agreed. Thanks, Andrea. Okay, Intelligence now."

Barnes looked over at Tina. She held his gaze for a moment, and if she'd interpreted the meaning as *Please give me something*, then she didn't disappoint.

"Okay, so . . . bit like SOCO, really, the SIR is geared around trying to put some names in the hat for our suspect, which, given where we are, means coming up with a list of all possibilities and then trying to whittle it down. The MO is pretty specific, so we've drawn up a list of ViSOR offenders and OCG nominals and broken it down into three parts: those living locally conforming to their reporting conditions, those released from prison in the last six months, and those that have dropped off grid. The bad news is that the list is pretty long — longer than your average *Guardian* reader will be comfortable with, actually."

She glanced at Andrea.

"To whittle it down, we're cross-referencing that list with known connections to Class A drug supply, on the basis that the cocaine found at Scene One, the car showroom, is from the same batch that washed ashore on 6 January."

It was both a jolting reminder to Barnes and an indication that his brain was verging on full. He made a note in his book to follow up on the case of the missing PC, Pete Lamb.

"On that basis, and based on the victim profiles, we're looking at drugs debts, reprisal attacks, ongoing feuds, that kind of thing. All the victims were well known to us, which is both a blessing and a curse — there is a lot of data to wade through."

"What if," Barnes said, "it's a rising-tide MO? That is, the perpetrator hasn't used this level of violence before, and might not yet appear in the ViSOR classification?"

Tina shrugged. "Then if we get nowhere, we widen the list systematically. Same as the prison releases during the last six months; that gets us nowhere, we extend it to a year."

"Fair enough," Barnes said.

"Now, there's three bits you're going to be interested in," she said. "First of all, we pulled off an ANPR dump of all vehicle hits in an umbrella around the crime scenes for the preceding twelve hours — less where that overlapped with peak daytime traffic. The list is long, but with the emergence of further victims we looked first at patterns to establish whether any vehicles appeared in more than one list, and we got a hit."

"Go on," Barnes said.

"A rental car — a black Volkswagen Passat estate RF13 CZG. Went through the town centre at 0102 hrs, forty-seven minutes before the 999 call to ambulance reporting the first body in the showroom. The same car pinged near Beachy Head at 0307 hrs on 14 January 2015, four hours before Victim Two was found. And the hat-trick: it hit again heading east out of Eastbourne on 20 January, fifty-one minutes before we got the first call on Victim Three."

"Have we gone loud with that car?"

"Yep," Tina said. "All alerts. If it hits a camera anywhere in the country, the Force control room for that area will deploy ARVs to find it."

"And it hasn't come to notice yet?"

Tina shook her head. "No, sorry. No documented movements since Victim Three was discovered."

"Gone to ground, maybe," someone said.

"Or he's ditched the car," said someone else.

"Both are possible," Tina said. "We've built a full inventory of its movements since the first of December and are working through it for patterns. Other than proximity to the three scenes, nothing has jumped out yet."

Tina began to distribute papers.

"All indications are that this is the genuine vehicle, rather than a clone. It was rented from the Stansted Airport branch of Enterprise Rent-A-Car at 0910 hrs on 5 January 2015.

"We've got details of the hirer and the credit card, but with no match on preliminary checks on any of our systems. There's a strong indication that the rental was made with fake ID."

"That and the beached cocaine link plays to the OCG angle, even if the MOs don't scream contract murder," Barnes said. "Your average garden-variety disemboweller might not have the connections to obtain decent fake ID — or the inclination, if they're preoccupied with howling at the moon. What about CCTV from the Stansted branch?" Barnes said.

"That's proving more difficult."

"They're being obstructive?"

"Not exactly, but it's just slow. We are getting the bum's rush a bit. They don't know how to work the system, or they need to talk to head office, or the person we need is on leave, or they want a DPA waiver, *blah blah blah*."

Barnes turned to the OET manager.

"Get two DCs up to Stansted on blue lights. Today. Take a warrant. Excavate the whole system if you have to. I want that footage. I'll get a call put in to their regional compliance manager while you're en route. Don't put your pen away, either. What's next, Tina?"

"Well, second point of interest is the timeline of movements of Victim One, Liam Lawrence. The day before his body was found, he was involved in a fight in the Curzon cinema during a screening — some disagreement that began in the auditorium and ended up in the foyer. The deceased and one other man. The proprietor, a Rahul Prabh, reported it on 101 after both parties had left; by all accounts, it was queued for a unit, but we never got there."

Barnes looked at the OET rep.

"Already on it, boss," he said, not looking up.

"Get a full statement off Mr Prabh. Cognitive for preference. E-fit too — or, preferably, a freehand sketch likeness. CCTV too. That could be our killer. Tina, back to you."

"Third, we got the recording of the 999 call from ambo."

Tina nodded at Haven, who clicked something on her laptop and plugged a cable into the side of it for the conference screen hookup.

"Have you listened to it?" Barnes asked.

"Yeah. It's brief," Tina said.

"Does it give us anything?"

Tina thought for a moment. "Personally, I don't think so. Male, local accent, reasonably well-spoken, probably thirties or forties. But the ambulance call taker could have told you that without the recording."

"Could it be a match with the description given by Mr Prabh?"

"Well, maybe. But even if you knew the voice, I think it's sketchy."

Barnes looked over Haven's shoulder as the recording arrived in her inbox as an email attachment a moment later.

There was no doubt about it, when Tina Guestling — Flagstaff — became involved, things began to happen.

The recording began to play out of the conference screen's speakers.

Static on the line. Then the trill of the incoming call.

Ambulance control. Is the patient breathing?

Only just. Meads Road, next to the town hall. The old Caffyns garage. In the boarded-up showroom.

What is your name, please, sir?

Don't spare the whip. He's not got long. He's been well and truly gutted.

Sir . . .

End.

He played it again.

Definitely male, middle thirties probably, local accent. An educated voice, as Tina had said. Muffled, something around his face or dropped over the receiver. It didn't sound like the caller was trying to disguise his voice beyond the muffling, but no way to be totally sure.

He played it again, and looked around the room.

"What do we think?" he said.

"If we had a suspect you could probably do a side-by-side voiceprint analysis, but as for a speculative search, I would say forget it," Brynn said. "There's no fingerprint database equivalent for voiceprints. And of course, even if you did identify someone from the voice alone, without any other evidence they'll just claim they broke in for shelter and found the body."

Barnes fought to not roll his eyes. He wanted to end this on a positive note.

"Okay, thanks all. This is great work, Tina, and there's plenty for us to be doing. I'll speak to Gold later about resources, so if you've got something you think needs prioritising but can't service, flag it and we'll bring out the big guns. See you back here in twelve hours. That'll be all."

The team moved out of the conference room with an energy that Barnes attributed entirely to Tina's input. He waited till they had gone, and then headed upstairs to the SIO's office.

He knew he had to speak to — confront — Samson Kane, but couldn't settle on the best approach. Gold — Theresa Baily — probably needed to know, plus in an ideal universe he would have sought Marlon Choudhury's counsel, but the DCI was still in hospital and barely able to communicate.

And you still haven't been to see him, Barnes thought.

Barnes glanced down at his mobile and saw a text message from Kane.

Sent you an email about cover tonight. Sorry.

Speak of the devil, Barnes thought. He knew what the email said before he even opened it. It was a long thread — several plaintive exchanges about sickness and poorly mothers and last-minute trials being listed and immovable training, the long and short of it being that Kane had forwarded it to Barnes with an instruction — albeit one disguised as a request — that he would have to cover the on-call DI rota again tonight.

Barnes composed a reply: *Okay, noted. You know Op Limekiln now has THREE bodies, though, right?* then deleted the second sentence before he clicked SEND.

He shook his head at nobody in particular, then brought up the recording of the 999 call again.

He hit the *play* button and watched as the yellow line indicating the soundwave began to jerk and twitch in time with the sounds coming from the computer's ancient speakers. Barnes watched the progress slider at the bottom of the screen, moving rapidly in step with the brief duration of the call.

He played it again, but this time rearranged the windows on his screen and deliberately placed Duke Kenley's photograph alongside the recording — a black window with a flat yellow line at the bottom.

He played it again, staring at Kenley's image as the yellow line flickered like a flame.

He played it again, and again, and again, fixing his gaze on the eyes.

Is it you, you bastard?

He closed his eyes to concentrate on the sound of the voice. Did he know it — or not? To his irritation, he realised that, for all his tunnel vision — or tunnel hearing — he hadn't spent enough time in Duquesne Kenley's presence to give a conclusive answer. And besides, even if he did conclusively claim that it was a stone bonker match, any half-decent defence lawyer would rip his identification apart. It certainly wouldn't even get to court without some solid corroborative evidence.

He couldn't be sure.

But he knew someone who could.

CHAPTER FORTY-FIVE

"Thank you for agreeing to see me," Barnes said. "By rights I thought you would hate my guts."

"I didn't think I had much of a choice."

"Well," Barnes said, "I suppose that's true. You didn't, but then, neither did we. You know, if you'd said no."

Barnes and DC Natalie Morgan were facing each other across a table in the Western View, a restaurant whose main floor featured floor-to-ceiling glass, together with a viewing platform cut into the rocks overhanging the promenade that somehow resembled the lair of a Bond villain.

There was a low hubbub of voices and the clink of crockery in the background. They were seated by a window, a whole load of sea and sky visible beyond the wooden decked terrace, the horizon slicing through the middle like a dark blue vein.

A waitress brought their drinks — tea for Barnes, some kind of herbal concoction for Morgan. She dunked the bag and stirred the glass mug thoughtfully. She looked good, Barnes thought — fresh-faced, new clothes, magazine-cover hair, a general glow that fell somewhere between merely healthy and radiant. Not the look of someone trapped in a fissure alone in Death Valley, with her kid and her law enforcement career on one side and some kind of *amour fou* with a man who was all-kinds-of-wrong on the other.

"So, do you?" Barnes said. "Hate my guts?"

Morgan shrugged. "I suppose I would, if I thought you were forcing me to continue with the deception. But, the fact remains, Kenley guessed off the bat that I wouldn't choose him over my career, and that if I'd agreed to see him, it was on a survey-and-report basis."

"And he was fine with that?"

She nodded. "He said he would take whatever he could get. 'Betray me if you have to,' were his exact words. He said in any case he would never have told me anything about what he did, for my own protection."

"That stands to reason."

"Look, I've been honest with you, and I've been honest with him. So, yeah, all in all I'm feeling pretty comfortable with myself, all things considered."

Barnes thought about this. "Is he keeping his nose clean?"

"Didn't you hear what I just said?"

"Because if he wasn't, that could compromise you, even if he didn't tell you anything about it."

"You sound like PSD."

"Well, DCI Choudhury is still in hospital, so I'm afraid I'm the next best thing."

"I . . . I didn't know that. Is he okay?"

"He had a stroke. It's too early to say what the prognosis might be."

"I'm sorry. You were . . . are . . ."

Barnes looked out of the window, where a strip of cloud had momentarily covered the sun.

"I'm sorry too. I was sort of hoping he'd go the distance. I've come to rely on that, somewhat. Anyway, back to Kenley."

"I've barely seen him," she said.

"Barely?"

"Yeah. We had a few nights at an Airbnb when he got out — that was nice . . ."

She glazed over momentarily. Barnes resisted the urge to click his fingers in front of her.

". . . a handful of dinner dates. He's been to my place once — he didn't stay — and some phone calls. I haven't spoken to him in weeks."

"Text messages?"

"Not many. He doesn't like them. He figures it's easier for us to read his text messages than listen to his phone calls."

"He's not far wrong. Anyway, it can't have escaped your attention that we've been on the receiving end of the handiwork of a fairly indiscreet serial killer. We're in the midst of it, in fact. Op Limekiln."

Morgan chewed the inside of her lip.

"What are the odds of that?" Barnes continued. "Three weeks after Duke Kenley gets out of jail. Coincidental, no?"

"He didn't have anything to do with it."

Barnes raised an eyebrow.

"What's the motive?" she said. "Your series."

"We're not sure yet."

"He wouldn't kill unless it was a means to an end."

"Are you listening to yourself?"

"It wasn't him."

"A better question might be: how do we know you're telling us the truth?"

She shrugged. "I'll volunteer my phone records, bank statements, DNA samples and invite a voluntary search of my home and car. How's that? You could even bug the place, but I guarantee it would be the most boring radio show you've ever heard. Or you could take me at my word, and this could be one of those weird arrangements where a detective and a gangster live in relative harmony with only a monthly vetting interview to worry about."

"You do know we suspect him of at least two murders, yes?"

She didn't answer, but stopped dunking her bag.

"And there's a safeguarding consideration. You know, for your boy."

She shook her head, keeping it bowed.

"You would suit PSD," she said, eventually. "Your arsehole potential is bigger than I thought."

"I'm just waxing prophetic. Thinking to myself: what would Marlon do? Now, is there anything at all you would like to tell me?"

"If there was, I would tell you."

Barnes sipped his tea and looked out at the Channel.

"I suppose on the one hand, the only ones coming through the door in the middle of the night are going to be us," he said after a time. "The two members of the Keber group that really had the knives out for him are dead. Stratton Pearce was killed in front of me; Roxy Petrescu was found in a London hotel earlier this month. Shot dead."

She looked at him. Held his gaze. Wanting the truth. "Was it him?"

Barnes shrugged. "Pearce, a definite no. I was there. Roxy, who knows? It happened a week after he left prison, which feels a bit coincidental, but there's no evidence pointing to him."

"Tell me when and where it happened, and I'll tell you if he was with me."

Barnes looked at her: *you really want to go there?*

"My point is," he said, "that right now is the best opportunity he's going to get to clean up his life. Consign prison to history. Open an actual bank account. Be with you — honestly."

"What does that mean? Takeaways and movie nights?"

Barnes spread his hands. "Exactly that. Be with you in a way that doesn't necessitate his sweeping for bugs, or keeping a gun under the pillow, or you having to attend monthly vetting interviews. This is his one opportune moment. He won't get another."

Now it was Morgan's turn to look out at the sea. "Well, we both know he isn't going to go and become a trainee business manager at House of Fraser, don't we? He isn't a rat race kind of bloke."

Barnes placed a piece of folded paper on the table. "That's the timeline for Operation Limekiln. Have a look. Compare it with your phone bill, bank statements, things like that. Just satisfy yourself he couldn't have had anything to do with it. For your own peace of mind," he added.

Barnes stood up, and dropped a tip on the table.

"Oh, and there's this."

He took a CD-ROM out from his pocket bearing the Force crest and placed it on top of the tip.

"That's the 999 call to ambulance reporting the first body. One in the morning, in an abandoned garage. Have a listen. It's less than a minute long. Play it in the car, maybe."

He put his wallet away, and looked down at her. She kept her eyes on her cup.

"The tiniest thing, you will tell me, right? If there's a hair out of place. If you don't, you'll just drop yourself in the shit."

He buttoned his jacket and left the restaurant, leaving her looking at the sea.

CHAPTER FORTY-SIX

Barnes was not privy to the logistical conversations, but presumed some thought had gone into the location for the press conference. The obvious choice would have been HQ — decent lighting, plenty of space for the banners and backdrops, the wood panelling of the original main building adding an air of authoritative history. *Don't worry,* it would have conveyed, *we've got this. Killers will come and go, but we will always be here.*

But they had inexplicably opted for the nerve centre — Eastbourne's Major Incident Suite, chucking distance from the dump sites of all of their victims. The building featured a conference room on the ground floor, which had been repurposed for the briefing — all but three of the tables had been removed to make space for rows and rows of chairs. Only one of the three windows opened — and then only an inch or two, held in place as it was by a safety latch — and the sills were at least two feet deep, meaning they had inevitably been used to store old phones and broken pieces of computer equipment. The display stands bearing the Force logo were at least freestanding and self-sufficient, otherwise Barnes would have had visions of the Blu-Tack giving out on one corner just as the questions started.

Barnes peered through a gap in the frosted glass. It was immediately obvious that there weren't enough chairs. The nationals had hoovered up the first few rows, with locals, freelance and other stragglers pressing against the walls as they filed in, trying not to trip over camera equipment and trailing cables.

He felt a sudden surge of butterflies, and he didn't even have a speaking part. That had been made abundantly clear to him by Theresa Baily. Glover's successor was going to lead, with Kane chipping in intermittently. Barnes's role was to sit quietly and listen — some kind of symbolic *look how hard we're thrashing our detectives* totem, which was fine by him.

He disappeared into the bathroom to check his appearance and splash some water on his face. He'd made himself look as smart as possible, but the lack of sleep and long hours were still apparent, and he'd hoped this would bring some kind of kudos to bear, a demonstration of dedication or something. We are living this. Bleeding this. For just a second, he heard Gabby's voice. *You look like shit*, he said in Barnes's head. *That's good.*

When he came back out into the corridor, Baily and Kane were there, together with Andrea Hope from the media department, who was coordinating proceedings. Haven Banks was there also, laptop and clipboard in hand. The tension in the corridor was pronounced, and Kane seemed to be avoiding eye contact with everyone. He couldn't have failed to feel Barnes's stare boring into him. Haven looked more nervous than anybody.

Baily looked at her watch, nodded, and Andrea opened the door, standing aside to let them in. Kane went in first, followed by Baily, then Barnes, and they took their places at the table. Haven took a position off to the side, next to Andrea.

The cameras began to click and flash, reflecting off three full jugs of water accompanied by plastic cups, and the microphones arrayed on the tables made Barnes think of some kind of grey anemone. As they sat down, Barnes again stared hard at Kane, trying to catch his eye, but the superintendent was most definitely not playing.

Baily, sitting in the centre, kicked things off.

"Good afternoon, ladies and gentlemen. Thank you for attending this media briefing today, for Operation Limekiln. My name is Acting Assistant Chief Constable Theresa Baily; I am the Gold Commander for this operation. I'm joined here by the area neighbourhood commander, Superintendent Samson Kane, and the senior investigating officer, Detective Inspector Rutherford Barnes. I will speak for approximately ten minutes, following which we will take ten questions, which should be delivered in an orderly, composed fashion. Please remember that we are holding this briefing to ensure that the public are kept properly informed, but there will be some aspects we cannot discuss as this is very much a live, active investigation. After all, killers watch the news too."

Barnes had to admit, the authoritative tone was pretty impressive, especially as Baily had only been wearing the tipstaff-and-laurels combination on her shoulders for five minutes. Barnes couldn't quite reconcile this with the grief-stricken, hand-wringing, strung-out woman he'd found hovering by his car in the hospital grounds. She'd swallowed the Big Boss manual all right, no doubt about it.

"Operation Limekiln is an investigation into three separate homicides that have taken place across the Eastbourne area in the last three weeks. For a number of reasons, we believe that each of these homicides have been committed by the same individual. We are dealing with a series."

Barnes scanned the faces of the gathered journalists like a hawk watching from a clifftop. A few eyebrows went up, a few frowned, but most remained completely impassive.

"I want to start by extending my sincere condolences to the bereaved families of all the deceased. They are being assisted by specially trained officers, and we are here today with their support.

"The first victim, thirty-nine-year-old Liam Lawrence, was discovered on Saturday, 10 January 2015 at the disused Caffyns showroom in Saffrons Road. Cause of death was blood loss from multiple stab and slash wounds. We believe the victim died no more than an hour prior to being discovered.

"The second victim, forty-four-year-old Carl Jessop, was discovered on Wednesday, 14 January 2015 at the Treasure Island adventure park on Eastbourne seafront. Cause of death was blunt force trauma.

"Indications are that both victims were killed at or near the respective scenes, the significance of which remains a matter of close consideration.

"The third victim, fifty-six-year-old Terry Markham, was discovered again on Eastbourne seafront, at Holywell. The deceased's throat had been cut and he was suspended by the neck from a lamp post. This was a particularly distressing sight, as I'm sure you can imagine, and I must reiterate our previous communication that the publication of any images displaying this crime scene and the body in situ will be regarded as both grossly insensitive and an attempt to pervert the course of justice."

Baily let that hang for a moment. Some hands went up. Baily responded with a single index finger pointed at the ceiling.

"The investigation team is working at pace to identify the perpetrator. We are twenty-four-seven, open all hours. There are several promising leads and a healthy circulation of community intelligence, and I wish to reassure the wider public that is only a matter of time before we apprehend this individual. However, I encourage — in fact, beg — anyone who has any relevant or potentially relevant information, however small, to come forward immediately. It may not seem like much on its own, but it could be the missing piece of the jigsaw. Let us decide. Please, think of the families who have lost loved ones, and pick up the phone."

"Acting Assistant," a voice chirped up from the second row. "Will you refer yourselves to the IPCC if the man kills again before you are able to catch him?"

No hand, he just piped up. There was a moment when Baily looked like she might shut the man down and refer to her earlier request for politeness and decorum, but she looked like she'd been disarmed and distracted by the journalist's mode of address. "Acting Assistant", while not technically incorrect — well, it just didn't sound good.

Baily took a sip of water. Barnes couldn't shake the feeling that this looked like a sign of weakness. He looked at the journalist who had asked the question, but the man was frowning at his notes.

"I was coming to that. We've already done so," Baily said. "It's entirely appropriate to invite external scrutiny at an early stage."

"Does that mean you've messed up?" someone else said.

"That is a non sequitur," Baily said. "Transparency and accountability do not only apply when mistakes have been made; rather, they are a constant. Besides, is it not better to learn lessons at the earliest opportunity?"

"Meaning you've identified something you should have done better?"

"There is always learning," Baily said. "And that's three questions. We can take seven more."

She seemed to be getting into her stride. Barnes chanced a look at Andrea. Impeccably turned out as ever, she was leaning against the wall, hands clasped behind her back — and Barnes thought she looked a little grey.

"What guarantees can you give that the public are not in danger?" someone asked.

Barnes, not for the first time in the last twenty minutes, was glad he had been sworn to silence. Baily, on the other hand, eyed the journalist like they'd asked a fatuous question.

"We are looking for somebody whom we believe to have killed three men in as many weeks," she said slowly. "That person has not yet been identified, never mind apprehended."

"What about motive?" came a question from the front row. "Were the victims known to each other?"

"The investigation team is working on establishing a full victimology to include associations, movements and events of interest."

"If these are random attacks," somebody else asked, "are you saying we should all stay home and lock our doors?"

"We have additional resources being drafted in from across the region," Baily said. "You won't be able to turn a corner in the town centre without bumping into a police officer or seeing a patrol car. We will be out, at all hours, in all weathers, looking for this individual. Our primary concern is catching this killer before he kills again."

Barnes grimaced internally. He knew what was coming next.

"And what if you don't?"

Baily didn't answer. There was a split-second delay; Baily picked up her glass and sipped some water again — which was Kane's cue to pick up the baton.

"We have our very best people working on this. We are connected with the College of Policing, the IPCC and the National Crime Agency to ensure the best skills and experience in the country are supporting the investigative effort. We have profilers, forensic psychologists and behavioural experts advising our team. We will catch this killer."

"Acting Assistant, will you resign if there is another murder before you can make an arrest?"

This time, Baily visibly bristled.

"I have a job to do," she said. "My focus is on retaining strategic command of our overall response, not least the investigation and attendant manhunt, all of which are a team effort and greater than the sum of their parts. Individual CVs, career opportunities and what happens to who are not our concern right now — and nor should they be yours. With any major investigation there is a built-in review phase — but we are a way off that."

Baily eyed Andrea. It took a fraction of a second, but as her eyes had not moved from the cameras since they'd entered the room, it was a palpably obvious movement.

"Thank you, ladies and gentlemen," Andrea said, pushing herself off the wall. "We are done for today. We will convene again in the next twenty-four to forty-eight hours; sooner if there are major developments in the investigation. We are considering holding a confidential briefing. You will be kept updated."

"You said ten questions," somebody muttered. "That was eight."

"Actually, it was nine," Barnes said, as the three of them stood and made to exit. The microphones were still on, and all heads turned. The assembled journalists all stopped filing out and looked over at him.

Baily turned and stared at him. Barnes half expected red-hot lasers to come blasting out of her head.

"That will be all," Andrea said, puncturing the pregnant pause, and the exodus began to slowly resume.

Barnes stayed where he was, scanning the crowd.

The others, meanwhile, had stopped to look at Barnes.

Everyone, that is, except Superintendent Samson Kane, who just carried on walking until he was out of sight.

CHAPTER FORTY-SEVEN

Four down, one to go.
    Barnes looked down at Levi Sadler's body. He didn't know why people always said the dead looked like they were sleeping. A comfort thing, he supposed — they never did, even the ones that went naturally. When you were asleep, your body hummed internally, the mechanisms of a factory working a night shift to keep things ticking. When you died, the cogs stopped turning and you became . . . waste.
    The body was male, naked, sprawled on its back across an inflatable mattress with no bedding besides a grubby pillow. Even in the bedroom's half-light, the skin was visibly grey and mottled.
    It looked fairly straightforward — not least because the last few bodies Barnes had attended had practically had knives sticking out of their backs — with a belt fastened around the left arm and a syringe on the threadbare carpet, along with other makings.
    It was an uninviting council flat in Hampden Park, with rooms leading off the short hallway fed by the front door. The girlfriend was in the next room, giving her account of the night's activities to the on-duty DC. She'd been verging

on hysterical when Barnes arrived; now she was just crying. There was no food and barely any furniture, but there was at least nobody else in the flat, which made life easier. You start introducing children into scenes like this, Barnes thought, and everything gets turned up a notch.

The girlfriend's name was Tammy Wenthill, a regular fixture in the policing calendar. When Barnes had joined she'd been a thirteen-year-old tearaway ripping up her estate; from there, she graduated to both Class A drugs and the carousel of abusive men that supplied them. A clutch of children by different fathers, each one taken into care in turn. It was a wonder she herself was still alive — she'd always just bumped along, pecking for scraps, never really getting any worse but as sure as hell not getting any better.

Barnes moved around the mattress, being careful not to accidentally step — or, God forbid, trip and fall — on the body. There was barely any room between the mattress and the walls; it was a double room in the loosest sense of the word. He moved to the window and looked out. There were no curtains or nets, and the night was clear. The flat was at the rear of the block; at ground level there was a mass of untamed vegetation on a spread of waste ground leading all the way back to the bypass, but this flat was on the fourth floor, and the view out the back wasn't all that bad. Car lights moved steadily along the Golden Jubilee Way flyover, the carriage lights of a train visible as it passed underneath it and past the Willingdon Upper, its progress marked by rows of towering electricity pylons. In the distance, the black, rippling surface of Hydneye Lake was just about visible.

The voices from the room next door slowed down and then stopped, and the night DC appeared in the doorway, notebook in hand. He didn't look happy. The night rota had been stretched for months, which meant detectives from across all the commands had been brought in to cover. The DC's day job was in Child Protection, which meant a regular Monday-to-Friday week. Barnes couldn't blame him for being pissed off. Covering nights for main office was bad enough, but getting called out to a shithole like this one was just rude.

He opened his mouth to speak.

"How is she doing?" Barnes asked.

The night DC closed his mouth again. His expression quite obviously and contemptuously read, *Who gives a shit?*

"It's Tammy Wenthill," he said, as if that explained everything.

Barnes shrugged. "Nobody likes waking up next to a dead body."

The DC shrugged: *whatever*.

"Well, that's more or less what happened. Boyfriend is Levi Sadler. They've been together about a year. There's a baby somewhere in the mix, but Children's Services have it, according to her. She was pretty matter-of-fact on that point."

"Stands to reason."

"They were out in the pub for a few hours last night, scored, and came back here to fix. They fell asleep on the mattress; she woke up, found him cold and called the ambulance. Her take is that he was released from prison a few days ago, having done about nine months, and that he overcooked it. As in, he thought his tolerance would be at the same level as it was when he got put away. He was still using inside, she thinks, but the crap you get in there wouldn't have had the same effect."

"It's a plausible enough theory."

"I thought so too," the DC said, looking relieved. "There's no inconsistent injury, no forced entry, no signs of a struggle. He injected himself, according to her. She fixed first and was already sparko. Her story holds up."

"Okay. We'll print the syringe anyway, but otherwise leave her be. Where did they score the gear?"

"In the pub. The Windsor."

"Description of the dealer?"

"Nothing you could hang your hat on. White male in his late twenties in a baseball cap. Big build. She 'doesn't know him'. That was the only bit she was cagey about; she quite obviously knows who it is."

"Okay. Get undertakers rolling, I'll go and try to prise it out of her."

The DC didn't need telling twice. A DI at a scene involving a dead body telling you to jack up undertakers was the sound of a job being wound down — the DC probably hoped he'd be back in the office to finish up what he started and might even get home on time.

Barnes moved into the kitchen. It was about the size of two telephone kiosks side by side, with dirty chessboard lino and a melamine counter black with mould at the edges. The only thing it had going for it was a complete absence of pots, pans, cups — or, indeed, food to put in them. There was a large paper bag bearing the McDonald's logo next to the sink with rubbish piled high inside it, including two plastic forks sticking out of the top. Last night's romantic dinner, Barnes figured.

Tammy's face was tear-stained, but her expression was fixed in righteous defiance. She was wearing turquoise eyeshadow and thick mascara that had smeared all over her face. She didn't look up when Barnes entered, just stared at the fridge like a recalcitrant pupil in the headmistress's office.

Barnes checked himself. Just because she was upset didn't mean she wasn't going to kick off or be any more helpful than she usually was. The shock of waking up to find her boyfriend dead and cold next to her had probably worn off; by now the presence of the police was no more than just a colossal pain in the arse. Not only that, but self-preservation in the circles she moved in would be contingent on telling Barnes absolutely nothing.

Barnes sat down in a sticky vinyl chair opposite Tammy. She lit a cigarette and blew smoke in his face.

"Tammy."

"What?"

"Who was the dealer?"

She scoffed. "I ain't a grass."

"The man in the Windsor," Barnes said. "The one who sold you the gear. Who was he?"

"Are you deaf? I already told your mate I didn't know him. He was new. Not one of the usuals. Far as I know, he's already had his head caved in."

Barnes raised an eyebrow.

"Well, if he's moving in on someone else's patch and the first thing he does is push dirty gear, he ain't gonna last long, is he?"

"So why not tell me about him?"

"Why you so interested?"

"Tammy, I'm taking the syringe. I'm going to check the surface for your fingerprints."

She scoffed again. "Fill your boots."

"You do know the reason I'm here, yes? The duty DI has to attend all fatal drugs overdoses. It's my call whether we chalk it up to just one of those things, an occupational hazard that people like you face, or whether we put the balloon up and call it a homicide."

Tammy sprang to her feet, causing the chair legs to scrape on the lino and Barnes to wince.

"You fucking what?" She lit another cigarette and began pacing.

Her response was contrived, Barnes knew. An over-the-top reaction to the cops turning up the heat bought you time, enabled you to lawyer up, and maybe even, if you were really lucky, got the decision-maker to back down.

"I don't necessarily need your fingerprints on the syringe," Barnes said. "There's no reason at all I couldn't bring you in for supply, or even manslaughter."

Tammy looked for a moment like she was going to combust, then her body shook a little and she seemed to crumble.

The tears began again.

"I hate fuckin' piggers," she said to her cigarette.

"Come on, Tammy," Barnes said gently. "Sit down."

He pushed the chair towards her. After a moment, she did as she was told.

"I ain't lyin'," she said. "I don't know him. That ain't gonna change after ten hours in a cell."

"Ten?"

She raised an eyebrow and expelled smoke.

"Look," he continued. "I believe you. You don't know the name, that's fine. But if there's someone new moving contaminated drugs around the town, I need to know about it. I don't want anybody else ending up like poor Levi."

She eyeballed him from under a frown, like she knew he was trying to manipulate her.

"Give me a description, at least. I promise you it will go no further than me. No statement, nothing written down. Just information."

"What about me? What do I get for that?"

Barnes shrugged. "Depends on how good your information is. I can't give you cash, but I can put in a good word with the judge the next time you get lifted. Discreetly, of course," he added.

"I want that in writing."

Now it was Barnes's turn to raise an eyebrow.

"Documents get lost, Tammy. They fall into the wrong hands."

"Then I ain't saying nothin'."

"Okay. Suit yourself." He stood up. "See you at the inquest."

He made to go.

"Okay, okay," she said, exhaling like she had the weight of the world on her shoulders. "He was short. Stocky build. Heavy."

Barnes sat back down, making a point of leaving his notebook in his pocket.

"How old?"

"Twenties, I guess. Dark blue tracksuit. Brown baseball cap."

"Beard? Tattoos? Piercings?"

"No beard. Stubble. No tattoos that I saw."

"Hair?"

"I just told you: he was wearing a cap."

Barnes just looked at her. She sighed.

"Dark, I guess. It was shaved around the sides. Like, zero grade."

"Accent?"

"Not sure. Local, maybe."

"Did he say anything?"

"Hardly said a word."

"How did it go down? Did he have a runner?"

She gave a slight shake of the head. Barnes was careful. She was on thin ice now, and she knew it. He half expected a defence solicitor to come barrelling through the door yelling, *Stop, stop, stop!*

"My ears only, Tammy," he said.

"No. He was holding. We met him outside. Then he was gone."

"Anything else you remember about him?"

She shook her head. "Only that he was older."

"Than?"

"Than the usual bunch we get slinging. Thirteen-year-olds on their BMXs. They're everywhere. You wouldn't expect to see someone his age on the street."

Barnes's leg was bouncing up and down madly. He made himself stop it, then got up.

"Thanks, Tammy. That was very useful."

About as useful as a poke in the eye, he thought.

"No, wait," she said. "There was something else."

He turned to face her. "Yes?"

"The . . . guy."

"The dealer."

"He . . . he called Levi by name."

"He knew him?"

"No. Levi said he'd never seen him before. I asked him about it later."

"So he didn't know him. What are you saying, Tammy?"

"For Christ's sake!" she said, exasperated. This was no surprise to Barnes. He was using a tactic that should have come as no surprise to her. Reel them in with promises of nice words to judges and other rewards, then lose interest and leave when the information disappoints. They nearly always chased after you, pleading. From doubting to desperate in the blink of an eye.

"Levi might have just forgotten. He wasn't nature's sharpest mind."

He expected another outburst, but Tammy was looking at the ceiling, apparently replaying the scene in her mind.

"It wasn't like that," she said. "He spoke to him like . . . I don't know. Almost like he'd been looking for him."

There was a knock at the flat door, and Barnes heard the clanking metal and squeaking wheels of the undertakers' gurney.

"They're going to take Levi away now, Tammy. Is there anyone you want me to call? Anyone else you think would want to know that he's passed? Any family?"

She half stood, like she wanted to see him one last time, but then sat back down and lit another cigarette.

"Just get him out of here," she said, waving a hand. "I wish I'd never met the prick."

Barnes left the kitchen and watched the undertakers work quickly and efficiently. Besides the four flights of stairs and the unserviceable lift, it was an uncomplicated assignment — certainly compared with many. Barnes quietly admired them; all he had to really do was turn up and assess. He didn't physically have to get them out himself, and certainly not with the air of sympathy and calm that was the watchword of their profession.

He walked down the brightly lit stairwell and headed to his car. The two uniformed patrol constables that had taken the initial call were still around; Barnes told them to close down the scene and then follow the body to the mortuary, after which they could stand down.

Levi would soon be placed in a cold metal fridge next to his other three murder victims. Barnes felt like he should tell the pathologist to reserve space for a fifth.

He opened the car door, then looked up at the flat, his hand on the window frame, Tammy's description of the dealer on the lookout for Levi Sadler circling his brain.

He wanted to feel relief, that the chain of five had been broken, that the killer hadn't struck again, that the nightmare hadn't come true. This was an overdose, plain and simple. Nothing to suggest there was any connection at all with his peripatetic serial killer.

And if you believe that . . . he thought.

CHAPTER FORTY-EIGHT

Barnes's heartbeat was like pounding footsteps, his mind like a treadmill at full pelt. He drove home, having convened an early morning briefing with his team to bring some quick-time structure to the developments.

He parked on the driveway and looked up at the dark house. Much as he wanted to curl up behind Tamsin's warm, sleeping body, he knew there was absolutely no point trying to sleep, and even less in disturbing the girls, and so he locked the car and headed out on foot. The night was cold, but it was still and dry, and not unpleasant.

Motion helped his mind function. If you wanted your brain to work for you and start coming up with the goods, you needed to be moving. Sitting still was the death knell of creativity. He wondered if that was why he hated meetings so much.

The area he lived in was a pleasant one, made up of wide intersecting avenues and neat, well-kept bungalows. When he and Tamsin had met, they'd both had to shrug off the domiciles of their respective past lives before looking for somewhere they could choose together, and they'd ended up in Wannock, a quiet village on the edge of Eastbourne, more or less equidistant from the South Downs, the sea and the town centre. It ticked every box in the estate agent's spec list, but, to Barnes, the fact that he could walk for five minutes off road into Wannock Glen and lose himself in the unspoiled vegetation of Folkington, Filching and Jevington was a game changer. Not only that, but, if the fecund aroma of greenery drifted in the right way, you could catch the salt air from the coast four miles away. The fact that it was barely a mile from their house to the one he'd shared with his late first wife was one that hadn't played on his mind nearly as much as he'd feared.

A pub dealer hitherto unknown to Tammy Wenthill — that wasn't a distinction many could lay claim to. Tammy was part of the furniture, and anyone on the street she didn't know was worthy of mistrust and suspicion. The dealer had been "looking" for Levi, she thought, and the general vibe of the guy gave her the willies.

It was only one of several potential theories, but it was the only one that seemed to be growing any legs. Was the dealer in the pub their killer? Had he changed the MO just for the sheer bumfluffery of it? If so, Tammy Wenthill might be the only person to have seen their killer in the flesh.

The thought that she was in danger hit him so hard it stopped him dead in his tracks. He could hear nothing but his heartbeat in his ears and the night wind whispering to the trees and thickets that surrounded him. Over to the west, a silent pulse of lightning heated the sky over the Cuckmere Valley.

He was careful not to turn an ankle as he picked his way back over the uneven terrain as fast as he could. He called the control room as he started the engine; even so, he was still back at Tammy's flat a good eight minutes before the first patrol car.

The communal door was shut, and the "trades" door release button didn't work out of hours, but the general appearance of the entrance was pretty ropey, and it popped open after a couple of shoulder barges.

He barrelled up the stairwell — still brightly lit, even at two in the morning — up to Tammy's flat. No blood in the stairwell, no smashed glass, and the door was on its hinges. That was encouraging.

He hammered on the door, before realising that such a rude attempt meant one of two things in Tammy's book — a disgruntled supplier owed some money or the police coming to raid the place, which meant she was either going to come out fighting or hide and wait for it to be over.

There was a third possibility, of course — that she had fixed again and was dead to the world, figuratively if not literally.

The square of frosted glass in the centre of the door had a crescent-shaped hole in the corner about the size of a penny. Barnes put his mouth to it. There was a cool draught carrying the faint stink of Levi's passing.

"Tammy, it's DI Barnes. We spoke earlier. I just want to know you're okay. Open the door, please, or I'll have to force it."

Nothing. He waited one minute and then began to kick at the door — just as a bleary-eyed Tammy Wenthill pulled it open. She was in her pyjamas, a cigarette between her lips, her face screwed up from the rude awakening.

Barnes checked his kick before it connected with her, but he still stumbled and fell into the doorframe.

"What the fuck is going on?" she grumbled.

Barnes put his hands on his knees, surprised by his own relief.

"Are you all right?" she said.

He straightened up. Now she looked worried. There was no point trying to fudge this, he thought. As it was, she helped him out.

"This is about the dealer, isn't it? In the Windsor."

No flies on her, he thought. It was the first thing she went to.

"Can I step in?" Barnes said.

She pulled a face and then walked back into the flat, leaving the door open, just as blue lights began to strobe through the windows in the stairwell.

Tammy got as far as the kitchen, then turned to face Barnes in the doorway. He hovered in the hallway. Her face said *get to it*.

He swallowed. "I have . . . reason to believe that your life is in danger."

Her eyebrows went up, then she scoffed. "Because of some mad hatter pushing dirty gear?"

"Look, I can't go into the detail right now. But, yes, this is about the man in the Windsor. It might be nothing, but . . . you know, when I turned up here he was the first thing you mentioned. And you said yourself you thought he was looking for Levi."

"Yeah, well, he found him. And now Levi is dead. So, mission accomplished, as far as he's concerned, right?"

"I can't discount that the hotshot wasn't meant for you."

He didn't really think that was true, but it certainly seemed to focus her mind. Her eyes widened and her pale face looked almost ghostly in the flat's feeble light.

"Me? Why the hell would he want to kill me?"

"You tell me. Don't owe anybody any money, steal somebody's boyfriend, anything like that?"

She pursed her lips. "Even if I had, that's not how it would go down. Sneaking around in the shadows like that. Street people don't work like that."

Barnes frowned as a thought occurred to him.

"Did you fix from the same baggie?"

She shook her head. "I had my own."

"Okay. Look, I'll know more in the next couple of days about what it was he actually took. In the meantime, I think it would be sensible for you to stay in a hotel. Our expense, of course."

She scoffed again. "No way. You think I'm in danger now, that's a good way to make it a sure thing. I'll take my chances."

"I thought you might say that." He held out a business card. She refused it, and he put it back in his pocket. "I'll check in with you tomorrow or the day after. Get to a doctor. Try to stay clean. If there is bad gear in circulation, you don't want to take the risk."

She rolled her eyes. He'd made a note of her number from the ambulance 999 call log. He keyed it into his phone and dialled. The tinny sound of Katy Perry's "Firework" blared from the bedroom.

"Good," he said. "Keep your phone with you. Keep it charged. Don't blow me off and change the number. If you can, get someone over here to be with you. Or better still, go somewhere else. The hotel offer remains open until I know more about what went on."

She nodded.

"The patrol car that was here earlier is going to wait outside. Just for tonight. They won't disturb you."

He made to go.

"Hey."

He stopped at the doorway to the flat and turned back.

"Look, I . . . thanks for warning me."

* * *

Barnes stepped into the incident room and flicked the overhead lights on. The team needed to rest and recharge, of course, but the lack of activity, the emptiness, the fact that there was more activity outside the windows — out on the deserted Levels, Southbourne Lake and the golf course beyond — than in here, spoke volumes about his case. If the press — or, God forbid, the bosses — were given an insider's spotlight on the mechanics of a serial killer investigation and saw this inertia — complete with the lights off — they'd kill each other to get in first with the *CLUELESS COPS* headline.

Maybe he was out of his depth. Maybe it was as simple as that. He could just admit it — underqualified, didn't have the experience, whatever — and throw the towel in. He could go back to managing a team treading their way through case files of burglaries and tinpot assaults, like hamsters on a wheel.

He knew what the answer would be. He'd be told to stop his mithering and crack the fuck on. No senior command wanted to put a substandard detective in charge of a case like this, but the fact remained that Barnes was as good as they had, and they all knew it. A generation of major crime SIOs had retired at more or less the same time a couple of years earlier, taking their wealth of experience with them. A couple had died not long after leaving; Barnes didn't know the others. In any case, it wasn't a tap they could just turn back on. Back in the early twenty-first century you could catch three or four murders a year and add them to your CV, but then they had started to dry up. He supposed it was a good thing — no one was going to complain about a declining murder rate, even if it did mean your senior investigators didn't have the flying hours under their belt when they did happen.

And besides, he didn't really believe it. Case for case, he'd worked more homicides than any other DI in the Force, never mind the division. Colleagues, loved ones, innocents — he'd been front and centre for practically all of them. He'd worked the kidnap of his own family from this very incident room, for God's sake. Not only that, but he knew that this case was still a tinderbox and not cold by any stretch — it only took a phone call from an analyst, a blink-and-you'll-miss-it sighting from a dog walker who nearly didn't bother to call in, a twist of new Crimestoppers information — or, of course, another body — and the whole thing could erupt in a blaze.

He looked down at his work phone. Countless missed calls, voicemails, text messages. He didn't have the inclination to go through all of them. The important ones would keep trying. The rest would just be noise.

As if to punctuate the point, Tina's number appeared on the screen as he was looking at it. He had quite a few missed calls from her — since about the time the Levi Sadler overdose came in, as it happened.

"Hi, Tina."

"Boss? You still around?"

"Yes, still on. Just got back from number four."

"Levi Sadler?"

"Yes, that's him."

"Anything in it?"

"I want to be relieved by the fact that it was just an OD. Nothing on the surface. Just looks like he wanted to celebrate getting out of prison but misjudged how much his tolerance levels had dropped. But that's too much to hope for. Too much of a coincidence."

"You're thinking someone deliberately injected him?"

"Not 'someone'. *Him*."

"You don't think it was the girlfriend?"

"Tammy? It's possible, but I doubt it. I spent some time with her — nothing out of place, other than she was unusually verbose. I didn't expect the usual tricks to work, but she surprised me."

"One to go, then."

And I still haven't confronted Samson Kane, Barnes thought.

"Hold on, I can check ANPR for the rental Passat. Give me a sec."

Barnes gave her Tammy Wenthill's address and the times of both the 999 call and the drug deal in the Windsor pub, and heard a keyboard clacking in the background.

"One hit," she said. "Eastbourne town centre an hour after the time she says the deal happened."

"Why am I not surprised?" Barnes said. "How the hell haven't we found that car yet? We might need to go to the national media on this."

"Want me to speak to Andrea?"

"No, I'll do it. What about Lee Flathill?" he said. "They had any luck with finding him?"

"Not so far. And even if they do, the police have been his sworn enemy since he was toilet-trained. They try to give him an Osman, he'll tell them to shove it up their wotsits."

"Even so, we need to up the ante. There's an immediate threat to his life; we need his bank accounts, phone movements, APWs, media appeal — the works. He's next, Tina, and may only have days, if not hours."

"Okay. Leave that with me, I'll sort it." He heard her fingers tapping a keyboard in the background. "What do you want the media appeal to say?"

"I don't know, anything. Say he's a suicidal missing person and we just want to know he's okay. Less chance of litigation and more chance he'll see it and come in, if only to correct us."

"Got it. Anyway, that's not why I'm calling you."

"Go on."

"Sketch likeness back on Liam Lawrence's cinema assailant. Ten years from now I'll be able to scan it like a fingerprint and run an automatic comparison against all the images on our database. But for now we're going to have to go old school and put posters up. I've emailed it to you."

"Ok, fantastic. Anything on the CCTV from the hire car office?"

"Still working on that."

Barnes's phone began the strange double trill of another incoming call. He looked at the display and inhaled. Natalie Morgan. It was one in the morning.

"Tina, I'll call you back. Great work."

He ended the call and accepted the inbound call without accidentally hanging up, which was no small miracle.

"Natalie?"

"Boss. I didn't wake you up, did I?" Her voice was tight, brittle, small.

"No, you didn't. What's up? Are you okay?"

"I looked at that timeline you sent me," she said, and Barnes could tell she'd been crying. "The night . . . the first victim was found."

"Yes."

"Kenley was with me. At the Airbnb I mentioned."

Barnes felt his heart sink a little. "All night?"

"No."

Barnes felt like he'd been stung, but he kept it under wraps. She was clearly fragile.

"Go on, Natalie," he said, softly. "You're doing the right thing."

"He left after midnight. Maybe closer to one. We were in bed. He crept out. He must have thought I was asleep."

"What time did he get back?"

"I don't know. I left. I gave it an hour, then packed my stuff and left. I've not returned his calls since."

"Okay. Okay, Natalie. Good work. Are you all right? Do you want to come in and debrief in person? I'm on all night." Barnes was still processing. He wasn't quite sure what to say.

"There's something else."

"Oh yes?"

"The voice on the recording. The 999 call."

"Yes?" Barnes stood rigid, the phone pressed hard to the side of his head.

"It's him. Kenley. Kenley made that call."

"You're sure?"

"One hundred per cent."

CHAPTER FORTY-NINE

Kenley muttered to himself and lit another cigarette. He was slowly narrowing down the list of potential suspects for whoever had ripped off his cocaine, but it was slow going, and no more scientific than keeping a vigil outside the gates of the police station and gradually reducing the list of possibles based on set variables — destination, time and pattern of movements, even mode of transport. The two things going against him were that, without Liam Lawrence, he couldn't even get a physical description of the thief, plus there was no guarantee that he even worked here. He might be Metpol, NCA, BTP, and enjoyed commuting from the seaside.

It didn't make sense to him. In prison, he had been able to generate the contacts and the intelligence to both zero in on and get in front of his nemesis, Roxy Petrescu — and Roxy had been an international ghost. Now, on the outside, the first contact he'd established had watched his own guts being hauled out within twenty-four hours of meeting Kenley, which seemed to have put other prospective candidates off applying for the job.

He gave it up. This was getting him nowhere. He'd practically been living in the rental car — he needed to find a hotel, clean up, get a bottle of something strong and either pay for some company or make one last attempt to reconnect with Natalie. Once he'd scratched that particular itch, he could regroup and go about his attempts to track down the cocaine-stealing cop in a slightly more ordered, strategic way.

He made a tactical detour back to the Probation-approved flophouse he had a room in just off Marine Parade — for show as much as anything — and then walked half a mile or so inland to a convenience store off Seaside for milk, beer, pastries and a newspaper. He shoved them all in a basket and was standing in the queue when his phone buzzed in his pocket. He pulled it out, and tried to ignore the rather adolescent heart-skipping feeling of seeing a new text message from Natalie, the first one in yonks.

He opened it.

It just said: *Kenley? x*

He frowned, thumb hovering over the device as he tried to work out her meaning, and by turns, a suitable reply.

He paid for his shopping while simultaneously typing, *U ok?*

He headed for the door, not taking his eyes from the phone.

She messaged again: *I'm sorry x*

Kenley frowned, confused. "What the . . . ?"

The automatic doors to the shop slid open.

Kenley looked up from his phone, and stopped.

Blocking the way was a man in a navy blue suit, hands by his sides, feet shoulder-width apart as if setting his stance for some kind of impact.

It took a second or two, but Kenley recognised him.

"Good morning, Duquesne," said DI Rutherford Barnes.

"What's this about?" Kenley said.

Barnes reached into his pocket with one hand, and pulled out a piece of paper. He unfolded it, and held it up.

Kenley squinted. It was a pencil likeness of an angry-looking face. He was never going to admit it out loud, but it was a pretty fucking good likeness.

Barnes reached behind his back with the other hand, and produced a pair of handcuffs that he held up and dangled off a finger. "Shall we?"

Kenley nodded towards the picture. "Looks nothing like me."

Kenley's phone buzzed again, and he instinctively looked down at it. He swiped the screen to unlock the phone — as he did so, four uniformed officers, two on each side, moved swiftly in from the left and right and took Kenley to the ground. The handcuffs went on with a metal chatter, while one of the officers grabbed Kenley's phone from his hand while it was still active, and promptly cancelled the auto-lock feature.

Kenley found his cheek mashed into the pavement. Hands roughly went through his pockets and pulled out his car keys. Out of the corner of his eye he saw one of the officers waving the keys around until the rental — which he'd parked on the other side of the street — made a *blip-blip* sound with the hazards going.

"Found his car."

Barnes stepped forwards. "Duquesne Kenley, you're under arrest for the murders of Liam Lawrence, Terry Markham, Levi Sadler and Carl Jessop. You do not have to say anything, but it may harm your defence if you do not mention when questioned something that you later rely on in court. Anything you do say may be given in evidence."

His teeth scraping the concrete, Kenley grinned. "Sorry, Rutherford. You've got the wrong man."

CHAPTER FIFTY

Find Samson Kane.

It wasn't the usual way for a DI to contact an ACC, but this was not a usual situation. Barnes sent the text message to Theresa Baily and then stepped into the interview room, closing out the echoing chatter of the custody block's main atrium. The windowless grey room was lit by a pale white bulb, and still bore the faint stink of the previous occupants. It had clearly been a long interview.

Barnes sat down at the table, spent some time arranging his papers, and then logged into the video recording system to start the interview.

Kenley sat opposite. His arms were folded, his face cocksure and defiant, but being shoehorned into a paper suit had taken the edge off ever so slightly. Barnes recognised the solicitor, an entirely dislikeable Australian named Peverell, who had long, rabbit-white hair swept back over his head, a battered leather jacket and tiny, yellowing eyes behind tinted spectacles. He made a show of being ensconced in his notes, but Barnes could tell he was hyper-tuned to the tension in the room.

Barnes opened the interview and went through the preamble — PACE rights, caution, Kenley's right to access a copy of the recording.

Then he sat back in his chair and braced for *no comment*.

Barnes opened his mouth.

"You've got the wrong man," Kenley said.

"Go on," Barnes said.

"I didn't kill anybody. I don't know those names you mentioned. I could prove it, but . . . I don't have to. *You* have to prove I *did* do it."

Barnes placed the sketch likeness down on the table. "These things are done by a real artist. We use a freelancer. So much better than those digital e-fits, which just look like sex dolls. This one is uncanny. He's got the hair spot on."

"Probably copied it off a photograph."

"The witness providing the description says that this person—" Barnes jabbed a vertical index finger onto the picture — "beat up Liam Lawrence less than twenty-four hours before he was murdered."

"That doesn't mean I killed him."

"You were there at the scene. He was still alive when you called the ambulance."

"Why would you say I called the ambulance? How could you possibly know that?"

Barnes pressed a button and inserted the working copy CD of the ambulance's 999 call into the drawer of the player.

Ambulance control. Is the patient breathing?

Only just. Meads Road, next to the town hall. The old Caffyns garage. In the boarded-up showroom.

What is your name, please, sir?

Don't spare the whip. He's not got long. He's been well and truly gutted.

Sir . . .

"Could be anyone."

"Natalie Morgan, Kenley. She says one hundred per cent that this is your voice."

"Yeah well, a woman with an axe to grind would say anything."

"She also said you were with her in bed the night Liam Lawrence died. She says you left around midnight and didn't come back."

Barnes left that hanging for a moment. He saw Kenley swallow.

"How would she know the time?"

"She was awake, Kenley."

Kenley opened his mouth. Barnes followed up with another jab before he could speak.

"The same rental car was seen near the first three crime scenes a matter of hours before the bodies were discovered. The same car, Kenley."

"But not the one you caught me with today, though, right?"

"Rentals can be chopped in, switched up, changed round. That's Murder 101. The point is, the hire agreement was in the name of Ben Blackwater. That's one of your documented aliases, Kenley. No, better, it's your *real name*, isn't it?"

Kenley's brow furrowed.

"You're saying I've got the wrong man. I'm saying that if that's true, then the real killer has stitched you up like a kipper. This does not look good for you."

"Do you have any CCTV from the car rental transaction, officer?" Peverell didn't look up from his scribbling.

Barnes looked directly at Kenley. "That CCTV is inbound, Kenley. Any minute now."

"We look forward to it with a keen sense of anticipation," Peverell said.

Barnes ignored him, and leaned across the table. "You do know those names, Kenley. You know all of them. I have reason to believe that there is one more named individual at risk. I think the killer — you — are working your way through that list, and you are going to stay in a cell until I can be sure that individual is safe."

"Officer, I don't think that is entirely—"

Barnes finally looked at Peverell. "It's time for you to leave."

Peverell's eyes widened, then he looked to Kenley and back to Barnes, an incredulous *the sheer audacity* smile on his face.

Barnes held his stare, and the smile slowly dropped.

"You cannot be serious."

"I'm always serious," Barnes said, and stood up.

"On what grounds?"

"On the grounds that this is no longer an evidential interview. We'll resume that later. This is now an intelligence interview, and your services are no longer required."

Barnes stopped the recording, walked to the door and held it open.

"This is a bloody outrage, mate. I want to speak to the superintendent."

"It's funny you should say that," Barnes said. "So do I."

He looked directly at Kenley.

"It's alright, chap," Kenley said to Peverell. "You can chip off. I'll call you when I need you."

Peverell slowly gathered his things and blustered his way out, dialling a number on his phone and making loud indignant noises into it as he walked off down the corridor.

Barnes shut the door and sat down again.

"Well, that was—" Kenley began.

"You were friends with Samson Kane. All those years ago."

Kenley's eyes widened: *How could you possibly know that?*

"He and I visited you in prison back — when, a year ago? Two? You go back all those years and nobody said anything to me about your teenage bromance. Including him."

"That sounds like something you should ask him about."

"I would, if I could find him."

"Sounds like he should be in this chair, not me."

"You were friends at school. He used to get beaten up by his stepfather, Lee, protecting his mother. He was in and out of the cells for one reason or another. Now all the people that wronged him — wronged both of you — are turning up dead. He drifted to the police, you drifted the other way. If anyone's got the capability, the track record — the *practice* — to take another life in anger, it's you."

"So you say."

"Did you know Roxy Petrescu is dead?"

"Who?" Kenley said, eyeing Barnes closely.

"Don't worry. If I wanted to ask you about that I'd have to get your brief back in here. But there's no evidence linking you to it, even with all the safety nets that Probation supposedly drop over what violent criminals get up to when they reintegrate with society. Just seems odd it happened so soon after you were released."

"The world is a small place. Full of coincidences."

Barnes began to arrange photographs of the bodies on the table.

Liam Lawrence — a pile of intestines on a steel mortuary table.

Carl Jessop — a heap of skin and clothing dumped in the freezing rain.

Terry Markham — a dead silhouette swinging gently by the neck, the hulk of the Seven Sisters behind him bathed in early morning light.

And Levi Sadler — shut down by a hotshot.

Kenley looked down.

"You really think I did this? Come on, Rutherford, really?"

Barnes suddenly leaned across the table.

"Liam Lawrence, Carl Jessop, Terry Markham and Levi Sadler. You knew them all as a boy. Now they're all dead."

"I . . ."

"Lee Flathill, Kenley. Where is he? What have you done with him? Is he dangling by his feet in a lock-up somewhere? Have you and Kane got together to settle a twenty-year score?"

"That's not my style, Rutherford. I'm strictly business. And I think you know that."

Barnes exhaled heavily, then stood up, opened the door and called the solicitor back in.

It took a while, because the thought of being ejected and then re-summoned like a subordinate yo-yo was clearly sticking in Peverell's craw, and he shuffled back down the corridor like a lightning rod of anger.

He sat down, sullen, and Barnes restarted the interview.

"You've just flushed your prosecution case down the toilet," Peverell said to Barnes. "You do know that?"

"Don't worry," Kenley said, as he gave Peverell a gentle elbow in the ribs. "You didn't miss anything."

He grinned at Barnes, who restarted the recording and resumed the interview.

He'd only just got through the preamble when there was a sharp knock at the door. Barnes cursed under his breath. He heard heavy, almost laboured breathing.

"It's all go today," Kenley said.

"I'm in the middle of an interview," Barnes said, not turning around, not taking his eyes from Kenley.

"I know. Sorry. For the benefit of the tape, Sergeant Mike Butcher, custody officer, entering the interview at 1227 hrs."

Barnes paused the recording. "What do you want, Mike?"

Butcher bent down till he was inches from Barnes's ear. "Call for you at the bridge, boss."

"Didn't you tell them I was in interview?"

"It's Tina Guestling. You're going to want to take it. She says it sounds like it might be number five."

* * *

The Curzon had been on borrowed time ever since the multiplex down at the Crumbles had opened in 1990, but its demise had rapidly hastened in the few short weeks since Duke Kenley smashed Liam Lawrence's head into a full-length glass display cabinet. Almost overnight, repeat pattern-posters covered the new chipboard hoardings on the windows and doors, and the concrete pillars that gated the now-opaque front doors were wrapped in spirals of garish advertisements. *GYLLENHAAL/ NIGHTCRAWLER* was still emblazoned on the white *Now Showing* display board in vivid red letters, some four months after its release. It seemed somehow appropriate.

There had been talk in the papers of reopening the cinema as a bingo hall, or of razing it to make way for a new block of student halls of residence, or of turning it into some form of chic-modern drinking den. In any event, two short weeks after Liam Lawrence had been cut to ribbons, the site had already been fenced off awaiting demolition.

Barnes made his way to the scene; when he arrived, the building was still ablaze, and didn't look to be abating any time soon. Trumpton looked like they had it more or less under control, but to Barnes's mind it looked like it had been burning rather longer than he felt comfortable with.

Both ends of Langney Road had been cordoned off and every residence within the cordon was being evacuated under the watchful command of Georgia Brass — did that woman ever catch a break? More pumps seemed to be arriving every minute and were converging on the scene in a parade of red steel; Barnes had counted six when something heavy thumped into his shoulder from behind, knocking him off balance.

"Hey, get out of the way." A massive firefighter shoulder-barged past Barnes as he ran towards the building to help a colleague with a hose. "No civilians inside the cordon."

Barnes reached inside his jacket for his warrant card, but the firefighter was already gone. There was nothing more he could do until the fire was out, and even then, he'd have to wait for the building to cool sufficiently for the fire investigators and Scenes-of-Crime to get inside. Even here, almost a hundred feet from the building itself — and technically *outside* the cordon, thank you very much, Mr Fire and Rescue — the heat was like a wall.

He wanted to give the fire crews a heads-up. Unlike them, he wasn't starting with a blank canvas. Unlike them, he knew — not a guess, he *knew* — they would find a body.

And he knew who it was.

* * *

Barnes made his way back to the incident room. Tina Guestling — Flagstaff — and the rest of the Op Limekiln team were there. The room was rigid with tension.

"Boss, I've got a feed from control room CCTV on the monitors," Tina said.

She fiddled with a control pad and joystick, and brought up images of the Curzon from various angles on nine different screens. Tentacles of flame were punching through the windows and roof of the art deco building like some orange creature trying to escape from within, while thin, rather feeble looking white lines of water streamed from the firefighters' hoses.

"This is now?" Barnes said.

Tina nodded. "This is a live stream. No pun intended," she added.

"What does this have to do with Lee Flathill?"

"Couple of guys were going at it outside. Squaring up. They realised they were turning heads, and one dragged the other inside the cinema — presumably to carry on their beef in private."

"I don't mean to sound cynical, but that's a daily occurrence in that part of town."

"Agreed. We didn't start getting 999 calls until the fire started. It was only when we pitched up on scene and started canvassing that the information about the two men arguing came out."

"And definitely Lee?"

Tina shrugged. "He was named as one of the two. He's pretty well known around town."

"Do we have footage of the fight?"

"We do, but it's not brilliant. Time-lapse footage. Operators are working on getting us a copy. Georgia Brass is pulling CCTV from shops opposite the scene."

Barnes put his hands on his hips and looked at the floor. He'd failed.

"That's a full house," he said. "And unless this fight happened before Duquesne Kenley got arrested, it can't be him."

Tina gently placed a hand on his shoulder. "He might still be an accomplice."

"He was in a police cell. There is no better alibi."

"Barnes, there's plenty we can do. We can interrogate his phone, social media, vehicle movements. There could be enough for a conspiracy charge."

But Barnes wasn't hearing her.

"He was right," he said. "Kenley was right. We've got the wrong man."

***

His head down, Barnes walked slowly down Hammonds Drive, past timber yards, scaffolding lorries and bleeping forklifts. He looked at his watch. There was still plenty of time left on Duquesne Kenley's custody clock before he needed to trouble a superintendent for an extension, and he intended to use every minute of it.

He looked at his phone. As always, there were a ton of missed calls, including a boatload from Andrea Hope. Much as he enjoyed listening to her sugar-dusted Roedean tones, she was his conduit to the newspapers, and was not likely to be bringing him good news.

He brought up Samson Kane's number. He didn't expect the superintendent to answer, but he still couldn't bring himself to dial the number. Baily hadn't called him back either, but, he supposed, ACCs were busy people.

When he arrived at the custody centre, Peverell and Kenley were still in the interview room. Barnes opened the door and was nearly sick — both of them were wearing identical, shit-eating grins.

Peverell stood and made a show of gathering his belongings. He was clearly going to enjoy this.

"Well, thank you both for your time. I trust you will send me the custody log and release papers when my client is reacquainted with his liberty."

"When that happens, I surely will," Barnes said from the doorway. "There's a few niceties to get through yet."

Peverell's face fell. His pink skin turned red; under his white, swept-back hair he looked a little like a snow monkey.

"What . . . can you possibly mean?"

"Your client is being held on a quadruple-murder charge. You don't think I'm just going to turn him loose?"

Peverell sat back down. "This . . . is an outrage."

"You said that earlier."

"Inspector, I must insist I speak with your superintendent. You were expecting a fifth victim to be located. As far as I can make out, that has just happened — while my client was in your custody. If that doesn't prove beyond reasonable doubt that he is innocent, then what the sheer buggery does?"

"Until I've interrogated his phone, his computer, his social media and his bank accounts and am completely satisfied he isn't part of a conspiracy, then he will remain here until I have completely exhausted all my options to extend his detention."

"But—"

"As a minimum, he will be in a cell until the fire is out and the scene has cooled sufficiently for me to get in there and see what we have. If there's a body, then there's a whole load more questions to ask."

"Inspector—"

Kenley put a hand on Peverell's forearm. Unlike that of his brief, Kenley's grin hadn't slipped.

"It's alright, Rob. Save your breath. I can kick it here for a bit. I wonder if the settlements for wrongful imprisonment lawsuits are calculated by the hour."

Peverell nodded, and then pushed past Barnes and went to sit in the consulting room, where he began another series of loud phone calls.

Barnes took Kenley back to the bridge in silence, and caught the eye of a jailer.

"This one back in the traps, please. I'll be back in a few hours."

"Right you are, boss. Got a summary of interview for the log?"

Barnes eyed Kenley. "All offences denied."

CHAPTER FIFTY-ONE

Barnes spent the next few hours in the incident room, largely pacing. Fire and Rescue had got the blaze under control, but it was going to be anything up to twenty-four hours before it was cool enough to get in and have a look. He thought about sitting down and starting to sketch out an investigative policy, but couldn't concentrate.

"Barnes?"

He turned round. Tina was standing there, one hand resting on her cane.

"Why don't you go home for a bit?"

"You're joking, surely."

"We need you on your game. Take advantage of the lulls."

He shook his head. "I can't."

She held out a brown A4 envelope.

"What's this?" he said.

"CCTV stills from the rental car agency."

He looked at her, then ripped it open. The lack of excitement in her voice already told him what he was going to see.

The stills were pretty good quality. The car rental office was busy in the image — a camera mounted from a top corner of the room, showing three heads behind the counter and five or so customers milling around in the waiting area.

Their man was standing at the counter. Short, white, commando T-shirt clinging to his heavy frame, and jeans. Face largely obscured by a baseball cap, but still obviously younger than Barnes had been thinking. A good match for Tammy Wenthill's description of the mysterious hotshot dealer in the Windsor pub.

But not Duquesne Kenley.

Not Samson Kane either, which was a small shred of relief.

But not the man in the cells.

"FIB are speaking with the NCA and the Crime Faculty. Looking at trying to explore some of the facial recognition capabilities that are in development."

"You need to be able to see a face for that."

"We're trying."

Barnes reinserted the images into the envelope and handed them back.

"Think he's done?" she said. "If we find Lee Flathill in the cinema, the list is complete. What does he do now?"

"I don't know," Barnes said. "But I'm going to take your advice. I'm going home."

* * *

When Barnes had crept into bed, he'd hoped for a quick turnaround; that is, get in without disturbing anyone, then wake early and sneak out before anyone else stirred.

He took Tamsin a cup of tea and gently kissed her ear, and had almost enacted his plan — debating whether or not to chance firing up the percolator before he left the house — but, as he slipped his shoes on, he was thwarted by the sound of little footsteps.

He looked up, one foot on a kitchen chair, toothbrush still wedged in his mouth, and saw Ellie in the doorway in her

Octonauts pyjamas. She was rubbing her eyes, Paddington trailing along behind her.

"Where you going, Daddy?"

"Just work, honey," he said, ignoring the sudden tension in his brain. She usually called him Barnes, but sometimes — when she was half-asleep, in fact — it just slipped out. He knew he should correct her, but sometimes it just felt like it would do more harm than good. "How come you're up? It's a quarter to six in the morning."

"I heard you."

He went over to her and lifted her up. "Well, I'm sorry I woke you," he said, sitting her on the counter.

"I don't want you to go to work."

"I know, but—"

"Will you take me with you?"

"Certainly one day we could . . . wait. Are you bigger?"

She perked up, puffing her chest out. "I growed. While I was sleeping."

Barnes took a step back. "Wow, I . . . I think you actually did."

It was slight, but she was definitely taller, and her chin looked ever so slightly less soft. Just how much had he missed of this?

"Listen, I'm going to make a couple of calls," he said. "Are you hungry?"

She nodded. He lifted her down and sat her at the kitchen table. She eyed him over her cereal while he made three separate calls on his mobile, totalling — he knew, because he counted — seven minutes. When they were over, he pocketed the phone and Ellie began to tell him, unbidden, the story of her week in some detail, and Barnes felt the sting of being briefed on stuff he really should have known first-hand, and sooner.

"You have to take me to school today," she announced suddenly.

"I . . ." and then he stopped. She was right. It was his day to take Maggie and Ellie to school.

Arriving at work after the school run at nine in the morning — or, in some cases, a little after — was something Barnes had taken a while to get used to, not least because the earliest office arrivals scored the most points in the great unspoken who-works-hardest competition. Barnes had long given up trying to score second-guessed brownie points in the promotion bunfight, but he nevertheless liked being in early to be fully briefed and ready for when the phone rang and some senior officer wanted to know the minutiae of an overnight case — sometimes because they needed to know, and sometimes because keeping CID middle managers on their toes in a state of constant nervous tension was good sport. He'd squared with it pretty quickly, however, and figured that time spent being impatient and rushing to leave the playground were experiences that the girls would inevitably remember. The job would just have to cope without him for half an hour.

Besides, doing the school run one day a week was a scaled-down stab at normality. There'd been a period when Maggie wouldn't leave his side. After her ordeal at the hands of an operation only a year so previously, cooked up by an unholy alliance comprising Tamsin's ex-husband and Barnes's now-deceased nemesis, Stratton Pearce. On the surface of it, she'd recovered remarkably well, but the scars were like the tides — on some days they were calm and invisible, on others they lashed the shore and roared as they did so. As Tamsin had said, Barnes had been the one to find her and get her to safety, and it was some considerable time before she'd felt able to be in the presence of an adult without either her mother or Barnes being present — preferably both.

He made tea and brought Ellie a second bowl of Cheerios, and she chatted to him for another half an hour or so, by which time Tamsin and Maggie were starting to stir. Tamsin shuffled in and wrapped her arms around Barnes's shoulders from behind. Her dressing gown smelled of hairspray and body lotion.

"Sorry to wake you," he said. "I'm getting them ready for school."

"No school today," she said, in a sleepy voice. "Inset day."

Ellie's eyes widened in surprise. "Yes!"

"Want to go to the zoo?" Barnes said, ruffling Ellie's hair.

Any doubts he might have had about such a spontaneous change of plan were banished by the delight lighting up her face.

Even on a January weekday, Drusillas would be busy, and so Barnes hustled them all to get ready and out the door posthaste in order to be somewhere near the front of the queue. Tamsin cobbled together rain macs and some packed lunches and in another forty-five minutes they were in the car.

They headed out of Eastbourne, the traffic slow and steady, and were enveloped by a sea of rolling green that the A27 bypass sliced through like a grey vein. As the road descended towards Alfriston and passed over the Cuckmere River, Barnes's eyes flicked to a layby on his left. There was a large bunch of flowers tied around the bridge's framework — recently replaced, Barnes noticed, as they passed. He tried not to dwell on it too much; he had already racked up too many colleagues that had fallen prematurely — certainly far more than one cop should experience in their lifetime — never mind those whose lives had been taken from them. He knew where the sites were, he knew the terrain and he knew the history — making him, he thought grimly, the area's most cheerless tour guide.

They ambled around the zoo, the girls squealing, Barnes taking comfort from the Seven Sisters forming a constant in the background of his field of vision, a canvas of splayed green fingers. Sun and rain lighthoused across the South Downs in scattered squares, the hills fading intermittently from dark to light and back again like something seen from the windows of a train carriage.

Ellie ticked off farm animals, reptiles, penguins and meerkats as they strolled, and Barnes found Tamsin's hand wriggling into his.

"This was a nice idea," she said, leaning her head on his shoulder.

"I'm at work so much," he said. "And none of you ever complain."

"You've got a lot going on," she said.

"There will always be something."

"Don't beat yourself up," she said. "Nobody else is."

He felt another stab of guilt. A little over a year earlier, both his wife and stepdaughters had been held hostage by Tamsin's ex-husband; Barnes had saved them, but he still held himself responsible for it happening at all. They all bore the scars, he knew, and yet all they seemed to remember was that he was the one that had gone to their rescue; and it seemed to have generated a line of goodwill credit that he didn't necessarily feel he deserved. He knew of plenty of wives in young marriages who had already tired of their husbands' job-pissed, always-in-the-office work absences, made all the less tolerable by the holier-than-thou mutterings about the nobility of the profession that it was all too easy to hide behind. Nothing was more unbearable than a self-righteous workaholic husband who thought their work was insurmountably important.

They made slow progress around the park and contemplated, over an ice cream, whether to blow off their remaining steam in the playground or make straight for the miniature railway ride. The showers were holding off and the sun, when it appeared, was surprisingly warm, and so they joined the end of the queue for the train ride, figuring that they could round off with twisting slides and banana boat swings.

They'd been in the queue a couple of minutes when Barnes felt his phone vibrate in his pocket, and he knew instinctively he should have left it at home. He ignored it, and it rang off. Then it rang again. And again.

"You okay?" Tamsin said. "You've suddenly got a thousand-yard stare."

He pulled the phone out, turned to her and kissed her forehead. "I have to get this. I'm sorry. Hold my place."

He stepped away from the queue and hovered on the edge of a sandpit with little yellow metal diggers and cranes that toddlers were operating with fierce concentration.

He looked down at the number — Tina.

He called back. A small person squealed in front of him as they worked out which of the three levers worked the corresponding parts of the excavating arm's joints.

"Boss? Thanks for calling back." She sounded breathless. "Sorry to bother you. Are you somewhere nice?"

"Just the zoo. What's up?"

"Fire called. They've managed to get into the cinema."

"They found a body?"

"What's left of one."

"Any ID?"

"No way."

"Okay, I'll be right there."

"Wait, there's more. We've been working back through the movements of the rental car. You know, the Passat."

"The one that Kenley hasn't been using." Barnes looked back over his shoulder at the queue. Tamsin was joking about something with the girls.

"It was in town about six hours before the fire started, which means it's been in the proximity of all of the murders."

"Andrea Hope's been calling me. I'm going to get that car on the national news."

"Oh, shit. You may not need to."

"Why?" Barnes scanned anxiously around him in case a particularly astute toddler was eavesdropping for some kind of tabloid exposé, but no one was paying any attention to him at all.

"It's just hit a camera, Northbound, out of town. And, by all accounts, driving like a maniac."

"Are we responding?"

"Control room's got units towards."

"I'll be right there."

CHAPTER FIFTY-TWO

Barnes went via the scene. He needed to *see* it.

When he got to the town centre, a bitter wind was barrelling up Terminus Road from the Channel. The fire incident commander was animated. Tina was right — they'd finally got the blaze out and the scene was safe enough, just about, to have a look at.

And they'd found what Barnes had been expecting them to find.

It was a curious sensation. The interior of the cinema was little more than a shell; despite this, the layout of the auditorium and its original purpose was still evident, with hulks of smoke-blackened seats and the tattered remains of the screen curtain. Above Barnes's head, the once-ornate Georgian ceiling rose and cornices looked as if they had been etched in charcoal.

"Where is it?" he said to the fire commander.

The commander didn't say anything, but pointed to the screen. He'd been reluctant to allow Barnes in for longer than a few minutes, but now the police were in, it was their show. This clearly bothered him.

Barnes went across, hopped up onto the low stage and moved to the edge. He turned back momentarily, and failed to prevent himself imagining an audience of dead people in the seats.

The body was immediately behind the screen. It was lying on its back, charred beyond recognition. The smell of burnt pork made Barnes's stomach lurch. There was an angry gash on its forehead which looked like a dollop of ketchup on a barbecued sausage.

The fire commander's hand went to his mouth.

"If you're going to vomit, do it outside," Barnes hissed.

The fire commander didn't need telling twice. He practically jumped off the stage.

"Keep to the edge of the auditorium," Barnes called after him. "This is a homicide enquiry now. We need a common scene route."

Barnes stood up. Alive, Lee Flathill had been huge, a steroid freak, maybe, but he didn't look like much now. The gold around his neck and fingers, now black, had turned white hot in the fire, and the metal had eaten into his skin. The tattoos were long gone, leaving only the remnants of puckered black flesh, hard and ridged like the bark of a tree.

Barnes would need dental comparisons and all that stuff for an official identification, but it was garnish. A tick-box exercise. This was Lee Flathill.

* * *

It had taken the better qualities of a seminary matriarch — in the form of Georgia Brass — to organise logistics and planning, the coroner's officer and the by-now-long-suffering pathologist. By the time Barnes got back to the station, the light was already fading, and the slight warmth brought by the crisp winter sun had disappeared completely.

The station was surprisingly quiet when Barnes arrived. An officer sprinted out of the station, nearly colliding with Barnes.

"Sorry," he said. He was a young constable, dressed in PSU overalls. He held his NATO helmet under one arm and a video camera under the other.

"Where're you off to in such a hurry?" Barnes asked.

The constable stopped and turned, his eyes dropping to Barnes's name badge before he answered. "Ashdown Forest, boss. Think they've got that murder suspect contained. He's proper tooled up, by all accounts. They're trying to negotiate now. I just hope they don't shoot him before I get there."

He ran off. Barnes felt drawn, Pied Piper fashion, to run behind him, but he fought this instinct and instead headed into the office. There was another job to do.

He collected his files. Tina had left him another envelope with a Post-it on the front:

Time-lapse stills of the fight outside the cinema before the fire. T x

Barnes had a quick look. They were grainy, poor quality, but the guy in the baseball cap was clearly the one on the rental car agency CCTV.

Their killer.

The other guy was even bigger, and Barnes made a tentative ID: Lee Flathill.

There was something else too. He couldn't quite put his finger on it, but it was something about the jawline, the build, the height.

There was a burst of activity from a personal radio someone had left on their desk. The words were mostly unintelligible, but the voice was animated, and Barnes caught clips of the transmission — words like "track", "containment" and "closing in".

He walked to the desk and switched the handset off. Typical CID. Go racing out of the station to get in on the action, and leave your radio behind.

Barnes walked down to the cell block. He didn't speak to the custody officer or any of the jailers other than to ask for some keys, and he continued on down past the bridge to the network of corridors that serviced the cells. It smelled like a hospital — disinfectant and shit — and there was a lonely looking cleaner mopping the floor at the end of one powerfully lit corridor.

He reached Kenley's cell, imagining the Levels on the other side of the window, rendered invisible by cubes of opaque four-inch-thick glass.

He opened the door hatch. It dropped with a *clang*. Kenley was sitting on the bunk, feet up, facing the door, fingers laced, arms resting on his knees. He was staring at the ceiling. His eyes dropped to Barnes's when the hatch opened.

Barnes opened the door.

Kenley didn't say anything.

"Got a minute?" Barnes said.

Kenley snorted. "Very funny."

Barnes entered the cell and sat on the bunk, which was no more than a metal box moulded into the walls and floor. There was a thin blue mattress and a safety blanket — Kenley had put both on the floor.

"A little unorthodox, no?" Kenley said.

"The rental car I mentioned in the interview," Barnes said. "It's involved in all five murders. Your brief asked about CCTV of the hire transaction. Well, it's back."

Kenley's eyebrows went up.

Barnes reached into his jacket and pulled out the envelope with the stills.

"You were right," Barnes said. "It's not you."

He laid the images out on the bunk — the CCTV from the car rental agency, but also the Polaroid he'd snapped of the burnt body in the cinema, and the stills of the fight outside the cinema.

Kenley didn't even look at them. Instead, he kept his eyes on Barnes's. Barnes gestured to the pictures with his eyes.

"Take a look," he said when Kenley still held his gaze.

Kenley's eyes dropped.

Barnes hadn't exactly expected Kenley to crow with glee, but he was unprepared for his reaction.

The corners of his mouth turned down. He swallowed, and began to breathe heavily through his nose. His eyes glistened wetly in the half-light.

Barnes stared at him, open-mouthed.

"Kenley?"

"We need to go for a drive," Kenley said.

Barnes, unsurprised but in a kind of trance, got up and led Kenley out to the bridge. He told the custody officer his murder suspect was being bailed out — the custody officer didn't object; he was quite happy to be shot of a quintuple murder suspect — and Barnes walked Kenley out of the secure area to the main public waiting area. Kenley was now technically at liberty — if he opted to bolt, Barnes would have little grounds to go after him.

Despite the whole building being relatively new, the public waiting area had quickly become an afterthought — donated sofas were arranged in a square around a chipboard coffee table which was itself strewn with the remnants of fast food containers. There were several well-thumbed magazines featuring outdated tabloid gossip that was now meaningless. The pockmarked plasterboard walls were covered with doodles and irreverence.

There was a cheap, wall-mounted television; Barnes suddenly tuned in to the fact it had started broadcasting a news item. Barnes stood on a chair and turned up the volume. He stayed on the chair while the headlines were read out.

He only caught the odd word, but the effect was immediate and obvious: yellow *BREAKING NEWS* ticker-tape scrolled across the screen; armed officers tooled up to the gills poked around in bushes with carbines, flanked by dog handlers, while the helicopter hovered watchfully overhead.

Barnes squinted at the image. It was a choppy, amateurish video — the operator was probably terrified of being shot. The footage changed. The scrolling ticker-tape remained, but the main image was replaced by a headshot of a face that was beginning to look extremely familiar.

They walked to Barnes's car; Barnes was momentarily thrown as to whether he should put Kenley in the back or the front, but raised no objections when Kenley opened the front door.

"Where are we going?" Barnes asked as he got in.

"North," was all Kenley said.

Kenley didn't speak until they were passing Uckfield and into the rolling green escarpments and sandy ridges of the Weald Basin. It was getting on for late afternoon, and shards of daylight were beginning to give way to dusk.

Kenley shifted in his seat so he was facing Barnes. "Got any smokes?"

Without speaking, Barnes handed him the regulation pack of Marlboro Lights that he kept for prisoner emergencies. "Me and Samson came to see you in prison. The two of us. My family were being held hostage and I pleaded with you to tell us what you knew, and you just laughed. He never told me he knew you."

"And when he came back again — alone, the second time — I told him where they were being held, which I wouldn't otherwise have done."

That jolted Barnes. He didn't know what to make of it. This double — if not quadruple — killer was responsible for saving his family?

"Forget about it," Kenley said, waving a hand as if he sensed Barnes's conflict. "I did it for purely selfish reasons. And as a favour to a friend. Not you," he added.

"You were friends?"

Kenley nodded slowly, like he was really considering the question.

"Samson was a good kid," Kenley said. "Came from nothing. I invited him to play cricket. Came over to compare trainers when I could have just yelled 'freak' like all the others.

"We were chalk and cheese. My dad was a surgeon. Nine times out of ten his dad, Lee, was never home, because he was in a cell, for knocking his mother about. His eight-months-pregnant mother. That blew my mind. I was pretty full of myself back then, but when I went over to his, I was like a wide-eyed little kid. I'd never seen anything like it. Me and him and Manny used to hang out in this camp we built at the back of the Courtlands industrial estate. It got wrecked by the townies, so we moved on. Happened in cycles."

"Manny?"

"His baby brother."

Barnes inhaled, as a thousand realities came flying into focus.

"He was three back then," Kenley continued. "Spent most of his time with Samson. Kept him away from trouble. He loved Samson. I got pretty close to him too."

Barnes pictured it. Kane reading his toddler brother a story, or building a Lego dinosaur, or playing video games, any kind of false normality to keep his mind away from the yelling and screaming going on downstairs.

"Lee made those boys' lives a misery. Lee — and his cronies."

"Liam Lawrence, Terry Markham, Levi Sadler and Carl Jessop."

"Bingo."

"Oh my God. The showroom, Treasure Island, the Italian Gardens. That's where you made all your camps."

"Turn right here," Kenley said. Barnes checked the mirror and turned off the A22 onto a yellowing, unmarked road that rumbled like an airstrip as they drove down it. The road was dead straight and looked as if it would lead towards some kind of life, but all Barnes could see were the rust-brown sides of the sprawling heathland of Ashdown Forest in the distance, patchworked with bracken and dotted with black skeletal firs. The place felt desolate, and brought *Apocalypse Now* to mind.

"Why would he come here? Is there another body? Of all the places he could have gone, he chose Ashdown Forest?"

Kenley shrugged. "Probably the only place he felt safe."

The firs that had been sporadically lining the roadside were now increasing in number, slowly becoming impervious to what little daylight existed as the forest thickened around the car.

They drove in silence for another ten minutes or so, until eventually Kenley said, "Stop the car."

Barnes pulled over onto the verge and stopped. As he turned the engine off, the faint thudding of the police helicopter became audible overhead.

It seemed to Barnes that they had arrived at nowhere in particular. He looked up and down the yellow, empty road. It faded to a point in front of him, and again to a point from the direction they had come.

The heathland was desolate, the sky the murky pale grey of a hard-boiled egg. They were surrounded on both sides by a forest of firs, but a mile or so further up the road the trees ended and the rolling escarpments led to the horizon. The wind was shrill with cold, and it numbed Barnes's face as it panted through the firs.

Kenley walked off to the side of the road and towards the lip of the forest. Barnes followed him, treading carefully on the uneven ground concealed below-knee-length blades of coarse grass. Kenley seemed to be walking effortlessly, with little regard for the terrain, and Barnes struggled to keep up with him.

"Hey, wait," Barnes panted, as Kenley disappeared into the gloom of the forest.

What little light was left disappeared under the canopy of firs, and Barnes pulled out his Maglite. It suddenly occurred to him that he was out in the middle of nowhere with a murder suspect, and no one knew where he was. He'd left his radio in the car.

Irony abounds, he thought.

He turned around. They'd only walked fifty yards or so, but the daylight they had left behind occupied only a small circle in his field of vision — the rest was black, like tunnel vision. He couldn't see the car.

He caught up with Kenley as the ground inclined more steeply. He grabbed his arm. "Where are you taking me?"

Kenley stopped and looked Barnes dead in the eye. His eyes were bright in the gloom.

"We're nearly there," he said, shrugging off Barnes's grip.

He picked his way up a steep bank, and Barnes followed him, impressed by his agility.

The forest was huge, and it seemed even larger because Barnes knew that beyond its natural perimeter there existed nothing but miles of empty sandstone and clay landscape stretching away in all directions.

There was no sign at all of human occupation — no litter, no friendly signposts, no time-worn paths or tracks defined by the footsteps of those that had gone before; none of those trappings of infrastructure to reassure you that someone, somewhere, must be looking out for you.

At the top of the bank Barnes could see pockets of pale light bursting through the foliage, and, beyond that, the low thudding noise of the helicopter, muffled and barely audible over the thousand hushing trees, but growing louder as he walked.

The undergrowth broke, and Barnes heaved a sigh of relief at the return of daylight. They found themselves on the edge of the forest, in a clearing overlooking a deep grassy basin.

In the clearing the dull thudding had sharpened up. Barnes looked up and shielded his as-yet unaccustomed eyes from the daylight. Two helicopters, in fact. One was dark blue and yellow, with the word *POLICE* on the side; the other silver, bearing the letters *SKY NEWS* in metallic red.

Barnes traced his line of vision down to the spot over which the machines hovered. Down in the basin, some two hundred feet below, near what looked like a makeshift camp, stood a lone man, surrounded by a circle of other men. Voices were faintly audible — it sounded like shouting.

Kenley passed Barnes a pair of binoculars from nowhere. Barnes slowly lifted them to his eyes, already guessing what he was about to see.

There was Manny, a strange hybrid of Samson Kane and Lee Flathill — but more the latter than the former. Zerograde haircut all over, T-shirt and combats clinging to his huge frame, a jacket tied around his waist.

He was holding a sawn-off twelve-bore turned on himself, the barrel pressing into his stomach. A phalanx of armed police surrounded him, weapons trained. They were all stationary apart from two, who edged almost imperceptibly forwards. Another officer, who wore a ballistic vest emblazoned with *POLICE* over a T-shirt and jeans, edged forwards from behind the line of armed officers, flanked by two AFOs holding full-length shields to protect him. Barnes pegged him as the hostage and crisis negotiator.

Kenley looked at Barnes, then nodded at something in the trees.

Barnes turned.

Samson Kane.

He was standing alone in the thicket of trees, wide-eyed and still, hugging himself, watching the tableau unfold in front of him.

Barnes made to go to him. Kenley held his arm to stop him, drilling Barnes with his eyes.

"They had another brother," Kenley said.

Barnes looked at him, his eyes wide with anticipation.

"Janet gave birth in the summer of 1993, when Manny was three. Lee drowned him in the bath when he was three weeks old. Manny never knew him. But Samson did."

Barnes looked down. Manny now had the shotgun pressed to his temple, and he lowered himself into a sitting position. He let out a sigh as he sat, as if he didn't think he'd ever get up again.

"What happened to Lee?"

"*You* should know that, surely. He claimed it was an accident. There wasn't enough to say it wasn't. He went to trial. Hung jury."

Barnes looked down at Manny in the basin, the weapon still held to his head. No one seemed to have moved, but

Barnes could have sworn the armed officers were closer to Manny than they had been a minute ago.

"I didn't see much of them after it happened. I moved out of town the second I was able to. But over the years I saw Manny from a distance every now and then as he turned into his dad. It was scary as hell. First the boxing classes, steaks by the truckload, the buzz cut — and then the 'roids."

Kenley shuddered.

"If his old man wasn't charcoal right now, you probably couldn't tell them apart. Sad, really. What's that song? 'Cat's in the Cradle'? Seems quite fitting here."

"But all this was years ago, Kenley. Why would Manny suddenly come out of the woodwork now?"

"Not a question I can answer, but my best guess is, someone's wound him up."

Barnes turned to face him. "Kenley, tell me you didn't have anything to do with the murders of those men."

The stereo sound of the helicopters, a constant up until now, suddenly halved. Barnes looked up and saw the news helicopter rearing off into the distance.

"Oh, shit," Kenley said. "They're going to shoot him."

Barnes made another attempt to go. This time, Kenley didn't try to stop him.

"I'm taking these," Barnes said, holding up the binoculars.

Barnes stumbled and staggered across the uneven forest floor, traversing a hundred yards or so until he reached Kane, alone in the gloom. It seemed to take forever.

Barnes didn't get too close. It seemed to take a moment for Kane to realise Barnes was there.

"You okay, boss? What are you doing out here by yourself?"

"I . . . I don't know," Kane said, still staring at the scene below. "The negotiator wanted me out of the way, but available. Close enough in case they thought I could help with the mediation, but not so close that he could see me."

Barnes looked down. The armed officers were now in a tight circle around Manny. Barnes looked back to where he had been standing, and was unsurprised to see that Kenley had vanished.

"We made a camp," Kane said, nodding towards the basin.

Barnes looked at Kane.

He raised the binoculars.

Manny's body was convulsed in sobs, the shotgun gradually lowering until the barrel was pointing at the ground.

He slowly sank to his knees and dropped the weapon, his head hanging forwards, staring at the ground.

Barnes exhaled heavily. Kane was frozen to the spot, his face pale.

One of the officers slung his weapon onto his back, and moved forwards to put the cuffs on Manny. The others kept their weapons aimed at him.

There was a flash of sudden movement as Manny made a grab for his waistband. He moved quickly — the pistol was already in his hand when the muzzles of three carbines silently flashed. At this distance, Manny was already dead on the grass before the sound of the three gunshots reached Barnes and Kane.

Kane said nothing. He slowly turned and began his descent back through the forest.

CHAPTER FIFTY-THREE

Marlon Choudhury was in a side room off the main ward, a huge brown bear of a man in a surgical gown hooked up to drips and monitors and things. Barnes wasn't sure if he was asleep or unconscious.

Barnes sat in a vinyl chair that smelled of bleach and soiled dressings. He'd positioned himself so that he could see Marlon's face; the DCI's head seemed to have naturally inclined itself towards the daylight. Through the window, the sun had disappeared behind a thin layer of cloud, turning the whole sky white. There was a small fountain in a once-sculpted garden two floors down, providing an endless trickle into a sad-looking pond.

The fountain, coupled with the metronomic bleeping of the machines surrounding the bed, had a strangely mesmerising effect on Barnes. It was not a place he liked coming to, but he also felt some of his tension ease as he watched Marlon Choudhury's huge chest rise and fall.

It had taken a few goes to do so without feeling self-conscious, but now Barnes was — after some gentle coaxing by one of the nurses — able to talk to Choudhury as if he were conscious. He decided to pick up where their last conversation had finished, which was centred around Barnes seeking promotion — a conversation Barnes had once thought he would never have again, with anyone.

"I thought about what you said," Barnes said. "I still don't know why I'd be doing it, but that doesn't mean I've dismissed it out of hand. I just . . . didn't think I'd ever entertain the idea again. It seems churlish, even mercenary, to think it might be a possibility just because Gabby Glover has gone. Maybe it's naive, but I still can't work out how one individual, regardless of their power, can have such a cliff-edge effect on someone's career.

"Tamsin thinks I should think about it too. She says I'd be good at it, but . . . I don't know. I mean, what does it actually mean? More hours, more responsibility, a bigger team to look after, nothing noticeable in my pay packet. And — here's the thing — promotion doesn't mean you've been recognised for being good at your job. At some stage up the ladder it ceases to be about how good you are and becomes more about how well you can operate politically, and whether your team thinks you're a complete buffoon or not — and even that is given limited weight. It doesn't automatically follow that a half-decent DI will make a half-decent DCI, and that's a level where the bosses can't afford risk. They can't afford people who play their own game, who don't acquiesce to the bureaucracy. It's not a place for wildcards.

"I know, I know, I can hear what you're saying. I'm just thinking about the negatives, I'm only halfway through my pensionable service, so why wouldn't I, et cetera. The truth is, though, Marlon, that when everyone gets around the boardroom table to discuss this year's contestants, yours will be a very lonely seat if you're putting me forward — even though Gabby won't be there to pour scorn on the idea. I can't think of anyone who would second it."

Barnes paused, allowing the bleeping to continue its steady rhythm. Even as he spoke, he pictured himself in front of an interview board, pictured the third pip on his tunic, pictured an email signature that read *Rutherford Barnes — Detective Chief Inspector*. Pictured being on a level footing with morons like Ed Shaw, his former boss.

That was the ego talking, though. If that same board asked him now why he wanted promotion, he would have to answer honestly: *I don't want it, but a few people said I should have a pop*; or, *That's up to you, really, isn't it? If you think I'm promotable, then go for it. If you don't, then let's all save our diary time*; or, *I thought it was about time someone said the emperor was naked*; and other similarly career-limiting responses.

Barnes stood up and took Choudhury's hand.

"I'll see you in a couple of days, Marlon. Next time I'll tell you about what went down in Ashdown Forest, and why Manny Flathill — Manny Kane — decided to flip out when he did. But not today. Rest up. Get yourself back to work. Lord knows we need you."

Barnes wasn't totally sure, but he thought he felt a slight pressure of Marlon Choudhury's hand when he mentioned Manny.

CHAPTER FIFTY-FOUR

Barnes sat in the empty incident room in the dark, headphones on. The CCTV monitors were still broadcasting a silent feed of the town centre. The empty platforms of the station and railway lines converging towards a point under Cavendish Bridge a mile or so in the distance, over which the sky was beginning to take on a pinkish tinge in the east. Wisps of steam rising from a vent behind a railway shed. Rows of silver chairs stacked on top of silver tables on the concourse. A clear pink dawn sullied only by the final wisps of black smoke curling away in the distance from the remnants of the Curzon.

Manny collapsing in a heap in the forest, dead before the bullet had exited his head.

Barnes was reviewing the video and transcript of the entirety of the attempt to negotiate a peaceful surrender with Manny Flathill.

The negotiator had done well in the circumstances. Conditions were freezing cold, the environment was hostile, and the subject himself, if not completely out of his tree, had most certainly been wired on something.

Despite his best efforts, the negotiator had been unable to keep Manny on simple cause-and-effect logic or a linear train of thought. Manny was all over the place — by turns ranting, crying, raging.

The transcript went on for pages. Barnes had to read it several times, circling and highlighting the sections he could work with. As he read, he remembered Gabby Glover's suicide note:

Liam Lawrence
Carl Jessop
Terry Markham
Lee Flathill
Levi Sadler
He is coming.

"He" being Manny. Glover had presumably been on the shitlist as well, and had checked himself out before Manny could lynch him, set him on fire or suck his eyeballs out with a hoover.

But why?

And then he found it. It had come in broken snippets, but just before he was shot, Manny had claimed that, back in the early 1990s, Glover had been the duty DI for both the bulk of the assaults on Janet Flathill by Lee — and also the SIO of the investigation into Lee drowning his newborn child. Manny's claim was that Glover, even then, had been a habitual cocaine user, and owed Lee and his cronies a good deal of money. Lee shaved points off the debt for every blind eye that Gabby turned.

Barnes put a hand to his mouth, bile rising. It was both a shock and it wasn't, and it still didn't explain why Manny had picked now to serve up revenge.

And then he realised why ACC Theresa Baily hadn't been returning his calls.

* * *

The old house at Police HQ was a neat, square Georgian redbrick building. The Union Jack was flying out the front, casting a rippling shadow across the neatly trimmed lawn.

Barnes opened the huge front door into the entrance lobby, which was adorned with World War rolls of honour alongside the tenures of past chief constables. The panelled walls were scattered with framed nineteenth-century photography and other memorabilia, including a bona fide suit of armour perched on the wide staircase.

He found Baily in her office. Her door was open, and she was typing furiously, the sound of the keys echoing out into the otherwise empty building. He looked at his watch. Half five. Early bath for the rest of them, clearly. Well, it was Friday.

She didn't immediately notice him, and he stood in the doorway for a moment, taking in the ten-foot windows, the polished oak conference table, the original fireplace. This would make an amazing country hotel one day, he thought.

She turned, started and then frowned.

"DI Barnes."

"Ma'am."

"Can I help you?"

He thought about this. She stayed sitting, and turned to face him.

"Do you know, I think you can."

He stepped inside, shutting the door, and she looked just a trifle uncomfortable. He stayed where he was in the absence of an invitation to sit — which was clearly not going to be forthcoming.

He nodded at the computer. "Getting your statement ready for the inquiry?"

"I beg your pardon?"

"Gabby told you, didn't he?"

"What?"

Barnes took the copy of the suicide note out of his pocket and read it out loud.

"*Liam Lawrence, Carl Jessop, Terry Markham, Lee Flathill, Levi Sadler. He is coming.*"

He put the note away again. Baily looked quite pale.

"You didn't know about the note," Barnes said, tilting his head. "Well, Gabby killed himself because his name should have been on that list too. As a reward for systematically failing to investigate any of the numerous assaults committed against Janet Flathill by her husband Lee, this crew of five kept Gabby in cocaine — and on a short leash — which enabled them to manipulate him into not investigating Lee for murdering his infant son. He neglected his duties throughout much of the 1990s, leading to at least two deaths — and yet somehow managed to bluster his way to ACC.

"But I still couldn't work out why Manny chose that particular time to do . . . what he did. Then I realised: *you* told him."

"You've got a bloody nerve—" Baily began.

"I think Gabby confessed to you — that's some heavy pillow talk, by the way — and then you realised his career would be over if it ever got out, and so you decided to sic Manny on him. You told him what Gabby had done — wound him up and watched him go. Gabby didn't fancy being burned alive, so he jumped out of a loft, creating an instant ACC vacancy for you to slot neatly into."

"This is pure fantasy, Inspector."

"And yet, here you are."

Her knuckles were white on the arms of her upholstered wooden captain's chair.

"That's why you brought me the box of his stuff, thinking the surveillance reports on his most hated officers would steer me into not investigating it too hard.

"Did you bank on him killing himself, or was that just an added bonus? If he hadn't, would you have kept the relationship going even after you'd taken his job? That's pretty brutal, I must say. DCI Choudhury is going to have quite the in-tray when he finally recovers. He's doing much better now, by the way. We almost had a conversation."

"I'm going to post you to the bloody Bognor property store."

He took a step forward and placed the note on the edge of the conference table.

"That's a copy. You can have that."

He opened the door, and then turned.

"Oh, one more thing. Are you going to tell Superintendent Samson Kane, or shall I?"

CHAPTER FIFTY-FIVE

Barnes found Tina waiting for him when he got back to the office. She was clutching a file, and looked anxious.

"What's up, Tina?"

"You okay, boss?"

He thought about this. "It's over."

She put the file on the table in front of him.

"Or is it?" he said.

"You need to look at this."

Barnes picked up the file. It contained phone records, transcripts of messages, financials, emails — all carefully indexed and annotated into a coherent narrative by the unfailingly meticulous Tina Flagstaff.

"Should I sit?" he said.

"I would."

He did as suggested, and felt his stomach start to sink as he read.

"Do you want me to get tactical up and running?" she said.

Barnes didn't look up. "I would."

* * *

PC Pete Lamb, his legs heavy, his brain feeling like melted butter, waited until nightfall and then clambered slowly up to the Beachy Head playing fields. He was sober, but felt ridiculously light-headed. Even when he stood still, the ground felt like it was undulating and the wind was piercing his head, and he had to concentrate bloody hard to keep away from the edge.

He removed the decorative foliage from the hide, and took the wooden hatch off. He lowered himself onto his belly, and reached down into the murk. He felt around for a moment or two, but couldn't feel anything.

He reached down a little further, making bloody sure he didn't overbalance, but his grasping fingers still closed around damp air.

"What the hell . . . ?"

He knew he hadn't been particularly frugal with either the money or the cocaine, but he knew for certain he damn well had more than nothing left.

There was only one possible explanation.

He'd been robbed.

Just as a football league list of possible suspects whirred through his brain, he heard footsteps behind him.

Flat on his belly and with one arm in a hole up to the shoulder, he was in the worst possible stance to react quickly to anything, and so could only sort of twist and jerk from his prone position.

Then he felt a boot on the small of his back. It applied increasing pressure until Lamb was pinned like a lab specimen to a piece of mounting card.

"Hello, PC Lamb," Kenley smiled. "You got my bricks?"

"Who's that?" Lamb said as he squirmed. "How the fuck d'you know who I am?"

"You're a disgrace to the uniform. I don't particularly like the police, but I have a sort of grudging respect for honest cops. Like your Rutherford Barnes. You, on the other hand, are the worst kind. Can you imagine your life if you ended up in prison?"

Lamb made another attempt to get up, but the boot drove him down and forwards, so now his head, arms and most of his shoulders were in the hole.

"Up to your neck in it, aren't you? Bit further forwards, Pete, and you'll be stuck there for ever. I wonder how deep it is. Pretty grim way to go, isn't it — a headstand in a sewer pipe that's not even wide enough for a fat man. You probably wouldn't be found for at least ten hours."

The fight suddenly went out of Lamb's body.

"What do you want?" he said, tears beginning to form somewhere in his head. "Are you going to kill me?"

"I'm not going to kill you, Pete. I'm going to *own* you. I took back the cash and blow, but it's light. So you're going to do a bit of community service and repay your debt. Once we're square — well, we can talk about that. In the meantime, I need to deliver this coke back to its rightful owner."

The boot was removed. Lamb smelled aftershave and felt a warm whisper near his ear.

"You're mine now," Kenley hissed.

* * *

Kenley left Pete Lamb in his hole and walked — strolled — over the cliff and back down the South Downs Way to his rental car. His phone rang as he walked. He frowned.

"Hello?"

"You helped him, didn't you?"

"Rutherford. It's nice to hear from you. What's up?"

"Jesus Christ, I must need my head examined. You helped him. You set him up, Manny. You told him where to find Carl, Liam, Lee and the others. You provided him with the blade that opened up Liam Lawrence. You helped him with how to evade capture. Told him about ANPR. Gave him some pretty shit murder methods. You called him the day before he found Lee outside the cinema."

"Are you asking me a question, Inspector?"

"Why did you do it?"

"Now that is a silly question. But I'll answer it: We were all pals, Rutherford. If one had asked the other to lie in front of a bus for them, we'd have all done it without hesitation. I just helped Manny scratch a twenty-two-year-old itch. Can you understand that, Rutherford? Would you do that for anyone? Would anyone do that for *you*?"

"You need to come in."

"There's no fun in that, Rutherford. Catch me if you can."

Kenley killed the call and carried on walking. He took a slow drive down the seafront, back to Langney Point and the ice cream kiosk at the Harbour Reach.

There was a reasonably strong north-easterly blowing, and he smelled the woman before she emerged from the shadows. Cigarettes, hairspray and perfume. She was very attractive, Kenley thought, but attractive women in this business were nothing but trouble.

"Have you got it?" she said.

He held out the rucksack. "That's all he left. He's either sold or snorted the rest."

"That isn't good."

He shrugged. "No more and no less than we were expecting. I've put him to work. We'll get it all back — and have a bit of fun doing so."

"We'd better. *You'd* better."

Kenley gave an exaggerated bow.

"Haven. Is that your real name?" he asked as she rifled through the rucksack.

"Don't ask stupid questions," she said, not looking up. "This is actually better than I thought. How long for the rest?"

Kenley shrugged. "Judging by the amount of crying he was doing, plus his contacts, plus abject fear, minus my cut, I'd say — a week?"

"Okay. We'll meet in a week. If it's late, that's a problem."

"It most certainly is. For both of us."

"What do you mean?"

"I'm not afraid of you, Haven Banks." Kenley gave her a broad grin, then turned on his heel and walked back to his car.

* * *

Haven watched him go. For a moment she thought about following him and goading him a bit more, but was distracted by the sound of Katy Perry's new single. She took out the phone. No number displayed, but she knew who it would be. Nobody else but Theresa Baily had this number.

She answered.

"Yes?"

"Are we good?" Baily asked.

Haven looked in the bag, then peered round the corner to make sure Kenley had actually gone. The lights stretched away along the promenade like a runway, the sea breathing in the invisible black, Beachy Head and the Seven Sisters looming up like a leviathan on the horizon.

"Yes," Haven said, permitting herself a smile. "We're good."

THE END

GLOSSARY OF POLICE TERMS

AFO — authorised firearms officer
APW — all ports warning
ARV — armed response vehicle
BTP — British Transport Police
CPR — cardiopulmonary resuscitation
CSM — crime scene manager
Cooper's Colours — a four-stage colour system (ranging through white-yellow-orange-red) indicating the incremental degrees of situational awareness and personal alertness in a combat situation; outlined in *Principles of Personal Defense* (2005) by Jeff Cooper (Paladin: Boulder, CO)
DPA — Data Protection Act
EGT — evidence gathering team
FLO — family liaison officer
G5 — Sussex code for sudden death call
  Gold Group — strategic meeting convened by a senior officer to oversee and manage major and critical incidents
HOLMES — Home Office Large Major Enquiry System

IED — improvised explosive device

IPCC — Independent Police Complaints Commission; phased out in 2018 and succeeded by the Independent Office for Police Conduct

Jam sandwich — dated slang term for a police patrol car

Metpol — Metropolitan Police

NAFIS — National Automated Fingerprint Identification System

NATO — North Atlantic Treaty Organisation

NCA — National Crime Agency

NDA — non-disclosure agreement

NDNAD — National DNA Database

OCG — organised crime group

OD — overdose

OET — outside enquiry team

Osman warning — issued by the police to individuals against whom there is intelligence of a credible threat to their life. The term arose from the *Osman v United Kingdom* (1998) case, and was superseded in 2016 by "Threat to life warning notice", following an appeal by the family about the use of the term.

PIP3 — Professionalising Investigation Programme Level 3; mandatory training and accreditation level required to be able to undertake the role of senior investigating officer for major and/or serious and organised crime

PIP4 — Professionalising Investigation Programme Level 4; a strategic oversight role providing independent advice, support and review for high-profile, complex, serious and organised or major crime investigations

PNC — Police National Computer

PND — Police National Database

PO — probation officer

POCA — Proceeds of Crime Act 2002; a piece of legislation that allows law enforcement to sequester assets that have been obtained via criminal means

PSU — police support unit; a specialist unit comprising one inspector, three sergeants and eighteen constables; deployed to violent offenders, search, serious public order incidents and other high-risk situations

RMS — records management system

RoLE — recognition of life extinct

SECAMB — South East Coast Ambulance Service

Sigwit — significant witness

SIO — senior investigating officer

SIR — strategic intelligence requirement

SIU — specialist investigations unit

SOCO — Scenes-of-Crime officer; now largely defunct in favour of "crime scene investigator" (CSI)

USP — unique selling point

ViSOR — Violent and Sex Offender Register

THE JOFFE BOOKS STORY

We began in 2014 when Jasper agreed to publish his mum's much-rejected romance novel and it became a bestseller.

Since then we've grown into the largest independent publisher in the UK. We're extremely proud to publish some of the very best writers in the world, including Joy Ellis, Faith Martin, Caro Ramsay, Helen Forrester, Simon Brett and Robert Goddard. Everyone at Joffe Books loves reading and we never forget that it all begins with the magic of an author telling a story.

We are proud to publish talented first-time authors, as well as established writers whose books we love introducing to a new generation of readers.

We won Trade Publisher of the Year at the Independent Publishing Awards in 2023. We have been shortlisted for Independent Publisher of the Year at the British Book Awards for the last four years, and were shortlisted for the Diversity and Inclusivity Award at the 2022 Independent Publishing Awards. In 2023 we were shortlisted for Publisher of the Year at the RNA Industry Awards.

We built this company with your help, and we love to hear from you, so please email us about absolutely anything bookish at feedback@joffebooks.com

If you want to receive free books every Friday and hear about all our new releases, join our mailing list: www.joffebooks.com/freebooks

And when you tell your friends about us, just remember: it's pronounced Joffe as in coffee or toffee!